A PRINCESS OF MARS

THE ANNOTATED EDITION

&

NEW TALES OF THE RED PLANET

All the best!
Dan Parson

WITH MY BACK AGAINST A GOLDEN THRONE, I FOUGHT ONCE AGAIN
FOR DEJAH THORIS.

A PRINCESS OF MARS

THE ANNOTATED EDITION

BY EDGAR RICE BURROUGHS

&

NEW TALES

OF THE

RED PLANET

STORIES BY
MATTHEW STOVER, DANIEL KEYS MORAN,
CHUCK ROSENTHAL, AARON PARRETT,
MARK D'ANNA AND MICHAEL KOGGE

WITH **ANNOTATIONS** BY AARON PARRETT
AND AN **INTRODUCTION** BY ROBERT B. ZEUSCHNER

SWORD
&
PLANET

A **Sword & Planet** original
published in Los Angeles, California
www.swordandplanet.net

Library of Congress Control Number: 2012936280

Publisher's Cataloging-In-Publication Data

```
Burroughs, Edgar Rice, 1875-1950.
   A princess of Mars : the annotated edition / by Edgar Rice Burroughs ; with
annotations by Aaron Parrett ; and an introduction by Robert B. Zeuschner ; [cover
and illustrations by Dan Parsons]. New tales of the red planet / stories by Matthew
Stover ... [et al.]. -- 1st ed.
   p. : ill. ; cm.
   Contents: Introduction / Robert B. Zeuschner -- A friend in Thark / Matthew
Stover -- Gentleman of Virginia / Michael Kogge -- The white apes of Iss / Mark
D'Anna -- Zero Mars / Aaron Parrett -- Uncle Jack / Daniel Keys Moran -- An island
in the moon / Chuck Rosenthal.
   A Princess of Mars was originally published: Chicago : A.C. McClurg, 1917.
   Includes bibliographical references.
   ISBN-13: 978-0-9854257-0-8
   ISBN-10: 0-9854257-0-9

   1. Burroughs, Edgar Rice, 1875-1950. Princess of Mars. 2. Mars (Planet)--
Fiction. 3. Science fiction. I. Parrett, Aaron. II. Zeuschner, Robert B., 1941-
III. Parsons, Dan. IV. Stover, Matthew Woodring. Friend in Thark. V. Kogge,
Michael. Gentleman of Virgina. VI. D'Anna, Mark. White apes of Iss. VII. Parrett,
Aaron. Zero Mars. VIII. Moran, Daniel Keys. Uncle Jack. IX. Rosenthal, Chuck,
1951- Island in the moon. X. Title. XI. Title: New tales of the red planet.

PS3503.U687 P76 2012                                            2012936280
813.52
```

For distribution and sale only in the United States of America.
First Edition
10 9 8 7 6 5 4 3 2 1

CONTENTS

INTRODUCTION

BY ROBERT B. ZEUSCHNER, PH.D.

This book which you hold in your hands is a tribute to the novel which first created and then explored a new genre of adventure fiction, the interplanetary romance. The story belongs to the tradition of Jules Verne, H. G. Wells, and the "lost race" novels of H. Rider Haggard, and is one cornerstone of what later became known as science fiction.

Our story begins in 1912, when a middle-aged man who was unable to feed his family turned to writing his daydreams down on paper. He submitted the first half of an exotic and fantastic adventure to a popular fiction magazine called *All-Story*. It was accepted and published as a serial entitled *Under the Moons of Mars*. The first installment appeared in February 1912 and continued for five more months. To readers of the pulps at the time, it seemed more exciting than the other serials being published—it had adventure, it had romance, and its Martian setting was literally "out of this world." The enthusiastic response convinced Burroughs to write more, and within a few years, he became one of the most popular and highest-paid authors of adventure fiction.

Fast-forward forty years later to May 1952, when one eleven-year-old boy who knew nothing of Burroughs or Barsoom eagerly opened a birthday present he had received in the mail from his grandmother. Inside were two books, one bound in bright red and one bound in green. The note said that these had belonged to his father thirty years before. One of the books was *The Son of Tarzan* and the other was *The Gods of Mars*, both by an author named Edgar Rice Burroughs.

By that time, I was a compulsive reader and I quickly climbed into the tree in our yard to read *The Gods of Mars*. I finished it that same night, hiding under the covers with a flashlight so that my parents wouldn't catch me awake. I'd never read anything so exciting and immediately fell in love with the heroine, the incomparable Dejah Thoris, princess of Helium. Luckily, there was more to the story. The back pages of the book listed other Burroughs novels, among them *A Princess of Mars*. Yet in 1952, almost all of Burroughs's books were out of print, and our local library had only two Tarzan tales and none of the Mars stories. But I needed to know what happened to lovely Dejah. I had to have more. More!

A few days later my dad drove me to an old used bookshop in Pasadena, The Book Nook. With two dollars earned from washing cars and mowing lawns, I bought *A Princess of Mars*. Although I didn't realize it at the time, it was the beginning of my life as a book collector. For the next decade, I would browse regularly through the many thrift shops and used bookstores which lined Colorado Boulevard in those days and would come home with more literary treasures, primarily novels by Edgar Rice Burroughs, Sax Rohmer, George Barr McCutcheon, Thorne Smith, Edgar Wallace and Talbot Mundy.

This was still the early 1950s. I did not know anything about first editions or dust jackets and most of my Burroughs treasures cost fifty cents apiece. Some were just a dime. Today we would call them reading copies. But to me, they were the doors to an alternative universe and my life was now filled with scantily-clad maidens in need of a hero to rescue them. My vocabulary expanded as I coped with the complex and unfamiliar English words in these books. It was the magical years of adolescence before high school, and I believed that I too could ride an eight-legged thoat, battle a green six-limbed Thark, impress the beautiful Dejah and free the world from the evildoers. After one day spent exploring dead cities and racing across the ochre sea bottoms of Mars, the very next day I could be in the fantasy jungles of Africa with Tarzan, gliding from one tree to another, using my sense of smell to detect the slightest hint of danger. Then I could travel to Venus, where I could climb trees that were miles tall and contained complex civilizations. Or I could explore Pellucidar, a hollowed-out realm in the center of the Earth, where the horizon flowed upward instead of down. In all of his stories, Burroughs brought the most outrageous and exciting worlds to life. What more could a kid ask?

Edgar Rice Burroughs was born on September 1, 1875, in Chicago. He was a bright and imaginative child. His father was a successful businessman who also had been a Union cavalry officer during the American Civil War, and young Edgar's imagination was stimulated by his father's stories of war and battle. At age thirteen, Burroughs traveled from Chicago to a cattle ranch in Idaho run by his elder brothers. It seems likely that here he absorbed the mystique of the noble cowboy, since in 1890 the "wild west" was still alive in people's living memories. A year later, Burroughs returned home to Chicago. However, his stubborn independence placed him in military school, where he displayed unusual skills in horsemanship. Upon graduation, he applied to West Point to be an officer, but was not accepted. Therefore, in May of 1896, Burroughs joined the U.S. Army and was assigned to Fort Grant in Arizona where he learned about Native Americans firsthand. The army released Burroughs in March of 1897 due to a heart murmur.

Soon after his stint in the army, he married his childhood sweetheart, Emma. But Burroughs had a problem: no matter how hard he tried, he was unable to support his wife and later, his two sons. He panned for gold and served as a railroad policemen. He sold stationary. He tried selling candy to drug stores, selling electric light bulbs to janitors, selling pencil sharpeners to schools, and he even pretended to be an accountant. He worked as a salesman peddling a cure for alcoholism until the Food and Drug Administration closed the business down. Finally, at age 35, he began to transfer his frustrations, nightmares and daydreams onto paper, an act which diverted his attention from the unpleasantness of his life. The result was the 1912 serial publication of *Under the Moons of Mars* in *All-Story* magazine, which in its later hardback edition of 1917 was renamed *A Princess of Mars*.

Burroughs's science-fiction story was perfect for the young men who comprised the majority of the pulp magazine audience. But it was the next published Burroughs tale that would establish him firmly as the most popular author of fantasy adventures in the world. The October 1912 story was *Tarzan of the Apes*, which was a genuine sensation in the pulp magazine world. It combined romance and adventure with a droll sense of humor. The letters columns of subsequent issues of *All-Story* were filled with requests for more Burroughs stories. Burroughs began to feel confident in this new way to earn a living. He wrote a second tale of John Carter, *The Gods of Mars* (1913), and then *The Warlord of Mars* a year later. These three comprise the first connected trilogy in science-fiction and are considered classics of the genre.

Other magazines wanted Burroughs to write for them. He was a good bargainer and played one magazine off against the other. Realizing the power he had, he began negotiating better and better rates, until he became the reigning monarch of pulp fantasy fiction for the next thirty years, demanding and receiving the highest payment possible. In fact, he became so successful that he was able to move his family from Chicago to southern California, and in 1919, he purchased a 540-acre ranch in the San Fernando Valley. The city which eventually grew around the ranch was given the name "Tarzana" in homage to his hero.

The story of *A Princess of Mars* did not arise out of a vacuum. As it was Burroughs's first novel, much of it bloomed from his own experiences. His military service in Arizona provided him with a strong understanding of the desert, the prime terrain of Mars. His heartfelt descriptions of the landscapes of "Barsoom," the name the native Martians used for their planet, evoked the majesty of the American West and Burroughs's own love for the mountains, rivers, and valleys of uncivilized nature. He also held a deep affection for animals, which manifested most clearly in John Carter's loyal companion, Woola.

Moreover, as an avid researcher, Burroughs based the technology and mechanics found in his stories on the best science of the time. In the early years of the twentieth century, respected astronomers suggested that life as we know it could survive on Mars. Famed businessman-turned-astronomer Percival Lowell even surmised that the crisscross terrestrial features he saw through his telescope were water canals constructed by intelligent Martian hands.

Where science left unanswered questions, Burroughs's fertile imagination did the rest. Over the eleven novels he set on Barsoom, he lent verisimilitude to his fantastical Mars by developing a vast history for the planet tracing back millennia, even inventing a Martian language, as J.R.R. Tolkien would do much later for Middle-earth. Burroughs populated his Mars with alien flora and fauna, warring tribes, nomadic marauders, and decaying empires—in toto, a civilization that was collapsing deeper and deeper into barbarism. Embellishing ideas from Lowell, Burroughs imagined that the ancient canals built to transport water had almost dried up and the atmosphere was depleting with each century. Life on Mars was a Darwinian struggle on a global scale, with each species teetering on the edge of extinction. A hero like John Carter was needed not only to save Martian princesses, but the planet itself.

The importance of *A Princess of Mars* cannot be overestimated in the history of American literature. If magazine editors could not afford to commission Burroughs for a story, they looked for writers who could pen tales of a similar quality. Many of those who cut their teeth hacking out pulp stories in the vein of Burroughs would later become masters of the genre, including authors like Robert Heinlein, Isaac Asimov, Robert E. Howard, Ray Bradbury, Fritz Leiber, Otis Adelbert Kline, Leigh Brackett, Jack Vance, and Philip José Farmer. Leigh Brackett's interplanetary stories of her character Eric John Stark, who some consider the true heir of John Carter, won her the job to pen the screenplay for *The Empire Strikes Back*. Robert E. Howard applied the same level of detail in creating the Hyborian Age of his hero, Conan, as his predecessor Burroughs did for Barsoom. Ray Bradbury, always proud to acknowledge his debt to Burroughs, went on to write such classics as *The Martian Chronicles* and *Fahrenheit 451*.

Nevertheless, Burroughs's influence does not end with the pulps—it goes well beyond the page. His imaginative descriptions of Barsoom and its creatures have inspired many dozens, perhaps hundreds of artists, most notably Frank Frazetta. Comics based on the *Mars* novels have printed since the early 1940s. Readers as diverse as astronomer Carl Sagan, primatologist Jane Goodall, and President Ronald Reagan—whose favorite author was Burroughs—cite Burroughs's novels as helping to inspire their careers.

Most apparent to the modern audience is Burroughs's impact on the movie industry. Filmmakers like Kerry and Kevin Conran, George Lucas, and James Cameron have all acknowledged their debts to John Carter. Any reader of Burroughs cannot miss the plot parallels of the John Carter stories with Cameron's *Avatar*, or the many references to Barsoom in George Lucas's *Star Wars*. Where would the warrior Jedi be without Burroughs's "jeddak," the wooly Banthas without "banth," or the evil Sith without the vile Barsoomian insects Burroughs dubbed the "sith"?

The *Mars* novels themselves have been contemplated as possible projects for the Hollywood studios almost since their publication. An animated serial adaptation almost happened in 1936, when Bob Clampett and John Coleman Burroughs prepared test footage for MGM. Unfortunately, their dream never came to fruition. Sales representatives determined that American audiences would be puzzled by movies about a man adventuring on Mars. It would take more than seventy-five years for Barsoom to reach the silver screen, when finally, in March 2012, Walt Disney Studios released one of its most beautiful and elaborate live-action films, *John Carter*, directed by *WALL•E's* Andrew Stanton.

What explains the continual appeal of Edgar Rice Burroughs and his Mars stories? Certainly, the romantic elements play an important role. In Burroughs's fiction, as was common in the genre, a beautiful and feisty damsel is rescued from overwhelming dangers by an honorable yet shy and inarticulate hero who performs phenomenal feats. Usually, true love conquers all. That said, many of the stories in the pulps followed the same structure and a majority of them are forgotten. What makes the creations of Edgar Rice Burroughs stand above the work of his peers is that his stories tap into the unconscious emotional desires of his readership, which at the time of publication was primarily male. Back then, as they do today, young men coming into adulthood want to impress the opposite gender, yet often lack the boldness, audacity, and skills to do so. They wish they could be like John Carter, and accomplish something great, hoping that the young lady will in turn recognize the latent hero within them. These are the same themes found in *Spider-Man* or other superhero comics: the universal desire for an ordinary boy to become a hero of legend.

Comparable to a superhero, the protagonists in Burroughs's books all live by a strong moral code. While physical beauty of form and figure is celebrated—as is an unembarrassed acceptance of nudity—the sexuality is implied, not explicit. The heroes and heroines know desire, but they also know the difference between duty and desire, and always do what they believe to be right. Like the noble cowboys of old, they value friendship above all, and prize honor and loyalty. Whenever John Carter of Mars, born a Virginia gentleman, sees someone facing unfair odds, he rushes in to help. Instinctively, the Burroughs hero stands up against injustice, no matter what the cost. They speak truth to power.

At first glance, a contemporary reader may question Burroughs's use of race in his books. Sadly, one cannot divorce history from fiction. Sometimes Burroughs employs stereotypes that were prevalent at the time yet are offensive today. But often Burroughs subverts these stereotypes. The white-skinned holy Therns of Barsoom are cannibals. The black-skinned First Born of Barsoom are of the highest intelligence and possess military skills which make them among the greatest of all the warriors and soldiers on Mars. Burroughs's greatest subversion of all is his attempt to unify the diversity of the Barsoom. Burroughs has his hero, John Carter, attempt to bring together the green men, the red men, the white-skinned Therns, the black-skinned First Born, and the yellow-skinned people of the north in brotherhood. A former soldier of Confederacy becomes an agent of equality.

Language is another hurdle for modern readers of Burroughs's novels. They may find his syntax and vocabulary archaic compared to what writers employ today. But one must remember that Burroughs's own sensibilities were formed well before the turn of the twentieth century—and most definitely before the flawed anti-hero became the protagonist of choice in western literature. In 1912, readers expected florid prose that fit the legendary deeds described. They believed that noble and well-educated characters should speak in elevated dialogue that was inspired by the poetry of Shakespeare and the King James Bible. Normally this style would turn off a contemporary audience, yet Burroughs possesses a unique gift that continues to connect him with a modern audience. His talent at writing extraordinary action sequences matches him with the best thriller writers of today.

Most of all, Burroughs's stubborn self-reliance shines through his characters, and may be the essential factor of his lasting appeal. While the threat of death to his heroes remains real, none of them ever quits. No situation is too terrible, no battle is ever hopeless. There is always a way out. The famous motto of the Burroughs hero, as quoted by John Carter—"I Still Live!"—has inspired generation after generation of young men and women never to surrender in the face of odds, however great. A certain eleven-year-old boy from Pasadena happily was one of them.

– Bob Zeuschner
February 20, 2012

A Princess of Mars

BY

Edgar Rice Burroughs

WITH **ANNOTATIONS** BY Aaron Parrett

To My Son
JACK

FOREWORD [1]

To the Reader of this Work:

In submitting Captain Carter's strange manuscript to you in book form, I believe that a few words relative to this remarkable personality will be of interest.

My first recollection of Captain Carter is of the few months he spent at my father's home in Virginia, just prior to the opening of the civil war. I was then a child of but five years, yet I well remember the tall, dark, smooth-faced, athletic man whom I called Uncle Jack.[2]

He seemed always to be laughing; and he entered into the sports of the children with the same hearty good fellowship he displayed toward those pastimes in which the men and women of his own age indulged; or he would sit for an hour at a time entertaining my old grandmother with stories of his strange, wild life in all parts of the world. We all loved him, and our slaves fairly worshipped the ground he trod.

He was a splendid specimen of manhood, standing a good two inches over six feet, broad of shoulder and narrow of hip, with the carriage of the trained fighting man. His features were regular and clear cut, his hair black and closely cropped, while his eyes were of a steel gray, reflecting a strong and loyal character, filled with fire and initiative. His manners were perfect, and his courtliness was that of a typical southern gentleman of the highest type.[3]

His horsemanship, especially after hounds, was a marvel and delight even in that country of magnificent horsemen. I have often heard my

---

[1] *A Princess of Mars* was first published as *Under the Moons of Mars* in *All-Story* magazine in four installments beginning in February 1912. It was Burroughs's first published work, though he used the pseudonym "Normal Bean," which was "corrected" by editors in publication as "Norman Bean."

[2] Burroughs inserts himself into the narrative to add a sense of authenticity to what would have been an very odd (and original) story in 1912. Nonetheless, the real Burroughs was born well after the American Civil War in 1875, which would make him around ten when he set the story.

[3] Very likely the inspiration for John Carter was Burroughs's mentor, Captain Charles King, from the Orchard Lake Military Academy in Michigan, where Burroughs was a member of the class of 1895. King was a graduate of West Point and a superb cavalryman in the wars against the Sioux and Apache in the 1870s. He not only regaled Burroughs with tales of combat, but taught him the finer points of horsemanship, which Burroughs mastered. See Robert Fenton, *The Big Swingers* (Prentice-Hall, 1967).

father caution him against his wild recklessness, but he would only laugh, and say that the tumble that killed him would be from the back of a horse yet unfoaled.

When the war broke out he left us, nor did I see him again for some fifteen or sixteen years. When he returned it was without warning, and I was much surprised to note that he had not aged apparently a moment, nor had he changed in any other outward way. He was, when others were with him, the same genial, happy fellow we had known of old, but when he thought himself alone I have seen him sit for hours gazing off into space, his face set in a look of wistful longing and hopeless misery; and at night he would sit thus looking up into the heavens, at what I did not know until I read his manuscript years afterward.

He told us that he had been prospecting and mining in Arizona part of the time since the war; and that he had been very successful was evidenced by the unlimited amount of money with which he was supplied. As to the details of his life during these years he was very reticent, in fact he would not talk of them at all.[4]

He remained with us for about a year and then went to New York, where he purchased a little place on the Hudson, where I visited him once a year on the occasions of my trips to the New York market—my father and I owning and operating a string of general stores throughout Virginia at that time. Captain Carter had a small but beautiful cottage, situated on a bluff overlooking the river, and during one of my last visits, in the winter of 1885, I observed he was much occupied in writing, I presume now, upon this manuscript.

He told me at this time that if anything should happen to him he wished me to take charge of his estate, and he gave me a key to a

---

[4] Western states enjoyed an influx of settlers from the east immediately following the American Civil War—many of them miners inspired by reports of major discoveries in the Sierra Nevada of California at Sutter's Mill in 1849 and Pike's Peak, Colorado in 1859. The Comstock Lode in Nevada was also discovered in 1859, and other major mining complexes, such as Butte, Montana, eventually known as "the richest hill on Earth," were first prospected in the years just after the Civil War. Many of the early western miners were former Confederate soldiers. Placer mining began in Arizona as early as the 1850s.

Burroughs's inspiration for Captain Carter's explorations in Arizona would most likely have been either the Congress Mine or the Lost Dutchman Mine, both discovered in central Arizona in 1870. The so-called "Lost Dutchman" saga (from a corruption of the word for "German") became an oft-repeated western legend involving a huge cache of Apache gold—and since John Carter also tangles with the Apaches in the first chapter, perhaps Burroughs had the Lost Dutchman story in mind.

compartment in the safe which stood in his study, telling me I would find his will there and some personal instructions which he had me pledge myself to carry out with absolute fidelity.

After I had retired for the night I have seen him from my window standing in the moonlight on the brink of the bluff overlooking the Hudson with his arms stretched out to the heavens as though in appeal. I thought at the time that he was praying, although I never understood that he was in the strict sense of the term a religious man.

Several months after I had returned home from my last visit, the first of March, 1886, I think, I received a telegram from him asking me to come to him at once. I had always been his favorite among the younger generation of Carters and so I hastened to comply with his demand.

I arrived at the little station, about a mile from his grounds, on the morning of March 4, 1886, and when I asked the livery man to drive me out to Captain Carter's he replied that if I was a friend of the Captain's he had some very bad news for me; the Captain had been found dead shortly after daylight that very morning by the watchman attached to an adjoining property.

For some reason this news did not surprise me, but I hurried out to his place as quickly as possible, so that I could take charge of the body and of his affairs.

I found the watchman who had discovered him, together with the local police chief and several townspeople, assembled in his little study. The watchman related the few details connected with the finding of the body, which he said had been still warm when he came upon it. It lay, he said, stretched full length in the snow with the arms outstretched above the head toward the edge of the bluff, and when he showed me the spot it flashed upon me that it was the identical one where I had seen him on those other nights, with his arms raised in supplication to the skies.

There were no marks of violence on the body, and with the aid of a local physician the coroner's jury quickly reached a decision of death from heart failure. Left alone in the study, I opened the safe and withdrew the contents of the drawer in which he had told me I would find my instructions. They were in part peculiar indeed, but I have followed them to each last detail as faithfully as I was able.

He directed that I remove his body to Virginia without embalming, and that he be laid in an open coffin within a tomb which he previously had had constructed and which, as I later learned, was well ventilated. The instructions impressed upon me that I must personally see that this was carried out just as he directed, even in secrecy if necessary.

His property was left in such a way that I was to receive the entire income for twenty-five years, when the principal was to become mine. His further instructions related to this manuscript which I was to retain sealed and unread, just as I found it, for eleven years; nor was I to divulge its contents until twenty-one years after his death.

A strange feature about the tomb, where his body still lies, is that the massive door is equipped with a single, huge gold-plated spring lock which can be opened *only from the inside.*[5]

Yours very sincerely,

EDGAR RICE BURROUGHS.

---

[5] By conveying to the reader the intriguing information that Carter's tomb can only be opened "*from the inside,*" Burroughs not only leaves the possibility hanging that Carter is not truly dead, but also cleverly suggests a "locked room mystery." This is a subgenre of the mystery genre, usually involving a crime committed within a locked room. The invention of the form is usually attributed to Edgar Allan Poe in his "Murders in the Rue Morgue" (1841), though other classics in the field include Gaston Leroux's *Mystery of the Yellow Room* (1907), Jacques Futrelle's "The Problem of Cell 13" (1905), and John Dickson Carr's "The Hollow Men" (1935). In Carter's case, the mystery is enhanced by his reappearance in later novels, thus "solving" the locked room problem.

CHAPTER I
ON THE ARIZONA HILLS

I am a very old man; how old I do not know. Possibly I am a hundred, possibly more; but I cannot tell because I have never aged as other men, nor do I remember any childhood. So far as I can recollect I have always been a man, a man of about thirty. I appear today as I did forty years and more ago, and yet I feel that I cannot go on living forever; that some day I shall die the real death from which there is no resurrection. I do not know why I should fear death, I who have died twice and am still alive; but yet I have the same horror of it as you who have never died, and it is because of this terror of death, I believe, that I am so convinced of my mortality.

And because of this conviction I have determined to write down the story of the interesting periods of my life and of my death. I cannot explain the phenomena; I can only set down here in the words of an ordinary soldier of fortune a chronicle of the strange events that befell me during the ten years that my dead body lay undiscovered in an Arizona cave.

I have never told this story, nor shall mortal man see this manuscript until after I have passed over for eternity. I know that the average human mind will not believe what it cannot grasp, and so I do not purpose being pilloried by the public, the pulpit, and the press, and held up as a colossal liar when I am but telling the simple truths which some day science will substantiate. Possibly the suggestions which I gained upon Mars, and the knowledge which I can set down in this chronicle, will aid in an earlier understanding of the mysteries of our sister planet; mysteries to you, but no longer mysteries to me.

My name is John Carter; I am better known as Captain Jack Carter of Virginia. At the close of the Civil War I found myself possessed of several hundred thousand dollars (Confederate) and a captain's commission in the cavalry arm of an army which no longer existed; the servant of a state which had vanished with the hopes of the South. Masterless, penniless, and with my only means of livelihood, fighting, gone, I determined to work my way to the southwest and attempt to retrieve my fallen fortunes in a search for gold.

I spent nearly a year prospecting in company with another Confederate officer, Captain James K. Powell of Richmond.[6] We were

---

[6] Is it possible that Burroughs named this Confederate soldier and sidekick to John Carter after Percival Lowell, contracting [P]ercival with Lowell to get Powell?

extremely fortunate, for late in the winter of 1865, after many hardships and privations, we located the most remarkable gold-bearing quartz vein that our wildest dreams had ever pictured. Powell, who was a mining engineer by education, stated that we had uncovered over a million dollars worth of ore in a trifle over three months.

As our equipment was crude in the extreme we decided that one of us must return to civilization, purchase the necessary machinery and return with a sufficient force of men properly to work the mine.

As Powell was familiar with the country, as well as with the mechanical requirements of mining we determined that it would be best for him to make the trip. It was agreed that I was to hold down our claim against the remote possibility of its being jumped by some wandering prospector.

On March 3, 1866, Powell and I packed his provisions on two of our burros, and bidding me good-bye he mounted his horse, and started down the mountainside toward the valley, across which led the first stage of his journey.

The morning of Powell's departure was, like nearly all Arizona mornings, clear and beautiful; I could see him and his little pack animals picking their way down the mountainside toward the valley, and all during the morning I would catch occasional glimpses of them as they topped a hog back or came out upon a level plateau. My last sight of Powell was about three in the afternoon as he entered the shadows of the range on the opposite side of the valley.

Some half hour later I happened to glance casually across the valley and was much surprised to note three little dots in about the same place I had last seen my friend and his two pack animals. I am not given to needless worrying, but the more I tried to convince myself that all was well with Powell, and that the dots I had seen on his trail were antelope or wild horses, the less I was able to assure myself.

Percival Lowell greatly influenced Burroughs's depictions of the Martian landscape. Lowell wrote three books devoted to Mars: *Mars* (1895), *Mars and Its Canals* (1906), and *Mars, the Abode of Life* (1908), all informed by his observations of the red planet from the observatory he constructed near Flagstaff, Arizona in 1894.

But Lowell's observations veered toward fantasy. Lowell misinterpreted astronomer Giovanni Schiaparelli's writings of the "canali" on Mars, an Italian word simply meaning "channels," which in no way implied human (or extraterrestrial) construction. The poor translation influenced Lowell's telescopic observations of Mars and helped sustain the misperception that Mars was a formerly lush planet now drying up, forcing its inhabitants to dig immense canals to move water about the surface (precisely the depiction Burroughs presents in his Martian cycle).

Since we had entered the territory we had not seen a hostile Indian, and we had, therefore, become careless in the extreme, and were wont to ridicule the stories we had heard of the great numbers of these vicious marauders that were supposed to haunt the trails, taking their toll in lives and torture of every white party which fell into their merciless clutches.

Powell, I knew, was well armed and, further, an experienced Indian fighter; but I too had lived and fought for years among the Sioux in the North, and I knew that his chances were small against a party of cunning trailing Apaches. Finally I could endure the suspense no longer, and, arming myself with my two Colt revolvers and a carbine, I strapped two belts of cartridges about me and catching my saddle horse, started down the trail taken by Powell in the morning.

As soon as I reached comparatively level ground I urged my mount into a canter and continued this, where the going permitted, until, close upon dusk, I discovered the point where other tracks joined those of Powell. They were the tracks of unshod ponies, three of them, and the ponies had been galloping.

I followed rapidly until, darkness shutting down, I was forced to await the rising of the moon, and given an opportunity to speculate on the question of the wisdom of my chase. Possibly I had conjured up impossible dangers, like some nervous old housewife, and when I should catch up with Powell would get a good laugh for my pains. However, I am not prone to sensitiveness, and the following of a sense of duty, wherever it may lead, has always been a kind of fetich with me throughout my life; which may account for the honors bestowed upon me by three republics and the decorations and friendships of an old and powerful emperor and several lesser kings, in whose service my sword has been red many a time.

About nine o'clock the moon was sufficiently bright for me to proceed on my way and I had no difficulty in following the trail at a fast walk, and in some places at a brisk trot until, about midnight, I reached the water hole where Powell had expected to camp. I came upon the spot unexpectedly, finding it entirely deserted, with no signs of having been recently occupied as a camp.

I was interested to note that the tracks of the pursuing horsemen, for such I was now convinced they must be, continued after Powell with only a brief stop at the hole for water; and always at the same rate of speed as his.

I was positive now that the trailers were Apaches and that they wished to capture Powell alive for the fiendish pleasure of the torture, so I urged my horse onward at a most dangerous pace, hoping against hope that I would catch up with the red rascals before they attacked him.

Further speculation was suddenly cut short by the faint report of two shots far ahead of me. I knew that Powell would need me now if ever, and I instantly urged my horse to his topmost speed up the narrow and difficult mountain trail.

I had forged ahead for perhaps a mile or more without hearing further sounds, when the trail suddenly debouched onto a small, open plateau near the summit of the pass. I had passed through a narrow, overhanging gorge just before entering suddenly upon this table land, and the sight which met my eyes filled me with consternation and dismay.

The little stretch of level land was white with Indian tepees, and there were probably half a thousand red warriors clustered around some object near the center of the camp. Their attention was so wholly riveted to this point of interest that they did not notice me, and I easily could have turned back into the dark recesses of the gorge and made my escape with perfect safety. The fact, however, that this thought did not occur to me until the following day removes any possible right to a claim to heroism to which the narration of this episode might possibly otherwise entitle me.

I do not believe that I am made of the stuff which constitutes heroes, because, in all of the hundreds of instances that my voluntary acts have placed me face to face with death, I cannot recall a single one where any alternative step to that I took occurred to me until many hours later. My mind is evidently so constituted that I am subconsciously forced into the path of duty without recourse to tiresome mental processes. However that may be, I have never regretted that cowardice is not optional with me.

In this instance I was, of course, positive that Powell was the center of attraction, but whether I thought or acted first I do not know, but within an instant from the moment the scene broke upon my view I had whipped out my revolvers and was charging down upon the entire army of warriors, shooting rapidly, and whooping at the top of my lungs. Singlehanded, I could not have pursued better tactics, for the red men, convinced by sudden surprise that not less than a regiment of regulars was upon them, turned and fled in every direction for their bows, arrows, and rifles.

The view which their hurried routing disclosed filled me with apprehension and with rage. Under the clear rays of the Arizona moon lay Powell, his body fairly bristling with the hostile arrows of the braves. That he was already dead I could not but be convinced, and yet I would have saved his body from mutilation at the hands of the Apaches as quickly as I would have saved the man himself from death.

Riding close to him I reached down from the saddle, and grasping his cartridge belt drew him up across the withers of my mount. A backward glance convinced me that to return by the way I had come would be more hazardous than to continue across the plateau, so, putting spurs to my poor beast, I made a dash for the opening to the pass which I could distinguish on the far side of the table land.

The Indians had by this time discovered that I was alone and I was pursued with imprecations, arrows, and rifle balls. The fact that it is difficult to aim anything but imprecations accurately by moonlight, that they were upset by the sudden and unexpected manner of my advent, and that I was a rather rapidly moving target saved me from the various deadly projectiles of the enemy and permitted me to reach the shadows of the surrounding peaks before an orderly pursuit could be organized.

My horse was traveling practically unguided as I knew that I had probably less knowledge of the exact location of the trail to the pass than he, and thus it happened that he entered a defile which led to the summit of the range and not to the pass which I had hoped would carry me to the valley and to safety. It is probable, however, that to this fact I owe my life and the remarkable experiences and adventures which befell me during the following ten years.

My first knowledge that I was on the wrong trail came when I heard the yells of the pursuing savages suddenly grow fainter and fainter far off to my left.

I knew then that they had passed to the left of the jagged rock formation at the edge of the plateau, to the right of which my horse had borne me and the body of Powell.

I drew rein on a little level promontory overlooking the trail below and to my left, and saw the party of pursuing savages disappearing around the point of a neighboring peak.

I knew the Indians would soon discover that they were on the wrong trail and that the search for me would be renewed in the right direction as soon as they located my tracks.

I had gone but a short distance further when what seemed to be an excellent trail opened up around the face of a high cliff. The trail was level and quite broad and led upward and in the general direction I wished to go. The cliff arose for several hundred feet on my right, and on my left was an equal and nearly perpendicular drop to the bottom of a rocky ravine.

I had followed this trail for perhaps a hundred yards when a sharp turn to the right brought me to the mouth of a large cave.[7] The opening was about four feet in height and three to four feet wide, and at this opening the trail ended.

It was now morning, and, with the customary lack of dawn which is a startling characteristic of Arizona, it had become daylight almost without warning.

Dismounting, I laid Powell upon the ground, but the most painstaking examination failed to reveal the faintest spark of life. I forced water from my canteen between his dead lips, bathed his face and rubbed his hands, working over him continuously for the better part of an hour in the face of the fact that I knew him to be dead.

I was very fond of Powell; he was thoroughly a man in every respect; a polished southern gentleman; a staunch and true friend; and it was with a feeling of the deepest grief that I finally gave up my crude endeavors at resuscitation.

Leaving Powell's body where it lay on the ledge I crept into the cave to reconnoiter. I found a large chamber, possibly a hundred feet in diameter and thirty or forty feet in height; a smooth and well-worn floor, and many other evidences that the cave had, at some remote period, been inhabited. The back of the cave was so lost in dense shadow that I could not distinguish whether there were openings into other apartments or not.

As I was continuing my examination I commenced to feel a pleasant drowsiness creeping over me which I attributed to the fatigue of my long and strenuous ride, and the reaction from the excitement of the fight and the pursuit. I felt comparatively safe in my present location as I knew that one man could defend the trail to the cave against an army.

I soon became so drowsy that I could scarcely resist the strong desire to throw myself on the floor of the cave for a few moments' rest, but I knew that this would never do, as it would mean certain death at the hands of my red friends, who might be upon me at any moment. With an effort I started toward the opening of the cave only to reel drunkenly against a side wall, and from there slip prone upon the floor.

---

[7] Arizona has over a thousand documented caves, including several of great repute, such as Lava River Cave and Grand Canyon Caverns (both near Flagstaff). Burroughs may have had in mind the Tonto Bridge cave, a secluded natural bridge that spans 400 feet across Pine Creek near Payson. As legend has it, prospector David Gowan "discovered" Tonto Bridge in 1877 while trying to escape from pursuing Apaches.

CHAPTER II
THE ESCAPE OF THE DEAD

A sense of delicious dreaminess overcame me, my muscles relaxed, and I was on the point of giving way to my desire to sleep when the sound of approaching horses reached my ears. I attempted to spring to my feet but was horrified to discover that my muscles refused to respond to my will. I was now thoroughly awake, but as unable to move a muscle as though turned to stone. It was then, for the first time, that I noticed a slight vapor filling the cave.[8] It was extremely tenuous and only noticeable against the opening which led to daylight. There also came to my nostrils a faintly pungent odor, and I could only assume that I had been overcome by some poisonous gas, but why I should retain my mental faculties and yet be unable to move I could not fathom.

I lay facing the opening of the cave and where I could see the short stretch of trail which lay between the cave and the turn of the cliff around which the trail led. The noise of the approaching horses had ceased, and I judged the Indians were creeping stealthily upon me along the little ledge which led to my living tomb. I remember that I hoped they would make short work of me as I did not particularly relish the thought of the innumerable things they might do to me if the spirit prompted them.[9]

I had not long to wait before a stealthy sound apprised me of their nearness, and then a war-bonneted, paint-streaked face was thrust cautiously around the shoulder of the cliff, and savage eyes looked into mine. That he could see me in the dim light of the cave I was sure for the early morning sun was falling full upon me through the opening.

The fellow, instead of approaching, merely stood and stared; his eyes bulging and his jaw dropped. And then another savage face appeared, and

---

[8] What kind of gas would produce such an effect? About the only common "gas" that Burroughs could have in mind would be diethyl ether, which was widely used as an anesthetic in the nineteenth and early twentieth centuries. The reported effects of ether are similar to what Burroughs describes here. See René Fülöp-Miller's *Triumph over Pain* (Bobbs-Merrill, 1938) for an excellent overview of the history of anesthesia containing descriptions of the effects of ether.

[9] Apaches were known for their cruelty, but was it justified? Edward Opler's 1941 book, *An Apache Life-way: The Economic, Social, and Religious Institutions of the Chiricahua Indians* (reprinted in 1994 by University of Nebraska Press) provides an excellent introduction to the culture. The last of the famous Apache attacks on settlers in Arizona and New Mexico (led by the famous Geronimo) were over by 1890. A less charitable and controversial account may be found in Gregory and Susan Michno's *A Fate Worse Than Death: Indian Captivities in the West 1830-1885* (Caxton, 2007).

a third and fourth and fifth, craning their necks over the shoulders of their fellows whom they could not pass upon the narrow ledge. Each face was the picture of awe and fear, but for what reason I did not know, nor did I learn until ten years later. That there were still other braves behind those who regarded me was apparent from the fact that the leaders passed back whispered word to those behind them.

Suddenly a low but distinct moaning sound issued from the recesses of the cave behind me, and, as it reached the ears of the Indians, they turned and fled in terror, panic-stricken. So frantic were their efforts to escape from the unseen thing behind me that one of the braves was hurled headlong from the cliff to the rocks below. Their wild cries echoed in the canyon for a short time, and then all was still once more.

The sound which had frightened them was not repeated, but it had been sufficient as it was to start me speculating on the possible horror which lurked in the shadows at my back. Fear is a relative term and so I can only measure my feelings at that time by what I had experienced in previous positions of danger and by those that I have passed through since; but I can say without shame that if the sensations I endured during the next few minutes were fear, then may God help the coward, for cowardice is of a surety its own punishment.

To be held paralyzed, with one's back toward some horrible and unknown danger from the very sound of which the ferocious Apache warriors turn in wild stampede, as a flock of sheep would madly flee from a pack of wolves, seems to me the last word in fearsome predicaments for a man who had ever been used to fighting for his life with all the energy of a powerful physique.

Several times I thought I heard faint sounds behind me as of somebody moving cautiously, but eventually even these ceased, and I was left to the contemplation of my position without interruption. I could but vaguely conjecture the cause of my paralysis, and my only hope lay in that it might pass off as suddenly as it had fallen upon me.

Late in the afternoon my horse, which had been standing with dragging rein before the cave, started slowly down the trail, evidently in search of food and water, and I was left alone with my mysterious unknown companion and the dead body of my friend, which lay just within my range of vision upon the ledge where I had placed it in the early morning.

From then until possibly midnight all was silence, the silence of the dead; then, suddenly, the awful moan of the morning broke upon my startled ears, and there came again from the black shadows the sound of a moving thing, and a faint rustling as of dead leaves. The shock to my already overstrained nervous system was terrible in the extreme, and with a superhuman effort I strove to break my awful bonds. It was an effort of the mind, of the will, of the nerves; not muscular, for I could not move even so much as my little finger, but none the less mighty for all that. And then something gave, there was a momentary feeling of nausea, a sharp click as of the snapping of a steel wire, and I stood with my back against the wall of the cave facing my unknown foe.

And then the moonlight flooded the cave, and there before me lay my own body as it had been lying all these hours, with the eyes staring toward the open ledge and the hands resting limply upon the ground.[10] I looked first at my lifeless clay there upon the floor of the cave and then down at myself in utter bewilderment; for there I lay clothed, and yet here I stood but naked as at the minute of my birth.

The transition had been so sudden and so unexpected that it left me for a moment forgetful of aught else than my strange metamorphosis. My first thought was, is this then death! Have I indeed passed over forever into that other life! But I could not well believe this, as I could feel my heart pounding against my ribs from the exertion of my efforts to release myself from the anaesthesis which had held me. My breath was coming in quick, short gasps, cold sweat stood out from every pore of my body, and the ancient experiment of pinching revealed the fact that I was anything other than a wraith.

Again was I suddenly recalled to my immediate surroundings by a repetition of the weird moan from the depths of the cave. Naked and unarmed as I was, I had no desire to face the unseen thing which menaced me.

My revolvers were strapped to my lifeless body which, for some unfathomable reason, I could not bring myself to touch. My carbine was in its boot, strapped to my saddle, and as my horse had wandered off I was left without means of defense. My only alternative seemed to lie in flight and my decision was crystallized by a recurrence of the rustling sound

---

[10] Here we have a classic depiction of the "out-of-body" experience. John Carter is anesthetized with a gas, feels himself leave his body, and then observes his corpse. Interestingly, reports of near-death experiences mirror some descriptions of alien abduction experiences.

Erling Holtsmark sees Carter's experience as an example of *katabasis*, or the journey of the hero to the underworld, with Odysseus's trip to Hades in Book XI of the *Odyssey*, or Aeneas's trip to the Underworld in Book VI of the *Aeneid* as obvious progenitors. See Holtsmark's *Edgar Rice Burroughs* (Twayne, 1986).

from the thing which now seemed, in the darkness of the cave and to my distorted imagination, to be creeping stealthily upon me.

Unable longer to resist the temptation to escape this horrible place I leaped quickly through the opening into the starlight of a clear Arizona night. The crisp, fresh mountain air outside the cave acted as an immediate tonic and I felt new life and new courage coursing through me. Pausing upon the brink of the ledge I upbraided myself for what now seemed to me wholly unwarranted apprehension. I reasoned with myself that I had lain helpless for many hours within the cave, yet nothing had molested me, and my better judgment, when permitted the direction of clear and logical reasoning, convinced me that the noises I had heard must have resulted from purely natural and harmless causes; probably the conformation of the cave was such that a slight breeze had caused the sounds I heard.

I decided to investigate, but first I lifted my head to fill my lungs with the pure, invigorating night air of the mountains. As I did so I saw stretching far below me the beautiful vista of rocky gorge, and level, cacti-studded flat, wrought by the moonlight into a miracle of soft splendor and wondrous enchantment.

Few western wonders are more inspiring than the beauties of an Arizona moonlit landscape; the silvered mountains in the distance, the strange lights and shadows upon hog back and arroyo, and the grotesque details of the stiff, yet beautiful cacti form a picture at once enchanting and inspiring; as though one were catching for the first time a glimpse of some dead and forgotten world, so different is it from the aspect of any other spot upon our earth.[11]

---

[11] Burroughs is astute to recognize the southwestern landscape as probably akin to Mars or other terrestrial planets (aside from Venus with its heavy atmosphere). As it happens, Apollo astronauts spent considerable time training in the highlands in Arizona. See Don E. Wilhelms's authoritative overview of the geological background of the Apollo moon missions, *To a Rocky Moon: A Geologist's History of Lunar Exploration* (University of Arizona Press, 1994).

Arizona was also the location chosen for Biosphere 2, a completely closed-off artificial environment that was designed in part to evaluate the possibility of establishing self-sustaining environment for travelers to Mars. See Nelson, M. and W. Dempster, "Living in Space: Results from Biosphere 2's Initial Closure, an Early Testbed for Closed Ecological Systems on Mars" (*American Astronautical Society: Science & Technology Series* Vol. 86, 1996).

In many ways, Antarctica presents a much more Mars-like environment and scientists have also set up analogue Mars habitats there as well. See Robert Zubrin's *Mars on Earth* (Tarcher, 2003).

As I stood thus meditating, I turned my gaze from the landscape to the heavens where the myriad stars formed a gorgeous and fitting canopy for the wonders of the earthly scene. My attention was quickly riveted by a large red star close to the distant horizon. As I gazed upon it I felt a spell of overpowering fascination—it was Mars, the god of war, and for me, the fighting man, it had always held the power of irresistible enchantment. As I gazed at it on that far-gone night it seemed to call across the unthinkable void, to lure me to it, to draw me as the lodestone attracts a particle of iron.

My longing was beyond the power of opposition; I closed my eyes, stretched out my arms toward the god of my vocation and felt myself drawn with the suddenness of thought through the trackless immensity of space. There was an instant of extreme cold and utter darkness.

CHAPTER III
MY ADVENT ON MARS

I opened my eyes upon a strange and weird landscape. I knew that I was on Mars; not once did I question either my sanity or my wakefulness. I was not asleep, no need for pinching here; my inner consciousness told me as plainly that I was upon Mars as your conscious mind tells you that you are upon Earth. You do not question the fact; neither did I.

I found myself lying prone upon a bed of yellowish, mosslike vegetation which stretched around me in all directions for interminable miles. I seemed to be lying in a deep, circular basin, along the outer verge of which I could distinguish the irregularities of low hills.

It was midday, the sun was shining full upon me and the heat of it was rather intense upon my naked body, yet no greater than would have been true under similar conditions on an Arizona desert.[12] Here and there were slight outcroppings of quartz-bearing rock which glistened in the sunlight; and a little to my left, perhaps a hundred yards, appeared a low, walled enclosure about four feet in height. No water, and no other vegetation than the moss was in evidence, and as I was somewhat thirsty I determined to do a little exploring.

Springing to my feet I received my first Martian surprise, for the effort, which on Earth would have brought me standing upright, carried me into the Martian air to the height of about three yards. I alighted softly upon the ground, however, without appreciable shock or jar. Now commenced a series of evolutions which even then seemed ludicrous in the extreme. I found that I must learn to walk all over again, as the muscular exertion which carried me easily and safely upon Earth played strange antics with me upon Mars.[13]

---

[12] In actuality, the mid-day sun on Mars in summertime would produce temperatures of only around 70 degrees Fahrenheit at the surface, while the ambient air temperature would be around 32 degrees. The temperatures at the poles are colder than anything on Earth, routinely reaching −195 degrees Fahrenheit. The average temperature on Mars is −80 degrees Fahrenheit. See *World Book Encyclopedia* (2006). For a more accurate description of conditions on Mars and what it would take to survive, see Robert Zubrin's *How to Live on Mars: A Trusty Guidebook to Surviving and Thriving on the Red Planet* (Three Rivers Press, 2008).

[13] Just as Jules Verne in *A Trip to the Moon* (1865) accurately imagined what weightlessness during the journey to the Moon would be like, Burroughs imagines more or less accurately what effect the reduced gravity on Mars would have on a human accustomed to Earth gravity. Naturally Burroughs exaggerates the effects, but a 200 lb. man would weigh only 80 lbs. on Mars. Since he would be able to apply the

Instead of progressing in a sane and dignified manner, my attempts to walk resulted in a variety of hops which took me clear of the ground a couple of feet at each step and landed me sprawling upon my face or back at the end of each second or third hop. My muscles, perfectly attuned and accustomed to the force of gravity on Earth, played the mischief with me in attempting for the first time to cope with the lesser gravitation and lower air pressure on Mars.

I was determined, however, to explore the low structure which was the only evidence of habitation in sight, and so I hit upon the unique plan of reverting to first principles in locomotion, creeping. I did fairly well at this and in a few moments had reached the low, encircling wall of the enclosure.

There appeared to be no doors or windows upon the side nearest me, but as the wall was but about four feet high I cautiously gained my feet and peered over the top upon the strangest sight it had ever been given me to see.

The roof of the enclosure was of solid glass about four or five inches in thickness, and beneath this were several hundred large eggs, perfectly round and snowy white. The eggs were nearly uniform in size being about two and one-half feet in diameter.

Five or six had already hatched and the grotesque caricatures which sat blinking in the sunlight were enough to cause me to doubt my sanity. They seemed mostly head, with little scrawny bodies, long necks and six legs, or, as I afterward learned, two legs and two arms, with an intermediary pair of limbs which could be used at will either as arms or legs. Their eyes were set at the extreme sides of their heads a trifle above the center and protruded in such a manner that they could be directed either forward or back and also independently of each other, thus permitting this queer animal to look in any direction, or in two directions at once, without the necessity of turning the head.[14]

The ears, which were slightly above the eyes and closer together, were small, cup-shaped antennae, protruding not more than an inch on these young specimens. Their noses were but longitudinal slits in the center of their faces, midway between their mouths and ears.

---

same force in a leap under different gravitational conditions, a broad jump of 10 feet on Earth would mean that on Mars he could now leap 25 feet.

[14] Burroughs's close familiarity with the horse possibly inspired his description of the Martians' vision. The horse, which possesses the largest eye of any Earth land animal, has a range of vision of about 350 degrees, of which 18 percent is binocular. In other words, a horse is able to see in any direction except directly behind itself.

There was no hair on their bodies, which were of a very light yellowish-green color. In the adults, as I was to learn quite soon, this color deepens to an olive green and is darker in the male than in the female. Further, the heads of the adults are not so out of proportion to their bodies as in the case of the young.

The iris of the eyes is blood red, as in Albinos, while the pupil is dark. The eyeball itself is very white, as are the teeth. These latter add a most ferocious appearance to an otherwise fearsome and terrible countenance, as the lower tusks curve upward to sharp points which end about where the eyes of earthly human beings are located. The whiteness of the teeth is not that of ivory, but of the snowiest and most gleaming of china. Against the dark background of their olive skins their tusks stand out in a most striking manner, making these weapons present a singularly formidable appearance.

Most of these details I noted later, for I was given but little time to speculate on the wonders of my new discovery. I had seen that the eggs were in the process of hatching, and as I stood watching the hideous little monsters break from their shells I failed to note the approach of a score of full-grown Martians from behind me.

Coming, as they did, over the soft and soundless moss, which covers practically the entire surface of Mars with the exception of the frozen areas at the poles and the scattered cultivated districts, they might have captured me easily, but their intentions were far more sinister. It was the rattling of the accouterments of the foremost warrior which warned me.

On such a little thing my life hung that I often marvel that I escaped so easily. Had not the rifle of the leader of the party swung from its fastenings beside his saddle in such a way as to strike against the butt of his great metal-shod spear I should have snuffed out without ever knowing that death was near me. But the little sound caused me to turn, and there upon me, not ten feet from my breast, was the point of that huge spear, a spear forty feet long, tipped with gleaming metal, and held low at the side of a mounted replica of the little devils I had been watching.

But how puny and harmless they now looked beside this huge and terrific incarnation of hate, of vengeance and of death. The man himself, for such I may call him, was fully fifteen feet in height and, on Earth, would have weighed some four hundred pounds. He sat his mount as we sit a horse, grasping the animal's barrel with his lower limbs, while the hands of his two right arms held his immense spear low at the side of his mount; his two left arms were outstretched laterally to help preserve his balance, the thing he rode having neither bridle or reins of any description for guidance.

And his mount! How can earthly words describe it! It towered ten feet at the shoulder; had four legs on either side; a broad flat tail, larger at the tip than at the root, and which it held straight out behind while running; a gaping mouth which split its head from its snout to its long, massive neck.

Like its master, it was entirely devoid of hair, but was of a dark slate color and exceeding smooth and glossy. Its belly was white, and its legs shaded from the slate of its shoulders and hips to a vivid yellow at the feet. The feet themselves were heavily padded and nailless, which fact had also contributed to the noiselessness of their approach, and, in common with a multiplicity of legs, is a characteristic feature of the fauna of Mars. The highest type of man and one other animal, the only mammal existing on Mars, alone have well-formed nails, and there are absolutely no hoofed animals in existence there.

Behind this first charging demon trailed nineteen others, similar in all respects, but, as I learned later, bearing individual characteristics peculiar to themselves; precisely as no two of us are identical although we are all cast in a similar mold. This picture, or rather materialized nightmare, which I have described at length, made but one terrible and swift impression on me as I turned to meet it.

Unarmed and naked as I was, the first law of nature manifested itself in the only possible solution of my immediate problem, and that was to get out of the vicinity of the point of the charging spear. Consequently I gave a very earthly and at the same time superhuman leap to reach the top of the Martian incubator, for such I had determined it must be.

My effort was crowned with a success which appalled me no less than it seemed to surprise the Martian warriors, for it carried me fully thirty feet into the air and landed me a hundred feet from my pursuers and on the opposite side of the enclosure.

I alighted upon the soft moss easily and without mishap, and turning saw my enemies lined up along the further wall. Some were surveying me with expressions which I afterward discovered marked extreme astonishment, and the others were evidently satisfying themselves that I had not molested their young.

They were conversing together in low tones, and gesticulating and pointing toward me. Their discovery that I had not harmed the little Martians, and that I was unarmed, must have caused them to look upon me with less ferocity; but, as I was to learn later, the thing which weighed most in my favor was my exhibition of hurdling.

While the Martians are immense, their bones are very large and they are muscled only in proportion to the gravitation which they must overcome. The result is that they are infinitely less agile and less powerful, in proportion to their weight, than an Earth man, and I doubt that were one of them suddenly to be transported to Earth he could lift his own weight from the ground; in fact, I am convinced that he could not do so.

My feat then was as marvelous upon Mars as it would have been upon Earth, and from desiring to annihilate me they suddenly looked upon me as a wonderful discovery to be captured and exhibited among their fellows.

The respite my unexpected agility had given me permitted me to formulate plans for the immediate future and to note more closely the appearance of the warriors, for I could not disassociate these people in my mind from those other warriors who, only the day before, had been pursuing me.

I noted that each was armed with several other weapons in addition to the huge spear which I have described. The weapon which caused me to decide against an attempt at escape by flight was what was evidently a rifle of some description, and which I felt, for some reason, they were peculiarly efficient in handling.

These rifles were of a white metal stocked with wood, which I learned later was a very light and intensely hard growth much prized on Mars, and entirely unknown to us denizens of Earth. The metal of the barrel is an alloy composed principally of aluminum and steel which they have learned to temper to a hardness far exceeding that of the steel with which we are familiar. The weight of these rifles is comparatively little, and with the small caliber, explosive, radium projectiles which they use, and the great length of the barrel, they are deadly in the extreme and at ranges which would be unthinkable on Earth.[15] The theoretic effective radius of this rifle is three hundred miles, but the best they can do in actual service when equipped with their wireless finders and sighters is but a trifle over two hundred miles.[16]

---

[15] Aluminum rifles that shoot radioactive bullets seems fanciful, but many modern rifle barrels are machined from aluminum (much more lightweight than steel). In recent military conflicts around the world, controversy has developed in response to bullets made of "depleted uranium" (DU), which does not seem too much different from Burroughs's invention.

[16] Here Burroughs is being somewhat fanciful: if the Martian held the rifle level and

This is quite far enough to imbue me with great respect for the Martian firearm, and some telepathic force must have warned me against an attempt to escape in broad daylight from under the muzzles of twenty of these death-dealing machines.[17]

The Martians, after conversing for a short time, turned and rode away in the direction from which they had come, leaving one of their number alone by the enclosure. When they had covered perhaps two hundred yards they halted, and turning their mounts toward us sat watching the warrior by the enclosure.

He was the one whose spear had so nearly transfixed me, and was evidently the leader of the band, as I had noted that they seemed to have moved to their present position at his direction. When his force had come to a halt he dismounted, threw down his spear and small arms, and came around the end of the incubator toward me, entirely unarmed and as naked as I, except for the ornaments strapped upon his head, limbs, and breast.

When he was within about fifty feet of me he unclasped an enormous metal armlet, and holding it toward me in the open palm of his hand, addressed me in a clear, resonant voice, but in a language, it is needless to say, I could not understand. He then stopped as though waiting for my

---

fired from shoulder level (10–12 feet), the muzzle velocity would have to be over a million feet per second which would produce a recoil that would surely kill even the stoutest Martian. Since Burroughs qualifies the range with the word "theoretically," he may have had in mind something like the 42 cm German howitzer dubbed "Big Bertha." This massive piece of siege artillery invented just prior to World War I was fired in a parabolic arc and could achieve distances of almost 8 miles. The siege artillery the Japanese used in the Sino-Russian war of 1905 consisted of 28 cm howitzers, which could achieve a range of about 6 miles. Since Martian gravity is only about 40 percent of Earth's, a Martian could aim his rifle at a 45-degree angle (to achieve the optimal parabolic arc). Assuming the rifle had a muzzle velocity of about 4200 feet per second, the projectile would travel over 250 miles before hitting Martian soil. Burroughs's "theoretical" qualifier probably refers to the lack of accuracy such a shot would entail.

[17] This is foreshadowing, as it turns out, that Carter is adept at telepathy. "Telepathy," from the Greek meaning "feeling at a distance," began first to appear in psychological and philosophical literature in the 1880s, and was by the turn of the century, a popular topic of parlor conversation. H.G. Wells's The War of the Worlds (1898), considered by many to be an influence on Burroughs, depicts the Martians as telepathic. Among other early appearances of telepathy in fiction is George Griffith's crime story, A Mayfair Magician (1905). Telepathy is a staple of science fiction, though some would say it is on the verge of losing its fantastic status and inching closer to reality with recent breakthroughs in neural imaging.

reply, pricking up his antennae-like ears and cocking his strange-looking eyes still further toward me.

As the silence became painful I concluded to hazard a little conversation on my own part, as I had guessed that he was making overtures of peace. The throwing down of his weapons and the withdrawing of his troop before his advance toward me would have signified a peaceful mission anywhere on Earth, so why not, then, on Mars!

Placing my hand over my heart I bowed low to the Martian and explained to him that while I did not understand his language, his actions spoke for the peace and friendship that at the present moment were most dear to my heart. Of course I might have been a babbling brook for all the intelligence my speech carried to him, but he understood the action with which I immediately followed my words.

Stretching my hand toward him, I advanced and took the armlet from his open palm, clasping it about my arm above the elbow; smiled at him and stood waiting. His wide mouth spread into an answering smile, and locking one of his intermediary arms in mine we turned and walked back toward his mount. At the same time he motioned his followers to advance. They started toward us on a wild run, but were checked by a signal from him. Evidently he feared that were I to be really frightened again I might jump entirely out of the landscape.

He exchanged a few words with his men, motioned to me that I would ride behind one of them, and then mounted his own animal. The fellow designated reached down two or three hands and lifted me up behind him on the glossy back of his mount, where I hung on as best I could by the belts and straps which held the Martian's weapons and ornaments.

The entire cavalcade then turned and galloped away toward the range of hills in the distance.

CHAPTER IV

A PRISONER

We had gone perhaps ten miles when the ground began to rise very rapidly. We were, as I was later to learn, nearing the edge of one of Mars' long-dead seas, in the bottom of which my encounter with the Martians had taken place.[18]

In a short time we gained the foot of the mountains, and after traversing a narrow gorge came to an open valley, at the far extremity of which was a low table land upon which I beheld an enormous city. Toward this we galloped, entering it by what appeared to be a ruined roadway leading out from the city, but only to the edge of the table land, where it ended abruptly in a flight of broad steps.

Upon closer observation I saw as we passed them that the buildings were deserted, and while not greatly decayed had the appearance of not having been tenanted for years, possibly for ages. Toward the center of the city was a large plaza, and upon this and in the buildings immediately surrounding it were camped some nine or ten hundred creatures of the same breed as my captors, for such I now considered them despite the suave manner in which I had been trapped.

With the exception of their ornaments all were naked. The women varied in appearance but little from the men, except that their tusks were much larger in proportion to their height, in some instances curving nearly to their high-set ears. Their bodies were smaller and lighter in color, and their fingers and toes bore the rudiments of nails, which were entirely lacking among the males. The adult females ranged in height from ten to twelve feet.

---

[18] The geography of Mars is extreme: its canyons are deeper than anything on Earth and its mountain ranges are higher than the Himalayas. Olympus Mons on Mars, at 14 miles high, dwarfs Earth's Mount Everest, which is 5.5 miles high, and makes Olympus Mons the highest mountain known on any planet in our solar system. It is a shield volcano, much like the volcanoes making the Hawaiian islands. (Mauna Kea, if measured from the floor of the ocean to its summit would be the tallest mountain on Earth at 33,000 feet).

Mars also contains deep canyons and what are called "outflow channels" that indicate ancient floods far greater in magnitude than anything measured on Earth. The Kasei Valles channels, for example, are thousands of kilometers across. Valles Marineris is a system of canyons on Mars that plunge to depths of over 4 miles and stretch 2400 miles across the surface of Mars in what looks like a large gash (visible on many photographs of the red planet).

The children were light in color, even lighter than the women, and all looked precisely alike to me, except that some were taller than others; older, I presumed.

I saw no signs of extreme age among them, nor is there any appreciable difference in their appearance from the age of maturity, about forty, until, at about the age of one thousand years, they go voluntarily upon their last strange pilgrimage down the river Iss, which leads no living Martian knows whither and from whose bosom no Martian has ever returned, or would be allowed to live did he return after once embarking upon its cold, dark waters.

Only about one Martian in a thousand dies of sickness or disease, and possibly about twenty take the voluntary pilgrimage. The other nine hundred and seventy-nine die violent deaths in duels, in hunting, in aviation and in war; but perhaps by far the greatest death loss comes during the age of childhood, when vast numbers of the little Martians fall victims to the great white apes of Mars.

The average life expectancy of a Martian after the age of maturity is about three hundred years, but would be nearer the one-thousand mark were it not for the various means leading to violent death. Owing to the waning resources of the planet it evidently became necessary to counteract the increasing longevity which their remarkable skill in therapeutics and surgery produced, and so human life has come to be considered but lightly on Mars, as is evidenced by their dangerous sports and the almost continual warfare between the various communities.

There are other and natural causes tending toward a diminution of population, but nothing contributes so greatly to this end as the fact that no male or female Martian is ever voluntarily without a weapon of destruction.

As we neared the plaza and my presence was discovered we were immediately surrounded by hundreds of the creatures who seemed anxious to pluck me from my seat behind my guard. A word from the leader of the party stilled their clamor, and we proceeded at a trot across the plaza to the entrance of as magnificent an edifice as mortal eye has rested upon.

The building was low, but covered an enormous area. It was constructed of gleaming white marble inlaid with gold and brilliant stones which sparkled and scintillated in the sunlight. The main entrance was some hundred feet in width and projected from the building proper to form a huge canopy above the entrance hall. There was no stairway, but a gentle incline to the first floor of the building opened into an enormous chamber encircled by galleries.

On the floor of this chamber, which was dotted with highly carved wooden desks and chairs, were assembled about forty or fifty male Martians around the steps of a rostrum. On the platform proper squatted an enormous warrior heavily loaded with metal ornaments, gay-colored feathers and beautifully wrought leather trappings ingeniously set with precious stones. From his shoulders depended a short cape of white fur lined with brilliant scarlet silk.

What struck me as most remarkable about this assemblage and the hall in which they were congregated was the fact that the creatures were entirely out of proportion to the desks, chairs, and other furnishings; these being of a size adapted to human beings such as I, whereas the great bulks of the Martians could scarcely have squeezed into the chairs, nor was there room beneath the desks for their long legs. Evidently, then, there were other denizens on Mars than the wild and grotesque creatures into whose hands I had fallen, but the evidences of extreme antiquity which showed all around me indicated that these buildings might have belonged to some long-extinct and forgotten race in the dim antiquity of Mars.

Our party had halted at the entrance to the building, and at a sign from the leader I had been lowered to the ground. Again locking his arm in mine, we had proceeded into the audience chamber. There were few formalities observed in approaching the Martian chieftain. My captor merely strode up to the rostrum, the others making way for him as he advanced. The chieftain rose to his feet and uttered the name of my escort who, in turn, halted and repeated the name of the ruler followed by his title.

At the time, this ceremony and the words they uttered meant nothing to me, but later I came to know that this was the customary greeting between green Martians. Had the men been strangers, and therefore unable to exchange names, they would have silently exchanged ornaments, had their missions been peaceful—otherwise they would have exchanged shots, or have fought out their introduction with some other of their various weapons.

My captor, whose name was Tars Tarkas, was virtually the vice-chieftain of the community, and a man of great ability as a statesman and warrior. He evidently explained briefly the incidents connected with his expedition, including my capture, and when he had concluded the chieftain addressed me at some length.

I replied in our good old English tongue merely to convince him that neither of us could understand the other; but I noticed that when I smiled slightly on concluding, he did likewise. This fact, and the similar occurrence during my first talk with Tars Tarkas, convinced me that we had at least something in common; the ability to smile, therefore to laugh; denoting a sense of humor. But I was to learn that the Martian smile is merely perfunctory, and that the Martian laugh is a thing to cause strong men to blanch in horror.

The ideas of humor among the green men of Mars are widely at variance with our conceptions of incitants to merriment. The death agonies of a fellow being are, to these strange creatures provocative of the wildest hilarity, while their chief form of commonest amusement is to inflict death on their prisoners of war in various ingenious and horrible ways.

The assembled warriors and chieftains examined me closely, feeling my muscles and the texture of my skin. The principal chieftain then evidently signified a desire to see me perform, and, motioning me to follow, he started with Tars Tarkas for the open plaza.

Now, I had made no attempt to walk, since my first signal failure, except while tightly grasping Tars Tarkas' arm, and so now I went skipping and flitting about among the desks and chairs like some monstrous grasshopper. After bruising myself severely, much to the amusement of the Martians, I again had recourse to creeping, but this did not suit them and I was roughly jerked to my feet by a towering fellow who had laughed most heartily at my misfortunes.

As he banged me down upon my feet his face was bent close to mine and I did the only thing a gentleman might do under the circumstances of brutality, boorishness, and lack of consideration for a stranger's rights; I swung my fist squarely to his jaw and he went down like a felled ox. As he sunk to the floor I wheeled around with my back toward the nearest desk, expecting to be overwhelmed by the vengeance of his fellows, but determined to give them as good a battle as the unequal odds would permit before I gave up my life.

My fears were groundless, however, as the other Martians, at first struck dumb with wonderment, finally broke into wild peals of laughter and applause. I did not recognize the applause as such, but later, when I had become acquainted with their customs, I learned that I had won what they seldom accord, a manifestation of approbation.

The fellow whom I had struck lay where he had fallen, nor did any of his mates approach him. Tars Tarkas advanced toward me, holding out one of his arms, and we thus proceeded to the plaza without further mishap. I did not, of course, know the reason for which we had come to the open, but I was not long in being enlightened. They first repeated the word "sak" a number of times, and then Tars Tarkas made several jumps, repeating the same word before each leap; then, turning to me, he said, "sak!" I saw what they were after, and gathering myself together I "sakked" with such marvelous success that I cleared a good hundred and fifty feet; nor did I this time, lose my equilibrium, but landed squarely upon my feet without falling. I then returned by easy jumps of twenty-five or thirty feet to the little group of warriors.

My exhibition had been witnessed by several hundred lesser Martians, and they immediately broke into demands for a repetition, which the chieftain then ordered me to make; but I was both hungry and thirsty, and determined on the spot that my only method of salvation was to demand the consideration from these creatures which they evidently would not voluntarily accord. I therefore ignored the repeated commands to "sak," and each time they were made I motioned to my mouth and rubbed my stomach.

Tars Tarkas and the chief exchanged a few words, and the former, calling to a young female among the throng, gave her some instructions and motioned me to accompany her. I grasped her proffered arm and together we crossed the plaza toward a large building on the far side.

My fair companion was about eight feet tall, having just arrived at maturity, but not yet to her full height. She was of a light olive-green color, with a smooth, glossy hide. Her name, as I afterward learned, was Sola, and she belonged to the retinue of Tars Tarkas. She conducted me to a spacious chamber in one of the buildings fronting on the plaza, and which, from the litter of silks and furs upon the floor, I took to be the sleeping quarters of several of the natives.

The room was well lighted by a number of large windows and was beautifully decorated with mural paintings and mosaics, but upon all there seemed to rest that indefinable touch of the finger of antiquity which convinced me that the architects and builders of these wondrous creations had nothing in common with the crude half-brutes which now occupied them.

Sola motioned me to be seated upon a pile of silks near the center of the room, and, turning, made a peculiar hissing sound, as though signaling to someone in an adjoining room. In response to her call I obtained my first sight of a new Martian wonder. It waddled in on its ten short legs, and squatted down before the girl like an obedient puppy. The thing was about the size of a Shetland pony, but its head bore a slight resemblance to that of a frog, except that the jaws were equipped with three rows of long, sharp tusks.

CHAPTER V

I ELUDE MY WATCH DOG

Sola stared into the brute's wicked-looking eyes, muttered a word or two of command, pointed to me, and left the chamber. I could not but wonder what this ferocious-looking monstrosity might do when left alone in such close proximity to such a relatively tender morsel of meat; but my fears were groundless, as the beast, after surveying me intently for a moment, crossed the room to the only exit which led to the street, and lay down full length across the threshold.

This was my first experience with a Martian watch dog, but it was destined not to be my last, for this fellow guarded me carefully during the time I remained a captive among these green men; twice saving my life, and never voluntarily being away from me a moment.

While Sola was away I took occasion to examine more minutely the room in which I found myself captive. The mural painting depicted scenes of rare and wonderful beauty; mountains, rivers, lake, ocean, meadow, trees and flowers, winding roadways, sun-kissed gardens—scenes which might have portrayed earthly views but for the different colorings of the vegetation. The work had evidently been wrought by a master hand, so subtle the atmosphere, so perfect the technique; yet nowhere was there a representation of a living animal, either human or brute, by which I could guess at the likeness of these other and perhaps extinct denizens of Mars.

While I was allowing my fancy to run riot in wild conjecture on the possible explanation of the strange anomalies which I had so far met with on Mars, Sola returned bearing both food and drink. These she placed on the floor beside me, and seating herself a short ways off regarded me intently. The food consisted of about a pound of some solid substance of the consistency of cheese and almost tasteless, while the liquid was apparently milk from some animal.[19] It was not unpleasant to the taste, though slightly acid, and I learned in a short time to prize it very highly. It came, as I later discovered, not from an animal, as there is only one mammal on Mars and that one very rare indeed, but from a large plant which grows practically without water, but seems to distill its plentiful supply of milk from the products of the soil, the moisture of the air, and

---

[19] What Burroughs describes as the mainstay of Martian foodstuffs sounds much like tofu. According to the Soy Info Center, tofu was first mentioned in the US in 1821 (Philadelphia), and the first commercial production began in San Francisco in 1878, although it remained relatively unknown in this country until the mid-twentieth century.

the rays of the sun. A single plant of this species will give eight or ten quarts of milk per day.

After I had eaten I was greatly invigorated, but feeling the need of rest I stretched out upon the silks and was soon asleep. I must have slept several hours, as it was dark when I awoke, and I was very cold. I noticed that someone had thrown a fur over me, but it had become partially dislodged and in the darkness I could not see to replace it. Suddenly a hand reached out and pulled the fur over me, shortly afterwards adding another to my covering.

I presumed that my watchful guardian was Sola, nor was I wrong. This girl alone, among all the green Martians with whom I came in contact, disclosed characteristics of sympathy, kindliness, and affection; her ministrations to my bodily wants were unfailing, and her solicitous care saved me from much suffering and many hardships.

As I was to learn, the Martian nights are extremely cold, and as there is practically no twilight or dawn, the changes in temperature are sudden and most uncomfortable, as are the transitions from brilliant daylight to darkness. The nights are either brilliantly illumined or very dark, for if neither of the two moons of Mars happen to be in the sky almost total darkness results, since the lack of atmosphere, or, rather, the very thin atmosphere, fails to diffuse the starlight to any great extent; on the other hand, if both of the moons are in the heavens at night the surface of the ground is brightly illuminated.[20]

Both of Mars' moons are vastly nearer her than is our moon to Earth; the nearer moon being but about five thousand miles distant, while the further is but little more than fourteen thousand miles away, against the nearly one-quarter million miles which separate us from our moon. The nearer moon of Mars makes a complete revolution around the planet in a little over seven and one-half hours, so that she may be seen hurtling through the sky like some huge meteor two or three times each night, revealing all her phases during each transit of the heavens.[21]

---

[20] Burroughs is correct about lack of twilight or dawn, as there is not much of an atmosphere to create these phenomena. (The Martian atmosphere is 1/100th as dense as Earth's). Nighttime temperatures on Mars can be quite cold: 150 degrees Fahrenheit below zero, even at the equator.

[21] The two Martian moons, Phobos and Deimos, are named after the sons of Ares, the Greek god of war. Phobos was fear, and Deimos was dread. (Ares became Mars in Roman mythology.)

As for the science, Burroughs again is close. Phobos, the larger, inner moon (22 km) orbits at roughly 5,800 miles and crosses the sky in about 7 hours. Deimos, the outer, smaller moon (12 km) orbits at 14,600 miles and takes around 30 hours (more

The further moon revolves about Mars in something over thirty and one-quarter hours, and with her sister satellite makes a nocturnal Martian scene one of splendid and weird grandeur. And it is well that nature has so graciously and abundantly lighted the Martian night, for the green men of Mars, being a nomadic race without high intellectual development, have but crude means for artificial lighting; depending principally upon torches, a kind of candle, and a peculiar oil lamp which generates a gas and burns without a wick.

This last device produces an intensely brilliant far-reaching white light, but as the natural oil which it requires can only be obtained by mining in one of several widely separated and remote localities it is seldom used by these creatures whose only thought is for today, and whose hatred for manual labor has kept them in a semi-barbaric state for countless ages.

After Sola had replenished my coverings I again slept, nor did I awaken until daylight. The other occupants of the room, five in number, were all females, and they were still sleeping, piled high with a motley array of silks and furs. Across the threshold lay stretched the sleepless guardian brute, just as I had last seen him on the preceding day; apparently he had not moved a muscle; his eyes were fairly glued upon me, and I fell to wondering just what might befall me should I endeavor to escape.

I have ever been prone to seek adventure and to investigate and experiment where wiser men would have left well enough alone. It therefore now occurred to me that the surest way of learning the exact attitude of this beast toward me would be to attempt to leave the room. I felt fairly secure in my belief that I could escape him should he pursue me once I was outside the building, for I had begun to take great pride in my ability as a jumper. Furthermore, I could see from the shortness of his legs that the brute himself was no jumper and probably no runner.

Slowly and carefully, therefore, I gained my feet, only to see that my watcher did the same; cautiously I advanced toward him, finding that by moving with a shuffling gait I could retain my balance as well as make reasonably rapid progress. As I neared the brute he backed cautiously away from me, and when I had reached the open he moved to one side to let me pass. He then fell in behind me and followed about ten paces in my rear as I made my way along the deserted street.

than two nights) to cross. Since Phobos crosses the sky at least once a night, observers on Mars would witness a lunar eclipse virtually every night.

Evidently his mission was to protect me only, I thought, but when we reached the edge of the city he suddenly sprang before me, uttering strange sounds and baring his ugly and ferocious tusks. Thinking to have some amusement at his expense, I rushed toward him, and when almost upon him sprang into the air, alighting far beyond him and away from the city. He wheeled instantly and charged me with the most appalling speed I had ever beheld. I had thought his short legs a bar to swiftness, but had he been coursing with greyhounds the latter would have appeared as though asleep on a door mat. As I was to learn, this is the fleetest animal on Mars, and owing to its intelligence, loyalty, and ferocity is used in hunting, in war, and as the protector of the Martian man.

I quickly saw that I would have difficulty in escaping the fangs of the beast on a straightaway course, and so I met his charge by doubling in my tracks and leaping over him as he was almost upon me. This maneuver gave me a considerable advantage, and I was able to reach the city quite a bit ahead of him, and as he came tearing after me I jumped for a window about thirty feet from the ground in the face of one of the buildings overlooking the valley.

Grasping the sill I pulled myself up to a sitting posture without looking into the building, and gazed down at the baffled animal beneath me. My exultation was short-lived, however, for scarcely had I gained a secure seat upon the sill than a huge hand grasped me by the neck from behind and dragged me violently into the room. Here I was thrown upon my back, and beheld standing over me a colossal ape-like creature, white and hairless except for an enormous shock of bristly hair upon its head.

CHAPTER VI
A FIGHT THAT WON FRIENDS

The thing, which more nearly resembled our earthly men than it did the Martians I had seen, held me pinioned to the ground with one huge foot, while it jabbered and gesticulated at some answering creature behind me. This other, which was evidently its mate, soon came toward us, bearing a mighty stone cudgel with which it evidently intended to brain me.

The creatures were about ten or fifteen feet tall, standing erect, and had, like the green Martians, an intermediary set of arms or legs, midway between their upper and lower limbs. Their eyes were close together and non-protruding; their ears were high set, but more laterally located than those of the Martians, while their snouts and teeth were strikingly like those of our African gorilla. Altogether they were not unlovely when viewed in comparison with the green Martians.

The cudgel was swinging in the arc which ended upon my upturned face when a bolt of myriad-legged horror hurled itself through the doorway full upon the breast of my executioner. With a shriek of fear the ape which held me leaped through the open window, but its mate closed in a terrific death struggle with my preserver, which was nothing less than my faithful watch-thing; I cannot bring myself to call so hideous a creature a dog.

As quickly as possible I gained my feet and backing against the wall I witnessed such a battle as it is vouchsafed few beings to see. The strength, agility, and blind ferocity of these two creatures is approached by nothing known to earthly man. My beast had an advantage in his first hold, having sunk his mighty fangs far into the breast of his adversary; but the great arms and paws of the ape, backed by muscles far transcending those of the Martian men I had seen, had locked the throat of my guardian and slowly were choking out his life, and bending back his head and neck upon his body, where I momentarily expected the former to fall limp at the end of a broken neck.

In accomplishing this the ape was tearing away the entire front of its breast, which was held in the vise-like grip of the powerful jaws. Back and forth upon the floor they rolled, neither one emitting a sound of fear or pain. Presently I saw the great eyes of my beast bulging completely from their sockets and blood flowing from its nostrils. That he was weakening perceptibly was evident, but so also was the ape, whose struggles were growing momentarily less.

Suddenly I came to myself and, with that strange instinct which seems ever to prompt me to my duty, I seized the cudgel, which had fallen to the floor at the commencement of the battle, and swinging it with all the power of my earthly arms I crashed it full upon the head of the ape, crushing his skull as though it had been an eggshell.[22]

Scarcely had the blow descended when I was confronted with a new danger. The ape's mate, recovered from its first shock of terror, had returned to the scene of the encounter by way of the interior of the building. I glimpsed him just before he reached the doorway and the sight of him, now roaring as he perceived his lifeless fellow stretched upon the floor, and frothing at the mouth, in the extremity of his rage, filled me, I must confess, with dire forebodings.

I am ever willing to stand and fight when the odds are not too overwhelmingly against me, but in this instance I perceived neither glory nor profit in pitting my relatively puny strength against the iron muscles and brutal ferocity of this enraged denizen of an unknown world; in fact, the only outcome of such an encounter, so far as I might be concerned, seemed sudden death.

I was standing near the window and I knew that once in the street I might gain the plaza and safety before the creature could overtake me; at least there was a chance for safety in flight, against almost certain death should I remain and fight however desperately.

It is true I held the cudgel, but what could I do with it against his four great arms? Even should I break one of them with my first blow, for I figured that he would attempt to ward off the cudgel, he could reach out and annihilate me with the others before I could recover for a second attack.

In the instant that these thoughts passed through my mind I had turned to make for the window, but my eyes alighting on the form of my erstwhile guardian threw all thoughts of flight to the four winds. He lay gasping upon the floor of the chamber, his great eyes fastened upon me in what seemed a pitiful appeal for protection. I could not withstand that look, nor could I, on second thought, have deserted my rescuer without giving as good an account of myself in his behalf as he had in mine.

---

[22] Burroughs was well versed in the classics, and many of his graphic scenes of violence seem inspired by similar descriptions, equally graphic, from Homer's *Iliad*.

Without more ado, therefore, I turned to meet the charge of the infuriated bull ape. He was now too close upon me for the cudgel to prove of any effective assistance, so I merely threw it as heavily as I could at his advancing bulk. It struck him just below the knees, eliciting a howl of pain and rage, and so throwing him off his balance that he lunged full upon me with arms wide stretched to ease his fall.

Again, as on the preceding day, I had recourse to earthly tactics, and swinging my right fist full upon the point of his chin I followed it with a smashing left to the pit of his stomach. The effect was marvelous, for, as I lightly sidestepped, after delivering the second blow, he reeled and fell upon the floor doubled up with pain and gasping for wind. Leaping over his prostrate body, I seized the cudgel and finished the monster before he could regain his feet.

As I delivered the blow a low laugh rang out behind me, and, turning, I beheld Tars Tarkas, Sola, and three or four warriors standing in the doorway of the chamber. As my eyes met theirs I was, for the second time, the recipient of their zealously guarded applause.

My absence had been noted by Sola on her awakening, and she had quickly informed Tars Tarkas, who had set out immediately with a handful of warriors to search for me. As they had approached the limits of the city they had witnessed the actions of the bull ape as he bolted into the building, frothing with rage.

They had followed immediately behind him, thinking it barely possible that his actions might prove a clew to my whereabouts and had witnessed my short but decisive battle with him. This encounter, together with my set-to with the Martian warrior on the previous day and my feats of jumping placed me upon a high pinnacle in their regard. Evidently devoid of all the finer sentiments of friendship, love, or affection, these people fairly worship physical prowess and bravery, and nothing is too good for the object of their adoration as long as he maintains his position by repeated examples of his skill, strength, and courage.

Sola, who had accompanied the searching party of her own volition, was the only one of the Martians whose face had not been twisted in laughter as I battled for my life. She, on the contrary, was sober with apparent solicitude and, as soon as I had finished the monster, rushed to me and carefully examined my body for possible wounds or injuries. Satisfying herself that I had come off unscathed she smiled quietly, and, taking my hand, started toward the door of the chamber.

Tars Tarkas and the other warriors had entered and were standing over the now rapidly reviving brute which had saved my life, and whose life I, in turn, had rescued. They seemed to be deep in argument, and finally one of them addressed me, but remembering my ignorance of his language turned back to Tars Tarkas, who, with a word and gesture, gave some command to the fellow and turned to follow us from the room.

There seemed something menacing in their attitude toward my beast, and I hesitated to leave until I had learned the outcome. It was well I did so, for the warrior drew an evil looking pistol from its holster and was on the point of putting an end to the creature when I sprang forward and struck up his arm. The bullet striking the wooden casing of the window exploded, blowing a hole completely through the wood and masonry.

I then knelt down beside the fearsome-looking thing, and raising it to its feet motioned for it to follow me. The looks of surprise which my actions elicited from the Martians were ludicrous; they could not understand, except in a feeble and childish way, such attributes as gratitude and compassion. The warrior whose gun I had struck up looked enquiringly at Tars Tarkas, but the latter signed that I be left to my own devices, and so we returned to the plaza with my great beast following close at heel, and Sola grasping me tightly by the arm.

I had at least two friends on Mars; a young woman who watched over me with motherly solicitude, and a dumb brute which, as I later came to know, held in its poor ugly carcass more love, more loyalty, more gratitude than could have been found in the entire five million green Martians who rove the deserted cities and dead sea bottoms of Mars.[23]

---

[23] The surface area of Earth (minus the oceans and Antarctica) is about 52.6 million square miles, and since the world population is around 7 billion, this yields a population density of about 130 people per square mile. In Burroughs's depiction of Mars, virtually the entire planet is inhabitable, so the population density of Barsoom is dramatically lower than on Earth. Mars has a surface area of about 90 million square miles, which means the population density of the green Martians would be .44 per square mile—about half the population density of Alaska!

I TURNED TO MEET THE CHARGE OF THE INFURIATED BULL APE.

CHAPTER VII
CHILD-RAISING ON MARS

After a breakfast, which was an exact replica of the meal of the preceding day and an index of practically every meal which followed while I was with the green men of Mars, Sola escorted me to the plaza, where I found the entire community engaged in watching or helping at the harnessing of huge mastodonian animals to great three-wheeled chariots. There were about two hundred and fifty of these vehicles, each drawn by a single animal, any one of which, from their appearance, might easily have drawn the entire wagon train when fully loaded.

The chariots themselves were large, commodious, and gorgeously decorated. In each was seated a female Martian loaded with ornaments of metal, with jewels and silks and furs, and upon the back of each of the beasts which drew the chariots was perched a young Martian driver. Like the animals upon which the warriors were mounted, the heavier draft animals wore neither bit nor bridle, but were guided entirely by telepathic means.[24]

This power is wonderfully developed in all Martians, and accounts largely for the simplicity of their language and the relatively few spoken words exchanged even in long conversations. It is the universal language of Mars, through the medium of which the higher and lower animals of this world of paradoxes are able to communicate to a greater or less extent, depending upon the intellectual sphere of the species and the development of the individual.[25]

As the cavalcade took up the line of march in single file, Sola dragged me into an empty chariot and we proceeded with the procession toward the point by which I had entered the city the day before. At the head of the caravan rode some two hundred warriors, five abreast, and a like number

---

[24] As we shall see, telepathy plays a critical role in several of Carter's harrowing escapes and rescues.

[25] Webster's provides a three-fold definition of "paradox," with the primary sense indicating an assertion contrary to conventional opinion. Indeed, the Greek word means something like "contrary to thought." The word also can refer to a statement that, while appearing to be true on its face, can be shown to contradict itself. The word then also refers to anything that exhibits contradictory qualities. *The Oxford Companion to Philosophy* (1995) offers a rather lengthy discussion of the three senses of the word and the fundamental importance of the problem to philosophy. Throughout *A Princess of Mars*, Burroughs conveys the idea that Martian culture is paradoxical at least in the latter sense of manifesting inconsistent qualities.

brought up the rear, while twenty-five or thirty outriders flanked us on either side.

Every one but myself—men, women, and children—were heavily armed, and at the tail of each chariot trotted a Martian hound, my own beast following closely behind ours; in fact, the faithful creature never left me voluntarily during the entire ten years I spent on Mars. Our way led out across the little valley before the city, through the hills, and down into the dead sea bottom which I had traversed on my journey from the incubator to the plaza. The incubator, as it proved, was the terminal point of our journey this day, and, as the entire cavalcade broke into a mad gallop as soon as we reached the level expanse of sea bottom, we were soon within sight of our goal.

On reaching it the chariots were parked with military precision on the four sides of the enclosure, and half a score of warriors, headed by the enormous chieftain, and including Tars Tarkas and several other lesser chiefs, dismounted and advanced toward it. I could see Tars Tarkas explaining something to the principal chieftain, whose name, by the way, was, as nearly as I can translate it into English, Lorquas Ptomel, Jed; jed being his title.

I was soon appraised of the subject of their conversation, as, calling to Sola, Tars Tarkas signed for her to send me to him. I had by this time mastered the intricacies of walking under Martian conditions, and quickly responding to his command I advanced to the side of the incubator where the warriors stood.

As I reached their side a glance showed me that all but a very few eggs had hatched, the incubator being fairly alive with the hideous little devils. They ranged in height from three to four feet, and were moving restlessly about the enclosure as though searching for food.

As I came to a halt before him, Tars Tarkas pointed over the incubator and said, "Sak." I saw that he wanted me to repeat my performance of yesterday for the edification of Lorquas Ptomel, and, as I must confess that my prowess gave me no little satisfaction, I responded quickly, leaping entirely over the parked chariots on the far side of the incubator. As I returned, Lorquas Ptomel grunted something at me, and turning to his warriors gave a few words of command relative to the incubator. They paid no further attention to me and I was thus permitted to remain close and watch their operations, which consisted in breaking an opening in the wall of the incubator large enough to permit of the exit of the young Martians.

On either side of this opening the women and the younger Martians, both male and female, formed two solid walls leading out through the chariots and quite away into the plain beyond. Between these walls the little Martians scampered, wild as deer; being permitted to run the full length of the aisle, where they were captured one at a time by the women and older children; the last in the line capturing the first little one to reach the end of the gauntlet, her opposite in the line capturing the second, and so on until all the little fellows had left the enclosure and been appropriated by some youth or female. As the women caught the young they fell out of line and returned to their respective chariots, while those who fell into the hands of the young men were later turned over to some of the women.

I saw that the ceremony, if it could be dignified by such a name, was over, and seeking out Sola I found her in our chariot with a hideous little creature held tightly in her arms.

The work of rearing young, green Martians consists solely in teaching them to talk, and to use the weapons of warfare with which they are loaded down from the very first year of their lives. Coming from eggs in which they have lain for five years, the period of incubation, they step forth into the world perfectly developed except in size. Entirely unknown to their mothers, who, in turn, would have difficulty in pointing out the fathers with any degree of accuracy, they are the common children of the community, and their education devolves upon the females who chance to capture them as they leave the incubator.

Their foster mothers may not even have had an egg in the incubator, as was the case with Sola, who had not commenced to lay, until less than a year before she became the mother of another woman's offspring. But this counts for little among the green Martians, as parental and filial love is as unknown to them as it is common among us. I believe this horrible system which has been carried on for ages is the direct cause of the loss of all the finer feelings and higher humanitarian instincts among these poor creatures.[26] From birth they know no father or mother love, they know not

---

[26] Throughout the Martian cycle, Burroughs deplores the devolution of the Martian races, invoking sociological ideas widely in circulation at the end of the nineteenth century and early twentieth century about the decay and degradation of human qualities because of our interference with nature. The fear of degeneration, atavism, and regression gained traction in the late nineteenth century through the work of Cesare Lombroso, although Bénédict August Morel in 1857 published a book on the subject, *Treatise on the Physical, Intellectual, and Moral Degeneration of the Human Species*, two years before Darwin put out *Origin of Species* (1859). Moreover, the French naturalist Georges-Louis Leclerc (Comte de Buffon) had intimated some of the

the meaning of the word home; they are taught that they are only suffered to live until they can demonstrate by their physique and ferocity that they are fit to live. Should they prove deformed or defective in any way they are promptly shot; nor do they see a tear shed for a single one of the many cruel hardships they pass through from earliest infancy.

I do not mean that the adult Martians are unnecessarily or intentionally cruel to the young, but theirs is a hard and pitiless struggle for existence upon a dying planet, the natural resources of which have dwindled to a point where the support of each additional life means an added tax upon the community into which it is thrown.

By careful selection they rear only the hardiest specimens of each species, and with almost supernatural foresight they regulate the birth rate to merely offset the loss by death.[27]

Each adult Martian female brings forth about thirteen eggs each year, and those which meet the size, weight, and specific gravity tests are hidden in the recesses of some subterranean vault where the temperature is too low for incubation. Every year these eggs are carefully examined by a council of twenty chieftains, and all but about one hundred of the most perfect are destroyed out of each yearly supply. At the end of five years

---

same concepts earlier in the eighteenth century.

Lombroso actually synthesized ideas from Darwin and Morel in a book that inaugurated the science of criminology called *Criminal Man* in 1876 (Italian title: *L'uomo delinquente*). Lombroso's description of the "criminal type" as a "throwback"—a man who was a reversion to a past race, born out of time and would have been normal had he been born at some earlier point—accords rather well with Burroughs's descriptions of the green Martians in various places throughout *A Princess of Mars*. The red Martians are the most civilized and advanced race on Mars, and are the product of the ancient (and superior) white Martians, yellow Martians, and black Martians mixing together as the Martian seas dried up 500,000 years ago. On the one hand, Burroughs strikes a progressive note in inverting some of the prejudicial hierarchies of Earth (making red men, for example, superior to whites), but on the other hand, few biologists today would consider "race" a meaningful concept, as all humans are one species and share the same DNA. The characteristics of race (skin color, hair color, eye shape) are all superficial and adaptations that change relatively rapidly depending on the human environment. See Luigi Luca Cavalli-Sforza, *Genes, People, Languages* (North Point, 2000). For an overview of the impact of Social Darwinism on American culture, see Richard Hofstadter, *Social Darwinism in American Thought* (revised ed., Beacon, 1955).

[27] Burroughs similarly describes ideas of eugenics as popularized by Francis Galton beginning in the 1880s, and in the twentieth century by Margaret Sanger, although she did not work publically until after *Under the Moons of Mars* had been published. Burroughs also anticipates similar treatment that Aldous Huxley gives this topic in *Brave New World* (1932).

about five hundred almost perfect eggs have been chosen from the thousands brought forth. These are then placed in the almost air-tight incubators to be hatched by the sun's rays after a period of another five years. The hatching which we had witnessed today was a fairly representative event of its kind, all but about one per cent of the eggs hatching in two days. If the remaining eggs ever hatched we knew nothing of the fate of the little Martians. They were not wanted, as their offspring might inherit and transmit the tendency to prolonged incubation, and thus upset the system which has maintained for ages and which permits the adult Martians to figure the proper time for return to the incubators, almost to an hour.

The incubators are built in remote fastnesses, where there is little or no likelihood of their being discovered by other tribes. The result of such a catastrophe would mean no children in the community for another five years. I was later to witness the results of the discovery of an alien incubator.

The community of which the green Martians with whom my lot was cast formed a part was composed of some thirty thousand souls. They roamed an enormous tract of arid and semi-arid land between forty and eighty degrees south latitude, and bounded on the east and west by two large fertile tracts. Their headquarters lay in the southwest corner of this district, near the crossing of two of the so-called Martian canals.

As the incubator had been placed far north of their own territory in a supposedly uninhabited and unfrequented area, we had before us a tremendous journey, concerning which I, of course, knew nothing.

After our return to the dead city I passed several days in comparative idleness. On the day following our return all the warriors had ridden forth early in the morning and had not returned until just before darkness fell. As I later learned, they had been to the subterranean vaults in which the eggs were kept and had transported them to the incubator, which they had then walled up for another five years, and which, in all probability, would not be visited again during that period.

The vaults which hid the eggs until they were ready for the incubator were located many miles south of the incubator, and would be visited yearly by the council of twenty chieftains. Why they did not arrange to build their vaults and incubators nearer home has always been a mystery to me, and, like many other Martian mysteries, unsolved and unsolvable by earthly reasoning and customs.

Sola's duties were now doubled, as she was compelled to care for the young Martian as well as for me, but neither one of us required much attention, and as we were both about equally advanced in Martian education, Sola took it upon herself to train us together.

Her prize consisted in a male about four feet tall, very strong and physically perfect; also, he learned quickly, and we had considerable amusement, at least I did, over the keen rivalry we displayed. The Martian language, as I have said, is extremely simple, and in a week I could make all my wants known and understand nearly everything that was said to me. Likewise, under Sola's tutelage, I developed my telepathic powers so that I shortly could sense practically everything that went on around me.

What surprised Sola most in me was that while I could catch telepathic messages easily from others, and often when they were not intended for me, no one could read a jot from my mind under any circumstances. At first this vexed me, but later I was very glad of it, as it gave me an undoubted advantage over the Martians.

CHAPTER VIII
A FAIR CAPTIVE FROM THE SKY

The third day after the incubator ceremony we set forth toward home, but scarcely had the head of the procession debouched into the open ground before the city than orders were given for an immediate and hasty return. As though trained for years in this particular evolution, the green Martians melted like mist into the spacious doorways of the nearby buildings, until, in less than three minutes, the entire cavalcade of chariots, mastodons and mounted warriors was nowhere to be seen.

Sola and I had entered a building upon the front of the city, in fact, the same one in which I had had my encounter with the apes, and, wishing to see what had caused the sudden retreat, I mounted to an upper floor and peered from the window out over the valley and the hills beyond; and there I saw the cause of their sudden scurrying to cover. A huge craft, long, low, and gray-painted, swung slowly over the crest of the nearest hill. Following it came another, and another, and another, until twenty of them, swinging low above the ground, sailed slowly and majestically toward us.

Each carried a strange banner swung from stem to stern above the upper works, and upon the prow of each was painted some odd device that gleamed in the sunlight and showed plainly even at the distance at which we were from the vessels.[28] I could see figures crowding the forward decks and upper works of the air craft. Whether they had discovered us or simply were looking at the deserted city I could not say, but in any event they received a rude reception, for suddenly and without warning the green Martian warriors fired a terrific volley from the windows of the buildings facing the little valley across which the great ships were so peacefully advancing.

Instantly the scene changed as by magic; the foremost vessel swung broadside toward us, and bringing her guns into play returned our fire, at the same time moving parallel to our front for a short distance and then turning back with the evident intention of completing a great circle which would bring her up to position once more opposite our firing line; the other vessels followed in her wake, each one opening upon us as she swung into position. Our own fire never diminished, and I doubt if twenty-

---

[28] Because Mars has such a thin atmosphere, objects at a distance would be clearer (and appear much closer) than on Earth. This was a noticeable problem for the Apollo astronauts on the moon, which has no atmosphere at all. See Wilhelms's *To a Rocky Moon.*

five per cent of our shots went wild. It had never been given me to see such deadly accuracy of aim, and it seemed as though a little figure on one of the craft dropped at the explosion of each bullet, while the banners and upper works dissolved in spurts of flame as the irresistible projectiles of our warriors mowed through them.

The fire from the vessels was most ineffectual, owing, as I afterward learned, to the unexpected suddenness of the first volley, which caught the ship's crews entirely unprepared and the sighting apparatus of the guns unprotected from the deadly aim of our warriors.

It seems that each green warrior has certain objective points for his fire under relatively identical circumstances of warfare. For example, a proportion of them, always the best marksmen, direct their fire entirely upon the wireless finding and sighting apparatus of the big guns of an attacking naval force; another detail attends to the smaller guns in the same way; others pick off the gunners; still others the officers; while certain other quotas concentrate their attention upon the other members of the crew, upon the upper works, and upon the steering gear and propellers.

Twenty minutes after the first volley the great fleet swung trailing off in the direction from which it had first appeared. Several of the craft were limping perceptibly, and seemed but barely under the control of their depleted crews. Their fire had ceased entirely and all their energies seemed focused upon escape. Our warriors then rushed up to the roofs of the buildings which we occupied and followed the retreating armada with a continuous fusillade of deadly fire.

One by one, however, the ships managed to dip below the crests of the outlying hills until only one barely moving craft was in sight. This had received the brunt of our fire and seemed to be entirely unmanned, as not a moving figure was visible upon her decks. Slowly she swung from her course, circling back toward us in an erratic and pitiful manner. Instantly the warriors ceased firing, for it was quite apparent that the vessel was entirely helpless, and, far from being in a position to inflict harm upon us, she could not even control herself sufficiently to escape.

As she neared the city the warriors rushed out upon the plain to meet her, but it was evident that she still was too high for them to hope to reach her decks. From my vantage point in the window I could see the bodies of her crew strewn about, although I could not make out what manner of creatures they might be. Not a sign of life was manifest upon her as she drifted slowly with the light breeze in a southeasterly direction.

She was drifting some fifty feet above the ground, followed by all but some hundred of the warriors who had been ordered back to the roofs to cover the possibility of a return of the fleet, or of reinforcements. It soon became evident that she would strike the face of the buildings about a mile south of our position, and as I watched the progress of the chase I saw a number of warriors gallop ahead, dismount and enter the building she seemed destined to touch.

As the craft neared the building, and just before she struck, the Martian warriors swarmed upon her from the windows, and with their great spears eased the shock of the collision, and in a few moments they had thrown out grappling hooks and the big boat was being hauled to ground by their fellows below.

After making her fast, they swarmed the sides and searched the vessel from stem to stern. I could see them examining the dead sailors, evidently for signs of life, and presently a party of them appeared from below dragging a little figure among them. The creature was considerably less than half as tall as the green Martian warriors, and from my balcony I could see that it walked erect upon two legs and surmised that it was some new and strange Martian monstrosity with which I had not as yet become acquainted.

They removed their prisoner to the ground and then commenced a systematic rifling of the vessel. This operation required several hours, during which time a number of the chariots were requisitioned to transport the loot, which consisted in arms, ammunition, silks, furs, jewels, strangely carved stone vessels, and a quantity of solid foods and liquids, including many casks of water, the first I had seen since my advent upon Mars.

After the last load had been removed the warriors made lines fast to the craft and towed her far out into the valley in a southwesterly direction. A few of them then boarded her and were busily engaged in what appeared, from my distant position, as the emptying of the contents of various carboys upon the dead bodies of the sailors and over the decks and works of the vessel.

This operation concluded, they hastily clambered over her sides, sliding down the guy ropes to the ground. The last warrior to leave the deck turned and threw something back upon the vessel, waiting an instant to note the outcome of his act. As a faint spurt of flame rose from the point where the missile struck he swung over the side and was quickly upon the ground. Scarcely had he alighted than the guy ropes were simultaneous released, and the great warship, lightened by the removal of the loot, soared majestically into the air, her decks and upper works a mass of roaring flames.

Slowly she drifted to the southeast, rising higher and higher as the flames ate away her wooden parts and diminished the weight upon her. Ascending to the roof of the building I watched her for hours, until finally she was lost in the dim vistas of the distance. The sight was awe-inspiring in the extreme as one contemplated this mighty floating funeral pyre, drifting unguided and unmanned through the lonely wastes of the Martian heavens; a derelict of death and destruction, typifying the life story of these strange and ferocious creatures into whose unfriendly hands fate had carried it.

Much depressed, and, to me, unaccountably so, I slowly descended to the street. The scene I had witnessed seemed to mark the defeat and annihilation of the forces of a kindred people, rather than the routing by our green warriors of a horde of similar, though unfriendly, creatures. I could not fathom the seeming hallucination, nor could I free myself from it; but somewhere in the innermost recesses of my soul I felt a strange yearning toward these unknown foemen, and a mighty hope surged through me that the fleet would return and demand a reckoning from the green warriors who had so ruthlessly and wantonly attacked it.

Close at my heel, in his now accustomed place, followed Woola, the hound, and as I emerged upon the street Sola rushed up to me as though I had been the object of some search on her part. The cavalcade was returning to the plaza, the homeward march having been given up for that day; nor, in fact, was it recommenced for more than a week, owing to the fear of a return attack by the air craft.

Lorquas Ptomel was too astute an old warrior to be caught upon the open plains with a caravan of chariots and children, and so we remained at the deserted city until the danger seemed passed.

As Sola and I entered the plaza a sight met my eyes which filled my whole being with a great surge of mingled hope, fear, exultation, and depression, and yet most dominant was a subtle sense of relief and happiness; for just as we neared the throng of Martians I caught a glimpse of the prisoner from the battle craft who was being roughly dragged into a nearby building by a couple of green Martian females.

And the sight which met my eyes was that of a slender, girlish figure, similar in every detail to the earthly women of my past life. She did not see me at first, but just as she was disappearing through the portal of the building which was to be her prison she turned, and her eyes met mine. Her face was oval and beautiful in the extreme, her every feature was finely chiseled and exquisite, her eyes large and lustrous and her head surmounted by a mass of coal black, waving hair, caught loosely into a strange yet becoming coiffure. Her skin was of a light reddish copper color, against which the crimson glow of her cheeks and the ruby of her beautifully molded lips shone with a strangely enhancing effect.

She was as destitute of clothes as the green Martians who accompanied her; indeed, save for her highly wrought ornaments she was entirely naked, nor could any apparel have enhanced the beauty of her perfect and symmetrical figure.[29]

As her gaze rested on me her eyes opened wide in astonishment, and she made a little sign with her free hand; a sign which I did not, of course, understand. Just a moment we gazed upon each other, and then the look of hope and renewed courage which had glorified her face as she discovered me, faded into one of utter dejection, mingled with loathing and contempt. I realized I had not answered her signal, and ignorant as I was of Martian customs, I intuitively felt that she had made an appeal for succor and protection which my unfortunate ignorance had prevented me from answering. And then she was dragged out of my sight into the depths of the deserted edifice.

---

[29] This is a pretty racy description for 1912, and was the sort of stuff that fueled the imaginations of many an adolescent in the early twentieth century. Earlier novels, such as the perennial bestseller *She* by H. Rider Haggard (1887), with its titillating description of Queen Ayesha, set the pace for later work by Burroughs and the multitude of other writers who worked in the pulps from 1896 to the 1940s. One of the best overviews of the genre is still Ron Goulart's *Cheap Thrills: An Informal History of the Pulp Magazine* (Arlington House, 1972), although a new, updated edition has come out (Hermes Press, 2007).

CHAPTER IX
I LEARN THE LANGUAGE

As I came back to myself I glanced at Sola, who had witnessed this encounter and I was surprised to note a strange expression upon her usually expressionless countenance. What her thoughts were I did not know, for as yet I had learned but little of the Martian tongue; enough only to suffice for my daily needs.[30]

As I reached the doorway of our building a strange surprise awaited me. A warrior approached bearing the arms, ornaments, and full accouterments of his kind. These he presented to me with a few unintelligible words, and a bearing at once respectful and menacing.

Later, Sola, with the aid of several of the other women, remodeled the trappings to fit my lesser proportions, and after they completed the work I went about garbed in all the panoply of war.[31]

From then on Sola instructed me in the mysteries of the various weapons, and with the Martian young I spent several hours each day practicing upon the plaza. I was not yet proficient with all the weapons, but my great familiarity with similar earthly weapons made me an unusually apt pupil, and I progressed in a very satisfactory manner.

The training of myself and the young Martians was conducted solely by the women, who not only attend to the education of the young in the arts of individual defense and offense, but are also the artisans who produce every manufactured article wrought by the green Martians. They make the powder, the cartridges, the firearms; in fact everything of value is produced by the females. In time of actual warfare they form a part of the reserves, and when the necessity arises fight with even greater intelligence and ferocity than the men.[32]

---

[30] But Carter has told us he has already developed a facility with telepathy, which raises an issue at the heart of many modern linguistic debates: is thought possible without language? For an excellent introduction to the subject, see Steven Pinker's *The Language Instinct* (William Morrow, 1994).

[31] Surely Burroughs has here in mind the famous passage in Book XVIII of the *Iliad* describing the armor of Achilles, which Virgil later echoes in Book VIII of the *Aeneid* when he describes the armor of Aeneas.

[32] Burroughs strikes an unusual feminist note here, which contrasts with the more common "damsel in distress" portrayal. Perhaps he was influenced by Plato, who in the *Republic* suggests that women can and should be trained (and train others) as soldiers.

The men are trained in the higher branches of the art of war; in strategy and the maneuvering of large bodies of troops. They make the laws as they are needed; a new law for each emergency. They are unfettered by precedent in the administration of justice. Customs have been handed down by ages of repetition, but the punishment for ignoring a custom is a matter for individual treatment by a jury of the culprit's peers, and I may say that justice seldom misses fire, but seems rather to rule in inverse ratio to the ascendency of law. In one respect at least the Martians are a happy people; they have no lawyers.[33]

I did not see the prisoner again for several days subsequent to our first encounter, and then only to catch a fleeting glimpse of her as she was being conducted to the great audience chamber where I had had my first meeting with Lorquas Ptomel. I could not but note the unnecessary harshness and brutality with which her guards treated her; so different from the almost maternal kindliness which Sola manifested toward me, and the respectful attitude of the few green Martians who took the trouble to notice me at all.

I had observed on the two occasions when I had seen her that the prisoner exchanged words with her guards, and this convinced me that they spoke, or at least could make themselves understood by a common language. With this added incentive I nearly drove Sola distracted by my importunities to hasten on my education and within a few more days I had mastered the Martian tongue sufficiently well to enable me to carry on a passable conversation and to fully understand practically all that I heard.

At this time our sleeping quarters were occupied by three or four females and a couple of the recently hatched young, beside Sola and her youthful ward, myself, and Woola the hound. After they had retired for the night it was customary for the adults to carry on a desultory conversation for a short time before lapsing into sleep, and now that I could understand their language I was always a keen listener, although I never proffered any remarks myself.

On the night following the prisoner's visit to the audience chamber the conversation finally fell upon this subject, and I was all ears on the instant.

---

[33] One of the most often quoted lines from the entire Burroughs canon. It recalls slightly Shakespeare's line from *Henry the Sixth*, "The first thing we do, let's kill all the lawyers," or Ambrose Bierce's definition from *The Devil's Dictionary* (published in 1906 as *The Cynic's Word Book*; reprinted with the new title in 1911. See Marc Galanter's book *Lowering the Bar: Lawyer Jokes and Legal Culture* (University of Wisconsin Press, 2006) for a comprehensive treatment of lawyers as objects of contempt in American culture.

I had feared to question Sola relative to the beautiful captive, as I could not but recall the strange expression I had noted upon her face after my first encounter with the prisoner. That it denoted jealousy I could not say, and yet, judging all things by mundane standards as I still did, I felt it safer to affect indifference in the matter until I learned more surely Sola's attitude toward the object of my solicitude.

Sarkoja, one of the older women who shared our domicile, had been present at the audience as one of the captive's guards, and it was toward her the question turned.

"When," asked one of the women, "will we enjoy the death throes of the red one? or does Lorquas Ptomel, Jed, intend holding her for ransom?"

"They have decided to carry her with us back to Thark, and exhibit her last agonies at the great games before Tal Hajus," replied Sarkoja.

"What will be the manner of her going out?" inquired Sola. "She is very small and very beautiful; I had hoped that they would hold her for ransom."

Sarkoja and the other women grunted angrily at this evidence of weakness on the part of Sola.

"It is sad, Sola, that you were not born a million years ago," snapped Sarkoja, "when all the hollows of the land were filled with water, and the peoples were as soft as the stuff they sailed upon. In our day we have progressed to a point where such sentiments mark weakness and atavism.[34] It will not be well for you to permit Tars Tarkas to learn that you hold such degenerate sentiments, as I doubt that he would care to entrust such as you with the grave responsibilities of maternity."

"I see nothing wrong with my expression of interest in this red woman," retorted Sola. "She has never harmed us, nor would she should we have fallen into her hands. It is only the men of her kind who war upon us, and I have ever thought that their attitude toward us is but the reflection of ours toward them. They live at peace with all their fellows, except when duty calls upon them to make war, while we are at peace with none; forever warring among our own kind as well as upon the red men, and even in our own communities the individuals fight amongst themselves. Oh, it is one continual, awful period of bloodshed from the time we break the shell until we gladly embrace the bosom of the river of mystery, the dark and ancient Iss which carries us to an unknown, but at least no more frightful and terrible existence! Fortunate indeed is he who

---

[34] On "atavism" and "degenerate" sentiments, see note 26.

meets his end in an early death.[35] Say what you please to Tars Tarkas, he can mete out no worse fate to me than a continuation of the horrible existence we are forced to lead in this life."

This wild outbreak on the part of Sola so greatly surprised and shocked the other women, that, after a few words of general reprimand, they all lapsed into silence and were soon asleep. One thing the episode had accomplished was to assure me of Sola's friendliness toward the poor girl, and also to convince me that I had been extremely fortunate in falling into her hands rather than those of some of the other females. I knew that she was fond of me, and now that I had discovered that she hated cruelty and barbarity I was confident that I could depend upon her to aid me and the girl captive to escape, provided of course that such a thing was within the range of possibilities.

I did not even know that there were any better conditions to escape to, but I was more than willing to take my chances among people fashioned after my own mold rather than to remain longer among the hideous and bloodthirsty green men of Mars. But where to go, and how, was as much of a puzzle to me as the age-old search for the spring of eternal life has been to earthly men since the beginning of time.[36]

I decided that at the first opportunity I would take Sola into my confidence and openly ask her to aid me, and with this resolution strong upon me I turned among my silks and furs and slept the dreamless and refreshing sleep of Mars.

---

[35] This sentiment has a long lineage, dating back to at least Sophocles, if not earlier. Burroughs was certainly familiar with Plautus's line, "*Quem dii diligunt, adulescens moritur*" ("Those whom the gods especially love die young"). Nietzsche's account of the Greek myth of Silenus in *The Birth of Tragedy* (1872) describes how the demigod told Midas that "What is best of all is utterly beyond your reach: not to be born, not to be, to be nothing. But the second best for you is—to die soon." (See *The Basic Writings of Nietzsche*, trans. Kaufmann, p. 42).

[36] This recalls Genesis as well as the older *Epic of Gilgamesh*, which had been translated into English in 1870.

CHAPTER X
CHAMPION AND CHIEF

Early the next morning I was astir. Considerable freedom was allowed me, as Sola had informed me that so long as I did not attempt to leave the city I was free to go and come as I pleased. She had warned me, however, against venturing forth unarmed, as this city, like all other deserted metropolises of an ancient Martian civilization, was peopled by the great white apes of my second day's adventure.

In advising me that I must not leave the boundries of the city Sola had explained that Woola would prevent this anyway should I attempt it, and she warned me most urgently not to arouse his fierce nature by ignoring his warnings should I venture too close to the forbidden territory. His nature was such, she said, that he would bring me back into the city dead or alive should I persist in opposing him; "preferably dead," she added.

On this morning I had chosen a new street to explore when suddenly I found myself at the limits of the city. Before me were low hills pierced by narrow and inviting ravines. I longed to explore the country before me, and, like the pioneer stock from which I sprang, to view what the landscape beyond the encircling hills might disclose from the summits which shut out my view.[37]

It also occurred to me that this would prove an excellent opportunity to test the qualities of Woola. I was convinced that the brute loved me; I had seen more evidences of affection in him than in any other Martian animal, man or beast, and I was sure that gratitude for the acts that had twice saved his life would more than outweigh his loyalty to the duty imposed upon him by cruel and loveless masters.

As I approached the boundary line Woola ran anxiously before me, and thrust his body against my legs. His expression was pleading rather than ferocious, nor did he bare his great tusks or utter his fearful guttural warnings. Denied the friendship and companionship of my kind, I had developed considerable affection for Woola and Sola, for the normal earthly man must have some outlet for his natural affections, and so I decided upon an appeal to a like instinct in this great brute, sure that I would not be disappointed.

---

[37] The phrase "pioneer stock" reminds us that Carter, though a Virginian by birth, emigrated westward, very much in the spirit of exploration. In many ways, the generic elements of science fiction and the Western overlap—both genres often involve the urge to explore new lands (worlds), for example.

I had never petted nor fondled him, but now I sat upon the ground and putting my arms around his heavy neck I stroked and coaxed him, talking in my newly acquired Martian tongue as I would have to my hound at home, as I would have talked to any other friend among the lower animals. His response to my manifestation of affection was remarkable to a degree; he stretched his great mouth to its full width, baring the entire expanse of his upper rows of tusks and wrinkling his snout until his great eyes were almost hidden by the folds of flesh. If you have ever seen a collie smile you may have some idea of Woola's facial distortion.

He threw himself upon his back and fairly wallowed at my feet; jumped up and sprang upon me, rolling me upon the ground by his great weight; then wriggling and squirming around me like a playful puppy presenting its back for the petting it craves. I could not resist the ludicrousness of the spectacle, and holding my sides I rocked back and forth in the first laughter which had passed my lips in many days; the first, in fact, since the morning Powell had left camp when his horse, long unused, had precipitately and unexpectedly bucked him off headforemost into a pot of frijoles.

My laughter frightened Woola, his antics ceased and he crawled pitifully toward me, poking his ugly head far into my lap; and then I remembered what laughter signified on Mars—torture, suffering, death. Quieting myself, I rubbed the poor old fellow's head and back, talked to him for a few minutes, and then in an authoritative tone commanded him to follow me, and arising started for the hills.

There was no further question of authority between us; Woola was my devoted slave from that moment hence, and I his only and undisputed master. My walk to the hills occupied but a few minutes, and I found nothing of particular interest to reward me. Numerous brilliantly colored and strangely formed wild flowers dotted the ravines and from the summit of the first hill I saw still other hills stretching off toward the north, and rising, one range above another, until lost in mountains of quite respectable dimensions; though I afterward found that only a few peaks on all Mars exceed four thousand feet in height; the suggestion of magnitude was merely relative.[38]

My morning's walk had been large with importance to me for it had resulted in a perfect understanding with Woola, upon whom Tars Tarkas

---

[38] Burroughs was off the mark with Mars' mountains. Olympus Mons soars to 16 miles, Arsia Mons to 9 miles, and Ascraeus Mons to nearly 11 miles. Since Mars has no oceans to provide "sea level," the measurements refer to elevation above the surrounding plains.

relied for my safe keeping. I now knew that while theoretically a prisoner I was virtually free, and I hastened to regain the city limits before the defection of Woola could be discovered by his erstwhile masters. The adventure decided me never again to leave the limits of my prescribed stamping grounds until I was ready to venture forth for good and all, as it would certainly result in a curtailment of my liberties, as well as the probable death of Woola, were we to be discovered.

On regaining the plaza I had my third glimpse of the captive girl. She was standing with her guards before the entrance to the audience chamber, and as I approached she gave me one haughty glance and turned her back full upon me. The act was so womanly, so earthly womanly, that though it stung my pride it also warmed my heart with a feeling of companionship; it was good to know that someone else on Mars beside myself had human instincts of a civilized order, even though the manifestation of them was so painful and mortifying.

Had a green Martian woman desired to show dislike or contempt she would, in all likelihood, have done it with a sword thrust or a movement of her trigger finger; but as their sentiments are mostly atrophied it would have required a serious injury to have aroused such passions in them.[39] Sola, let me add, was an exception; I never saw her perform a cruel or uncouth act, or fail in uniform kindliness and good nature. She was indeed, as her fellow Martian had said of her, an atavism; a dear and precious reversion to a former type of loved and loving ancestor.

Seeing that the prisoner seemed the center of attraction I halted to view the proceedings. I had not long to wait for presently Lorquas Ptomel and his retinue of chieftains approached the building and, signing the guards to follow with the prisoner entered the audience chamber. Realizing that I was a somewhat favored character, and also convinced that the warriors did not know of my proficiency in their language, as I had pleaded with Sola to keep this a secret on the grounds that I did not wish to be forced to talk with the men until I had perfectly mastered the Martian tongue, I chanced an attempt to enter the audience chamber and listen to the proceedings.

The council squatted upon the steps of the rostrum, while below them stood the prisoner and her two guards. I saw that one of the women was Sarkoja, and thus understood how she had been present at the hearing of the preceding day, the results of which she had reported to the occupants of our dormitory last night. Her attitude toward the captive was most

---

[39] See note 26.

harsh and brutal. When she held her, she sunk her rudimentary nails into the poor girl's flesh, or twisted her arm in a most painful manner. When it was necessary to move from one spot to another she either jerked her roughly, or pushed her headlong before her. She seemed to be venting upon this poor defenseless creature all the hatred, cruelty, ferocity, and spite of her nine hundred years, backed by unguessable ages of fierce and brutal ancestors.

The other woman was less cruel because she was entirely indifferent; if the prisoner had been left to her alone, and fortunately she was at night, she would have received no harsh treatment, nor, by the same token would she have received any attention at all.

As Lorquas Ptomel raised his eyes to address the prisoner they fell on me and he turned to Tars Tarkas with a word, and gesture of impatience. Tars Tarkas made some reply which I could not catch, but which caused Lorquas Ptomel to smile; after which they paid no further attention to me.

"What is your name?" asked Lorquas Ptomel, addressing the prisoner.

"Dejah Thoris, daughter of Mors Kajak of Helium."

"And the nature of your expedition?" he continued.

"It was a purely scientific research party sent out by my father's father, the Jeddak of Helium, to rechart the air currents, and to take atmospheric density tests," replied the fair prisoner, in a low, well-modulated voice.

"We were unprepared for battle," she continued, "as we were on a peaceful mission, as our banners and the colors of our craft denoted. The work we were doing was as much in your interests as in ours, for you know full well that were it not for our labors and the fruits of our scientific operations there would not be enough air or water on Mars to support a single human life. For ages we have maintained the air and water supply at practically the same point without an appreciable loss, and we have done this in the face of the brutal and ignorant interference of your green men.

"Why, oh, why will you not learn to live in amity with your fellows, must you ever go on down the ages to your final extinction but little above the plane of the dumb brutes that serve you! A people without written language, without art, without homes, without love; the victim of eons of the horrible community idea. Owning everything in common, even to your women and children, has resulted in your owning nothing in common. You hate each other as you hate all else except yourselves. Come back to the ways of our common ancestors, come back to the light of kindliness and fellowship. The way is open to you, you will find the hands of the red men stretched out to aid you. Together we may do still more to regenerate our dying planet. The granddaughter of the greatest and mightiest of the red jeddaks has asked you. Will you come?"[40]

Lorquas Ptomel and the warriors sat looking silently and intently at the young woman for several moments after she had ceased speaking. What was passing in their minds no man may know, but that they were moved I truly believe, and if one man high among them had been strong enough to rise above custom, that moment would have marked a new and mighty era for Mars.

I saw Tars Tarkas rise to speak, and on his face was such an expression as I had never seen upon the countenance of a green Martian warrior. It bespoke an inward and mighty battle with self, with heredity, with age-old custom, and as he opened his mouth to speak, a look almost of benignity, of kindliness, momentarily lighted up his fierce and terrible countenance.

What words of moment were to have fallen from his lips were never spoken, as just then a young warrior, evidently sensing the trend of thought among the older men, leaped down from the steps of the rostrum, and striking the frail captive a powerful blow across the face, which felled her to the floor, placed his foot upon her prostrate form and turning toward the assembled council broke into peals of horrid, mirthless laughter.

For an instant I thought Tars Tarkas would strike him dead, nor did the aspect of Lorquas Ptomel augur any too favorably for the brute, but the mood passed, their old selves reasserted their ascendency, and they smiled. It was portentous however that they did not laugh aloud, for the brute's act constituted a side-splitting witticism according to the ethics which rule green Martian humor.

That I have taken moments to write down a part of what occurred as that blow fell does not signify that I remained inactive for any such length of time. I think I must have sensed something of what was coming, for I realize now that I was crouched as for a spring as I saw the blow aimed at her beautiful, upturned, pleading face, and ere the hand descended I was halfway across the hall.

Scarcely had his hideous laugh rang out but once, when I was upon him. The brute was twelve feet in height and armed to the teeth, but I

[40] Burroughs was a confirmed Republican all his life, and had been exposed to the political activism of the famous socialist Eugene Debs in Chicago in the 1890s. Hofstadter makes clear in his book *Social Darwinism in American Thought* (1955) that the social Darwinism popularized by Herbert Spencer between 1870 and 1906 was especially popular with conservatives.

believe that I could have accounted for the whole roomful in the terrific intensity of my rage. Springing upward, I struck him full in the face as he turned at my warning cry and then as he drew his short-sword I drew mine and sprang up again upon his breast, hooking one leg over the butt of his pistol and grasping one of his huge tusks with my left hand while I delivered blow after blow upon his enormous chest.

He could not use his short-sword to advantage because I was too close to him, nor could he draw his pistol, which he attempted to do in direct opposition to Martian custom which says that you may not fight a fellow warrior in private combat with any other than the weapon with which you are attacked. In fact he could do nothing but make a wild and futile attempt to dislodge me. With all his immense bulk he was little if any stronger than I, and it was but the matter of a moment or two before he sank, bleeding and lifeless, to the floor.

Dejah Thoris had raised herself upon one elbow and was watching the battle with wide, staring eyes. When I had regained my feet I raised her in my arms and bore her to one of the benches at the side of the room.

Again no Martian interfered with me, and tearing a piece of silk from my cape I endeavored to staunch the flow of blood from her nostrils. I was soon successful as her injuries amounted to little more than an ordinary nosebleed, and when she could speak she placed her hand upon my arm and looking up into my eyes, said:

"Why did you do it? You who refused me even friendly recognition in the first hour of my peril! And now you risk your life and kill one of your companions for my sake. I cannot understand. What strange manner of man are you, that you consort with the green men, though your form is that of my race, while your color is little darker than that of the white ape? Tell me, are you human, or are you more than human?"[41]

"It is a strange tale," I replied, "too long to attempt to tell you now, and one which I so much doubt the credibility of myself that I fear to hope that others will believe it. Suffice it, for the present, that I am your friend, and, so far as our captors will permit, your protector and your servant."

"Then you too are a prisoner? But why, then, those arms and the regalia of a Tharkian chieftain? What is your name? Where your country?"

"Yes, Dejah Thoris, I too am a prisoner; my name is John Carter, and I claim Virginia, one of the United States of America, Earth, as my home;

---

[41] This recalls Nietzsche's conception of the *Übermensch*, or "Overman," another late nineteenth century conception developed with aplomb in early twentieth-century science fiction. The most notable example is Olaf Stapledon's *Odd John* (1935).

but why I am permitted to wear arms I do not know, nor was I aware that my regalia was that of a chieftain."

We were interrupted at this juncture by the approach of one of the warriors, bearing arms, accouterments and ornaments, and in a flash one of her questions was answered and a puzzle cleared up for me. I saw that the body of my dead antagonist had been stripped, and I read in the menacing yet respectful attitude of the warrior who had brought me these trophies of the kill the same demeanor as that evinced by the other who had brought me my original equipment, and now for the first time I realized that my blow, on the occasion of my first battle in the audience chamber had resulted in the death of my adversary.

The reason for the whole attitude displayed toward me was now apparent; I had won my spurs, so to speak, and in the crude justice, which always marks Martian dealings, and which, among other things, has caused me to call her the planet of paradoxes, I was accorded the honors due a conqueror; the trappings and the position of the man I killed. In truth, I was a Martian chieftain, and this I learned later was the cause of my great freedom and my toleration in the audience chamber.

As I had turned to receive the dead warrior's chattels I had noticed that Tars Tarkas and several others had pushed forward toward us, and the eyes of the former rested upon me in a most quizzical manner. Finally he addressed me:

"You speak the tongue of Barsoom quite readily for one who was deaf and dumb to us a few short days ago. Where did you learn it, John Carter?"

"You, yourself, are responsible, Tars Tarkas," I replied, "in that you furnished me with an instructress of remarkable ability; I have to thank Sola for my learning."

"She has done well," he answered, "but your education in other respects needs considerable polish. Do you know what your unprecedented temerity would have cost you had you failed to kill either of the two chieftains whose metal you now wear?"

"I presume that that one whom I had failed to kill, would have killed me," I answered, smiling.

"No, you are wrong. Only in the last extremity of self-defense would a Martian warrior kill a prisoner; we like to save them for other purposes," and his face bespoke possibilities that were not pleasant to dwell upon.

"But one thing can save you now," he continued. "Should you, in recognition of your remarkable valor, ferocity, and prowess, be considered by Tal Hajus as worthy of his service you may be taken into the community and become a full-fledged Tharkian. Until we reach the headquarters of Tal Hajus it is the will of Lorquas Ptomel that you be accorded the respect your acts have earned you. You will be treated by us as a Tharkian chieftain, but you must not forget that every chief who ranks you is responsible for your safe delivery to our mighty and most ferocious ruler. I am done."

"I hear you, Tars Tarkas," I answered. "As you know I am not of Barsoom; your ways are not my ways, and I can only act in the future as I have in the past, in accordance with the dictates of my conscience and guided by the standards of mine own people. If you will leave me alone I will go in peace, but if not, let the individual Barsoomians with whom I must deal either respect my rights as a stranger among you, or take whatever consequences may befall. Of one thing let us be sure, whatever may be your ultimate intentions toward this unfortunate young woman, whoever would offer her injury or insult in the future must figure on making a full accounting to me. I understand that you belittle all sentiments of generosity and kindliness, but I do not, and I can convince your most doughty warrior that these characteristics are not incompatible with an ability to fight."

Ordinarily I am not given to long speeches, nor ever before had I descended to bombast, but I had guessed at the keynote which would strike an answering chord in the breasts of the green Martians, nor was I wrong, for my harangue evidently deeply impressed them, and their attitude toward me thereafter was still further respectful.

Tars Tarkas himself seemed pleased with my reply, but his only comment was more or less enigmatical—"And I think I know Tal Hajus, Jeddak of Thark."

I now turned my attention to Dejah Thoris, and assisting her to her feet I turned with her toward the exit, ignoring her hovering guardian harpies as well as the inquiring glances of the chieftains. Was I not now a chieftain also! Well, then, I would assume the responsibilities of one. They did not molest us, and so Dejah Thoris, Princess of Helium, and John Carter, gentleman of Virginia, followed by the faithful Woola, passed through utter silence from the audience chamber of Lorquas Ptomel, Jed among the Tharks of Barsoom.

CHAPTER XI
WITH DEJAH THORIS

As we reached the open the two female guards who had been detailed to watch over Dejah Thoris hurried up and made as though to assume custody of her once more. The poor child shrank against me and I felt her two little hands fold tightly over my arm. Waving the women away, I informed them that Sola would attend the captive hereafter, and I further warned Sarkoja that any more of her cruel attentions bestowed upon Dejah Thoris would result in Sarkoja's sudden and painful demise.

My threat was unfortunate and resulted in more harm than good to Dejah Thoris, for, as I learned later, men do not kill women upon Mars, nor women, men. So Sarkoja merely gave us an ugly look and departed to hatch up deviltries against us.

I soon found Sola and explained to her that I wished her to guard Dejah Thoris as she had guarded me; that I wished her to find other quarters where they would not be molested by Sarkoja, and I finally informed her that I myself would take up my quarters among the men.

Sola glanced at the accouterments which were carried in my hand and slung across my shoulder.

"You are a great chieftain now, John Carter," she said, "and I must do your bidding, though indeed I am glad to do it under any circumstances. The man whose metal you carry was young, but he was a great warrior, and had by his promotions and kills won his way close to the rank of Tars Tarkas, who, as you know, is second to Lorquas Ptomel only. You are eleventh, there are but ten chieftains in this community who rank you in prowess."

"And if I should kill Lorquas Ptomel?" I asked.

"You would be first, John Carter; but you may only win that honor by the will of the entire council that Lorquas Ptomel meet you in combat, or should he attack you, you may kill him in self-defense, and thus win first place."

I laughed, and changed the subject. I had no particular desire to kill Lorquas Ptomel, and less to be a jed among the Tharks.

I accompanied Sola and Dejah Thoris in a search for new quarters, which we found in a building nearer the audience chamber and of far more pretentious architecture than our former habitation. We also found in this building real sleeping apartments with ancient beds of highly wrought metal swinging from enormous gold chains depending from the marble ceilings. The decoration of the walls was most elaborate, and, unlike the frescoes in the other buildings I had examined, portrayed many human figures in the compositions. These were of people like myself, and of a much lighter color than Dejah Thoris. They were clad in graceful, flowing robes, highly ornamented with metal and jewels, and their luxuriant hair was of a beautiful golden and reddish bronze. The men were beardless and only a few wore arms. The scenes depicted for the most part, a fair-skinned, fair-haired people at play.

Dejah Thoris clasped her hands with an exclamation of rapture as she gazed upon these magnificent works of art, wrought by a people long extinct; while Sola, on the other hand, apparently did not see them.

We decided to use this room, on the second floor and overlooking the plaza, for Dejah Thoris and Sola, and another room adjoining and in the rear for the cooking and supplies. I then dispatched Sola to bring the bedding and such food and utensils as she might need, telling her that I would guard Dejah Thoris until her return.

As Sola departed Dejah Thoris turned to me with a faint smile.

"And whereto, then, would your prisoner escape should you leave her, unless it was to follow you and crave your protection, and ask your pardon for the cruel thoughts she has harbored against you these past few days?"

"You are right," I answered, "there is no escape for either of us unless we go together."

"I heard your challenge to the creature you call Tars Tarkas, and I think I understand your position among these people, but what I cannot fathom is your statement that you are not of Barsoom."

"In the name of my first ancestor, then," she continued, "where may you be from? You are like unto my people, and yet so unlike. You speak my language, and yet I heard you tell Tars Tarkas that you had but learned it recently. All Barsoomians speak the same tongue from the ice-clad south to the ice-clad north, though their written languages differ.[42] Only in the

---

[42] Because Martian history far exceeds Earth history (Martian civilization dates back at least 500,000 years before the present, whereas Earth civilization dates back fewer than 10,000 years), Burroughs can speculate about the fate of linguistic development. A common concern among modern linguists is that through language extinction and processes of globalization, all of Earth's inhabitants may eventually speak a common language; for example, something perhaps called Sino-Spanglish.

    Other theorists argue that dialects and new languages are constantly springing up. In his book, *English as a Global Language* (Cambridge University Press, 1997), linguist David Crystal is a chief proponent of the view that, owing to the proliferation of technology connecting practically every community on the globe, we will all speak a common language. Alternatively, other linguists insist that new dialects spawning

valley Dor, where the river Iss empties into the lost sea of Korus, is there supposed to be a different language spoken, and, except in the legends of our ancestors, there is no record of a Barsoomian returning up the river Iss, from the shores of Korus in the valley of Dor. Do not tell me that you have thus returned! They would kill you horribly anywhere upon the surface of Barsoom if that were true; tell me it is not!"

Her eyes were filled with a strange, weird light; her voice was pleading, and her little hands, reached up upon my breast, were pressed against me as though to wring a denial from my very heart.

"I do not know your customs, Dejah Thoris, but in my own Virginia a gentleman does not lie to save himself; I am not of Dor; I have never seen the mysterious Iss; the lost sea of Korus is still lost, so far as I am concerned. Do you believe me?"

And then it struck me suddenly that I was very anxious that she should believe me. It was not that I feared the results which would follow a general belief that I had returned from the Barsoomian heaven or hell, or whatever it was. Why was it, then! Why should I care what she thought? I looked down at her; her beautiful face upturned, and her wonderful eyes opening up the very depth of her soul; and as my eyes met hers I knew why, and—I shuddered.

A similar wave of feeling seemed to stir her; she drew away from me with a sigh, and with her earnest, beautiful face turned up to mine, she whispered: "I believe you, John Carter; I do not know what a 'gentleman' is, nor have I ever heard before of Virginia; but on Barsoom no man lies; if he does not wish to speak the truth he is silent.[43] Where is this Virginia, your country, John Carter?" she asked, and it seemed that this fair name of my fair land had never sounded more beautiful than as it fell from those perfect lips on that far-gone day.

---

distinct languages will continue in the future, just as they have in the past. See Salikoko Mufwene's *The Ecology of Language Evolution* (Cambridge University Press, 2001).

[43] Does this mean women can lie? And is a culture devoid of lying even possible? See Allison Kornet, "The Truth About Lying" (*Psychology Today*, 1 May 1997). For philosophers, this points to the paradox of the Epimenides the Liar, a Cretan who insisted that "all Cretans were liars," which is a key problem of epistemology.

At least three Hollywood movies explore what life would be like if a person was unable to lie, most recently the Jim Carrey vehicle, *Liar, Liar* (1997). Earlier films include the 1929 *Nothing But the Truth*, and the 1941 remake of the same name (starring Bob Hope). Perhaps Burroughs has this problem in mind when he calls Mars a planet of paradoxes.

"I am of another world," I answered, "the great planet Earth, which revolves about our common sun and next within the orbit of your Barsoom, which we know as Mars. How I came here I cannot tell you, for I do not know; but here I am, and since my presence has permitted me to serve Dejah Thoris I am glad that I am here."

She gazed at me with troubled eyes, long and questioningly. That it was difficult to believe my statement I well knew, nor could I hope that she would do so however much I craved her confidence and respect. I would much rather not have told her anything of my antecedents, but no man could look into the depth of those eyes and refuse her slightest behest.

Finally she smiled, and, rising, said: "I shall have to believe even though I cannot understand. I can readily perceive that you are not of the Barsoom of today; you are like us, yet different—but why should I trouble my poor head with such a problem, when my heart tells me that I believe because I wish to believe!"[44]

It was good logic, good, earthly, feminine logic, and if it satisfied her I certainly could pick no flaws in it. As a matter of fact it was about the only kind of logic that could be brought to bear upon my problem. We fell into a general conversation then, asking and answering many questions on each side. She was curious to learn of the customs of my people and displayed a remarkable knowledge of events on Earth. When I questioned her closely on this seeming familiarity with earthly things she laughed, and cried out:

"Why, every school boy on Barsoom knows the geography, and much concerning the fauna and flora, as well as the history of your planet fully as well as of his own. Can we not see everything which takes place upon Earth, as you call it; is it not hanging there in the heavens in plain sight?"

This baffled me, I must confess, fully as much as my statements had confounded her; and I told her so. She then explained in general the instruments her people had used and been perfecting for ages, which permit them to throw upon a screen a perfect image of what is transpiring upon any planet and upon many of the stars. These pictures are so perfect in detail that, when photographed and enlarged, objects no greater than a blade of grass may be distinctly recognized. I afterward, in Helium, saw many of these pictures, as well as the instruments which produced them.[45]

---

[44] Burroughs's depiction of this sort of specious reasoning ("I believe because I wish to believe") as "feminine logic" seems unquestionably sexist, even if Carter accedes to it. The phrase is possibly a vague echo of Anselm's *fides intellectum quaerens*," or "faith seeking understanding," a theological stance in which faith precedes reason.

[45] An interesting aspect of Martian technology is that they are aware of life not merely

"If, then, you are so familiar with earthly things," I asked, "why is it that you do not recognize me as identical with the inhabitants of that planet?"

She smiled again as one might in bored indulgence of a questioning child.

"Because, John Carter," she replied, "nearly every planet and star having atmospheric conditions at all approaching those of Barsoom, shows forms of animal life almost identical with you and me; and, further, Earth men, almost without exception, cover their bodies with strange, unsightly pieces of cloth, and their heads with hideous contraptions the purpose of which we have been unable to conceive; while you, when found by the Tharkian warriors, were entirely undisfigured and unadorned.[46]

"The fact that you wore no ornaments is a strong proof of your un-Barsoomian origin, while the absence of grotesque coverings might cause a doubt as to your earthliness."

I then narrated the details of my departure from the Earth, explaining that my body there lay fully clothed in all the, to her, strange garments of mundane dwellers. At this point Sola returned with our meager belongings and her young Martian protege, who, of course, would have to share the quarters with them.

Sola asked us if we had had a visitor during her absence, and seemed much surprised when we answered in the negative. It seemed that as she had mounted the approach to the upper floors where our quarters were located, she had met Sarkoja descending. We decided that she must have

---

on Earth, but other planets (see note 46), and that they can observe details with amazing clarity, as if watching live television. Burroughs may have in mind the famous hoax perpetrated in the *New York Sun* in 1835, in which the hoaxers claimed that the greatest living astronomer of his day, Sir John Herschel, had created a telescope so powerful as to be able to see bison and other mammals on the moon. The hoax inspired Edgar Allan Poe to write "The Unparalleled Adventure of Hans Pfall" (1835), a story about a balloon trip to the moon, which some critics point to as one of the first works of science fiction.

[46] The idea that stars and planets are other worlds that potentially support life is a much older proposition than most people think. Lucian (ca. 200 CE) wrote two narratives about traveling to the moon in which he encounters both lunar beings and solar beings (*Vera Historia* and *Icaromenippus*). Thomas Aquinas and other medieval philosophers in the twelfth century debated the issue, the consensus reached seeming to indicate that many scholastics accepted it as inevitable. Since 2007, thanks to the Hubble Telescope, scientists are now aware of at least 700 extrasolar planets, and in December of 2011, astronomers discovered the first extrasolar and potentially Earth-like planet in a system 600 light years away. Whether or not extraterrestrial intelligent life would resemble human beings at all is a matter of broad debate.

been eavesdropping, but as we could recall nothing of importance that had passed between us we dismissed the matter as of little consequence, merely promising ourselves to be warned to the utmost caution in the future.

Dejah Thoris and I then fell to examining the architecture and decorations of the beautiful chambers of the building we were occupying. She told me that these people had presumably flourished over a hundred thousand years before. They were the early progenitors of her race, but had mixed with the other great race of early Martians, who were very dark, almost black, and also with the reddish yellow race which had flourished at the same time.

These three great divisions of the higher Martians had been forced into a mighty alliance as the drying up of the Martian seas had compelled them to seek the comparatively few and always diminishing fertile areas, and to defend themselves, under new conditions of life, against the wild hordes of green men.

Ages of close relationship and intermarrying had resulted in the race of red men, of which Dejah Thoris was a fair and beautiful daughter. During the ages of hardships and incessant warring between their own various races, as well as with the green men, and before they had fitted themselves to the changed conditions, much of the high civilization and many of the arts of the fair-haired Martians had become lost; but the red race of today has reached a point where it feels that it has made up in new discoveries and in a more practical civilization for all that lies irretrievably buried with the ancient Barsoomians, beneath the countless intervening ages.[47]

These ancient Martians had been a highly cultivated and literary race, but during the vicissitudes of those trying centuries of readjustment to new conditions, not only did their advancement and production cease entirely, but practically all their archives, records, and literature were lost.[48]

Dejah Thoris related many interesting facts and legends concerning this lost race of noble and kindly people. She said that the city in which we were camping was supposed to have been a center of commerce and culture known as Korad. It had been built upon a beautiful, natural harbor, landlocked by magnificent hills. The little valley on the west front

---

[47] See note 26 for background on Burroughs's overview of Martian racial hierarchy.

[48] Paralleling humanity's loss of much that was written in antiquity, the Martian civilization has lost many primary records of its past.

of the city, she explained, was all that remained of the harbor, while the pass through the hills to the old sea bottom had been the channel through which the shipping passed up to the city's gates.

The shores of the ancient seas were dotted with just such cities, and lesser ones, in diminishing numbers, were to be found converging toward the center of the oceans, as the people had found it necessary to follow the receding waters until necessity had forced upon them their ultimate salvation, the so-called Martian canals.[49]

We had been so engrossed in exploration of the building and in our conversation that it was late in the afternoon before we realized it. We were brought back to a realization of our present conditions by a messenger bearing a summons from Lorquas Ptomel directing me to appear before him forthwith. Bidding Dejah Thoris and Sola farewell, and commanding Woola to remain on guard, I hastened to the audience chamber, where I found Lorquas Ptomel and Tars Tarkas seated upon the rostrum.

---

[49] Percival Lowell's misperception of Schiaparelli's Mars account is well documented, and has been discussed in many quarters—as an example of the importance of accurate translation to the progression of science. For a full account, see Paul Chambers's *Life on Mars: The Complete Story* (Blandford, 1999), which contains a section devoted to Schiaparelli and Lowell, as well a thorough account of the actual NASA missions to Mars and their discoveries.

Chapter XII

A Prisoner with Power

As I entered and saluted, Lorquas Ptomel signaled me to advance, and, fixing his great, hideous eyes upon me, addressed me thus:

"You have been with us a few days, yet during that time you have by your prowess won a high position among us. Be that as it may, you are not one of us; you owe us no allegiance.

"Your position is a peculiar one," he continued; "you are a prisoner and yet you give commands which must be obeyed; you are an alien and yet you are a Tharkian chieftain; you are a midget and yet you can kill a mighty warrior with one blow of your fist. And now you are reported to have been plotting to escape with another prisoner of another race; a prisoner who, from her own admission, half believes you are returned from the valley of Dor. Either one of these accusations, if proved, would be sufficient grounds for your execution, but we are a just people and you shall have a trial on our return to Thark, if Tal Hajus so commands.

"But," he continued, in his fierce guttural tones, "if you run off with the red girl it is I who shall have to account to Tal Hajus; it is I who shall have to face Tars Tarkas, and either demonstrate my right to command, or the metal from my dead carcass will go to a better man, for such is the custom of the Tharks.

"I have no quarrel with Tars Tarkas; together we rule supreme the greatest of the lesser communities among the green men; we do not wish to fight between ourselves; and so if you were dead, John Carter, I should be glad. Under two conditions only, however, may you be killed by us without orders from Tal Hajus; in personal combat in self-defense, should you attack one of us, or were you apprehended in an attempt to escape.

"As a matter of justice I must warn you that we only await one of these two excuses for ridding ourselves of so great a responsibility. The safe delivery of the red girl to Tal Hajus is of the greatest importance. Not in a thousand years have the Tharks made such a capture; she is the granddaughter of the greatest of the red jeddaks, who is also our bitterest enemy. I have spoken. The red girl told us that we were without the softer sentiments of humanity, but we are a just and truthful race. You may go."

Turning, I left the audience chamber. So this was the beginning of Sarkoja's persecution! I knew that none other could be responsible for this report which had reached the ears of Lorquas Ptomel so quickly, and now I recalled those portions of our conversation which had touched upon escape and upon my origin.

Sarkoja was at this time Tars Tarkas' oldest and most trusted female. As such she was a mighty power behind the throne, for no warrior had the confidence of Lorquas Ptomel to such an extent as did his ablest lieutenant, Tars Tarkas.

However, instead of putting thoughts of possible escape from my mind, my audience with Lorquas Ptomel only served to center my every faculty on this subject. Now, more than before, the absolute necessity for escape, in so far as Dejah Thoris was concerned, was impressed upon me, for I was convinced that some horrible fate awaited her at the headquarters of Tal Hajus.

As described by Sola, this monster was the exaggerated personification of all the ages of cruelty, ferocity, and brutality from which he had descended. Cold, cunning, calculating; he was, also, in marked contrast to most of his fellows, a slave to that brute passion which the waning demands for procreation upon their dying planet has almost stilled in the Martian breast.[50]

The thought that the divine Dejah Thoris might fall into the clutches of such an abysmal atavism started the cold sweat upon me. Far better that we save friendly bullets for ourselves at the last moment, as did those brave frontier women of my lost land, who took their own lives rather than fall into the hands of the Indian braves.[51]

As I wandered about the plaza lost in my gloomy forebodings Tars Tarkas approached me on his way from the audience chamber. His demeanor toward me was unchanged, and he greeted me as though we had not just parted a few moments before.

"Where are your quarters, John Carter?" he asked.

"I have selected none," I replied. "It seemed best that I quartered either by myself or among the other warriors, and I was awaiting an

---

[50] Erling Holtsmark suggests that Burroughs is responsible for solidifying the notion in early twentieth-century literature that one of the marks of brute atavism is the obsession with sex—or sexual appetite.

[51] The notion of women committing suicide to avoid torture or "dishonor" at the hands of an enemy is a recurrent theme in literature. In The Franklin's Tale of *The Canterbury Tales*, Chaucer recounts numerous examples of noble Greek and Roman women who killed themselves to avoid rape or torture. Rumors and reports of American frontier women doing the same to avoid suffering at the hands of their Indian captors appear frequently in the literature. The so-called "Indian Captivity Narrative" refers to an entire subgenre of American literature. See Nancy Chu's essay, "Women in the Frontier Dime Novel" (*Books at Iowa* 33, 1980).

opportunity to ask your advice. As you know," and I smiled, "I am not yet familiar with all the customs of the Tharks."

"Come with me," he directed, and together we moved off across the plaza to a building which I was glad to see adjoined that occupied by Sola and her charges.

"My quarters are on the first floor of this building," he said, "and the second floor also is fully occupied by warriors, but the third floor and the floors above are vacant; you may take your choice of these.

"I understand," he continued, "that you have given up your woman to the red prisoner. Well, as you have said, your ways are not our ways, but you can fight well enough to do about as you please, and so, if you wish to give your woman to a captive, it is your own affair; but as a chieftain you should have those to serve you, and in accordance with our customs you may select any or all the females from the retinues of the chieftains whose metal you now wear."

I thanked him, but assured him that I could get along very nicely without assistance except in the matter of preparing food, and so he promised to send women to me for this purpose and also for the care of my arms and the manufacture of my ammunition, which he said would be necessary. I suggested that they might also bring some of the sleeping silks and furs which belonged to me as spoils of combat, for the nights were cold and I had none of my own.

He promised to do so, and departed. Left alone, I ascended the winding corridor to the upper floors in search of suitable quarters. The beauties of the other buildings were repeated in this, and, as usual, I was soon lost in a tour of investigation and discovery.

I finally chose a front room on the third floor, because this brought me nearer to Dejah Thoris, whose apartment was on the second floor of the adjoining building, and it flashed upon me that I could rig up some means of communication whereby she might signal me in case she needed either my services or my protection.

Adjoining my sleeping apartment were baths, dressing rooms, and other sleeping and living apartments, in all some ten rooms on this floor. The windows of the back rooms overlooked an enormous court, which formed the center of the square made by the buildings which faced the four contiguous streets, and which was now given over to the quartering of the various animals belonging to the warriors occupying the adjoining buildings.

While the court was entirely overgrown with the yellow, moss-like vegetation which blankets practically the entire surface of Mars, yet numerous fountains, statuary, benches, and pergola-like contraptions bore witness to the beauty which the court must have presented in bygone times, when graced by the fair-haired, laughing people whom stern and unalterable cosmic laws had driven not only from their homes, but from all except the vague legends of their descendants.[52]

One could easily picture the gorgeous foliage of the luxuriant Martian vegetation which once filled this scene with life and color; the graceful figures of the beautiful women, the straight and handsome men; the happy frolicking children—all sunlight, happiness and peace. It was difficult to realize that they had gone; down through ages of darkness, cruelty, and ignorance, until their hereditary instincts of culture and humanitarianism had risen ascendant once more in the final composite race which now is dominant upon Mars.

My thoughts were cut short by the advent of several young females bearing loads of weapons, silks, furs, jewels, cooking utensils, and casks of food and drink, including considerable loot from the air craft. All this, it seemed, had been the property of the two chieftains I had slain, and now, by the customs of the Tharks, it had become mine. At my direction they placed the stuff in one of the back rooms, and then departed, only to return with a second load, which they advised me constituted the balance of my goods. On the second trip they were accompanied by ten or fifteen other women and youths, who, it seemed, formed the retinues of the two chieftains.

They were not their families, nor their wives, nor their servants; the relationship was peculiar, and so unlike anything known to us that it is most difficult to describe. All property among the green Martians is owned in common by the community, except the personal weapons, ornaments and sleeping silks and furs of the individuals. These alone can one claim undisputed right to, nor may he accumulate more of these than are required for his actual needs. The surplus he holds merely as custodian,

---

[52] This sounds like a version of Epicureanism or stoicism. Burroughs was no doubt acquainted with *De Rerum Natura*, one of the most influential of ancient Roman philosophical works, written by Lucretius (ca 100–55 BCE). In it, Lucretius articulates the essential tenets of the Epicureanism that so influenced Virgil in the *Aeneid*. Akin to, but often at odds with, stoicism, Epicureanism advocated a sort of determinism occasionally complicated by a random "swerve" (*clinamen*), which Burroughs also seems to refer to in other passages in *A Princess of Mars*. See note 57.

and it is passed on to the younger members of the community as necessity demands.[53]

The women and children of a man's retinue may be likened to a military unit for which he is responsible in various ways, as in matters of instruction, discipline, sustenance, and the exigencies of their continual roamings and their unending strife with other communities and with the red Martians. His women are in no sense wives. The green Martians use no word corresponding in meaning with this earthly word. Their mating is a matter of community interest solely, and is directed without reference to natural selection.[54] The council of chieftains of each community control the matter as surely as the owner of a Kentucky racing stud directs the scientific breeding of his stock for the improvement of the whole.

In theory it may sound well, as is often the case with theories, but the results of ages of this unnatural practice, coupled with the community interest in the offspring being held paramount to that of the mother, is shown in the cold, cruel creatures, and their gloomy, loveless, mirthless existence.

It is true that the green Martians are absolutely virtuous, both men and women, with the exception of such degenerates as Tal Hajus; but better far a finer balance of human characteristics even at the expense of a slight and occasional loss of chastity.

Finding that I must assume responsibility for these creatures, whether I would or not, I made the best of it and directed them to find quarters on the upper floors, leaving the third floor to me. One of the girls I charged with the duties of my simple cuisine, and directed the others to take up the various activities which had formerly constituted their vocations. Thereafter I saw little of them, nor did I care to.

---

[53] That all property is owned in common sounds dangerously communist. The Martian attitudes about women and children and communal child-rearing have some precedent in Plato's Republic. It is interesting that a political conservative like Burroughs seems to extol the idea of communal ownership (compare to note 40, above).

[54] Burroughs was speculating on topics that were all the buzz in 1912. The First International Congress of Eugenics was held that year, inspired in part by books such as Ernst Haeckel's *Riddle of the Universe* (1899), which promoted many social Darwinist ideas including eugenics. Burroughs may have been familiar with Haeckel's book, since it was translated into English in 1901. See note 26.

CHAPTER XIII
LOVE-MAKING ON MARS[55]

Following the battle with the air ships, the community remained within the city for several days, abandoning the homeward march until they could feel reasonably assured that the ships would not return; for to be caught on the open plains with a cavalcade of chariots and children was far from the desire of even so warlike a people as the green Martians.

During our period of inactivity, Tars Tarkas had instructed me in many of the customs and arts of war familiar to the Tharks, including lessons in riding and guiding the great beasts which bore the warriors. These creatures, which are known as thoats, are as dangerous and vicious as their masters, but when once subdued are sufficiently tractable for the purposes of the green Martians.

Two of these animals had fallen to me from the warriors whose metal I wore, and in a short time I could handle them quite as well as the native warriors. The method was not at all complicated. If the thoats did not respond with sufficient celerity to the telepathic instructions of their riders they were dealt a terrific blow between the ears with the butt of a pistol, and if they showed fight this treatment was continued until the brutes either were subdued, or had unseated their riders.

In the latter case it became a life and death struggle between the man and the beast. If the former were quick enough with his pistol he might live to ride again, though upon some other beast; if not, his torn and mangled body was gathered up by his women and burned in accordance with Tharkian custom.

My experience with Woola determined me to attempt the experiment of kindness in my treatment of my thoats. First I taught them that they could not unseat me, and even rapped them sharply between the ears to impress upon them my authority and mastery. Then, by degrees, I won their confidence in much the same manner as I had adopted countless times with my many mundane mounts. I was ever a good hand with animals, and by inclination, as well as because it brought more lasting and satisfactory results, I was always kind and humane in my dealings with the

---

[55] "Love-making" suggests a rather more titillating subject for this chapter than actually appears, but that is a result of the vagaries of idiom changing through time: although Merriam-Webster's most recent dictionary still lists "courtship" as the primary meaning for "lovemaking," most modern readers will tend to take the phrase for its secondary meaning of "sexual intercourse." Rather than an overview of Martian coitus, however, Burroughs simply describes Carter wooing Dejah Thoris.

lower orders. I could take a human life, if necessary, with far less compunction than that of a poor, unreasoning, irresponsible brute.

In the course of a few days my thoats were the wonder of the entire community. They would follow me like dogs, rubbing their great snouts against my body in awkward evidence of affection, and respond to my every command with an alacrity and docility which caused the Martian warriors to ascribe to me the possession of some earthly power unknown on Mars.

"How have you bewitched them?" asked Tars Tarkas one afternoon, when he had seen me run my arm far between the great jaws of one of my thoats which had wedged a piece of stone between two of his teeth while feeding upon the moss-like vegetation within our court yard.

"By kindness," I replied. "You see, Tars Tarkas, the softer sentiments have their value, even to a warrior. In the height of battle as well as upon the march I know that my thoats will obey my every command, and therefore my fighting efficiency is enhanced, and I am a better warrior for the reason that I am a kind master. Your other warriors would find it to the advantage of themselves as well as of the community to adopt my methods in this respect. Only a few days since you, yourself, told me that these great brutes, by the uncertainty of their tempers, often were the means of turning victory into defeat, since, at a crucial moment, they might elect to unseat and rend their riders."

"Show me how you accomplish these results," was Tars Tarkas' only rejoinder.

And so I explained as carefully as I could the entire method of training I had adopted with my beasts, and later he had me repeat it before Lorquas Ptomel and the assembled warriors. That moment marked the beginning of a new existence for the poor thoats, and before I left the community of Lorquas Ptomel I had the satisfaction of observing a regiment of as tractable and docile mounts as one might care to see. The effect on the precision and celerity of the military movements was so remarkable that Lorquas Ptomel presented me with a massive anklet of gold from his own leg, as a sign of his appreciation of my service to the horde.

On the seventh day following the battle with the air craft we again took up the march toward Thark, all probability of another attack being deemed remote by Lorquas Ptomel.

During the days just preceding our departure I had seen but little of Dejah Thoris, as I had been kept very busy by Tars Tarkas with my lessons in the art of Martian warfare, as well as in the training of my thoats. The few times I had visited her quarters she had been absent, walking upon the streets with Sola, or investigating the buildings in the near vicinity of the plaza. I had warned them against venturing far from the plaza for fear of the great white apes, whose ferocity I was only too well acquainted with. However, since Woola accompanied them on all their excursions, and as Sola was well armed, there was comparatively little cause for fear.

On the evening before our departure I saw them approaching along one of the great avenues which lead into the plaza from the east. I advanced to meet them, and telling Sola that I would take the responsibility for Dejah Thoris' safekeeping, I directed her to return to her quarters on some trivial errand. I liked and trusted Sola, but for some reason I desired to be alone with Dejah Thoris, who represented to me all that I had left behind upon Earth in agreeable and congenial companionship. There seemed bonds of mutual interest between us as powerful as though we had been born under the same roof rather than upon different planets, hurtling through space some forty-eight million miles apart.

That she shared my sentiments in this respect I was positive, for on my approach the look of pitiful hopelessness left her sweet countenance to be replaced by a smile of joyful welcome, as she placed her little right hand upon my left shoulder in true red Martian salute.

"Sarkoja told Sola that you had become a true Thark," she said, "and that I would now see no more of you than of any of the other warriors."

"Sarkoja is a liar of the first magnitude," I replied, "notwithstanding the proud claim of the Tharks to absolute verity."

Dejah Thoris laughed.

"I knew that even though you became a member of the community you would not cease to be my friend; 'A warrior may change his metal, but not his heart,' as the saying is upon Barsoom."

"I think they have been trying to keep us apart," she continued, "for whenever you have been off duty one of the older women of Tars Tarkas' retinue has always arranged to trump up some excuse to get Sola and me out of sight. They have had me down in the pits below the buildings helping them mix their awful radium powder, and make their terrible projectiles. You know that these have to be manufactured by artificial light, as exposure to sunlight always results in an explosion. You have noticed that their bullets explode when they strike an object? Well, the opaque, outer coating is broken by the impact, exposing a glass cylinder, almost solid, in the forward end of which is a minute particle of radium powder. The moment the sunlight, even though diffused, strikes this powder it explodes with a violence which nothing can withstand. If you ever witness a night battle you will note the absence of these explosions, while the morning following the battle will be filled at sunrise with the sharp detonations of exploding missiles fired the preceding night. As a rule, however, non-exploding projectiles are used at night."[56]

While I was much interested in Dejah Thoris' explanation of this wonderful adjunct to Martian warfare, I was more concerned by the immediate problem of their treatment of her. That they were keeping her away from me was not a matter for surprise, but that they should subject her to dangerous and arduous labor filled me with rage.

"Have they ever subjected you to cruelty and ignominy, Dejah Thoris?" I asked, feeling the hot blood of my fighting ancestors leap in my veins as I awaited her reply.

"Only in little ways, John Carter," she answered. "Nothing that can harm me outside my pride. They know that I am the daughter of ten thousand jeddaks, that I trace my ancestry straight back without a break to the builder of the first great waterway, and they, who do not even know their own mothers, are jealous of me. At heart they hate their horrid fates, and so wreak their poor spite on me who stand for everything they have not, and for all they most crave and never can attain. Let us pity them, my chieftain, for even though we die at their hands we can afford them pity, since we are greater than they and they know it."

Had I known the significance of those words "my chieftain," as applied by a red Martian woman to a man, I should have had the surprise of my life, but I did not know at that time, nor for many months thereafter. Yes, I still had much to learn upon Barsoom.

"I presume it is the better part of wisdom that we bow to our fate with as good grace as possible, Dejah Thoris; but I hope, nevertheless, that I may be present the next time that any Martian, green, red, pink, or violet, has the temerity to even so much as frown on you, my princess."

---

[56] Burroughs's original footnote in the text: "I have used the word radium in describing this powder because in the light of recent discoveries on Earth I believe it to be a mixture of which radium is the base. In Captain Carter's manuscript it is mentioned always by the name used in the written language of Helium and is spelled in hieroglyphics which it would be difficult and useless to reproduce." Burroughs here and elsewhere exploits a relatively recent scientific discovery in his use of radium as the primary Martian power source. Though famously discovered in 1898 by the Curies, radium had only been isolated as a pure metal in 1910. A million times more radioactive than uranium, it is also much rarer.

Dejah Thoris caught her breath at my last words, and gazed upon me with dilated eyes and quickening breath, and then, with an odd little laugh, which brought roguish dimples to the corners of her mouth, she shook her head and cried:

"What a child! A great warrior and yet a stumbling little child."

"What have I done now?" I asked, in sore perplexity.

"Some day you shall know, John Carter, if we live; but I may not tell you. And I, the daughter of Mors Kajak, son of Tardos Mors, have listened without anger," she soliloquized in conclusion.

Then she broke out again into one of her gay, happy, laughing moods; joking with me on my prowess as a Thark warrior as contrasted with my soft heart and natural kindliness.

"I presume that should you accidentally wound an enemy you would take him home and nurse him back to health," she laughed.

"That is precisely what we do on Earth," I answered. "At least among civilized men."

This made her laugh again. She could not understand it, for, with all her tenderness and womanly sweetness, she was still a Martian, and to a Martian the only good enemy is a dead enemy; for every dead foeman means so much more to divide between those who live.

I was very curious to know what I had said or done to cause her so much perturbation a moment before and so I continued to importune her to enlighten me.

"No," she exclaimed, "it is enough that you have said it and that I have listened. And when you learn, John Carter, and if I be dead, as likely I shall be ere the further moon has circled Barsoom another twelve times, remember that I listened and that I—smiled."

It was all Greek to me, but the more I begged her to explain the more positive became her denials of my request, and, so, in very hopelessness, I desisted.

Day had now given away to night and as we wandered along the great avenue lighted by the two moons of Barsoom, and with Earth looking down upon us out of her luminous green eye, it seemed that we were alone in the universe, and I, at least, was content that it should be so.

The chill of the Martian night was upon us, and removing my silks I threw them across the shoulders of Dejah Thoris. As my arm rested for an instant upon her I felt a thrill pass through every fiber of my being such as contact with no other mortal had even produced; and it seemed to me that she had leaned slightly toward me, but of that I was not sure. Only I knew that as my arm rested there across her shoulders longer than the act of adjusting the silk required she did not draw away, nor did she speak. And so, in silence, we walked the surface of a dying world, but in the breast of one of us at least had been born that which is ever oldest, yet ever new.

I loved Dejah Thoris. The touch of my arm upon her naked shoulder had spoken to me in words I would not mistake, and I knew that I had loved her since the first moment that my eyes had met hers that first time in the plaza of the dead city of Korad.

CHAPTER XIV
A DUEL TO THE DEATH

My first impulse was to tell her of my love, and then I thought of the helplessness of her position wherein I alone could lighten the burdens of her captivity, and protect her in my poor way against the thousands of hereditary enemies she must face upon our arrival at Thark. I could not chance causing her additional pain or sorrow by declaring a love which, in all probability she did not return. Should I be so indiscreet, her position would be even more unbearable than now, and the thought that she might feel that I was taking advantage of her helplessness, to influence her decision was the final argument which sealed my lips.

"Why are you so quiet, Dejah Thoris?" I asked. "Possibly you would rather return to Sola and your quarters."

"No," she murmured, "I am happy here. I do not know why it is that I should always be happy and contented when you, John Carter, a stranger, are with me; yet at such times it seems that I am safe and that, with you, I shall soon return to my father's court and feel his strong arms about me and my mother's tears and kisses on my cheek."

"Do people kiss, then, upon Barsoom?" I asked, when she had explained the word she used, in answer to my inquiry as to its meaning.

"Parents, brothers, and sisters, yes; and," she added in a low, thoughtful tone, "lovers."

"And you, Dejah Thoris, have parents and brothers and sisters?"

"Yes."

"And a—lover?"

She was silent, nor could I venture to repeat the question.

"The man of Barsoom," she finally ventured, "does not ask personal questions of women, except his mother, and the woman he has fought for and won."

"But I have fought—" I started, and then I wished my tongue had been cut from my mouth; for she turned even as I caught myself and ceased, and drawing my silks from her shoulder she held them out to me, and without a word, and with head held high, she moved with the carriage of the queen she was toward the plaza and the doorway of her quarters.

I did not attempt to follow her, other than to see that she reached the building in safety, but, directing Woola to accompany her, I turned disconsolately and entered my own house. I sat for hours cross-legged, and cross-tempered, upon my silks meditating upon the queer freaks chance plays upon us poor devils of mortals.[57]

So this was love! I had escaped it for all the years I had roamed the five continents and their encircling seas; in spite of beautiful women and urging opportunity; in spite of a half-desire for love and a constant search for my ideal, it had remained for me to fall furiously and hopelessly in love with a creature from another world, of a species similar possibly, yet not identical with mine. A woman who was hatched from an egg, and whose span of life might cover a thousand years; whose people had strange customs and ideas; a woman whose hopes, whose pleasures, whose standards of virtue and of right and wrong might vary as greatly from mine as did those of the green Martians.

Yes, I was a fool, but I was in love, and though I was suffering the greatest misery I had ever known I would not have had it otherwise for all the riches of Barsoom. Such is love, and such are lovers wherever love is known.

To me, Dejah Thoris was all that was perfect; all that was virtuous and beautiful and noble and good. I believed that from the bottom of my heart, from the depth of my soul on that night in Korad as I sat cross-legged upon my silks while the nearer moon of Barsoom raced through the western sky toward the horizon, and lighted up the gold and marble, and jeweled mosaics of my world-old chamber, and I believe it today as I sit at my desk in the little study overlooking the Hudson. Twenty years have intervened; for ten of them I lived and fought for Dejah Thoris and her people, and for ten I have lived upon her memory.

The morning of our departure for Thark dawned clear and hot, as do all Martian mornings except for the six weeks when the snow melts at the poles.

I sought out Dejah Thoris in the throng of departing chariots, but she turned her shoulder to me, and I could see the red blood mount to her cheek. With the foolish inconsistency of love I held my peace when I might have plead ignorance of the nature of my offense, or at least the gravity of it, and so have effected, at worst, a half conciliation.

My duty dictated that I must see that she was comfortable, and so I glanced into her chariot and rearranged her silks and furs. In doing so I noted with horror that she was heavily chained by one ankle to the side of the vehicle.

---

[57] Burroughs seems to have in mind something like Lucretius's *clinamen*, or a random "swerve" in the unfolding of destiny. See note 52.

"What does this mean?" I cried, turning to Sola.

"Sarkoja thought it best," she answered, her face betokening her disapproval of the procedure.

Examining the manacles I saw that they fastened with a massive spring lock.

"Where is the key, Sola? Let me have it."

"Sarkoja wears it, John Carter," she answered.

I turned without further word and sought out Tars Tarkas, to whom I vehemently objected to the unnecessary humiliations and cruelties, as they seemed to my lover's eyes, that were being heaped upon Dejah Thoris.

"John Carter," he answered, "if ever you and Dejah Thoris escape the Tharks it will be upon this journey. We know that you will not go without her. You have shown yourself a mighty fighter, and we do not wish to manacle you, so we hold you both in the easiest way that will yet ensure security. I have spoken."

I saw the strength of his reasoning at a flash, and knew that it were futile to appeal from his decision, but I asked that the key be taken from Sarkoja and that she be directed to leave the prisoner alone in future.

"This much, Tars Tarkas, you may do for me in return for the friendship that, I must confess, I feel for you."

"Friendship?" he replied. "There is no such thing, John Carter; but have your will. I shall direct that Sarkoja cease to annoy the girl, and I myself will take the custody of the key."

"Unless you wish me to assume the responsibility," I said, smiling.

He looked at me long and earnestly before he spoke.

"Were you to give me your word that neither you nor Dejah Thoris would attempt to escape until after we have safely reached the court of Tal Hajus you might have the key and throw the chains into the river Iss."

"It were better that you held the key, Tars Tarkas," I replied

He smiled, and said no more, but that night as we were making camp I saw him unfasten Dejah Thoris' fetters himself.

With all his cruel ferocity and coldness there was an undercurrent of something in Tars Tarkas which he seemed ever battling to subdue. Could it be a vestige of some human instinct come back from an ancient forbear to haunt him with the horror of his people's ways!

As I was approaching Dejah Thoris' chariot I passed Sarkoja, and the black, venomous look she accorded me was the sweetest balm I had felt for many hours. Lord, how she hated me! It bristled from her so palpably that one might almost have cut it with a sword.

A few moments later I saw her deep in conversation with a warrior named Zad; a big, hulking, powerful brute, but one who had never made a kill among his own chieftains, and a second name only with the metal of some chieftain. It was this custom which entitled me to the names of either of the chieftains I had killed; in fact, some of the warriors addressed me as Dotar Sojat, a combination of the surnames of the two warrior chieftains whose metal I had taken, or, in other words, whom I had slain in fair fight.

As Sarkoja talked with Zad he cast occasional glances in my direction, while she seemed to be urging him very strongly to some action. I paid little attention to it at the time, but the next day I had good reason to recall the circumstances, and at the same time gain a slight insight into the depths of Sarkoja's hatred and the lengths to which she was capable of going to wreak her horrid vengeance on me.

Dejah Thoris would have none of me again on this evening, and though I spoke her name she neither replied, nor conceded by so much as the flutter of an eyelid that she realized my existence. In my extremity I did what most other lovers would have done; I sought word from her through an intimate. In this instance it was Sola whom I intercepted in another part of camp.

"What is the matter with Dejah Thoris?" I blurted out at her. "Why will she not speak to me?"

Sola seemed puzzled herself, as though such strange actions on the part of two humans were quite beyond her, as indeed they were, poor child.

"She says you have angered her, and that is all she will say, except that she is the daughter of a jed and the granddaughter of a jeddak and she has been humiliated by a creature who could not polish the teeth of her grandmother's sorak."

I pondered over this report for some time, finally asking, "What might a sorak be, Sola?"

"A little animal about as big as my hand, which the red Martian women keep to play with," explained Sola.

Not fit to polish the teeth of her grandmother's cat! I must rank pretty low in the consideration of Dejah Thoris, I thought; but I could not help laughing at the strange figure of speech, so homely and in this respect so earthly. It made me homesick, for it sounded very much like "not fit to polish her shoes." And then commenced a train of thought quite new to me. I began to wonder what my people at home were doing. I had not seen them for years. There was a family of Carters in Virginia who claimed close relationship with me; I was supposed to be a great uncle, or something of the kind equally foolish. I could pass anywhere for twenty-five to thirty years of age, and to be a great uncle always seemed the height of incongruity, for my thoughts and feelings were those of a boy. There was two little kiddies in the Carter family whom I had loved and who had thought there was no one on Earth like Uncle Jack; I could see them just as plainly, as I stood there under the moonlit skies of Barsoom, and I longed for them as I had never longed for any mortals before.[58] By nature a wanderer, I had never known the true meaning of the word home, but the great hall of the Carters had always stood for all that the word did mean to me, and now my heart turned toward it from the cold and unfriendly peoples I had been thrown amongst. For did not even Dejah Thoris despise me! I was a low creature, so low in fact that I was not even fit to polish the teeth of her grandmother's cat; and then my saving sense of humor came to my rescue, and laughing I turned into my silks and furs and slept upon the moon-haunted ground the sleep of a tired and healthy fighting man.

We broke camp the next day at an early hour and marched with only a single halt until just before dark. Two incidents broke the tediousness of the march. About noon we espied far to our right what was evidently an incubator, and Lorquas Ptomel directed Tars Tarkas to investigate it. The latter took a dozen warriors, including myself, and we raced across the velvety carpeting of moss to the little enclosure.

It was indeed an incubator, but the eggs were very small in comparison with those I had seen hatching in ours at the time of my arrival on Mars.

Tars Tarkas dismounted and examined the enclosure minutely, finally announcing that it belonged to the green men of Warhoon and that the cement was scarcely dry where it had been walled up.

"They cannot be a day's march ahead of us," he exclaimed, the light of battle leaping to his fierce face.

The work at the incubator was short indeed. The warriors tore open the entrance and a couple of them, crawling in, soon demolished all the eggs with their short-swords. Then remounting we dashed back to join the cavalcade. During the ride I took occasion to ask Tars Tarkas if these

---

[58] Calling himself "Uncle Jack," John Carter refers to Burroughs as one of his ostensible nephews.

Warhoons whose eggs we had destroyed were a smaller people than his Tharks.

"I noticed that their eggs were so much smaller than those I saw hatching in your incubator," I added.

He explained that the eggs had just been placed there; but, like all green Martian eggs, they would grow during the five-year period of incubation until they obtained the size of those I had seen hatching on the day of my arrival on Barsoom. This was indeed an interesting piece of information, for it had always seemed remarkable to me that the green Martian women, large as they were, could bring forth such enormous eggs as I had seen the four-foot infants emerging from. As a matter of fact, the new-laid egg is but little larger than an ordinary goose egg, and as it does not commence to grow until subjected to the light of the sun the chieftains have little difficulty in transporting several hundreds of them at one time from the storage vaults to the incubators.

Shortly after the incident of the Warhoon eggs we halted to rest the animals, and it was during this halt that the second of the day's interesting episodes occurred. I was engaged in changing my riding cloths from one of my thoats to the other, for I divided the day's work between them, when Zad approached me, and without a word struck my animal a terrific blow with his long-sword.

I did not need a manual of green Martian etiquette to know what reply to make, for, in fact, I was so wild with anger that I could scarcely refrain from drawing my pistol and shooting him down for the brute he was; but he stood waiting with drawn long-sword, and my only choice was to draw my own and meet him in fair fight with his choice of weapons or a lesser one.

This latter alternative is always permissible, therefore I could have used my short-sword, my dagger, my hatchet, or my fists had I wished, and been entirely within my rights, but I could not use firearms or a spear while he held only his long-sword.

I chose the same weapon he had drawn because I knew he prided himself upon his ability with it, and I wished, if I worsted him at all, to do it with his own weapon. The fight that followed was a long one and delayed the resumption of the march for an hour. The entire community surrounded us, leaving a clear space about one hundred feet in diameter for our battle.

Zad first attempted to rush me down as a bull might a wolf, but I was much too quick for him, and each time I side-stepped his rushes he would go lunging past me, only to receive a nick from my sword upon his arm or back. He was soon streaming blood from a half dozen minor wounds, but I could not obtain an opening to deliver an effective thrust. Then he changed his tactics, and fighting warily and with extreme dexterity, he tried to do by science what he was unable to do by brute strength. I must admit that he was a magnificent swordsman, and had it not been for my greater endurance and the remarkable agility the lesser gravitation of Mars lent me I might not have been able to put up the creditable fight I did against him.

We circled for some time without doing much damage on either side; the long, straight, needle-like swords flashing in the sunlight, and ringing out upon the stillness as they crashed together with each effective parry. Finally Zad, realizing that he was tiring more than I, evidently decided to close in and end the battle in a final blaze of glory for himself; just as he rushed me a blinding flash of light struck full in my eyes, so that I could not see his approach and could only leap blindly to one side in an effort to escape the mighty blade that it seemed I could already feel in my vitals. I was only partially successful, as a sharp pain in my left shoulder attested, but in the sweep of my glance as I sought to again locate my adversary, a sight met my astonished gaze which paid me well for the wound the temporary blindness had caused me. There, upon Dejah Thoris' chariot stood three figures, for the purpose evidently of witnessing the encounter above the heads of the intervening Tharks. There were Dejah Thoris, Sola, and Sarkoja, and as my fleeting glance swept over them a little tableau was presented which will stand graven in my memory to the day of my death.

As I looked, Dejah Thoris turned upon Sarkoja with the fury of a young tigress and struck something from her upraised hand; something which flashed in the sunlight as it spun to the ground. Then I knew what had blinded me at that crucial moment of the fight, and how Sarkoja had found a way to kill me without herself delivering the final thrust. Another thing I saw, too, which almost lost my life for me then and there, for it took my mind for the fraction of an instant entirely from my antagonist; for, as Dejah Thoris struck the tiny mirror from her hand, Sarkoja, her face livid with hatred and baffled rage, whipped out her dagger and aimed a terrific blow at Dejah Thoris; and then Sola, our dear and faithful Sola, sprang between them; the last I saw was the great knife descending upon her shielding breast.

My enemy had recovered from his thrust and was making it extremely interesting for me, so I reluctantly gave my attention to the work in hand, but my mind was not upon the battle.

We rushed each other furiously time after time, 'til suddenly, feeling the sharp point of his sword at my breast in a thrust I could neither parry nor escape, I threw myself upon him with outstretched sword and with all the weight of my body, determined that I would not die alone if I could prevent it. I felt the steel tear into my chest, all went black before me, my head whirled in dizziness, and I felt my knees giving beneath me.

I SOUGHT OUT DEJAH THORIS IN THE THRONG OF DEPARTING
CHARIOTS.

CHAPTER XV
SOLA TELLS ME HER STORY

When consciousness returned, and, as I soon learned, I was down but a moment, I sprang quickly to my feet searching for my sword, and there I found it, buried to the hilt in the green breast of Zad, who lay stone dead upon the ochre moss of the ancient sea bottom. As I regained my full senses I found his weapon piercing my left breast, but only through the flesh and muscles which cover my ribs, entering near the center of my chest and coming out below the shoulder. As I had lunged I had turned so that his sword merely passed beneath the muscles, inflicting a painful but not dangerous wound.

Removing the blade from my body I also regained my own, and turning my back upon his ugly carcass, I moved, sick, sore, and disgusted, toward the chariots which bore my retinue and my belongings. A murmur of Martian applause greeted me, but I cared not for it.

Bleeding and weak I reached my women, who, accustomed to such happenings, dressed my wounds, applying the wonderful healing and remedial agents which make only the most instantaneous of death blows fatal. Give a Martian woman a chance and death must take a back seat. They soon had me patched up so that, except for weakness from loss of blood and a little soreness around the wound, I suffered no great distress from this thrust which, under earthly treatment, undoubtedly would have put me flat on my back for days.

As soon as they were through with me I hastened to the chariot of Dejah Thoris, where I found my poor Sola with her chest swathed in bandages, but apparently little the worse for her encounter with Sarkoja, whose dagger it seemed had struck the edge of one of Sola's metal breast ornaments and, thus deflected, had inflicted but a slight flesh wound.

As I approached I found Dejah Thoris lying prone upon her silks and furs, her lithe form wracked with sobs. She did not notice my presence, nor did she hear me speaking with Sola, who was standing a short distance from the vehicle.

"Is she injured?" I asked of Sola, indicating Dejah Thoris by an inclination of my head.

"No," she answered, "she thinks that you are dead."

"And that her grandmother's cat may now have no one to polish its teeth?" I queried, smiling.

"I think you wrong her, John Carter," said Sola. "I do not understand either her ways or yours, but I am sure the granddaughter of ten thousand jeddaks would never grieve like this over any who held but the highest claim upon her affections. They are a proud race, but they are just, as are all Barsoomians, and you must have hurt or wronged her grievously that she will not admit your existence living, though she mourns you dead.

"Tears are a strange sight upon Barsoom," she continued, "and so it is difficult for me to interpret them. I have seen but two people weep in all my life, other than Dejah Thoris; one wept from sorrow, the other from baffled rage. The first was my mother, years ago before they killed her; the other was Sarkoja, when they dragged her from me today."

"Your mother!" I exclaimed, "but, Sola, you could not have known your mother, child."

"But I did. And my father also," she added. "If you would like to hear the strange and un-Barsoomian story come to the chariot tonight, John Carter, and I will tell you that of which I have never spoken in all my life before. And now the signal has been given to resume the march, you must go."

"I will come tonight, Sola," I promised. "Be sure to tell Dejah Thoris I am alive and well. I shall not force myself upon her, and be sure that you do not let her know I saw her tears. If she would speak with me I but await her command."

Sola mounted the chariot, which was swinging into its place in line, and I hastened to my waiting thoat and galloped to my station beside Tars Tarkas at the rear of the column.

We made a most imposing and awe-inspiring spectacle as we strung out across the yellow landscape; the two hundred and fifty ornate and brightly colored chariots, preceded by an advance guard of some two hundred mounted warriors and chieftains riding five abreast and one hundred yards apart, and followed by a like number in the same formation, with a score or more of flankers on either side; the fifty extra mastodons, or heavy draught animals, known as zitidars, and the five or six hundred extra thoats of the warriors running loose within the hollow square formed by the surrounding warriors.[59] The gleaming metal and jewels of the gorgeous ornaments of the men and women, duplicated in the trappings of the zitidars and thoats, and interspersed with the flashing colors of magnificent silks and furs and feathers, lent a barbaric splendor

---

[59] Perhaps Burroughs here has in mind Herodotus's famous description of the army of Xerxes from the *Histories*.

to the caravan which would have turned an East Indian potentate green with envy.

The enormous broad tires of the chariots and the padded feet of the animals brought forth no sound from the moss-covered sea bottom; and so we moved in utter silence, like some huge phantasmagoria, except when the stillness was broken by the guttural growling of a goaded zitidar, or the squealing of fighting thoats. The green Martians converse but little, and then usually in monosyllables, low and like the faint rumbling of distant thunder.

We traversed a trackless waste of moss which, bending to the pressure of broad tire or padded foot, rose up again behind us, leaving no sign that we had passed. We might indeed have been the wraiths of the departed dead upon the dead sea of that dying planet for all the sound or sign we made in passing. It was the first march of a large body of men and animals I had ever witnessed which raised no dust and left no spoor; for there is no dust upon Mars except in the cultivated districts during the winter months, and even then the absence of high winds renders it almost unnoticeable.[60]

We camped that night at the foot of the hills we had been approaching for two days and which marked the southern boundary of this particular sea. Our animals had been two days without drink, nor had they had water for nearly two months, not since shortly after leaving Thark; but, as Tars Tarkas explained to me, they require but little and can live almost indefinitely upon the moss which covers Barsoom, and which, he told me, holds in its tiny stems sufficient moisture to meet the limited demands of the animals.

After partaking of my evening meal of cheese-like food and vegetable milk I sought out Sola, whom I found working by the light of a torch upon some of Tars Tarkas' trappings. She looked up at my approach, her face lighting with pleasure and with welcome.

"I am glad you came," she said; "Dejah Thoris sleeps and I am lonely. Mine own people do not care for me, John Carter; I am too unlike them. It is a sad fate, since I must live my life amongst them, and I often wish that I were a true green Martian woman, without love and without hope; but I have known love and so I am lost.

---

[60] Mars is known for its immense dust storms. Because of the thinness of the atmosphere and the absolute lack of rain, dust can remain airborne for years. The Mariner IX probe landed in the midst of a major dust storm that lasted a month in 1971. Global storms seen by the Hubble telescope in 2001 produced dust that did not settle for two years.

"I promised to tell you my story, or rather the story of my parents. From what I have learned of you and the ways of your people I am sure that the tale will not seem strange to you, but among green Martians it has no parallel within the memory of the oldest living Thark, nor do our legends hold many similar tales.

"My mother was rather small, in fact too small to be allowed the responsibilities of maternity, as our chieftains breed principally for size. She was also less cold and cruel than most green Martian women, and caring little for their society, she often roamed the deserted avenues of Thark alone, or went and sat among the wild flowers that deck the nearby hills, thinking thoughts and wishing wishes which I believe I alone among Tharkian women today may understand, for am I not the child of my mother?

"And there among the hills she met a young warrior, whose duty it was to guard the feeding zitidars and thoats and see that they roamed not beyond the hills. They spoke at first only of such things as interest a community of Tharks, but gradually, as they came to meet more often, and, as was now quite evident to both, no longer by chance, they talked about themselves, their likes, their ambitions and their hopes. She trusted him and told him of the awful repugnance she felt for the cruelties of their kind, for the hideous, loveless lives they must ever lead, and then she waited for the storm of denunciation to break from his cold, hard lips; but instead he took her in his arms and kissed her.

"They kept their love a secret for six long years. She, my mother, was of the retinue of the great Tal Hajus, while her lover was a simple warrior, wearing only his own metal. Had their defection from the traditions of the Tharks been discovered both would have paid the penalty in the great arena before Tal Hajus and the assembled hordes.

"The egg from which I came was hidden beneath a great glass vessel upon the highest and most inaccessible of the partially ruined towers of ancient Thark. Once each year my mother visited it for the five long years it lay there in the process of incubation. She dared not come oftener, for in the mighty guilt of her conscience she feared that her every move was watched. During this period my father gained great distinction as a warrior and had taken the metal from several chieftains. His love for my mother had never diminished, and his own ambition in life was to reach a point where he might wrest the metal from Tal Hajus himself, and thus, as ruler of the Tharks, be free to claim her as his own, as well as, by the might of his power, protect the child which otherwise would be quickly dispatched should the truth become known.

"It was a wild dream, that of wresting the metal from Tal Hajus in five short years, but his advance was rapid, and he soon stood high in the councils of Thark. But one day the chance was lost forever, in so far as it could come in time to save his loved ones, for he was ordered away upon a long expedition to the ice-clad south, to make war upon the natives there and despoil them of their furs, for such is the manner of the green Barsoomian; he does not labor for what he can wrest in battle from others.

"He was gone for four years, and when he returned all had been over for three; for about a year after his departure, and shortly before the time for the return of an expedition which had gone forth to fetch the fruits of a community incubator, the egg had hatched. Thereafter my mother continued to keep me in the old tower, visiting me nightly and lavishing upon me the love the community life would have robbed us both of. She hoped, upon the return of the expedition from the incubator, to mix me with the other young assigned to the quarters of Tal Hajus, and thus escape the fate which would surely follow discovery of her sin against the ancient traditions of the green men.

"She taught me rapidly the language and customs of my kind, and one night she told me the story I have told to you up to this point, impressing upon me the necessity for absolute secrecy and the great caution I must exercise after she had placed me with the other young Tharks to permit no one to guess that I was further advanced in education than they, nor by any sign to divulge in the presence of others my affection for her, or my knowledge of my parentage; and then drawing me close to her she whispered in my ear the name of my father.

"And then a light flashed out upon the darkness of the tower chamber, and there stood Sarkoja, her gleaming, baleful eyes fixed in a frenzy of loathing and contempt upon my mother. The torrent of hatred and abuse she poured out upon her turned my young heart cold in terror. That she had heard the entire story was apparent, and that she had suspected something wrong from my mother's long nightly absences from her quarters accounted for her presence there on that fateful night.

"One thing she had not heard, nor did she know, the whispered name of my father. This was apparent from her repeated demands upon my mother to disclose the name of her partner in sin, but no amount of abuse or threats could wring this from her, and to save me from needless torture she lied, for she told Sarkoja that she alone knew nor would she even tell her child.

"With final imprecations, Sarkoja hastened away to Tal Hajus to report her discovery, and while she was gone my mother, wrapping me in the silks and furs of her night coverings, so that I was scarcely noticeable, descended to the streets and ran wildly away toward the outskirts of the city, in the direction which led to the far south, out toward the man whose protection she might not claim, but on whose face she wished to look once more before she died.

"As we neared the city's southern extremity a sound came to us from across the mossy flat, from the direction of the only pass through the hills which led to the gates, the pass by which caravans from either north or south or east or west would enter the city. The sounds we heard were the squealing of thoats and the grumbling of zitidars, with the occasional clank of arms which announced the approach of a body of warriors. The thought uppermost in her mind was that it was my father returned from his expedition, but the cunning of the Thark held her from headlong and precipitate flight to greet him.

"Retreating into the shadows of a doorway she awaited the coming of the cavalcade which shortly entered the avenue, breaking its formation and thronging the thoroughfare from wall to wall. As the head of the procession passed us the lesser moon swung clear of the overhanging roofs and lit up the scene with all the brilliancy of her wondrous light. My mother shrank further back into the friendly shadows, and from her hiding place saw that the expedition was not that of my father, but the returning caravan bearing the young Tharks. Instantly her plan was formed, and as a great chariot swung close to our hiding place she slipped stealthily in upon the trailing tailboard, crouching low in the shadow of the high side, straining me to her bosom in a frenzy of love.

"She knew, what I did not, that never again after that night would she hold me to her breast, nor was it likely we would ever look upon each other's face again. In the confusion of the plaza she mixed me with the other children, whose guardians during the journey were now free to relinquish their responsibility. We were herded together into a great room, fed by women who had not accompanied the expedition, and the next day we were parceled out among the retinues of the chieftains.

"I never saw my mother after that night. She was imprisoned by Tal Hajus, and every effort, including the most horrible and shameful torture, was brought to bear upon her to wring from her lips the name of my father; but she remained steadfast and loyal, dying at last amidst the laughter of Tal Hajus and his chieftains during some awful torture she was undergoing.

"I learned afterwards that she told them that she had killed me to save me from a like fate at their hands, and that she had thrown my body to the white apes. Sarkoja alone disbelieved her, and I feel to this day that she suspects my true origin, but does not dare expose me, at the present, at all events, because she also guesses, I am sure, the identity of my father.

"When he returned from his expedition and learned the story of my mother's fate I was present as Tal Hajus told him; but never by the quiver of a muscle did he betray the slightest emotion; only he did not laugh as Tal Hajus gleefully described her death struggles. From that moment on he was the cruelest of the cruel, and I am awaiting the day when he shall win the goal of his ambition, and feel the carcass of Tal Hajus beneath his foot, for I am as sure that he but waits the opportunity to wreak a terrible vengeance, and that his great love is as strong in his breast as when it first transfigured him nearly forty years ago, as I am that we sit here upon the edge of a world-old ocean while sensible people sleep, John Carter."

"And your father, Sola, is he with us now?" I asked.

"Yes," she replied, "but he does not know me for what I am, nor does he know who betrayed my mother to Tal Hajus. I alone know my father's name, and only I and Tal Hajus and Sarkoja know that it was she who carried the tale that brought death and torture upon her he loved."

We sat silent for a few moments, she wrapped in the gloomy thoughts of her terrible past, and I in pity for the poor creatures whom the heartless, senseless customs of their race had doomed to loveless lives of cruelty and of hate. Presently she spoke.

"John Carter, if ever a real man walked the cold, dead bosom of Barsoom you are one. I know that I can trust you, and because the knowledge may someday help you or him or Dejah Thoris or myself, I am going to tell you the name of my father, nor place any restrictions or conditions upon your tongue. When the time comes, speak the truth if it seems best to you. I trust you because I know that you are not cursed with the terrible trait of absolute and unswerving truthfulness, that you could lie like one of your own Virginia gentlemen if a lie would save others from sorrow or suffering. My father's name is Tars Tarkas."[61]

---

[61] The inability to lie poses many interesting logical problems. Could a key to Carter's telepathic superiority among the Martians be his human capacity to lie?

CHAPTER XVI
WE PLAN ESCAPE

The remainder of our journey to Thark was uneventful. We were twenty days upon the road, crossing two sea bottoms and passing through or around a number of ruined cities, mostly smaller than Korad. Twice we crossed the famous Martian waterways, or canals, so-called by our earthly astronomers. When we approached these points a warrior would be sent far ahead with a powerful field glass, and if no great body of red Martian troops was in sight we would advance as close as possible without chance of being seen and then camp until dark, when we would slowly approach the cultivated tract, and, locating one of the numerous, broad highways which cross these areas at regular intervals, creep silently and stealthily across to the arid lands upon the other side. It required five hours to make one of these crossings without a single halt, and the other consumed the entire night, so that we were just leaving the confines of the high-walled fields when the sun broke out upon us.

Crossing in the darkness, as we did, I was unable to see but little, except as the nearer moon, in her wild and ceaseless hurtling through the Barsoomian heavens, lit up little patches of the landscape from time to time, disclosing walled fields and low, rambling buildings, presenting much the appearance of earthly farms. There were many trees, methodically arranged, and some of them were of enormous height; there were animals in some of the enclosures, and they announced their presence by terrified squealings and snortings as they scented our queer, wild beasts and wilder human beings.

Only once did I perceive a human being, and that was at the intersection of our crossroad with the wide, white turnpike which cuts each cultivated district longitudinally at its exact center. The fellow must have been sleeping beside the road, for, as I came abreast of him, he raised upon one elbow and after a single glance at the approaching caravan leaped shrieking to his feet and fled madly down the road, scaling a nearby wall with the agility of a scared cat.[62] The Tharks paid him not the slightest attention; they were not out upon the warpath, and the only sign that I had that they had seen him was a quickening of the pace of the caravan as we hastened toward the bordering desert which marked our entrance into the realm of Tal Hajus.

---

[62] "Turnpike" is a term Americans in the western states may be unfamiliar with, meaning a main road, usually a paved highway. It is commonly used in the eastern United States, often for toll roads (e.g., the New Jersey Turnpike).

Not once did I have speech with Dejah Thoris, as she sent no word to me that I would be welcome at her chariot, and my foolish pride kept me from making any advances. I verily believe that a man's way with women is in inverse ratio to his prowess among men.[63] The weakling and the saphead have often great ability to charm the fair sex, while the fighting man who can face a thousand real dangers unafraid, sits hiding in the shadows like some frightened child.

Just thirty days after my advent upon Barsoom we entered the ancient city of Thark, from whose long-forgotten people this horde of green men have stolen even their name. The hordes of Thark number some thirty thousand souls, and are divided into twenty-five communities. Each community has its own jed and lesser chieftains, but all are under the rule of Tal Hajus, Jeddak of Thark. Five communities make their headquarters at the city of Thark, and the balance are scattered among other deserted cities of ancient Mars throughout the district claimed by Tal Hajus.

We made our entry into the great central plaza early in the afternoon. There were no enthusiastic friendly greetings for the returned expedition. Those who chanced to be in sight spoke the names of warriors or women with whom they came in direct contact, in the formal greeting of their kind, but when it was discovered that they brought two captives a greater interest was aroused, and Dejah Thoris and I were the centers of inquiring groups.

We were soon assigned to new quarters, and the balance of the day was devoted to settling ourselves to the changed conditions. My home now was upon an avenue leading into the plaza from the south, the main artery down which we had marched from the gates of the city. I was at the far end of the square and had an entire building to myself. The same grandeur of architecture which was so noticeable a characteristic of Korad was in evidence here, only, if that were possible, on a larger and richer scale. My quarters would have been suitable for housing the greatest of earthly emperors, but to these queer creatures nothing about a building appealed to them but its size and the enormity of its chambers; the larger the building, the more desirable; and so Tal Hajus occupied what must have been an enormous public building, the largest in the city, but entirely unfitted for residence purposes; the next largest was reserved for Lorquas Ptomel, the next for the jed of a lesser rank, and so on to the bottom of the list of five jeds. The warriors occupied the buildings with the chieftains to whose retinues they belonged; or, if they preferred, sought shelter among

---

[63] A man's prowess with women is in inverse ratio to his prowess among men. Perhaps we should dub this Burroughs's Wallflower Theorem.

any of the thousands of untenanted buildings in their own quarter of town; each community being assigned a certain section of the city. The selection of building had to be made in accordance with these divisions, except in so far as the jeds were concerned, they all occupying edifices which fronted upon the plaza.

When I had finally put my house in order, or rather seen that it had been done, it was nearing sunset, and I hastened out with the intention of locating Sola and her charges, as I had determined upon having speech with Dejah Thoris and trying to impress on her the necessity of our at least patching up a truce until I could find some way of aiding her to escape. I searched in vain until the upper rim of the great red sun was just disappearing behind the horizon and then I spied the ugly head of Woola peering from a second-story window on the opposite side of the very street where I was quartered, but nearer the plaza.

Without waiting for a further invitation I bolted up the winding runway which led to the second floor, and entering a great chamber at the front of the building was greeted by the frenzied Woola, who threw his great carcass upon me, nearly hurling me to the floor; the poor old fellow was so glad to see me that I thought he would devour me, his head split from ear to ear, showing his three rows of tusks in his hobgoblin smile.

Quieting him with a word of command and a caress, I looked hurriedly through the approaching gloom for a sign of Dejah Thoris, and then, not seeing her, I called her name. There was an answering murmur from the far corner of the apartment, and with a couple of quick strides I was standing beside her where she crouched among the furs and silks upon an ancient carved wooden seat. As I waited she rose to her full height and looking me straight in the eye said:

"What would Dotar Sojat, Thark, of Dejah Thoris his captive?"[64]

"Dejah Thoris, I do not know how I have angered you. It was furtherest from my desire to hurt or offend you, whom I had hoped to protect and comfort. Have none of me if it is your will, but that you must aid me in effecting your escape, if such a thing be possible, is not my request, but my command. When you are safe once more at your father's court you may do with me as you please, but from now on until that day I am your master, and you must obey and aid me."

She looked at me long and earnestly and I thought that she was softening toward me.

---

[64] "Dotar Sojat," the Barsoomian name for John Carter, is derived from the names of the two Thark soldiers he bested. See Chapter 14.

"I understand your words, Dotar Sojat," she replied, "but you I do not understand. You are a queer mixture of child and man, of brute and noble.[65] I only wish that I might read your heart."

"Look down at your feet, Dejah Thoris; it lies there now where it has lain since that other night at Korad, and where it will ever lie beating alone for you until death stills it forever."

She took a little step toward me, her beautiful hands outstretched in a strange, groping gesture.

"What do you mean, John Carter?" she whispered. "What are you saying to me?"

"I am saying what I had promised myself that I would not say to you, at least until you were no longer a captive among the green men; what from your attitude toward me for the past twenty days I had thought never to say to you; I am saying, Dejah Thoris, that I am yours, body and soul, to serve you, to fight for you, and to die for you. Only one thing I ask of you in return, and that is that you make no sign, either of condemnation or of approbation of my words until you are safe among your own people, and that whatever sentiments you harbor toward me they be not influenced or colored by gratitude; whatever I may do to serve you will be prompted solely from selfish motives, since it gives me more pleasure to serve you than not."[66]

"I will respect your wishes, John Carter, because I understand the motives which prompt them, and I accept your service no more willingly than I bow to your authority; your word shall be my law. I have twice wronged you in my thoughts and again I ask your forgiveness."

Further conversation of a personal nature was prevented by the entrance of Sola, who was much agitated and wholly unlike her usual calm and possessed self.

"That horrible Sarkoja has been before Tal Hajus," she cried, "and from what I heard upon the plaza there is little hope for either of you."

"What do they say?" inquired Dejah Thoris.

"That you will be thrown to the wild calots [dogs] in the great arena as soon as the hordes have assembled for the yearly games."

---

[65] Since Burroughs has earlier described Mars as a planet of paradoxes, it is fitting that Dejah should reel off a list of paradoxical character traits exhibited by John Carter himself.

[66] Carter's request to Dejah is reminiscent of chivalric romances in which the lover pledges troth with no expectation of requital.

"Sola," I said, "you are a Thark, but you hate and loathe the customs of your people as much as we do. Will you not accompany us in one supreme effort to escape? I am sure that Dejah Thoris can offer you a home and protection among her people, and your fate can be no worse among them than it must ever be here."

"Yes," cried Dejah Thoris, "come with us, Sola, you will be better off among the red men of Helium than you are here, and I can promise you not only a home with us, but the love and affection your nature craves and which must always be denied you by the customs of your own race. Come with us, Sola; we might go without you, but your fate would be terrible if they thought you had connived to aid us. I know that even that fear would not tempt you to interfere in our escape, but we want you with us, we want you to come to a land of sunshine and happiness, amongst a people who know the meaning of love, of sympathy, and of gratitude. Say that you will, Sola; tell me that you will."

"The great waterway which leads to Helium is but fifty miles to the south," murmured Sola, half to herself; "a swift thoat might make it in three hours; and then to Helium it is five hundred miles, most of the way through thinly settled districts. They would know and they would follow us. We might hide among the great trees for a time, but the chances are small indeed for escape. They would follow us to the very gates of Helium, and they would take toll of life at every step; you do not know them."

"Is there no other way we might reach Helium?" I asked. "Can you not draw me a rough map of the country we must traverse, Dejah Thoris?"

"Yes," she replied, and taking a great diamond from her hair she drew upon the marble floor the first map of Barsoomian territory I had ever seen. It was crisscrossed in every direction with long straight lines, sometimes running parallel and sometimes converging toward some great circle. The lines, she said, were waterways; the circles, cities; and one far to the northwest of us she pointed out as Helium. There were other cities closer, but she said she feared to enter many of them, as they were not all friendly toward Helium.

Finally, after studying the map carefully in the moonlight which now flooded the room, I pointed out a waterway far to the north of us which also seemed to lead to Helium.

"Does not this pierce your grandfather's territory?" I asked.

"Yes," she answered, "but it is two hundred miles north of us; it is one of the waterways we crossed on the trip to Thark."

"They would never suspect that we would try for that distant waterway," I answered, "and that is why I think that it is the best route for our escape."[67]

Sola agreed with me, and it was decided that we should leave Thark this same night; just as quickly, in fact, as I could find and saddle my thoats. Sola was to ride one and Dejah Thoris and I the other; each of us carrying sufficient food and drink to last us for two days, since the animals could not be urged too rapidly for so long a distance.

I directed Sola to proceed with Dejah Thoris along one of the less frequented avenues to the southern boundary of the city, where I would overtake them with the thoats as quickly as possible; then, leaving them to gather what food, silks, and furs we were to need, I slipped quietly to the rear of the first floor, and entered the courtyard, where our animals were moving restlessly about, as was their habit, before settling down for the night.

In the shadows of the buildings and out beneath the radiance of the Martian moons moved the great herd of thoats and zitidars, the latter grunting their low gutturals and the former occasionally emitting the sharp squeal which denotes the almost habitual state of rage in which these creatures passed their existence. They were quieter now, owing to the absence of man, but as they scented me they became more restless and their hideous noise increased. It was risky business, this entering a paddock of thoats alone and at night; first, because their increasing noisiness might warn the nearby warriors that something was amiss, and also because for the slightest cause, or for no cause at all some great bull thoat might take it upon himself to lead a charge upon me.

Having no desire to awaken their nasty tempers upon such a night as this, where so much depended upon secrecy and dispatch, I hugged the shadows of the buildings, ready at an instant's warning to leap into the safety of a nearby door or window. Thus I moved silently to the great gates which opened upon the street at the back of the court, and as I neared the exit I called softly to my two animals. How I thanked the kind providence which had given me the foresight to win the love and confidence of these wild dumb brutes, for presently from the far side of the court I saw two huge bulks forcing their way toward me through the surging mountains of flesh.

---

[67] The gamble to try for a much further route of escape than expected recalls the wily Hannibal who attacked Rome from the north by crossing the Alps with his elephants.

They came quite close to me, rubbing their muzzles against my body and nosing for the bits of food it was always my practice to reward them with. Opening the gates I ordered the two great beasts to pass out, and then slipping quietly after them I closed the portals behind me.

I did not saddle or mount the animals there, but instead walked quietly in the shadows of the buildings toward an unfrequented avenue which led toward the point I had arranged to meet Dejah Thoris and Sola. With the noiselessness of disembodied spirits we moved stealthily along the deserted streets, but not until we were within sight of the plain beyond the city did I commence to breathe freely. I was sure that Sola and Dejah Thoris would find no difficulty in reaching our rendezvous undetected, but with my great thoats I was not so sure for myself, as it was quite unusual for warriors to leave the city after dark; in fact there was no place for them to go within any but a long ride.

I reached the appointed meeting place safely, but as Dejah Thoris and Sola were not there I led my animals into the entrance hall of one of the large buildings. Presuming that one of the other women of the same household may have come in to speak to Sola, and so delayed their departure, I did not feel any undue apprehension until nearly an hour had passed without a sign of them, and by the time another half hour had crawled away I was becoming filled with grave anxiety. Then there broke upon the stillness of the night the sound of an approaching party, which, from the noise, I knew could be no fugitives creeping stealthily toward liberty. Soon the party was near me, and from the black shadows of my entranceway I perceived a score of mounted warriors, who, in passing, dropped a dozen words that fetched my heart clean into the top of my head.

"He would likely have arranged to meet them just without the city, and so—" I heard no more, they had passed on; but it was enough. Our plan had been discovered, and the chances for escape from now on to the fearful end would be small indeed. My one hope now was to return undetected to the quarters of Dejah Thoris and learn what fate had overtaken her, but how to do it with these great monstrous thoats upon my hands, now that the city probably was aroused by the knowledge of my escape was a problem of no mean proportions.

Suddenly an idea occurred to me, and acting on my knowledge of the construction of the buildings of these ancient Martian cities with a hollow court within the center of each square, I groped my way blindly through the dark chambers, calling the great thoats after me. They had difficulty in negotiating some of the doorways, but as the buildings fronting the city's principal exposures were all designed upon a magnificent scale, they were able to wriggle through without sticking fast; and thus we finally made the inner court where I found, as I had expected, the usual carpet of moss-like vegetation which would prove their food and drink until I could return them to their own enclosure. That they would be as quiet and contented here as elsewhere I was confident, nor was there but the remotest possibility that they would be discovered, as the green men had no great desire to enter these outlying buildings, which were frequented by the only thing, I believe, which caused them the sensation of fear-the great white apes of Barsoom.

Removing the saddle trappings, I hid them just within the rear doorway of the building through which we had entered the court, and, turning the beasts loose, quickly made my way across the court to the rear of the buildings upon the further side, and thence to the avenue beyond. Waiting in the doorway of the building until I was assured that no one was approaching, I hurried across to the opposite side and through the first doorway to the court beyond; thus, crossing through court after court with only the slight chance of detection which the necessary crossing of the avenues entailed, I made my way in safety to the courtyard in the rear of Dejah Thoris' quarters.

Here, of course, I found the beasts of the warriors who quartered in the adjacent buildings, and the warriors themselves I might expect to meet within if I entered; but, fortunately for me, I had another and safer method of reaching the upper story where Dejah Thoris should be found, and, after first determining as nearly as possible which of the buildings she occupied, for I had never observed them before from the court side, I took advantage of my relatively great strength and agility and sprang upward until I grasped the sill of a second-story window which I thought to be in the rear of her apartment. Drawing myself inside the room I moved stealthily toward the front of the building, and not until I had quite reached the doorway of her room was I made aware by voices that it was occupied.

I did not rush headlong in, but listened without to assure myself that it was Dejah Thoris and that it was safe to venture within. It was well indeed that I took this precaution, for the conversation I heard was in the low gutturals of men, and the words which finally came to me proved a most timely warning. The speaker was a chieftain and he was giving orders to four of his warriors.

"And when he returns to this chamber," he was saying, "as he surely will when he finds she does not meet him at the city's edge, you four are to spring upon him and disarm him. It will require the combined strength of all of you to do it if the reports they bring back from Korad are correct. When you have him fast bound bear him to the vaults beneath the jeddak's quarters and chain him securely where he may be found when Tal Hajus wishes him. Allow him to speak with none, nor permit any other to enter this apartment before he comes. There will be no danger of the girl returning, for by this time she is safe in the arms of Tal Hajus, and may all her ancestors have pity upon her, for Tal Hajus will have none; the great Sarkoja has done a noble night's work. I go, and if you fail to capture him when he comes, I commend your carcasses to the cold bosom of Iss."

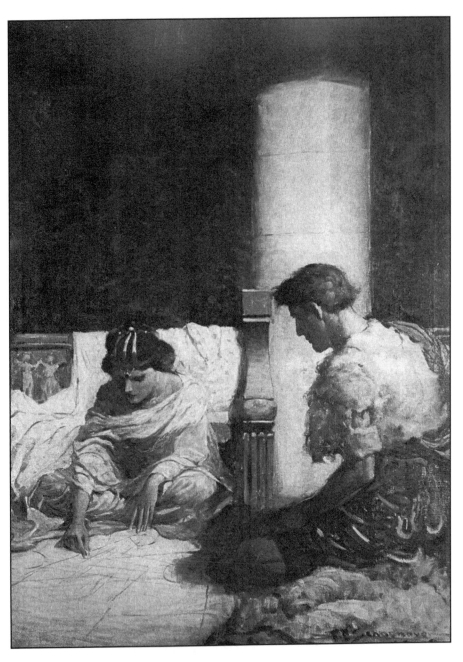

SHE DREW UPON THE MARBLE FLOOR THE FIRST MAP OF THE
BARSOOMIAN TERRITORY I HAD EVER SEEN.

CHAPTER XVII
A COSTLY RECAPTURE

As the speaker ceased he turned to leave the apartment by the door where I was standing, but I needed to wait no longer; I had heard enough to fill my soul with dread, and stealing quietly away I returned to the courtyard by the way I had come. My plan of action was formed upon the instant, and crossing the square and the bordering avenue upon the opposite side I soon stood within the courtyard of Tal Hajus.

The brilliantly lighted apartments of the first floor told me where first to seek, and advancing to the windows I peered within. I soon discovered that my approach was not to be the easy thing I had hoped, for the rear rooms bordering the court were filled with warriors and women. I then glanced up at the stories above, discovering that the third was apparently unlighted, and so decided to make my entrance to the building from that point. It was the work of but a moment for me to reach the windows above, and soon I had drawn myself within the sheltering shadows of the unlighted third floor.

Fortunately the room I had selected was untenanted, and creeping noiselessly to the corridor beyond I discovered a light in the apartments ahead of me. Reaching what appeared to be a doorway I discovered that it was but an opening upon an immense inner chamber which towered from the first floor, two stories below me, to the dome-like roof of the building, high above my head. The floor of this great circular hall was thronged with chieftains, warriors and women, and at one end was a great raised platform upon which squatted the most hideous beast I had ever put my eyes upon. He had all the cold, hard, cruel, terrible features of the green warriors, but accentuated and debased by the animal passions to which he had given himself over for many years. There was not a mark of dignity or pride upon his bestial countenance, while his enormous bulk spread itself out upon the platform where he squatted like some huge devil fish, his six limbs accentuating the similarity in a horrible and startling manner.

But the sight that froze me with apprehension was that of Dejah Thoris and Sola standing there before him, and the fiendish leer of him as he let his great protruding eyes gloat upon the lines of her beautiful figure.[68] She

---

[68] Burroughs's description of Tal Hajus seems to have inspired the unforgettable Jabba the Hutt (who keeps the lovely Princess Leia chained) in the George Lucas film *Return of the Jedi* (1983), the third installment of the original *Star Wars* series.

was speaking, but I could not hear what she said, nor could I make out the low grumbling of his reply. She stood there erect before him, her head high held, and even at the distance I was from them I could read the scorn and disgust upon her face as she let her haughty glance rest without sign of fear upon him. She was indeed the proud daughter of a thousand jeddaks, every inch of her dear, precious little body; so small, so frail beside the towering warriors around her, but in her majesty dwarfing them into insignificance; she was the mightiest figure among them and I verily believe that they felt it.

Presently Tal Hajus made a sign that the chamber be cleared, and that the prisoners be left alone before him. Slowly the chieftains, the warriors and the women melted away into the shadows of the surrounding chambers, and Dejah Thoris and Sola stood alone before the jeddak of the Tharks.

One chieftain alone had hesitated before departing; I saw him standing in the shadows of a mighty column, his fingers nervously toying with the hilt of his great-sword and his cruel eyes bent in implacable hatred upon Tal Hajus. It was Tars Tarkas, and I could read his thoughts as they were an open book for the undisguised loathing upon his face. He was thinking of that other woman who, forty years ago, had stood before this beast, and could I have spoken a word into his ear at that moment the reign of Tal Hajus would have been over; but finally he also strode from the room, not knowing that he left his own daughter at the mercy of the creature he most loathed.

Tal Hajus arose, and I, half fearing, half anticipating his intentions, hurried to the winding runway which led to the floors below. No one was near to intercept me, and I reached the main floor of the chamber unobserved, taking my station in the shadow of the same column that Tars Tarkas had but just deserted. As I reached the floor Tal Hajus was speaking.

"Princess of Helium, I might wring a mighty ransom from your people would I but return you to them unharmed, but a thousand times rather would I watch that beautiful face writhe in the agony of torture; it shall be long drawn out, that I promise you; ten days of pleasure were all too short to show the love I harbor for your race.[69] The terrors of your death shall haunt the slumbers of the red men through all the ages to come; they will shudder in the shadows of the night as their fathers tell them of the awful vengeance of the green men; of the power and might and hate and cruelty

---

[69] The sadistic Tal Hajus promises torture and hints suggestively of rape, a theme that Burroughs fully exploits in this chapter. See next note.

of Tal Hajus. But before the torture you shall be mine for one short hour, and word of that too shall go forth to Tardos Mors, Jeddak of Helium, your grandfather, that he may grovel upon the ground in the agony of his sorrow. Tomorrow the torture will commence; tonight thou art Tal Hajus'; come!"

He sprang down from the platform and grasped her roughly by the arm, but scarcely had he touched her than I leaped between them. My short-sword, sharp and gleaming was in my right hand; I could have plunged it into his putrid heart before he realized that I was upon him; but as I raised my arm to strike I thought of Tars Tarkas, and, with all my rage, with all my hatred, I could not rob him of that sweet moment for which he had lived and hoped all these long, weary years, and so, instead, I swung my good right fist full upon the point of his jaw. Without a sound he slipped to the floor as one dead.

In the same deathly silence I grasped Dejah Thoris by the hand, and motioning Sola to follow we sped noiselessly from the chamber and to the floor above. Unseen we reached a rear window and with the straps and leather of my trappings I lowered, first Sola and then Dejah Thoris to the ground below. Dropping lightly after them I drew them rapidly around the court in the shadows of the buildings, and thus we returned over the same course I had so recently followed from the distant boundary of the city.

We finally came upon my thoats in the courtyard where I had left them, and placing the trappings upon them we hastened through the building to the avenue beyond. Mounting, Sola upon one beast, and Dejah Thoris behind me upon the other, we rode from the city of Thark through the hills to the south.

Instead of circling back around the city to the northwest and toward the nearest waterway which lay so short a distance from us, we turned to the northeast and struck out upon the mossy waste across which, for two hundred dangerous and weary miles, lay another main artery leading to Helium.

No word was spoken until we had left the city far behind, but I could hear the quiet sobbing of Dejah Thoris as she clung to me with her dear head resting against my shoulder.

"If we make it, my chieftain, the debt of Helium will be a mighty one; greater than she can ever pay you; and should we not make it," she continued, "the debt is no less, though Helium will never know, for you have saved the last of our line from worse than death."[70]

---

[70] The phrase has been used at least since Gibbon to refer to rape, although torture is

I did not answer, but instead reached to my side and pressed the little fingers of her I loved where they clung to me for support, and then, in unbroken silence, we sped over the yellow, moonlit moss; each of us occupied with his own thoughts. For my part I could not be other than joyful had I tried, with Dejah Thoris' warm body pressed close to mine, and with all our unpassed danger my heart was singing as gaily as though we were already entering the gates of Helium.

Our earlier plans had been so sadly upset that we now found ourselves without food or drink, and I alone was armed. We therefore urged our beasts to a speed that must tell on them sorely before we could hope to sight the ending of the first stage of our journey.

We rode all night and all the following day with only a few short rests. On the second night both we and our animals were completely fagged, and so we lay down upon the moss and slept for some five or six hours, taking up the journey once more before daylight. All the following day we rode, and when, late in the afternoon we had sighted no distant trees, the mark of the great waterways throughout all Barsoom, the terrible truth flashed upon us—we were lost.

Evidently we had circled, but which way it was difficult to say, nor did it seem possible with the sun to guide us by day and the moons and stars by night. At any rate no waterway was in sight, and the entire party was almost ready to drop from hunger, thirst and fatigue. Far ahead of us and a trifle to the right we could distinguish the outlines of low mountains. These we decided to attempt to reach in the hope that from some ridge we might discern the missing waterway. Night fell upon us before we reached our goal, and, almost fainting from weariness and weakness, we lay down and slept.

---

implied as well. Burroughs's formulaic use of the concept no doubt stemmed from its association with Indian captivity narratives, and in fact is so pervasive in his novels that the phrase has come to be particularly with his work. The epitome occurs in *Tarzan of the Apes* (1914), wherein Burroughs writes of an ape who "threw [Jane] across his broad, hairy shoulders, and leaped back into the trees, bearing Jane Porter away to a fate a thousand time worse than death." Recall that John Carter himself expresses his anxiety over what the Apaches might do to him in the opening of the novel in Arizona.

    The television series *Firefly* (2002), a weird amalgamation of science fiction and western tropes, exploits the same fear in its depiction of "the reavers," a tribe of renegade spacemen roaming the edge of the galaxy who presumably rape, kill, and eat their unfortunate victims." One of the characters in the pilot episode describes the savagery of these reavers: "If they take the ship, they'll rape us to death, eat our flesh, and sew our skins into their clothing—and if we're very, very lucky, they'll do it in that order."

I was awakened early in the morning by some huge body pressing close to mine, and opening my eyes with a start I beheld my blessed old Woola snuggling close to me; the faithful brute had followed us across that trackless waste to share our fate, whatever it might be. Putting my arms about his neck I pressed my cheek close to his, nor am I ashamed that I did it, nor of the tears that came to my eyes as I thought of his love for me. Shortly after this Dejah Thoris and Sola awakened, and it was decided that we push on at once in an effort to gain the hills.

We had gone scarcely a mile when I noticed that my thoat was commencing to stumble and stagger in a most pitiful manner, although we had not attempted to force them out of a walk since about noon of the preceding day. Suddenly he lurched wildly to one side and pitched violently to the ground. Dejah Thoris and I were thrown clear of him and fell upon the soft moss with scarcely a jar; but the poor beast was in a pitiable condition, not even being able to rise, although relieved of our weight. Sola told me that the coolness of the night, when it fell, together with the rest would doubtless revive him, and so I decided not to kill him, as was my first intention, as I had thought it cruel to leave him alone there to die of hunger and thirst. Relieving him of his trappings, which I flung down beside him, we left the poor fellow to his fate, and pushed on with the one thoat as best we could. Sola and I walked, making Dejah Thoris ride, much against her will. In this way we had progressed to within about a mile of the hills we were endeavoring to reach when Dejah Thoris, from her point of vantage upon the thoat, cried out that she saw a great party of mounted men filing down from a pass in the hills several miles away. Sola and I both looked in the direction she indicated, and there, plainly discernible, were several hundred mounted warriors. They seemed to be headed in a southwesterly direction, which would take them away from us.

They doubtless were Thark warriors who had been sent out to capture us, and we breathed a great sigh of relief that they were traveling in the opposite direction. Quickly lifting Dejah Thoris from the thoat, I commanded the animal to lie down and we three did the same, presenting as small an object as possible for fear of attracting the attention of the warriors toward us.

We could see them as they filed out of the pass, just for an instant, before they were lost to view behind a friendly ridge; to us a most providential ridge; since, had they been in view for any great length of time, they scarcely could have failed to discover us. As what proved to be the last warrior came into view from the pass, he halted and, to our consternation, threw his small but powerful fieldglass to his eye and scanned the sea bottom in all directions. Evidently he was a chieftain, for in certain marching formations among the green men a chieftain brings up the extreme rear of the column. As his glass swung toward us our hearts stopped in our breasts, and I could feel the cold sweat start from every pore in my body.

Presently it swung full upon us and—stopped. The tension on our nerves was near the breaking point, and I doubt if any of us breathed for the few moments he held us covered by his glass; and then he lowered it and we could see him shout a command to the warriors who had passed from our sight behind the ridge. He did not wait for them to join him, however, instead he wheeled his thoat and came tearing madly in our direction.

There was but one slight chance and that we must take quickly. Raising my strange Martian rifle to my shoulder I sighted and touched the button which controlled the trigger; there was a sharp explosion as the missile reached its goal, and the charging chieftain pitched backward from his flying mount.

Springing to my feet I urged the thoat to rise, and directed Sola to take Dejah Thoris with her upon him and make a mighty effort to reach the hills before the green warriors were upon us. I knew that in the ravines and gullies they might find a temporary hiding place, and even though they died there of hunger and thirst it would be better so than that they fell into the hands of the Tharks. Forcing my two revolvers upon them as a slight means of protection, and, as a last resort, as an escape for themselves from the horrid death which recapture would surely mean, I lifted Dejah Thoris in my arms and placed her upon the thoat behind Sola, who had already mounted at my command.

"Good-bye, my princess," I whispered, "we may meet in Helium yet. I have escaped from worse plights than this," and I tried to smile as I lied.

"What," she cried, "are you not coming with us?"

"How may I, Dejah Thoris? Someone must hold these fellows off for a while, and I can better escape them alone than could the three of us together."

She sprang quickly from the thoat and, throwing her dear arms about my neck, turned to Sola, saying with quiet dignity: "Fly, Sola! Dejah Thoris remains to die with the man she loves."[71]

---

[71] Inasmuch as Burroughs's formula (according to Holtsmark) was the juxtaposition of *katabasis* with the pursuit of romantic love, we might say that here we have reached the climax of the novel: Dejah Thoris has professed her love for John Carter. Hence, his love requited, he has attained his central goal, and escape from the green Martians,

Those words are engraved upon my heart. Ah, gladly would I give up my life a thousand times could I only hear them once again; but I could not then give even a second to the rapture of her sweet embrace, and pressing my lips to hers for the first time, I picked her up bodily and tossed her to her seat behind Sola again, commanding the latter in peremptory tones to hold her there by force, and then, slapping the thoat upon the flank, I saw them borne away; Dejah Thoris struggling to the last to free herself from Sola's grasp.

Turning, I beheld the green warriors mounting the ridge and looking for their chieftain. In a moment they saw him, and then me; but scarcely had they discovered me than I commenced firing, lying flat upon my belly in the moss. I had an even hundred rounds in the magazine of my rifle, and another hundred in the belt at my back, and I kept up a continuous stream of fire until I saw all of the warriors who had been first to return from behind the ridge either dead or scurrying to cover.

My respite was short-lived however, for soon the entire party, numbering some thousand men, came charging into view, racing madly toward me. I fired until my rifle was empty and they were almost upon me, and then a glance showing me that Dejah Thoris and Sola had disappeared among the hills, I sprang up, throwing down my useless gun, and started away in the direction opposite to that taken by Sola and her charge.

If ever Martians had an exhibition of jumping, it was granted those astonished warriors on that day long years ago, but while it led them away from Dejah Thoris it did not distract their attention from endeavoring to capture me.

They raced wildly after me until, finally, my foot struck a projecting piece of quartz, and down I went sprawling upon the moss. As I looked up they were upon me, and although I drew my long-sword in an attempt to sell my life as dearly as possible, it was soon over. I reeled beneath their blows which fell upon me in perfect torrents; my head swam; all was black, and I went down beneath them to oblivion.

---

with Dejah in his arms, will furnish the dénouement.

CHAPTER XVIII
CHAINED IN WARHOON

It must have been several hours before I regained consciousness and I well remember the feeling of surprise which swept over me as I realized that I was not dead.

I was lying among a pile of sleeping silks and furs in the corner of a small room in which were several green warriors, and bending over me was an ancient and ugly female.

As I opened my eyes she turned to one of the warriors, saying,

"He will live, O Jed."

"'Tis well," replied the one so addressed, rising and approaching my couch, "he should render rare sport for the great games."

And now as my eyes fell upon him, I saw that he was no Thark, for his ornaments and metal were not of that horde. He was a huge fellow, terribly scarred about the face and chest, and with one broken tusk and a missing ear. Strapped on either breast were human skulls and depending from these a number of dried human hands.

His reference to the great games of which I had heard so much while among the Tharks convinced me that I had but jumped from purgatory into gehenna.[72]

After a few more words with the female, during which she assured him that I was now fully fit to travel, the jed ordered that we mount and ride after the main column.

I was strapped securely to as wild and unmanageable a thoat as I had ever seen, and, with a mounted warrior on either side to prevent the beast from bolting, we rode forth at a furious pace in pursuit of the column. My wounds gave me but little pain, so wonderfully and rapidly had the applications and injections of the female exercised their therapeutic powers, and so deftly had she bound and plastered the injuries.

Just before dark we reached the main body of troops shortly after they had made camp for the night. I was immediately taken before the leader, who proved to be the jeddak of the hordes of Warhoon.

---

[72] *Gehenna* is one of the words used in the King James Bible that has usually been translated as "hell," although originally it was merely a specific geographical designation for a valley in which corpses were incinerated outside of Jerusalem. The New Testament retains the image of *gehenna* as an unpleasant fate for the unrepentant. Christ, for example, in Mark 9:43 refers to *gehenna* as the place "where the fire is never quenched," which is obviously the source of the modern conception of hell as a fiery place.

Like the jed who had brought me, he was frightfully scarred, and also decorated with the breastplate of human skulls and dried dead hands which seemed to mark all the greater warriors among the Warhoons, as well as to indicate their awful ferocity, which greatly transcends even that of the Tharks.

The jeddak, Bar Comas, who was comparatively young, was the object of the fierce and jealous hatred of his old lieutenant, Dak Kova, the jed who had captured me, and I could not but note the almost studied efforts which the latter made to affront his superior.

He entirely omitted the usual formal salutation as we entered the presence of the jeddak, and as he pushed me roughly before the ruler he exclaimed in a loud and menacing voice.

"I have brought a strange creature wearing the metal of a Thark whom it is my pleasure to have battle with a wild thoat at the great games."

"He will die as Bar Comas, your jeddak, sees fit, if at all," replied the young ruler, with emphasis and dignity.

"If at all?" roared Dak Kova. "By the dead hands at my throat but he shall die, Bar Comas. No maudlin weakness on your part shall save him. O, would that Warhoon were ruled by a real jeddak rather than by a water-hearted weakling from whom even old Dak Kova could tear the metal with his bare hands!"

Bar Comas eyed the defiant and insubordinate chieftain for an instant, his expression one of haughty, fearless contempt and hate, and then without drawing a weapon and without uttering a word he hurled himself at the throat of his defamer.

I never before had seen two green Martian warriors battle with nature's weapons and the exhibition of animal ferocity which ensued was as fearful a thing as the most disordered imagination could picture. They tore at each others' eyes and ears with their hands and with their gleaming tusks repeatedly slashed and gored until both were cut fairly to ribbons from head to foot.

Bar Comas had much the better of the battle as he was stronger, quicker and more intelligent. It soon seemed that the encounter was done saving only the final death thrust when Bar Comas slipped in breaking away from a clinch. It was the one little opening that Dak Kova needed, and hurling himself at the body of his adversary he buried his single mighty tusk in Bar Comas' groin and with a last powerful effort ripped the young jeddak wide open the full length of his body, the great tusk finally wedging in the bones of Bar Comas' jaw. Victor and vanquished rolled limp and lifeless upon the moss, a huge mass of torn and bloody flesh.

Bar Comas was stone dead, and only the most herculean efforts on the part of Dak Kova's females saved him from the fate he deserved. Three days later he walked without assistance to the body of Bar Comas which, by custom, had not been moved from where it fell, and placing his foot upon the neck of his erstwhile ruler he assumed the title of Jeddak of Warhoon.

The dead jeddak's hands and head were removed to be added to the ornaments of his conqueror, and then his women cremated what remained, amid wild and terrible laughter.

The injuries to Dak Kova had delayed the march so greatly that it was decided to give up the expedition, which was a raid upon a small Thark community in retaliation for the destruction of the incubator, until after the great games, and the entire body of warriors, ten thousand in number, turned back toward Warhoon.

My introduction to these cruel and bloodthirsty people was but an index to the scenes I witnessed almost daily while with them. They are a smaller horde than the Tharks but much more ferocious. Not a day passed but that some members of the various Warhoon communities met in deadly combat. I have seen as high as eight mortal duels within a single day.

We reached the city of Warhoon after some three days march and I was immediately cast into a dungeon and heavily chained to the floor and walls. Food was brought me at intervals but owing to the utter darkness of the place I do not know whether I lay there days, or weeks, or months. It was the most horrible experience of all my life and that my mind did not give way to the terrors of that inky blackness has been a wonder to me ever since.[73] The place was filled with creeping, crawling things; cold, sinuous bodies passed over me when I lay down, and in the darkness I occasionally caught glimpses of gleaming, fiery eyes, fixed in horrible intentness upon me. No sound reached me from the world above and no word would my

---

[73] Burroughs's description of temporal disorientation accords with experiments in sensory deprivation carried out in subterranean caves. Without diurnal light cues, the body's circadian rhythms quickly become erratic and can produce disorientation and terror. Such deprivation can also cause what is called the Granzfeld effect, which consists of vivid hallucinations. Ancient Greeks sometimes purposely descended into caves in pursuit of "visions." See Yulia Ustinova's *Caves and the Ancient Greek Mind: Descending Underground in the Search for Ultimate Truth* (Oxford, 2009).

jailer vouchsafe when my food was brought to me, although I at first bombarded him with questions.

Finally all the hatred and maniacal loathing for these awful creatures who had placed me in this horrible place was centered by my tottering reason upon this single emissary who represented to me the entire horde of Warhoons.

I had noticed that he always advanced with his dim torch to where he could place the food within my reach and as he stooped to place it upon the floor his head was about on a level with my breast. So, with the cunning of a madman, I backed into the far corner of my cell when next I heard him approaching and gathering a little slack of the great chain which held me in my hand I waited his coming, crouching like some beast of prey. As he stooped to place my food upon the ground I swung the chain above my head and crashed the links with all my strength upon his skull. Without a sound he slipped to the floor, stone dead.

Laughing and chattering like the idiot I was fast becoming I fell upon his prostrate form my fingers feeling for his dead throat. Presently they came in contact with a small chain at the end of which dangled a number of keys. The touch of my fingers on these keys brought back my reason with the suddenness of thought. No longer was I a jibbering idiot, but a sane, reasoning man with the means of escape within my very hands.

As I was groping to remove the chain from about my victim's neck I glanced up into the darkness to see six pairs of gleaming eyes fixed, unwinking, upon me. Slowly they approached and slowly I shrank back from the awful horror of them. Back into my corner I crouched holding my hands palms out, before me, and stealthily on came the awful eyes until they reached the dead body at my feet. Then slowly they retreated but this time with a strange grating sound and finally they disappeared in some black and distant recess of my dungeon.

CHAPTER XIX

BATTLING IN THE ARENA

Slowly I regained my composure and finally essayed again to attempt to remove the keys from the dead body of my former jailer. But as I reached out into the darkness to locate it I found to my horror that it was gone. Then the truth flashed on me; the owners of those gleaming eyes had dragged my prize away from me to be devoured in their neighboring lair; as they had been waiting for days, for weeks, for months, through all this awful eternity of my imprisonment to drag my dead carcass to their feast.

For two days no food was brought me, but then a new messenger appeared and my incarceration went on as before, but not again did I allow my reason to be submerged by the horror of my position.

Shortly after this episode another prisoner was brought in and chained near me. By the dim torch light I saw that he was a red Martian and I could scarcely await the departure of his guards to address him. As their retreating footsteps died away in the distance, I called out softly the Martian word of greeting, kaor.

"Who are you who speaks out of the darkness?" he answered

"John Carter, a friend of the red men of Helium."

"I am of Helium," he said, "but I do not recall your name."

And then I told him my story as I have written it here, omitting only any reference to my love for Dejah Thoris. He was much excited by the news of Helium's princess and seemed quite positive that she and Sola could easily have reached a point of safety from where they left me. He said that he knew the place well because the defile through which the Warhoon warriors had passed when they discovered us was the only one ever used by them when marching to the south.

"Dejah Thoris and Sola entered the hills not five miles from a great waterway and are now probably quite safe," he assured me.

My fellow prisoner was Kantos Kan, a padwar (lieutenant) in the navy of Helium. He had been a member of the ill-fated expedition which had fallen into the hands of the Tharks at the time of Dejah Thoris' capture, and he briefly related the events which followed the defeat of the battleships.

Badly injured and only partially manned they had limped slowly toward Helium, but while passing near the city of Zodanga, the capital of Helium's hereditary enemies among the red men of Barsoom, they had been attacked by a great body of war vessels and all but the craft to which Kantos Kan belonged were either destroyed or captured. His vessel was chased for days by three of the Zodangan war ships but finally escaped during the darkness of a moonless night.

Thirty days after the capture of Dejah Thoris, or about the time of our coming to Thark, his vessel had reached Helium with about ten survivors of the original crew of seven hundred officers and men. Immediately seven great fleets, each of one hundred mighty war ships, had been dispatched to search for Dejah Thoris, and from these vessels two thousand smaller craft had been kept out continuously in futile search for the missing princess.

Two green Martian communities had been wiped off the face of Barsoom by the avenging fleets, but no trace of Dejah Thoris had been found. They had been searching among the northern hordes, and only within the past few days had they extended their quest to the south.

Kantos Kan had been detailed to one of the small one-man fliers and had had the misfortune to be discovered by the Warhoons while exploring their city. The bravery and daring of the man won my greatest respect and admiration. Alone he had landed at the city's boundary and on foot had penetrated to the buildings surrounding the plaza. For two days and nights he had explored their quarters and their dungeons in search of his beloved princess only to fall into the hands of a party of Warhoons as he was about to leave, after assuring himself that Dejah Thoris was not a captive there.

During the period of our incarceration Kantos Kan and I became well acquainted, and formed a warm personal friendship. A few days only elapsed, however, before we were dragged forth from our dungeon for the great games. We were conducted early one morning to an enormous amphitheater, which instead of having been built upon the surface of the ground was excavated below the surface. It had partially filled with debris so that how large it had originally been was difficult to say. In its present condition it held the entire twenty thousand Warhoons of the assembled hordes.[74]

---

[74] The description of the Warhoon arena sounds much like the Roman coliseums, although the largest of them, such as the Colosseum (the Flavian Ampitheatre) in the center of Rome, could seat over 50,000 spectators. The underground sections that held the gladiators and animals prior to their battles was called the *hypogeum* and is clearly visible in photographs of the Colosseum. Descriptions of the Colosseum and events held in the first and second centuries CE can be found in Pliny and Tacitus.

The arena was immense but extremely uneven and unkempt. Around it the Warhoons had piled building stone from some of the ruined edifices of the ancient city to prevent the animals and the captives from escaping into the audience, and at each end had been constructed cages to hold them until their turns came to meet some horrible death upon the arena.

Kantos Kan and I were confined together in one of the cages. In the others were wild calots, thoats, mad zitidars, green warriors, and women of other hordes, and many strange and ferocious wild beasts of Barsoom which I had never before seen. The din of their roaring, growling and squealing was deafening and the formidable appearance of any one of them was enough to make the stoutest heart feel grave forebodings.

Kantos Kan explained to me that at the end of the day one of these prisoners would gain freedom and the others would lie dead about the arena. The winners in the various contests of the day would be pitted against each other until only two remained alive; the victor in the last encounter being set free, whether animal or man. The following morning the cages would be filled with a new consignment of victims, and so on throughout the ten days of the games.

Shortly after we had been caged the amphitheater began to fill and within an hour every available part of the seating space was occupied. Dak Kova, with his jeds and chieftains, sat at the center of one side of the arena upon a large raised platform.

At a signal from Dak Kova the doors of two cages were thrown open and a dozen green Martian females were driven to the center of the arena. Each was given a dagger and then, at the far end, a pack of twelve calots, or wild dogs were loosed upon them.

As the brutes, growling and foaming, rushed upon the almost defenseless women I turned my head that I might not see the horrid sight. The yells and laughter of the green horde bore witness to the excellent quality of the sport and when I turned back to the arena, as Kantos Kan told me it was over, I saw three victorious calots, snarling and growling over the bodies of their prey. The women had given a good account of themselves.

Next a mad zitidar was loosed among the remaining dogs, and so it went throughout the long, hot, horrible day.

During the day I was pitted against first men and then beasts, but as I was armed with a long-sword and always outclassed my adversary in agility and generally in strength as well, it proved but child's play to me. Time and time again I won the applause of the bloodthirsty multitude, and toward the end there were cries that I be taken from the arena and be made a member of the hordes of Warhoon.

Finally there were but three of us left, a great green warrior of some far northern horde, Kantos Kan, and myself.

The other two were to battle and then I to fight the conqueror for the liberty which was accorded the final winner.

Kantos Kan had fought several times during the day and like myself had always proven victorious, but occasionally by the smallest of margins, especially when pitted against the green warriors. I had little hope that he could best his giant adversary who had mowed down all before him during the day. The fellow towered nearly sixteen feet in height, while Kantos Kan was some inches under six feet. As they advanced to meet one another I saw for the first time a trick of Martian swordsmanship which centered Kantos Kan's every hope of victory and life on one cast of the dice, for, as he came to within about twenty feet of the huge fellow he threw his sword arm far behind him over his shoulder and with a mighty sweep hurled his weapon point foremost at the green warrior. It flew true as an arrow and piercing the poor devil's heart laid him dead upon the arena.

Kantos Kan and I were now pitted against each other but as we approached to the encounter I whispered to him to prolong the battle until nearly dark in the hope that we might find some means of escape. The horde evidently guessed that we had no hearts to fight each other and so they howled in rage as neither of us placed a fatal thrust. Just as I saw the sudden coming of dark I whispered to Kantos Kan to thrust his sword between my left arm and my body. As he did so I staggered back clasping the sword tightly with my arm and thus fell to the ground with his weapon apparently protruding from my chest. Kantos Kan perceived my coup and stepping quickly to my side he placed his foot upon my neck and withdrawing his sword from my body gave me the final death blow through the neck which is supposed to sever the jugular vein, but in this instance the cold blade slipped harmlessly into the sand of the arena. In the darkness which had now fallen none could tell but that he had really finished me. I whispered to him to go and claim his freedom and then look for me in the hills east of the city, and so he left me.

When the amphitheater had cleared I crept stealthily to the top and as the great excavation lay far from the plaza and in an untenanted portion of the great dead city I had little trouble in reaching the hills beyond.

CHAPTER XX
IN THE ATMOSPHERE FACTORY

For two days I waited there for Kantos Kan, but as he did not come I started off on foot in a northwesterly direction toward a point where he had told me lay the nearest waterway. My only food consisted of vegetable milk from the plants which gave so bounteously of this priceless fluid.

Through two long weeks I wandered, stumbling through the nights guided only by the stars and hiding during the days behind some protruding rock or among the occasional hills I traversed. Several times I was attacked by wild beasts; strange, uncouth monstrosities that leaped upon me in the dark, so that I had ever to grasp my long-sword in my hand that I might be ready for them. Usually my strange, newly acquired telepathic power warned me in ample time, but once I was down with vicious fangs at my jugular and a hairy face pressed close to mine before I knew that I was even threatened.

What manner of thing was upon me I did not know, but that it was large and heavy and many-legged I could feel. My hands were at its throat before the fangs had a chance to bury themselves in my neck, and slowly I forced the hairy face from me and closed my fingers, vise-like, upon its windpipe.

Without sound we lay there, the beast exerting every effort to reach me with those awful fangs, and I straining to maintain my grip and choke the life from it as I kept it from my throat. Slowly my arms gave to the unequal struggle, and inch by inch the burning eyes and gleaming tusks of my antagonist crept toward me, until, as the hairy face touched mine again, I realized that all was over. And then a living mass of destruction sprang from the surrounding darkness full upon the creature that held me pinioned to the ground. The two rolled growling upon the moss, tearing and rending one another in a frightful manner, but it was soon over and my preserver stood with lowered head above the throat of the dead thing which would have killed me.

The nearer moon, hurtling suddenly above the horizon and lighting up the Barsoomian scene, showed me that my preserver was Woola, but from whence he had come, or how found me, I was at a loss to know. That I was glad of his companionship it is needless to say, but my pleasure at seeing him was tempered by anxiety as to the reason of his leaving Dejah Thoris. Only her death I felt sure, could account for his absence from her, so faithful I knew him to be to my commands.

By the light of the now brilliant moons I saw that he was but a shadow of his former self, and as he turned from my caress and commenced greedily to devour the dead carcass at my feet I realized that the poor fellow was more than half starved. I, myself, was in but little better plight but I could not bring myself to eat the uncooked flesh and I had no means of making a fire. When Woola had finished his meal I again took up my weary and seemingly endless wandering in quest of the elusive waterway.

At daybreak of the fifteenth day of my search I was overjoyed to see the high trees that denoted the object of my search. About noon I dragged myself wearily to the portals of a huge building which covered perhaps four square miles and towered two hundred feet in the air. It showed no aperture in the mighty walls other than the tiny door at which I sank exhausted, nor was there any sign of life about it.

I could find no bell or other method of making my presence known to the inmates of the place, unless a small round role in the wall near the door was for that purpose. It was of about the bigness of a lead pencil and thinking that it might be in the nature of a speaking tube I put my mouth to it and was about to call into it when a voice issued from it asking me whom I might be, where from, and the nature of my errand.

I explained that I had escaped from the Warhoons and was dying of starvation and exhaustion.

"You wear the metal of a green warrior and are followed by a calot, yet you are of the figure of a red man. In color you are neither green nor red. In the name of the ninth day, what manner of creature are you?"[75]

"I am a friend of the red men of Barsoom and I am starving. In the name of humanity open to us," I replied.

Presently the door commenced to recede before me until it had sunk into the wall fifty feet, then it stopped and slid easily to the left, exposing a short, narrow corridor of concrete, at the further end of which was another door, similar in every respect to the one I had just passed. No one was in sight, yet immediately we passed the first door it slid gently into place behind us and receded rapidly to its original position in the front wall of the building. As the door had slipped aside I had noted its great thickness, fully twenty feet, and as it reached its place once more after closing behind us, great cylinders of steel had dropped from the ceiling behind it and fitted their lower ends into apertures countersunk in the floor.

---

[75] This is surely a typo for the more usual Barsoomian oath, "In the name of the ninth ray!" The ninth ray, as we see in this chapter, is the key to the sustainability of the Martian atmosphere through Martian engineering.

A second and third door receded before me and slipped to one side as the first, before I reached a large inner chamber where I found food and drink set out upon a great stone table. A voice directed me to satisfy my hunger and to feed my calot, and while I was thus engaged my invisible host put me through a severe and searching cross-examination.

"Your statements are most remarkable," said the voice, on concluding its questioning, "but you are evidently speaking the truth, and it is equally evident that you are not of Barsoom. I can tell that by the conformation of your brain and the strange location of your internal organs and the shape and size of your heart."

"Can you see through me?" I exclaimed.

"Yes, I can see all but your thoughts, and were you a Barsoomian I could read those."

Then a door opened at the far side of the chamber and a strange, dried up, little mummy of a man came toward me. He wore but a single article of clothing or adornment, a small collar of gold from which depended upon his chest a great ornament as large as a dinner plate set solid with huge diamonds, except for the exact center which was occupied by a strange stone, an inch in diameter, that scintillated nine different and distinct rays; the seven colors of our earthly prism and two beautiful rays which, to me, were new and nameless. I cannot describe them any more than you could describe red to a blind man. I only know that they were beautiful in the extreme.

The old man sat and talked with me for hours, and the strangest part of our intercourse was that I could read his every thought while he could not fathom an iota from my mind unless I spoke.

I did not apprise him of my ability to sense his mental operations, and thus I learned a great deal which proved of immense value to me later and which I would never have known had he suspected my strange power, for the Martians have such perfect control of their mental machinery that they are able to direct their thoughts with absolute precision.

The building in which I found myself contained the machinery which produces that artificial atmosphere which sustains life on Mars. The secret of the entire process hinges on the use of the ninth ray, one of the beautiful scintillations which I had noted emanating from the great stone in my host's diadem.[76]

---

[76] The theme of an atmosphere engine on Mars necessary to sustain life also appears in the Paul Verhoeven film *Total Recall* (1990), loosely based on the Philip K. Dick Mars-based story "We Can Remember it for you Wholesale," although other elements of that film seem drawn from the Dick novel *The Martian Time Slip* (1964).

This ray is separated from the other rays of the sun by means of finely adjusted instruments placed upon the roof of the huge building, three-quarters of which is used for reservoirs in which the ninth ray is stored. This product is then treated electrically, or rather certain proportions of refined electric vibrations are incorporated with it, and the result is then pumped to the five principal air centers of the planet where, as it is released, contact with the ether of space transforms it into atmosphere.

There is always sufficient reserve of the ninth ray stored in the great building to maintain the present Martian atmosphere for a thousand years, and the only fear, as my new friend told me, was that some accident might befall the pumping apparatus.

He led me to an inner chamber where I beheld a battery of twenty radium pumps any one of which was equal to the task of furnishing all Mars with the atmosphere compound. For eight hundred years, he told me, he had watched these pumps which are used alternately a day each at a stretch, or a little over twenty-four and one-half Earth hours. He has one assistant who divides the watch with him. Half a Martian year, about three hundred and forty-four of our days, each of these men spend alone in this huge, isolated plant.

Every red Martian is taught during earliest childhood the principles of the manufacture of atmosphere, but only two at one time ever hold the secret of ingress to the great building, which, built as it is with walls a hundred and fifty feet thick, is absolutely unassailable, even the roof being guarded from assault by air craft by a glass covering five feet thick.

The only fear they entertain of attack is from the green Martians or some demented red man, as all Barsoomians realize that the very existence of every form of life of Mars is dependent upon the uninterrupted working of this plant.

One curious fact I discovered as I watched his thoughts was that the outer doors are manipulated by telepathic means. The locks are so finely adjusted that the doors are released by the action of a certain combination of thought waves. To experiment with my new-found toy I thought to surprise him into revealing this combination and so I asked him in a casual manner how he had managed to unlock the massive doors for me from the inner chambers of the building. As quick as a flash there leaped to his mind nine Martian sounds, but as quickly faded as he answered that this was a secret he must not divulge.

From then on his manner toward me changed as though he feared that he had been surprised into divulging his great secret, and I read suspicion and fear in his looks and thoughts, though his words were still fair.

Before I retired for the night he promised to give me a letter to a nearby agricultural officer who would help me on my way to Zodanga, which he said, was the nearest Martian city.

"But be sure that you do not let them know you are bound for Helium as they are at war with that country. My assistant and I are of no country, we belong to all Barsoom and this talisman which we wear protects us in all lands, even among the green men—though we do not trust ourselves to their hands if we can avoid it," he added.

"And so good-night, my friend," he continued, "may you have a long and restful sleep—yes, a long sleep."

And though he smiled pleasantly I saw in his thoughts the wish that he had never admitted me, and then a picture of him standing over me in the night, and the swift thrust of a long dagger and the half formed words, "I am sorry, but it is for the best good of Barsoom."

As he closed the door of my chamber behind him his thoughts were cut off from me as was the sight of him, which seemed strange to me in my little knowledge of thought transference.

What was I to do? How could I escape through these mighty walls? Easily could I kill him now that I was warned, but once he was dead I could no more escape, and with the stopping of the machinery of the great plant I should die with all the other inhabitants of the planet—all, even Dejah Thoris were she not already dead. For the others I did not give the snap of my finger, but the thought of Dejah Thoris drove from my mind all desire to kill my mistaken host.

Cautiously I opened the door of my apartment and, followed by Woola, sought the inner of the great doors. A wild scheme had come to me; I would attempt to force the great locks by the nine thought waves I had read in my host's mind.

Creeping stealthily through corridor after corridor and down winding runways which turned hither and thither I finally reached the great hall in which I had broken my long fast that morning. Nowhere had I seen my host, nor did I know where he kept himself by night.

I was on the point of stepping boldly out into the room when a slight noise behind me warned me back into the shadows of a recess in the corridor. Dragging Woola after me I crouched low in the darkness.

Presently the old man passed close by me, and as he entered the dimly lighted chamber which I had been about to pass through I saw that he held a long thin dagger in his hand and that he was sharpening it upon a stone. In his mind was the decision to inspect the radium pumps, which would take about thirty minutes, and then return to my bed chamber and finish me.

As he passed through the great hall and disappeared down the runway which led to the pump-room, I stole stealthily from my hiding place and crossed to the great door, the inner of the three which stood between me and liberty.

Concentrating my mind upon the massive lock I hurled the nine thought waves against it. In breathless expectancy I waited, when finally the great door moved softly toward me and slid quietly to one side. One after the other the remaining mighty portals opened at my command and Woola and I stepped forth into the darkness, free, but little better off than we had been before, other than that we had full stomachs.

Hastening away from the shadows of the formidable pile I made for the first crossroad, intending to strike the central turnpike as quickly as possible. This I reached about morning and entering the first enclosure I came to I searched for some evidences of a habitation.

There were low rambling buildings of concrete barred with heavy impassable doors, and no amount of hammering and hallooing brought any response. Weary and exhausted from sleeplessness I threw myself upon the ground commanding Woola to stand guard.

Some time later I was awakened by his frightful growlings and opened my eyes to see three red Martians standing a short distance from us and covering me with their rifles.

"I am unarmed and no enemy," I hastened to explain. "I have been a prisoner among the green men and am on my way to Zodanga. All I ask is food and rest for myself and my calot and the proper directions for reaching my destination."

They lowered their rifles and advanced pleasantly toward me placing their right hands upon my left shoulder, after the manner of their custom of salute, and asking me many questions about myself and my wanderings. They then took me to the house of one of them which was only a short distance away.

The buildings I had been hammering at in the early morning were occupied only by stock and farm produce, the house proper standing among a grove of enormous trees, and, like all red-Martian homes, had been raised at night some forty or fifty feet from the ground on a large round metal shaft which slid up or down within a sleeve sunk in the ground, and was operated by a tiny radium engine in the entrance hall of the building. Instead of bothering with bolts and bars for their dwellings, the red Martians simply run them up out of harm's way during the night. They also have private means for lowering or raising them from the ground without if they wish to go away and leave them.

These brothers, with their wives and children, occupied three similar houses on this farm. They did no work themselves, being government officers in charge. The labor was performed by convicts, prisoners of war, delinquent debtors and confirmed bachelors who were too poor to pay the high celibate tax which all red-Martian governments impose.

They were the personification of cordiality and hospitality and I spent several days with them, resting and recuperating from my long and arduous experiences.

When they had heard my story—I omitted all reference to Dejah Thoris and the old man of the atmosphere plant—they advised me to color my body to more nearly resemble their own race and then attempt to find employment in Zodanga, either in the army or the navy.

"The chances are small that your tale will be believed until after you have proven your trustworthiness and won friends among the higher nobles of the court. This you can most easily do through military service, as we are a warlike people on Barsoom," explained one of them, "and save our richest favors for the fighting man."

When I was ready to depart they furnished me with a small domestic bull thoat, such as is used for saddle purposes by all red Martians. The animal is about the size of a horse and quite gentle, but in color and shape an exact replica of his huge and fierce cousin of the wilds.

The brothers had supplied me with a reddish oil with which I anointed my entire body and one of them cut my hair, which had grown quite long, in the prevailing fashion of the time, square at the back and banged in front, so that I could have passed anywhere upon Barsoom as a full-fledged red Martian. My metal and ornaments were also renewed in the style of a Zodangan gentleman, attached to the house of Ptor, which was the family name of my benefactors.

They filled a little sack at my side with Zodangan money. The medium of exchange upon Mars is not dissimilar from our own except that the coins are oval. Paper money is issued by individuals as they require it and redeemed twice yearly. If a man issues more than he can redeem, the government pays his creditors in full and the debtor works out the amount upon the farms or in mines, which are all owned by the government. This suits everybody except the debtor as it has been a difficult thing to obtain sufficient voluntary labor to work the great isolated farm lands of Mars, stretching as they do like narrow ribbons from pole to pole, through wild stretches peopled by wild animals and wilder men.

When I mentioned my inability to repay them for their kindness to me they assured me that I would have ample opportunity if I lived long upon Barsoom, and bidding me farewell they watched me until I was out of sight upon the broad white turnpike.

THE OLD MAN SAT AND TALKED WITH ME FOR HOURS.

CHAPTER XXI
AN AIR SCOUT FOR ZODANGA

As I proceeded on my journey toward Zodanga many strange and interesting sights arrested my attention, and at the several farm houses where I stopped I learned a number of new and instructive things concerning the methods and manners of Barsoom.

The water which supplies the farms of Mars is collected in immense underground reservoirs at either pole from the melting ice caps, and pumped through long conduits to the various populated centers. Along either side of these conduits, and extending their entire length, lie the cultivated districts. These are divided into tracts of about the same size, each tract being under the supervision of one or more government officers.

Instead of flooding the surface of the fields, and thus wasting immense quantities of water by evaporation, the precious liquid is carried underground through a vast network of small pipes directly to the roots of the vegetation.[77] The crops upon Mars are always uniform, for there are no droughts, no rains, no high winds, and no insects, or destroying birds.

On this trip I tasted the first meat I had eaten since leaving Earth—large, juicy steaks and chops from the well-fed domestic animals of the farms. Also I enjoyed luscious fruits and vegetables, but not a single article of food which was exactly similar to anything on Earth. Every plant and flower and vegetable and animal has been so refined by ages of careful, scientific cultivation and breeding that the like of them on Earth dwindled into pale, gray, characterless nothingness by comparison.

At a second stop I met some highly cultivated people of the noble class and while in conversation we chanced to speak of Helium. One of the older men had been there on a diplomatic mission several years before and spoke with regret of the conditions which seemed destined ever to keep these two countries at war.

"Helium," he said, "rightly boasts the most beautiful women of Barsoom, and of all her treasures the wondrous daughter of Mors Kajak, Dejah Thoris, is the most exquisite flower.

---

[77] Underground irrigation to avoid evaporation. Burroughs seems to be describing the qanat, a system of underground irrigation designed over 2,500 years ago in Iran, and still used today in the Martian-like arid terrain of the Middle East.

"Why," he added, "the people really worship the ground she walks upon and since her loss on that ill-starred expedition all Helium has been draped in mourning.

"That our ruler should have attacked the disabled fleet as it was returning to Helium was but another of his awful blunders which I fear will sooner or later compel Zodanga to elevate a wiser man to his place."

"Even now, though our victorious armies are surrounding Helium, the people of Zodanga are voicing their displeasure, for the war is not a popular one, since it is not based on right or justice. Our forces took advantage of the absence of the principal fleet of Helium on their search for the princess, and so we have been able easily to reduce the city to a sorry plight. It is said she will fall within the next few passages of the further moon."

"And what, think you, may have been the fate of the princess, Dejah Thoris?" I asked as casually as possible.

"She is dead," he answered. "This much was learned from a green warrior recently captured by our forces in the south. She escaped from the hordes of Thark with a strange creature of another world, only to fall into the hands of the Warhoons. Their thoats were found wandering upon the sea bottom and evidences of a bloody conflict were discovered nearby."

While this information was in no way reassuring, neither was it at all conclusive proof of the death of Dejah Thoris, and so I determined to make every effort possible to reach Helium as quickly as I could and carry to Tardos Mors such news of his granddaughter's possible whereabouts as lay in my power.

Ten days after leaving the three Ptor brothers I arrived at Zodanga. From the moment that I had come in contact with the red inhabitants of Mars I had noticed that Woola drew a great amount of unwelcome attention to me, since the huge brute belonged to a species which is never domesticated by the red men. Were one to stroll down Broadway with a Numidian lion at his heels the effect would be somewhat similar to that which I should have produced had I entered Zodanga with Woola.

The very thought of parting with the faithful fellow caused me so great regret and genuine sorrow that I put it off until just before we arrived at the city's gates; but then, finally, it became imperative that we separate. Had nothing further than my own safety or pleasure been at stake no argument could have prevailed upon me to turn away the one creature upon Barsoom that had never failed in a demonstration of affection and loyalty; but as I would willingly have offered my life in the service of her in search of whom I was about to challenge the unknown dangers of this, to me, mysterious city, I could not permit even Woola's life to threaten the success of my venture, much less his momentary happiness, for I doubted not he soon would forget me. And so I bade the poor beast an affectionate farewell, promising him, however, that if I came through my adventure in safety that in some way I should find the means to search him out.[78]

He seemed to understand me fully, and when I pointed back in the direction of Thark he turned sorrowfully away, nor could I bear to watch him go; but resolutely set my face toward Zodanga and with a touch of heartsickness approached her frowning walls.

The letter I bore from them gained me immediate entrance to the vast, walled city. It was still very early in the morning and the streets were practically deserted. The residences, raised high upon their metal columns, resembled huge rookeries, while the uprights themselves presented the appearance of steel tree trunks. The shops as a rule were not raised from the ground nor were their doors bolted or barred, since thievery is practically unknown upon Barsoom. Assassination is the ever-present fear of all Barsoomians, and for this reason alone their homes are raised high above the ground at night, or in times of danger.

The Ptor brothers had given me explicit directions for reaching the point of the city where I could find living accommodations and be near the offices of the government agents to whom they had given me letters. My way led to the central square or plaza, which is a characteristic of all Martian cities.

The plaza of Zodanga covers a square mile and is bounded by the palaces of the jeddak, the jeds, and other members of the royalty and nobility of Zodanga, as well as by the principal public buildings, cafes, and shops.

As I was crossing the great square lost in wonder and admiration of the magnificent architecture and the gorgeous scarlet vegetation which carpeted the broad lawns I discovered a red Martian walking briskly toward me from one of the avenues. He paid not the slightest attention to me, but as he came abreast I recognized him, and turning I placed my hand upon his shoulder, calling out:

"Kaor, Kantos Kan!"

---

[78] One has to wonder whether Harlan Ellison had this Burroughs passage in mind when he wrote his novella *A Boy and His Dog* (1969), in which the protagonist makes a very different choice when faced with the prospect of losing either his lover or his boon companion.

Like lightning he wheeled and before I could so much as lower my hand the point of his long-sword was at my breast.

"Who are you?" he growled, and then as a backward leap carried me fifty feet from his sword he dropped the point to the ground and exclaimed, laughing,

"I do not need a better reply, there is but one man upon all Barsoom who can bounce about like a rubber ball. By the mother of the further moon, John Carter, how came you here, and have you become a Darseen that you can change your color at will?"

"You gave me a bad half minute my friend," he continued, after I had briefly outlined my adventures since parting with him in the arena at Warhoon. "Were my name and city known to the Zodangans I would shortly be sitting on the banks of the lost sea of Korus with my revered and departed ancestors. I am here in the interest of Tardos Mors, Jeddak of Helium, to discover the whereabouts of Dejah Thoris, our princess. Sab Than, prince of Zodanga, has her hidden in the city and has fallen madly in love with her. His father, Than Kosis, Jeddak of Zodanga, has made her voluntary marriage to his son the price of peace between our countries, but Tardos Mors will not accede to the demands and has sent word that he and his people would rather look upon the dead face of their princess than see her wed to any than her own choice, and that personally he would prefer being engulfed in the ashes of a lost and burning Helium to joining the metal of his house with that of Than Kosis. His reply was the deadliest affront he could have put upon Than Kosis and the Zodangans, but his people love him the more for it and his strength in Helium is greater today than ever.

"I have been here three days," continued Kantos Kan, "but I have not yet found where Dejah Thoris is imprisoned. Today I join the Zodangan navy as an air scout and I hope in this way to win the confidence of Sab Than, the prince, who is commander of this division of the navy, and thus learn the whereabouts of Dejah Thoris. I am glad that you are here, John Carter, for I know your loyalty to my princess and two of us working together should be able to accomplish much."

The plaza was now commencing to fill with people going and coming upon the daily activities of their duties. The shops were opening and the cafes filling with early morning patrons. Kantos Kan led me to one of these gorgeous eating places where we were served entirely by mechanical apparatus. No hand touched the food from the time it entered the building in its raw state until it emerged hot and delicious upon the tables before the guests, in response to the touching of tiny buttons to indicate their desires.

After our meal, Kantos Kan took me with him to the headquarters of the air-scout squadron and introducing me to his superior asked that I be enrolled as a member of the corps. In accordance with custom an examination was necessary, but Kantos Kan had told me to have no fear on this score as he would attend to that part of the matter. He accomplished this by taking my order for examination to the examining officer and representing himself as John Carter.

"This ruse will be discovered later," he cheerfully explained, "when they check up my weights, measurements, and other personal identification data, but it will be several months before this is done and our mission should be accomplished or have failed long before that time."

The next few days were spent by Kantos Kan in teaching me the intricacies of flying and of repairing the dainty little contrivances which the Martians use for this purpose.[79] The body of the one-man air craft is about sixteen feet long, two feet wide and three inches thick, tapering to a point at each end. The driver sits on top of this plane upon a seat constructed over the small, noiseless radium engine which propels it. The medium of buoyancy is contained within the thin metal walls of the body and consists of the eighth Barsoomian ray, or ray of propulsion, as it may be termed in view of its properties.

This ray, like the ninth ray, is unknown on Earth, but the Martians have discovered that it is an inherent property of all light no matter from what source it emanates. They have learned that it is the solar eighth ray which propels the light of the sun to the various planets, and that it is the individual eighth ray of each planet which "reflects," or propels the light thus obtained out into space once more. The solar eighth ray would be absorbed by the surface of Barsoom, but the Barsoomian eighth ray, which tends to propel light from Mars into space, is constantly streaming out from the planet constituting a force of repulsion of gravity which when confined is able to lift enormous weights from the surface of the ground.[80]

---

[79] The first true airplane flights having been accomplished only in 1903, flying was still very much a novelty in 1911. H.G. Wells wrote the amazingly prescient *The War in the Air* in 1907, but even as late as 1911, the French military theoretician Ferdinand Foch claimed that "airplanes are interesting toys, but of no military value." In fact, throughout the Mars saga, Burroughs understands quite well that the airplane is a machine tailor-made for executing the first principle of military strategy: seize the high ground, a principle especially inculcated in cavalry men.

[80] The eighth ray is Burroughs's fanciful version of an anti-gravity device, only slightly

It is this ray which has enabled them to so perfect aviation that battle ships far outweighing anything known upon Earth sail as gracefully and lightly through the thin air of Barsoom as a toy balloon in the heavy atmosphere of Earth.

During the early years of the discovery of this ray many strange accidents occurred before the Martians learned to measure and control the wonderful power they had found. In one instance, some nine hundred years before, the first great battle ship to be built with eighth ray reservoirs was stored with too great a quantity of the rays and she had sailed up from Helium with five hundred officers and men, never to return.

Her power of repulsion for the planet was so great that it had carried her far into space, where she can be seen today, by the aid of powerful telescopes, hurtling through the heavens ten thousand miles from Mars; a tiny satellite that will thus encircle Barsoom to the end of time.

The fourth day after my arrival at Zodanga I made my first flight, and as a result of it I won a promotion which included quarters in the palace of Than Kosis.

As I rose above the city I circled several times, as I had seen Kantos Kan do, and then throwing my engine into top speed I raced at terrific velocity toward the south, following one of the great waterways which enter Zodanga from that direction.

I had traversed perhaps two hundred miles in a little less than an hour when I descried far below me a party of three green warriors racing madly toward a small figure on foot which seemed to be trying to reach the confines of one of the walled fields.

Dropping my machine rapidly toward them, and circling to the rear of the warriors, I soon saw that the object of their pursuit was a red Martian wearing the metal of the scout squadron to which I was attached. A short distance away lay his tiny flier, surrounded by the tools with which he had evidently been occupied in repairing some damage when surprised by the green warriors.

They were now almost upon him; their flying mounts charging down on the relatively puny figure at terrific speed, while the warriors leaned low to the right, with their great metal-shod spears. Each seemed striving to be the first to impale the poor Zodangan and in another moment his fate would have been sealed had it not been for my timely arrival.

---

more convincing than say H.G. Wells's "cavorite" in *The First Men in the Moon* (1901).

Driving my fleet air craft at high speed directly behind the warriors I soon overtook them and without diminishing my speed I rammed the prow of my little flier between the shoulders of the nearest. The impact sufficient to have torn through inches of solid steel, hurled the fellow's headless body into the air over the head of his thoat, where it fell sprawling upon the moss. The mounts of the other two warriors turned squealing in terror, and bolted in opposite directions.

Reducing my speed I circled and came to the ground at the feet of the astonished Zodangan. He was warm in his thanks for my timely aid and promised that my day's work would bring the reward it merited, for it was none other than a cousin of the jeddak of Zodanga whose life I had saved.

We wasted no time in talk as we knew that the warriors would surely return as soon as they had gained control of their mounts. Hastening to his damaged machine we were bending every effort to finish the needed repairs and had almost completed them when we saw the two green monsters returning at top speed from opposite sides of us. When they had approached within a hundred yards their thoats again became unmanageable and absolutely refused to advance further toward the air craft which had frightened them.

The warriors finally dismounted and hobbling their animals advanced toward us on foot with drawn long-swords.

I advanced to meet the larger, telling the Zodangan to do the best he could with the other. Finishing my man with almost no effort, as had now from much practice become habitual with me, I hastened to return to my new acquaintance whom I found indeed in desperate straits.

He was wounded and down with the huge foot of his antagonist upon his throat and the great long-sword raised to deal the final thrust. With a bound I cleared the fifty feet intervening between us, and with outstretched point drove my sword completely through the body of the green warrior. His sword fell, harmless, to the ground and he sank limply upon the prostrate form of the Zodangan.

A cursory examination of the latter revealed no mortal injuries and after a brief rest he asserted that he felt fit to attempt the return voyage. He would have to pilot his own craft, however, as these frail vessels are not intended to convey but a single person.

Quickly completing the repairs we rose together into the still, cloudless Martian sky, and at great speed and without further mishap returned to Zodanga.

As we neared the city we discovered a mighty concourse of civilians and troops assembled upon the plain before the city. The sky was black with naval vessels and private and public pleasure craft, flying long streamers of gay-colored silks, and banners and flags of odd and picturesque design.

My companion signaled that I slow down, and running his machine close beside mine suggested that we approach and watch the ceremony, which, he said, was for the purpose of conferring honors on individual officers and men for bravery and other distinguished service. He then unfurled a little ensign which denoted that his craft bore a member of the royal family of Zodanga, and together we made our way through the maze of low-lying air vessels until we hung directly over the jeddak of Zodanga and his staff. All were mounted upon the small domestic bull thoats of the red Martians, and their trappings and ornamentation bore such a quantity of gorgeously colored feathers that I could not but be struck with the startling resemblance the concourse bore to a band of the red Indians of my own Earth.[81]

One of the staff called the attention of Than Kosis to the presence of my companion above them and the ruler motioned for him to descend. As they waited for the troops to move into position facing the jeddak the two talked earnestly together, the jeddak and his staff occasionally glancing up at me. I could not hear their conversation and presently it ceased and all dismounted, as the last body of troops had wheeled into position before their emperor. A member of the staff advanced toward the troops, and calling the name of a soldier commanded him to advance. The officer then recited the nature of the heroic act which had won the approval of the jeddak, and the latter advanced and placed a metal ornament upon the left arm of the lucky man.

Ten men had been so decorated when the aide called out,

"John Carter, air scout!"

Never in my life had I been so surprised, but the habit of military discipline is strong within me, and I dropped my little machine lightly to the ground and advanced on foot as I had seen the others do. As I halted before the officer, he addressed me in a voice audible to the entire assemblage of troops and spectators.

---

[81] As if we didn't see this coming, Burroughs associates the red Martians, decked out in their ceremonial costumes, with the "red men" of Earth. Burroughs's depiction of Native Americans seems to match the ambivalence typical of his age. On the one hand, the Apaches are depicted as bloodthirsty and violent demons, but then he also presents elements of the myth of the Noble Savage in the Martian cycle.

"In recognition, John Carter," he said, "of your remarkable courage and skill in defending the person of the cousin of the jeddak Than Kosis and, singlehanded, vanquishing three green warriors, it is the pleasure of our jeddak to confer on you the mark of his esteem."

Than Kosis then advanced toward me and placing an ornament upon me, said:

"My cousin has narrated the details of your wonderful achievement, which seems little short of miraculous, and if you can so well defend a cousin of the jeddak how much better could you defend the person of the jeddak himself. You are therefore appointed a padwar of The Guards and will be quartered in my palace hereafter."

I thanked him, and at his direction joined the members of his staff. After the ceremony I returned my machine to its quarters on the roof of the barracks of the air-scout squadron, and with an orderly from the palace to guide me I reported to the officer in charge of the palace.

CHAPTER XXII
I FIND DEJAH

The major-domo to whom I reported had been given instructions to station me near the person of the jeddak, who, in time of war, is always in great danger of assassination, as the rule that all is fair in war seems to constitute the entire ethics of Martian conflict.

He therefore escorted me immediately to the apartment in which Than Kosis then was. The ruler was engaged in conversation with his son, Sab Than, and several courtiers of his household, and did not perceive my entrance.

The walls of the apartment were completely hung with splendid tapestries which hid any windows or doors which may have pierced them. The room was lighted by imprisoned rays of sunshine held between the ceiling proper and what appeared to be a ground-glass false ceiling a few inches below.

My guide drew aside one of the tapestries, disclosing a passage which encircled the room, between the hangings and the walls of the chamber. Within this passage I was to remain, he said, so long as Than Kosis was in the apartment. When he left I was to follow. My only duty was to guard the ruler and keep out of sight as much as possible. I would be relieved after a period of four hours. The major-domo then left me.

The tapestries were of a strange weaving which gave the appearance of heavy solidity from one side, but from my hiding place I could perceive all that took place within the room as readily as though there had been no curtain intervening.

Scarcely had I gained my post than the tapestry at the opposite end of the chamber separated and four soldiers of The Guard entered, surrounding a female figure. As they approached Than Kosis the soldiers fell to either side and there standing before the jeddak and not ten feet from me, her beautiful face radiant with smiles, was Dejah Thoris.

Sab Than, Prince of Zodanga, advanced to meet her, and hand in hand they approached close to the jeddak. Than Kosis looked up in surprise, and, rising, saluted her.

"To what strange freak do I owe this visit from the Princess of Helium, who, two days ago, with rare consideration for my pride, assured me that she would prefer Tal Hajus, the green Thark, to my son?"

Dejah Thoris only smiled the more and with the roguish dimples playing at the corners of her mouth she made answer:

"From the beginning of time upon Barsoom it has been the prerogative of woman to change her mind as she listed and to dissemble in matters concerning her heart. That you will forgive, Than Kosis, as has your son. Two days ago I was not sure of his love for me, but now I am, and I have come to beg of you to forget my rash words and to accept the assurance of the Princess of Helium that when the time comes she will wed Sab Than, Prince of Zodanga."

"I am glad that you have so decided," replied Than Kosis. "It is far from my desire to push war further against the people of Helium, and, your promise shall be recorded and a proclamation to my people issued forthwith."

"It were better, Than Kosis," interrupted Dejah Thoris, "that the proclamation wait the ending of this war. It would look strange indeed to my people and to yours were the Princess of Helium to give herself to her country's enemy in the midst of hostilities."

"Cannot the war be ended at once?" spoke Sab Than. "It requires but the word of Than Kosis to bring peace. Say it, my father, say the word that will hasten my happiness, and end this unpopular strife."

"We shall see," replied Than Kosis, "how the people of Helium take to peace. I shall at least offer it to them."

Dejah Thoris, after a few words, turned and left the apartment, still followed by her guards.

Thus was the edifice of my brief dream of happiness dashed, broken, to the ground of reality. The woman for whom I had offered my life, and from whose lips I had so recently heard a declaration of love for me, had lightly forgotten my very existence and smilingly given herself to the son of her people's most hated enemy.

Although I had heard it with my own ears I could not believe it. I must search out her apartments and force her to repeat the cruel truth to me alone before I would be convinced, and so I deserted my post and hastened through the passage behind the tapestries toward the door by which she had left the chamber. Slipping quietly through this opening I discovered a maze of winding corridors, branching and turning in every direction.

Running rapidly down first one and then another of them I soon became hopelessly lost and was standing panting against a side wall when I heard voices near me. Apparently they were coming from the opposite side of the partition against which I leaned and presently I made out the tones of Dejah Thoris. I could not hear the words but I knew that I could not possibly be mistaken in the voice.

Moving on a few steps I discovered another passageway at the end of which lay a door. Walking boldly forward I pushed into the room only to find myself in a small antechamber in which were the four guards who had accompanied her. One of them instantly arose and accosted me, asking the nature of my business.

"I am from Than Kosis," I replied, "and wish to speak privately with Dejah Thoris, Princess of Helium."

"And your order?" asked the fellow.

I did not know what he meant, but replied that I was a member of The Guard, and without waiting for a reply from him I strode toward the opposite door of the antechamber, behind which I could hear Dejah Thoris conversing.

But my entrance was not to be so easily accomplished. The guardsman stepped before me, saying,

"No one comes from Than Kosis without carrying an order or the password. You must give me one or the other before you may pass."

"The only order I require, my friend, to enter where I will, hangs at my side," I answered, tapping my long-sword; "will you let me pass in peace or no?"

For reply he whipped out his own sword, calling to the others to join him, and thus the four stood, with drawn weapons, barring my further progress.

"You are not here by the order of Than Kosis," cried the one who had first addressed me, "and not only shall you not enter the apartments of the Princess of Helium but you shall go back to Than Kosis under guard to explain this unwarranted temerity. Throw down your sword; you cannot hope to overcome four of us," he added with a grim smile.

My reply was a quick thrust which left me but three antagonists and I can assure you that they were worthy of my metal. They had me backed against the wall in no time, fighting for my life. Slowly I worked my way to a corner of the room where I could force them to come at me only one at a time, and thus we fought upward of twenty minutes; the clanging of steel on steel producing a veritable bedlam in the little room.

The noise had brought Dejah Thoris to the door of her apartment, and there she stood throughout the conflict with Sola at her back peering over her shoulder. Her face was set and emotionless and I knew that she did not recognize me, nor did Sola.

Finally a lucky cut brought down a second guardsman and then, with only two opposing me, I changed my tactics and rushed them down after the fashion of my fighting that had won me many a victory. The third fell within ten seconds after the second, and the last lay dead upon the bloody floor a few moments later. They were brave men and noble fighters, and it grieved me that I had been forced to kill them, but I would have willingly depopulated all Barsoom could I have reached the side of my Dejah Thoris in no other way.

Sheathing my bloody blade I advanced toward my Martian Princess, who still stood mutely gazing at me without sign of recognition.

"Who are you, Zodangan?" she whispered. "Another enemy to harass me in my misery?"

"I am a friend," I answered, "a once cherished friend."

"No friend of Helium's princess wears that metal," she replied, "and yet the voice! I have heard it before; it is not—it cannot be—no, for he is dead."

"It is, though, my Princess, none other than John Carter," I said. "Do you not recognize, even through paint and strange metal, the heart of your chieftain?"

As I came close to her she swayed toward me with outstretched hands, but as I reached to take her in my arms she drew back with a shudder and a little moan of misery.

"Too late, too late," she grieved. "O my chieftain that was, and whom I thought dead, had you but returned one little hour before—but now it is too late, too late."[82]

"What do you mean, Dejah Thoris?" I cried. "That you would not have promised yourself to the Zodangan prince had you known that I lived?"

"Think you, John Carter, that I would give my heart to you yesterday and today to another? I thought that it lay buried with your ashes in the pits of Warhoon, and so today I have promised my body to another to save my people from the curse of a victorious Zodangan army."[83]

---

[82] Because Dejah Thoris believes Carter has died, she has agreed to marry another, leading to the classic tragic-romantic situation that has precedents in literature ranging from *Tristan and Isolde* to *The Winter's Tale*.

[83] Interestingly, Dejah, like a Platonic philosopher, distinguishes between body and soul or mind: "I have pledged my body to another to save my people." Her action recalls other acts of noble sacrifice, including the biblical story of Esther, although Burroughs might have had more specifically certain legends about the Carthaginian Dido (also called Elissa) in mind.

"But I am not dead, my princess. I have come to claim you, and all Zodanga cannot prevent it."

"It is too late, John Carter, my promise is given, and on Barsoom that is final. The ceremonies which follow later are but meaningless formalities. They make the fact of marriage no more certain than does the funeral cortege of a jeddak again place the seal of death upon him. I am as good as married, John Carter. No longer may you call me your princess. No longer are you my chieftain."[84]

"I know but little of your customs here upon Barsoom, Dejah Thoris, but I do know that I love you, and if you meant the last words you spoke to me that day as the hordes of Warhoon were charging down upon us, no other man shall ever claim you as his bride. You meant them then, my princess, and you mean them still! Say that it is true."

"I meant them, John Carter," she whispered. "I cannot repeat them now for I have given myself to another. Ah, if you had only known our ways, my friend," she continued, half to herself, "the promise would have been yours long months ago, and you could have claimed me before all others. It might have meant the fall of Helium, but I would have given my empire for my Tharkian chief."

Then aloud she said: "Do you remember the night when you offended me? You called me your princess without having asked my hand of me, and then you boasted that you had fought for me. You did not know, and I should not have been offended; I see that now. But there was no one to tell you what I could not, that upon Barsoom there are two kinds of women in the cities of the red men. The one they fight for that they may ask them in marriage; the other kind they fight for also, but never ask their hands. When a man has won a woman he may address her as his princess, or in any of the several terms which signify possession. You had fought for me, but had never asked me in marriage, and so when you called me your princess, you see," she faltered, "I was hurt, but even then,

---

[84] Dejah's insistence that the deed has been done through her mere verbal promise anticipates the philosophical investigation of "illocutionary declaration" by the philosopher John Austin, also referred to as a "performative speech act," in which the saying of an utterance effects an actual change in affairs. A commonly cited example would be when a judge or minister utters the statement, "I now pronounce you husband and wife." The making of the statement creates the actual condition of legal marriage. Dejah Thoris is explaining to Carter (no doubt due to the strict inability of Barsoomians to tell falsehoods) that her mere utterance of the promise to marry in effect creates the reality of marriage.

John Carter, I did not repulse you, as I should have done, until you made it doubly worse by taunting me with having won me through combat."[85]

"I do not need ask your forgiveness now, Dejah Thoris," I cried. "You must know that my fault was of ignorance of your Barsoomian customs. What I failed to do, through implicit belief that my petition would be presumptuous and unwelcome, I do now, Dejah Thoris; I ask you to be my wife, and by all the Virginian fighting blood that flows in my veins you shall be."

"No, John Carter, it is useless," she cried, hopelessly, "I may never be yours while Sab Than lives."

"You have sealed his death warrant, my princess—Sab Than dies."

"Nor that either," she hastened to explain. "I may not wed the man who slays my husband, even in self-defense. It is custom. We are ruled by custom upon Barsoom. It is useless, my friend. You must bear the sorrow with me. That at least we may share in common. That, and the memory of the brief days among the Tharks. You must go now, nor ever see me again. Good-bye, my chieftain that was."

Disheartened and dejected, I withdrew from the room, but I was not entirely discouraged, nor would I admit that Dejah Thoris was lost to me until the ceremony had actually been performed.

As I wandered along the corridors, I was as absolutely lost in the mazes of winding passageways as I had been before I discovered Dejah Thoris' apartments.

I knew that my only hope lay in escape from the city of Zodanga, for the matter of the four dead guardsmen would have to be explained, and as I could never reach my original post without a guide, suspicion would surely rest on me so soon as I was discovered wandering aimlessly through the palace.

Presently I came upon a spiral runway leading to a lower floor, and this I followed downward for several stories until I reached the doorway of a large apartment in which were a number of guardsmen. The walls of this room were hung with transparent tapestries behind which I secreted myself without being apprehended.

The conversation of the guardsmen was general, and awakened no interest in me until an officer entered the room and ordered four of the men to relieve the detail who were guarding the Princess of Helium. Now, I knew, my troubles would commence in earnest and indeed they were upon me all too soon, for it seemed that the squad had scarcely left the

---

[85] Dejah Thoris seems to be distinguishing between "wife" and "concubine."

guardroom before one of their number burst in again breathlessly, crying that they had found their four comrades butchered in the antechamber.

In a moment the entire palace was alive with people. Guardsmen, officers, courtiers, servants, and slaves ran helter-skelter through the corridors and apartments carrying messages and orders, and searching for signs of the assassin.

This was my opportunity and slim as it appeared I grasped it, for as a number of soldiers came hurrying past my hiding place I fell in behind them and followed through the mazes of the palace until, in passing through a great hall, I saw the blessed light of day coming in through a series of larger windows.

Here I left my guides, and, slipping to the nearest window, sought for an avenue of escape. The windows opened upon a great balcony which overlooked one of the broad avenues of Zodanga. The ground was about thirty feet below, and at a like distance from the building was a wall fully twenty feet high, constructed of polished glass about a foot in thickness. To a red Martian escape by this path would have appeared impossible, but to me, with my earthly strength and agility, it seemed already accomplished. My only fear was in being detected before darkness fell, for I could not make the leap in broad daylight while the court below and the avenue beyond were crowded with Zodangans.

Accordingly I searched for a hiding place and finally found one by accident, inside a huge hanging ornament which swung from the ceiling of the hall, and about ten feet from the floor. Into the capacious bowl-like vase I sprang with ease, and scarcely had I settled down within it than I heard a number of people enter the apartment. The group stopped beneath my hiding place and I could plainly overhear their every word.

"It is the work of Heliumites," said one of the men.

"Yes, O Jeddak, but how had they access to the palace? I could believe that even with the diligent care of your guardsmen a single enemy might reach the inner chambers, but how a force of six or eight fighting men could have done so unobserved is beyond me. We shall soon know, however, for here comes the royal psychologist."

Another man now joined the group, and, after making his formal greetings to his ruler, said:

"O mighty Jeddak, it is a strange tale I read in the dead minds of your faithful guardsmen. They were felled not by a number of fighting men, but by a single opponent."

He paused to let the full weight of this announcement impress his hearers, and that his statement was scarcely credited was evidenced by the impatient exclamation of incredulity which escaped the lips of Than Kosis.

"What manner of weird tale are you bringing me, Notan?" he cried.

"It is the truth, my Jeddak," replied the psychologist. "In fact the impressions were strongly marked on the brain of each of the four guardsmen. Their antagonist was a very tall man, wearing the metal of one of your own guardsmen, and his fighting ability was little short of marvelous for he fought fair against the entire four and vanquished them by his surpassing skill and superhuman strength and endurance. Though he wore the metal of Zodanga, my Jeddak, such a man was never seen before in this or any other country upon Barsoom.[86]

"The mind of the Princess of Helium whom I have examined and questioned was a blank to me, she has perfect control, and I could not read one iota of it. She said that she witnessed a portion of the encounter, and that when she looked there was but one man engaged with the guardsmen; a man whom she did not recognize as ever having seen."

"Where is my erstwhile savior?" spoke another of the party, and I recognized the voice of the cousin of Than Kosis, whom I had rescued from the green warriors. "By the metal of my first ancestor," he went on, "but the description fits him to perfection, especially as to his fighting ability."

"Where is this man?" cried Than Kosis. "Have him brought to me at once. What know you of him, cousin? It seemed strange to me now that I think upon it that there should have been such a fighting man in Zodanga, of whose name, even, we were ignorant before today. And his name too, John Carter, who ever heard of such a name upon Barsoom!"

Word was soon brought that I was nowhere to be found, either in the palace or at my former quarters in the barracks of the air-scout squadron. Kantos Kan, they had found and questioned, but he knew nothing of my whereabouts, and as to my past, he had told them he knew as little, since he had but recently met me during our captivity among the Warhoons.

"Keep your eyes on this other one," commanded Than Kosis. "He also is a stranger and likely as not they both hail from Helium, and where one is we shall sooner or later find the other. Quadruple the air patrol, and let

---

[86] This psychologist has the ability to read the minds of dead men—surely a first in science fiction! Seems akin to the nineteenth-century belief that the image of the murderer could be seen in, and photographed on, the eyes of the victim as a means of solving crimes. See Bill Jay's essay, "Images in the Eyes of the Dead."

every man who leaves the city by air or ground be subjected to the closest scrutiny."

Another messenger now entered with word that I was still within the palace walls.

"The likeness of every person who has entered or left the palace grounds today has been carefully examined," concluded the fellow, "and not one approaches the likeness of this new padwar of the guards, other than that which was recorded of him at the time he entered."

"Then we will have him shortly," commented Than Kosis contentedly, "and in the meanwhile we will repair to the apartments of the Princess of Helium and question her in regard to the affair. She may know more than she cared to divulge to you, Notan. Come."

They left the hall, and, as darkness had fallen without, I slipped lightly from my hiding place and hastened to the balcony. Few were in sight, and choosing a moment when none seemed near I sprang quickly to the top of the glass wall and from there to the avenue beyond the palace grounds.

Chapter XXIII
Lost in the Sky

Without effort at concealment I hastened to the vicinity of our quarters, where I felt sure I should find Kantos Kan. As I neared the building I became more careful, as I judged, and rightly, that the place would be guarded. Several men in civilian metal loitered near the front entrance and in the rear were others. My only means of reaching, unseen, the upper story where our apartments were situated was through an adjoining building, and after considerable maneuvering I managed to attain the roof of a shop several doors away.

Leaping from roof to roof, I soon reached an open window in the building where I hoped to find the Heliumite, and in another moment I stood in the room before him. He was alone and showed no surprise at my coming, saying he had expected me much earlier, as my tour of duty must have ended some time since.

I saw that he knew nothing of the events of the day at the palace, and when I had enlightened him he was all excitement. The news that Dejah Thoris had promised her hand to Sab Than filled him with dismay.

"It cannot be," he exclaimed. "It is impossible! Why no man in all Helium but would prefer death to the selling of our loved princess to the ruling house of Zodanga. She must have lost her mind to have assented to such an atrocious bargain. You, who do not know how we of Helium love the members of our ruling house, cannot appreciate the horror with which I contemplate such an unholy alliance."

"What can be done, John Carter?" he continued. "You are a resourceful man. Can you not think of some way to save Helium from this disgrace?"

"If I can come within sword's reach of Sab Than," I answered, "I can solve the difficulty in so far as Helium is concerned, but for personal reasons I would prefer that another struck the blow that frees Dejah Thoris."

Kantos Kan eyed me narrowly before he spoke.

"You love her!" he said. "Does she know it?"

"She knows it, Kantos Kan, and repulses me only because she is promised to Sab Than."

The splendid fellow sprang to his feet, and grasping me by the shoulder raised his sword on high, exclaiming:

"And had the choice been left to me I could not have chosen a more fitting mate for the first princess of Barsoom. Here is my hand upon your shoulder, John Carter, and my word that Sab Than shall go out at the point of my sword for the sake of my love for Helium, for Dejah Thoris, and for you. This very night I shall try to reach his quarters in the palace."

"How?" I asked. "You are strongly guarded and a quadruple force patrols the sky."

He bent his head in thought a moment, then raised it with an air of confidence.

"I only need to pass these guards and I can do it," he said at last. "I know a secret entrance to the palace through the pinnacle of the highest tower. I fell upon it by chance one day as I was passing above the palace on patrol duty. In this work it is required that we investigate any unusual occurrence we may witness, and a face peering from the pinnacle of the high tower of the palace was, to me, most unusual. I therefore drew near and discovered that the possessor of the peering face was none other than Sab Than. He was slightly put out at being detected and commanded me to keep the matter to myself, explaining that the passage from the tower led directly to his apartments, and was known only to him. If I can reach the roof of the barracks and get my machine I can be in Sab Than's quarters in five minutes; but how am I to escape from this building, guarded as you say it is?"

"How well are the machine sheds at the barracks guarded?" I asked.

"There is usually but one man on duty there at night upon the roof."

"Go to the roof of this building, Kantos Kan, and wait me there."

Without stopping to explain my plans I retraced my way to the street and hastened to the barracks. I did not dare to enter the building, filled as it was with members of the air-scout squadron, who, in common with all Zodanga, were on the lookout for me.

The building was an enormous one, rearing its lofty head fully a thousand feet into the air. But few buildings in Zodanga were higher than these barracks, though several topped it by a few hundred feet; the docks of the great battleships of the line standing some fifteen hundred feet from the ground, while the freight and passenger stations of the merchant squadrons rose nearly as high.

It was a long climb up the face of the building, and one fraught with much danger, but there was no other way, and so I essayed the task. The fact that Barsoomian architecture is extremely ornate made the feat much simpler than I had anticipated, since I found ornamental ledges and projections which fairly formed a perfect ladder for me all the way to the eaves of the building. Here I met my first real obstacle. The eaves projected nearly twenty feet from the wall to which I clung, and though I encircled the great building I could find no opening through them.

The top floor was alight, and filled with soldiers engaged in the pastimes of their kind; I could not, therefore, reach the roof through the building.

There was one slight, desperate chance, and that I decided I must take—it was for Dejah Thoris, and no man has lived who would not risk a thousand deaths for such as she.

Clinging to the wall with my feet and one hand, I unloosened one of the long leather straps of my trappings at the end of which dangled a great hook by which air sailors are hung to the sides and bottoms of their craft for various purposes of repair, and by means of which landing parties are lowered to the ground from the battleships.

I swung this hook cautiously to the roof several times before it finally found lodgment; gently I pulled on it to strengthen its hold, but whether it would bear the weight of my body I did not know. It might be barely caught upon the very outer verge of the roof, so that as my body swung out at the end of the strap it would slip off and launch me to the pavement a thousand feet below.

An instant I hesitated, and then, releasing my grasp upon the supporting ornament, I swung out into space at the end of the strap. Far below me lay the brilliantly lighted streets, the hard pavements, and death. There was a little jerk at the top of the supporting eaves, and a nasty slipping, grating sound which turned me cold with apprehension; then the hook caught and I was safe.

Clambering quickly aloft I grasped the edge of the eaves and drew myself to the surface of the roof above. As I gained my feet I was confronted by the sentry on duty, into the muzzle of whose revolver I found myself looking.

"Who are you and whence came you?" he cried.

"I am an air scout, friend, and very near a dead one, for just by the merest chance I escaped falling to the avenue below," I replied.

"But how came you upon the roof, man? No one has landed or come up from the building for the past hour. Quick, explain yourself, or I call the guard."

"Look you here, sentry, and you shall see how I came and how close a shave I had to not coming at all," I answered, turning toward the edge of the roof, where, twenty feet below, at the end of my strap, hung all my weapons.

The fellow, acting on impulse of curiosity, stepped to my side and to his undoing, for as he leaned to peer over the eaves I grasped him by his throat and his pistol arm and threw him heavily to the roof. The weapon dropped from his grasp, and my fingers choked off his attempted cry for assistance. I gagged and bound him and then hung him over the edge of the roof as I myself had hung a few moments before. I knew it would be morning before he would be discovered, and I needed all the time that I could gain.

Donning my trappings and weapons I hastened to the sheds, and soon had out both my machine and Kantos Kan's. Making his fast behind mine I started my engine, and skimming over the edge of the roof I dove down into the streets of the city far below the plane usually occupied by the air patrol. In less than a minute I was settling safely upon the roof of our apartment beside the astonished Kantos Kan.[87]

I lost no time in explanation, but plunged immediately into a discussion of our plans for the immediate future. It was decided that I was to try to make Helium while Kantos Kan was to enter the palace and dispatch Sab Than. If successful he was then to follow me. He set my compass for me, a clever little device which will remain steadfastly fixed upon any given point on the surface of Barsoom, and bidding each other farewell we rose together and sped in the direction of the palace which lay in the route which I must take to reach Helium.[88]

As we neared the high tower a patrol shot down from above, throwing its piercing searchlight full upon my craft, and a voice roared out a command to halt, following with a shot as I paid no attention to his hail. Kantos Kan dropped quickly into the darkness, while I rose steadily and at terrific speed raced through the Martian sky followed by a dozen of the air-scout craft which had joined the pursuit, and later by a swift cruiser carrying a hundred men and a battery of rapid-fire guns. By twisting and turning my little machine, now rising and now falling, I managed to elude their search-lights most of the time, but I was also losing ground by these tactics, and so I decided to hazard everything on a straight-away course and leave the result to fate and the speed of my machine.

Kantos Kan had shown me a trick of gearing, which is known only to the navy of Helium, that greatly increased the speed of our machines, so

---

[87] One of the most exciting and fast-paced parts of the book—these flying scenes are a kind of 1912 version of the extraordinary dogfights at the end of *Star Wars* (1977).

[88] This sounds somewhat like Global Positioning System technology (GPS) begun in the 1970s on Earth and now a standard part of automobile navigation.

that I felt sure I could distance my pursuers if I could dodge their projectiles for a few moments.

As I sped through the air the screeching of the bullets around me convinced me that only by a miracle could I escape, but the die was cast, and throwing on full speed I raced a straight course toward Helium.[89] Gradually I left my pursuers further and further behind, and I was just congratulating myself on my lucky escape, when a well-directed shot from the cruiser exploded at the prow of my little craft. The concussion nearly capsized her, and with a sickening plunge she hurtled downward through the dark night.

How far I fell before I regained control of the plane I do not know, but I must have been very close to the ground when I started to rise again, as I plainly heard the squealing of animals below me. Rising again I scanned the heavens for my pursuers, and finally making out their lights far behind me, saw that they were landing, evidently in search of me.

Not until their lights were no longer discernible did I venture to flash my little lamp upon my compass, and then I found to my consternation that a fragment of the projectile had utterly destroyed my only guide, as well as my speedometer. It was true I could follow the stars in the general direction of Helium, but without knowing the exact location of the city or the speed at which I was traveling my chances for finding it were slim.

Helium lies a thousand miles southwest of Zodanga, and with my compass intact I should have made the trip, barring accidents, in between four and five hours. As it turned out, however, morning found me speeding over a vast expanse of dead sea bottom after nearly six hours of continuous flight at high speed. Presently a great city showed below me, but it was not Helium, as that alone of all Barsoomian metropolises consists in two immense circular walled cities about seventy-five miles apart and would have been easily distinguishable from the altitude at which I was flying.

Believing that I had come too far to the north and west, I turned back in a southeasterly direction, passing during the forenoon several other large cities, but none resembling the description which Kantos Kan had given me of Helium. In addition to the twin-city formation of Helium, another distinguishing feature is the two immense towers, one of vivid

---

[89] Surely Burroughs has in mind Julius Caesar crossing the River Rubicon, where the Roman historian Suetonius attributes him with delivering one of the most famous lines in all of Latin literature, known to any schoolboy of the nineteenth century: "*alea iacta est*" ("the die is cast"). See Suetonuis's *The Twelve Caesars*.

scarlet rising nearly a mile into the air from the center of one of the cities, while the other, of bright yellow and of the same height, marks her sister.

CHAPTER XXIV
TARS TARKAS FINDS A FRIEND

About noon I passed low over a great dead city of ancient Mars, and as I skimmed out across the plain beyond I came full upon several thousand green warriors engaged in a terrific battle. Scarcely had I seen them than a volley of shots was directed at me, and with the almost unfailing accuracy of their aim my little craft was instantly a ruined wreck, sinking erratically to the ground.

I fell almost directly in the center of the fierce combat, among warriors who had not seen my approach so busily were they engaged in life and death struggles. The men were fighting on foot with long-swords, while an occasional shot from a sharpshooter on the outskirts of the conflict would bring down a warrior who might for an instant separate himself from the entangled mass.

As my machine sank among them I realized that it was fight or die, with good chances of dying in any event, and so I struck the ground with drawn long-sword ready to defend myself as I could.

I fell beside a huge monster who was engaged with three antagonists, and as I glanced at his fierce face, filled with the light of battle, I recognized Tars Tarkas the Thark. He did not see me, as I was a trifle behind him, and just then the three warriors opposing him, and whom I recognized as Warhoons, charged simultaneously. The mighty fellow made quick work of one of them, but in stepping back for another thrust he fell over a dead body behind him and was down and at the mercy of his foes in an instant. Quick as lightning they were upon him, and Tars Tarkas would have been gathered to his fathers in short order had I not sprung before his prostrate form and engaged his adversaries. I had accounted for one of them when the mighty Thark regained his feet and quickly settled the other.

He gave me one look, and a slight smile touched his grim lip as, touching my shoulder, he said,

"I would scarcely recognize you, John Carter, but there is no other mortal upon Barsoom who would have done what you have for me. I think I have learned that there is such a thing as friendship, my friend."

He said no more, nor was there opportunity, for the Warhoons were closing in about us, and together we fought, shoulder to shoulder, during all that long, hot afternoon, until the tide of battle turned and the remnant of the fierce Warhoon horde fell back upon their thoats, and fled into the gathering darkness.

Ten thousand men had been engaged in that titanic struggle, and upon the field of battle lay three thousand dead. Neither side asked or gave quarter, nor did they attempt to take prisoners.

On our return to the city after the battle we had gone directly to Tars Tarkas' quarters, where I was left alone while the chieftain attended the customary council which immediately follows an engagement.

As I sat awaiting the return of the green warrior I heard something move in an adjoining apartment, and as I glanced up there rushed suddenly upon me a huge and hideous creature which bore me backward upon the pile of silks and furs upon which I had been reclining. It was Woola—faithful, loving Woola. He had found his way back to Thark and, as Tars Tarkas later told me, had gone immediately to my former quarters where he had taken up his pathetic and seemingly hopeless watch for my return.

"Tal Hajus knows that you are here, John Carter," said Tars Tarkas, on his return from the jeddak's quarters; "Sarkoja saw and recognized you as we were returning. Tal Hajus has ordered me to bring you before him tonight. I have ten thoats, John Carter; you may take your choice from among them, and I will accompany you to the nearest waterway that leads to Helium. Tars Tarkas may be a cruel green warrior, but he can be a friend as well. Come, we must start."

"And when you return, Tars Tarkas?" I asked.

"The wild calots, possibly, or worse," he replied. "Unless I should chance to have the opportunity I have so long waited of battling with Tal Hajus."

"We will stay, Tars Tarkas, and see Tal Hajus tonight. You shall not sacrifice yourself, and it may be that tonight you can have the chance you wait."

He objected strenuously, saying that Tal Hajus often flew into wild fits of passion at the mere thought of the blow I had dealt him, and that if ever he laid his hands upon me I would be subjected to the most horrible tortures.

While we were eating I repeated to Tars Tarkas the story which Sola had told me that night upon the sea bottom during the march to Thark.

He said but little, but the great muscles of his face worked in passion and in agony at recollection of the horrors which had been heaped upon the only thing he had ever loved in all his cold, cruel, terrible existence.

He no longer demurred when I suggested that we go before Tal Hajus, only saying that he would like to speak to Sarkoja first. At his request I accompanied him to her quarters, and the look of venomous hatred she cast upon me was almost adequate recompense for any future misfortunes this accidental return to Thark might bring me.

"Sarkoja," said Tars Tarkas, "forty years ago you were instrumental in bringing about the torture and death of a woman named Gozava. I have just discovered that the warrior who loved that woman has learned of your part in the transaction. He may not kill you, Sarkoja, it is not our custom, but there is nothing to prevent him tying one end of a strap about your neck and the other end to a wild thoat, merely to test your fitness to survive and help perpetuate our race. Having heard that he would do this on the morrow, I thought it only right to warn you, for I am a just man. The river Iss is but a short pilgrimage, Sarkoja. Come, John Carter."

The next morning Sarkoja was gone, nor was she ever seen after.

In silence we hastened to the jeddak's palace, where we were immediately admitted to his presence; in fact, he could scarcely wait to see me and was standing erect upon his platform glowering at the entrance as I came in.

"Strap him to that pillar," he shrieked. "We shall see who it is dares strike the mighty Tal Hajus. Heat the irons; with my own hands I shall burn the eyes from his head that he may not pollute my person with his vile gaze."

"Chieftains of Thark," I cried, turning to the assembled council and ignoring Tal Hajus, "I have been a chief among you, and today I have fought for Thark shoulder to shoulder with her greatest warrior. You owe me, at least, a hearing. I have won that much today. You claim to be just people—"

"Silence," roared Tal Hajus. "Gag the creature and bind him as I command."

"Justice, Tal Hajus," exclaimed Lorquas Ptomel. "Who are you to set aside the customs of ages among the Tharks."

"Yes, justice!" echoed a dozen voices, and so, while Tal Hajus fumed and frothed, I continued.

"You are a brave people and you love bravery, but where was your mighty jeddak during the fighting today? I did not see him in the thick of battle; he was not there. He rends defenseless women and little children in his lair, but how recently has one of you seen him fight with men? Why, even I, a midget beside him, felled him with a single blow of my fist. Is it of such that the Tharks fashion their jeddaks? There stands beside me now a great Thark, a mighty warrior and a noble man. Chieftains, how sounds, Tars Tarkas, Jeddak of Thark?"

A roar of deep-toned applause greeted this suggestion.

"It but remains for this council to command, and Tal Hajus must prove his fitness to rule. Were he a brave man he would invite Tars Tarkas to combat, for he does not love him, but Tal Hajus is afraid; Tal Hajus, your jeddak, is a coward. With my bare hands I could kill him, and he knows it."

After I ceased there was tense silence, as all eyes were riveted upon Tal Hajus. He did not speak or move, but the blotchy green of his countenance turned livid, and the froth froze upon his lips.

"Tal Hajus," said Lorquas Ptomel in a cold, hard voice, "never in my long life have I seen a jeddak of the Tharks so humiliated. There could be but one answer to this arraignment. We wait it." And still Tal Hajus stood as though electrified.

"Chieftains," continued Lorquas Ptomel, "shall the jeddak, Tal Hajus, prove his fitness to rule over Tars Tarkas?"

There were twenty chieftains about the rostrum, and twenty swords flashed high in assent.

There was no alternative. That decree was final, and so Tal Hajus drew his long-sword and advanced to meet Tars Tarkas.

The combat was soon over, and, with his foot upon the neck of the dead monster, Tars Tarkas became jeddak among the Tharks.

His first act was to make me a full-fledged chieftain with the rank I had won by my combats the first few weeks of my captivity among them.

Seeing the favorable disposition of the warriors toward Tars Tarkas, as well as toward me, I grasped the opportunity to enlist them in my cause against Zodanga. I told Tars Tarkas the story of my adventures, and in a few words had explained to him the thought I had in mind.

"John Carter has made a proposal," he said, addressing the council, "which meets with my sanction. I shall put it to you briefly. Dejah Thoris, the Princess of Helium, who was our prisoner, is now held by the jeddak of Zodanga, whose son she must wed to save her country from devastation at the hands of the Zodangan forces.

"John Carter suggests that we rescue her and return her to Helium. The loot of Zodanga would be magnificent, and I have often thought that had we an alliance with the people of Helium we could obtain sufficient assurance of sustenance to permit us to increase the size and frequency of our hatchings, and thus become unquestionably supreme among the green men of all Barsoom. What say you?"

It was a chance to fight, an opportunity to loot, and they rose to the bait as a speckled trout to a fly.

For Tharks they were wildly enthusiastic, and before another half hour had passed twenty mounted messengers were speeding across dead sea bottoms to call the hordes together for the expedition.

In three days we were on the march toward Zodanga, one hundred thousand strong, as Tars Tarkas had been able to enlist the services of three smaller hordes on the promise of the great loot of Zodanga.

At the head of the column I rode beside the great Thark while at the heels of my mount trotted my beloved Woola.

We traveled entirely by night, timing our marches so that we camped during the day at deserted cities where, even to the beasts, we were all kept indoors during the daylight hours. On the march Tars Tarkas, through his remarkable ability and statesmanship, enlisted fifty thousand more warriors from various hordes, so that, ten days after we set out we halted at midnight outside the great walled city of Zodanga, one hundred and fifty thousand strong.

The fighting strength and efficiency of this horde of ferocious green monsters was equivalent to ten times their number of red men. Never in the history of Barsoom, Tars Tarkas told me, had such a force of green warriors marched to battle together. It was a monstrous task to keep even a semblance of harmony among them, and it was a marvel to me that he got them to the city without a mighty battle among themselves.[90]

But as we neared Zodanga their personal quarrels were submerged by their greater hatred for the red men, and especially for the Zodangans, who had for years waged a ruthless campaign of extermination against the green men, directing special attention toward despoiling their incubators.

Now that we were before Zodanga the task of obtaining entry to the city devolved upon me, and directing Tars Tarkas to hold his forces in two divisions out of earshot of the city, with each division opposite a large gateway, I took twenty dismounted warriors and approached one of the small gates that pierced the walls at short intervals. These gates have no regular guard, but are covered by sentries, who patrol the avenue that

---

[90] This episode recalls the alliance of the various Greek tribes in their combined assault on Troy in the *Iliad*. The actual destruction of Troy is not described in the *Iliad*, but is the subject of the opening of Virgil's *Aeneid*.

encircles the city just within the walls as our metropolitan police patrol their beats.

The walls of Zodanga are seventy-five feet in height and fifty feet thick. They are built of enormous blocks of carborundum, and the task of entering the city seemed, to my escort of green warriors, an impossibility. The fellows who had been detailed to accompany me were of one of the smaller hordes, and therefore did not know me.

Placing three of them with their faces to the wall and arms locked, I commanded two more to mount to their shoulders, and a sixth I ordered to climb upon the shoulders of the upper two. The head of the topmost warrior towered over forty feet from the ground.

In this way, with ten warriors, I built a series of three steps from the ground to the shoulders of the topmost man. Then starting from a short distance behind them I ran swiftly up from one tier to the next, and with a final bound from the broad shoulders of the highest I clutched the top of the great wall and quietly drew myself to its broad expanse. After me I dragged six lengths of leather from an equal number of my warriors. These lengths we had previously fastened together, and passing one end to the topmost warrior I lowered the other end cautiously over the opposite side of the wall toward the avenue below. No one was in sight, so, lowering myself to the end of my leather strap, I dropped the remaining thirty feet to the pavement below.

I had learned from Kantos Kan the secret of opening these gates, and in another moment my twenty great fighting men stood within the doomed city of Zodanga.

I found to my delight that I had entered at the lower boundary of the enormous palace grounds. The building itself showed in the distance a blaze of glorious light, and on the instant I determined to lead a detachment of warriors directly within the palace itself, while the balance of the great horde was attacking the barracks of the soldiery.

Dispatching one of my men to Tars Tarkas for a detail of fifty Tharks, with word of my intentions, I ordered ten warriors to capture and open one of the great gates while with the nine remaining I took the other. We were to do our work quietly, no shots were to be fired and no general advance made until I had reached the palace with my fifty Tharks. Our plans worked to perfection. The two sentries we met were dispatched to their fathers upon the banks of the lost sea of Korus, and the guards at both gates followed them in silence.

CHAPTER XXV
THE LOOTING OF ZODANGA

As the great gate where I stood swung open my fifty Tharks, headed by Tars Tarkas himself, rode in upon their mighty thoats. I led them to the palace walls, which I negotiated easily without assistance. Once inside, however, the gate gave me considerable trouble, but I finally was rewarded by seeing it swing upon its huge hinges, and soon my fierce escort was riding across the gardens of the jeddak of Zodanga.

As we approached the palace I could see through the great windows of the first floor into the brilliantly illuminated audience chamber of Than Kosis. The immense hall was crowded with nobles and their women, as though some important function was in progress. There was not a guard in sight without the palace, due, I presume, to the fact that the city and palace walls were considered impregnable, and so I came close and peered within.

At one end of the chamber, upon massive golden thrones encrusted with diamonds, sat Than Kosis and his consort, surrounded by officers and dignitaries of state. Before them stretched a broad aisle lined on either side with soldiery, and as I looked there entered this aisle at the far end of the hall, the head of a procession which advanced to the foot of the throne.

First there marched four officers of the jeddak's Guard bearing a huge salver on which reposed, upon a cushion of scarlet silk, a great golden chain with a collar and padlock at each end. Directly behind these officers came four others carrying a similar salver which supported the magnificent ornaments of a prince and princess of the reigning house of Zodanga.

At the foot of the throne these two parties separated and halted, facing each other at opposite sides of the aisle. Then came more dignitaries, and the officers of the palace and of the army, and finally two figures entirely muffled in scarlet silk, so that not a feature of either was discernible. These two stopped at the foot of the throne, facing Than Kosis. When the balance of the procession had entered and assumed their stations Than Kosis addressed the couple standing before him. I could not hear his words, but presently two officers advanced and removed the scarlet robe from one of the figures, and I saw that Kantos Kan had failed in his mission, for it was Sab Than, Prince of Zodanga, who stood revealed before me.

Than Kosis now took a set of the ornaments from one of the salvers and placed one of the collars of gold about his son's neck, springing the padlock fast. After a few more words addressed to Sab Than he turned to the other figure, from which the officers now removed the enshrouding silks, disclosing to my now comprehending view Dejah Thoris, Princess of Helium.

The object of the ceremony was clear to me; in another moment Dejah Thoris would be joined forever to the Prince of Zodanga. It was an impressive and beautiful ceremony, I presume, but to me it seemed the most fiendish sight I had ever witnessed, and as the ornaments were adjusted upon her beautiful figure and her collar of gold swung open in the hands of Than Kosis I raised my long-sword above my head, and, with the heavy hilt, I shattered the glass of the great window and sprang into the midst of the astonished assemblage. With a bound I was on the steps of the platform beside Than Kosis, and as he stood riveted with surprise I brought my long-sword down upon the golden chain that would have bound Dejah Thoris to another.

In an instant all was confusion; a thousand drawn swords menaced me from every quarter, and Sab Than sprang upon me with a jeweled dagger he had drawn from his nuptial ornaments. I could have killed him as easily as I might a fly, but the age-old custom of Barsoom stayed my hand, and grasping his wrist as the dagger flew toward my heart I held him as though in a vise and with my long-sword pointed to the far end of the hall.[91]

"Zodanga has fallen," I cried. "Look!"

All eyes turned in the direction I had indicated, and there, forging through the portals of the entranceway rode Tars Tarkas and his fifty warriors on their great thoats.

A cry of alarm and amazement broke from the assemblage, but no word of fear, and in a moment the soldiers and nobles of Zodanga were hurling themselves upon the advancing Tharks.

Thrusting Sab Than headlong from the platform, I drew Dejah Thoris to my side. Behind the throne was a narrow doorway and in this Than Kosis now stood facing me, with drawn long-sword. In an instant we were engaged, and I found no mean antagonist.

As we circled upon the broad platform I saw Sab Than rushing up the steps to aid his father, but, as he raised his hand to strike, Dejah Thoris sprang before him and then my sword found the spot that made Sab Than

---

[91] The battle scene here recalls the triumphant return of Odysseus to Ithaka and his relatively effortless slaughter of Penelope's suitors in the *Odyssey*.

jeddak of Zodanga. As his father rolled dead upon the floor the new jeddak tore himself free from Dejah Thoris' grasp, and again we faced each other. He was soon joined by a quartet of officers, and, with my back against a golden throne, I fought once again for Dejah Thoris. I was hard pressed to defend myself and yet not strike down Sab Than and, with him, my last chance to win the woman I loved. My blade was swinging with the rapidity of lightning as I sought to parry the thrusts and cuts of my opponents. Two I had disarmed, and one was down, when several more rushed to the aid of their new ruler, and to avenge the death of the old.

As they advanced there were cries of "The woman! The woman! Strike her down; it is her plot. Kill her! Kill her!"

Calling to Dejah Thoris to get behind me I worked my way toward the little doorway back of the throne, but the officers realized my intentions, and three of them sprang in behind me and blocked my chances for gaining a position where I could have defended Dejah Thoris against any army of swordsmen.

The Tharks were having their hands full in the center of the room, and I began to realize that nothing short of a miracle could save Dejah Thoris and myself, when I saw Tars Tarkas surging through the crowd of pygmies that swarmed about him. With one swing of his mighty longsword he laid a dozen corpses at his feet, and so he hewed a pathway before him until in another moment he stood upon the platform beside me, dealing death and destruction right and left.

The bravery of the Zodangans was awe-inspiring, not one attempted to escape, and when the fighting ceased it was because only Tharks remained alive in the great hall, other than Dejah Thoris and myself.

Sab Than lay dead beside his father, and the corpses of the flower of Zodangan nobility and chivalry covered the floor of the bloody shambles.

My first thought when the battle was over was for Kantos Kan, and leaving Dejah Thoris in charge of Tars Tarkas I took a dozen warriors and hastened to the dungeons beneath the palace. The jailers had all left to join the fighters in the throne room, so we searched the labyrinthine prison without opposition.

I called Kantos Kan's name aloud in each new corridor and compartment, and finally I was rewarded by hearing a faint response. Guided by the sound, we soon found him helpless in a dark recess.

He was overjoyed at seeing me, and to know the meaning of the fight, faint echoes of which had reached his prison cell. He told me that the air patrol had captured him before he reached the high tower of the palace, so that he had not even seen Sab Than.

We discovered that it would be futile to attempt to cut away the bars and chains which held him prisoner, so, at his suggestion I returned to search the bodies on the floor above for keys to open the padlocks of his cell and of his chains.

Fortunately among the first I examined I found his jailer, and soon we had Kantos Kan with us in the throne room.

The sounds of heavy firing, mingled with shouts and cries, came to us from the city's streets, and Tars Tarkas hastened away to direct the fighting without. Kantos Kan accompanied him to act as guide, the green warriors commencing a thorough search of the palace for other Zodangans and for loot, and Dejah Thoris and I were left alone.

She had sunk into one of the golden thrones, and as I turned to her she greeted me with a wan smile.

"Was there ever such a man!" she exclaimed. "I know that Barsoom has never before seen your like. Can it be that all Earth men are as you? Alone, a stranger, hunted, threatened, persecuted, you have done in a few short months what in all the past ages of Barsoom no man has ever done: joined together the wild hordes of the sea bottoms and brought them to fight as allies of a red Martian people."

"The answer is easy, Dejah Thoris," I replied smiling. "It was not I who did it, it was love, love for Dejah Thoris, a power that would work greater miracles than this you have seen."[92]

A pretty flush overspread her face and she answered,

"You may say that now, John Carter, and I may listen, for I am free."

"And more still I have to say, ere it is again too late," I returned. "I have done many strange things in my life, many things that wiser men would not have dared, but never in my wildest fancies have I dreamed of winning a Dejah Thoris for myself—for never had I dreamed that in all the universe dwelt such a woman as the Princess of Helium. That you are a princess does not abash me, but that you are you is enough to make me doubt my sanity as I ask you, my princess, to be mine."

"He does not need to be abashed who so well knew the answer to his plea before the plea were made," she replied, rising and placing her dear hands upon my shoulders, and so I took her in my arms and kissed her.

---

[92] Here we have an exposition of the Ovidian principle of *amor vincit omnia*, or "love conquers all."

And thus in the midst of a city of wild conflict, filled with the alarms of war; with death and destruction reaping their terrible harvest around her, did Dejah Thoris, Princess of Helium, true daughter of Mars, the God of War, promise herself in marriage to John Carter, Gentleman of Virginia.

Chapter XXVI
Through Carnage to Joy

Sometime later Tars Tarkas and Kantos Kan returned to report that Zodanga had been completely reduced. Her forces were entirely destroyed or captured, and no further resistance was to be expected from within. Several battleships had escaped, but there were thousands of war and merchant vessels under guard of Thark warriors.

The lesser hordes had commenced looting and quarreling among themselves, so it was decided that we collect what warriors we could, man as many vessels as possible with Zodangan prisoners and make for Helium without further loss of time.[93]

Five hours later we sailed from the roofs of the dock buildings with a fleet of two hundred and fifty battleships, carrying nearly one hundred thousand green warriors, followed by a fleet of transports with our thoats.

Behind us we left the stricken city in the fierce and brutal clutches of some forty thousand green warriors of the lesser hordes. They were looting, murdering, and fighting amongst themselves. In a hundred places they had applied the torch, and columns of dense smoke were rising above the city as though to blot out from the eye of heaven the horrid sights beneath.

In the middle of the afternoon we sighted the scarlet and yellow towers of Helium, and a short time later a great fleet of Zodangan battleships rose from the camps of the besiegers without the city, and advanced to meet us.

The banners of Helium had been strung from stem to stern of each of our mighty craft, but the Zodangans did not need this sign to realize that we were enemies, for our green Martian warriors had opened fire upon them almost as they left the ground. With their uncanny marksmanship they raked the on-coming fleet with volley after volley.

The twin cities of Helium, perceiving that we were friends, sent out hundreds of vessels to aid us, and then began the first real air battle I had ever witnessed.

The vessels carrying our green warriors were kept circling above the contending fleets of Helium and Zodanga, since their batteries were useless in the hands of the Tharks who, having no navy, have no skill in naval gunnery. Their small-arm fire, however, was most effective, and the

---

[93] The ransacking and pillage of Zondanga seems inspired by the descriptions of the collapse of Ilium (Troy) in the wake of the Greek invasion in the *Aeneid*.

final outcome of the engagement was strongly influenced, if not wholly determined, by their presence.

At first the two forces circled at the same altitude, pouring broadside after broadside into each other. Presently a great hole was torn in the hull of one of the immense battle craft from the Zodangan camp; with a lurch she turned completely over, the little figures of her crew plunging, turning and twisting toward the ground a thousand feet below; then with sickening velocity she tore after them, almost completely burying herself in the soft loam of the ancient sea bottom.[94]

A wild cry of exultation arose from the Heliumite squadron, and with redoubled ferocity they fell upon the Zodangan fleet. By a pretty maneuver two of the vessels of Helium gained a position above their adversaries, from which they poured upon them from their keel bomb batteries a perfect torrent of exploding bombs.

Then, one by one, the battleships of Helium succeeded in rising above the Zodangans, and in a short time a number of the beleaguering battleships were drifting hopeless wrecks toward the high scarlet tower of greater Helium. Several others attempted to escape, but they were soon surrounded by thousands of tiny individual fliers, and above each hung a monster battleship of Helium ready to drop boarding parties upon their decks.

Within but little more than an hour from the moment the victorious Zodangan squadron had risen to meet us from the camp of the besiegers the battle was over, and the remaining vessels of the conquered Zodangans were headed toward the cities of Helium under prize crews.

There was an extremely pathetic side to the surrender of these mighty fliers, the result of an age-old custom which demanded that surrender should be signalized by the voluntary plunging to earth of the commander of the vanquished vessel. One after another the brave fellows, holding their colors high above their heads, leaped from the towering bows of their mighty craft to an awful death.

Not until the commander of the entire fleet took the fearful plunge, thus indicating the surrender of the remaining vessels, did the fighting cease, and the useless sacrifice of brave men come to an end.

We now signaled the flagship of Helium's navy to approach, and when she was within hailing distance I called out that we had the Princess Dejah

---

[94] Though Burroughs claimed not to have read H.G. Wells, it is difficult to imagine that *The War in the Air* was in not some way a predecessor of this colossal air battle on Mars.

Thoris on board, and that we wished to transfer her to the flagship that she might be taken immediately to the city.

As the full import of my announcement bore in upon them a great cry arose from the decks of the flagship, and a moment later the colors of the Princess of Helium broke from a hundred points upon her upper works. When the other vessels of the squadron caught the meaning of the signals flashed them they took up the wild acclaim and unfurled her colors in the gleaming sunlight.

The flagship bore down upon us, and as she swung gracefully to and touched our side a dozen officers sprang upon our decks. As their astonished gaze fell upon the hundreds of green warriors, who now came forth from the fighting shelters, they stopped aghast, but at sight of Kantos Kan, who advanced to meet them, they came forward, crowding about him.

Dejah Thoris and I then advanced, and they had no eyes for other than her. She received them gracefully, calling each by name, for they were men high in the esteem and service of her grandfather, and she knew them well.

"Lay your hands upon the shoulder of John Carter," she said to them, turning toward me, "the man to whom Helium owes her princess as well as her victory today."

They were very courteous to me and said many kind and complimentary things, but what seemed to impress them most was that I had won the aid of the fierce Tharks in my campaign for the liberation of Dejah Thoris, and the relief of Helium.

"You owe your thanks more to another man than to me," I said, "and here he is; meet one of Barsoom's greatest soldiers and statesmen, Tars Tarkas, Jeddak of Thark."

With the same polished courtesy that had marked their manner toward me they extended their greetings to the great Thark, nor, to my surprise, was he much behind them in ease of bearing or in courtly speech. Though not a garrulous race, the Tharks are extremely formal, and their ways lend themselves amazingly well to dignified and courtly manners.

Dejah Thoris went aboard the flagship, and was much put out that I would not follow, but, as I explained to her, the battle was but partly won; we still had the land forces of the besieging Zodangans to account for, and I would not leave Tars Tarkas until that had been accomplished.

The commander of the naval forces of Helium promised to arrange to have the armies of Helium attack from the city in conjunction with our land attack, and so the vessels separated and Dejah Thoris was borne in triumph back to the court of her grandfather, Tardos Mors, Jeddak of Helium.

In the distance lay our fleet of transports, with the thoats of the green warriors, where they had remained during the battle. Without landing stages it was to be a difficult matter to unload these beasts upon the open plain, but there was nothing else for it, and so we put out for a point about ten miles from the city and began the task.

It was necessary to lower the animals to the ground in slings and this work occupied the remainder of the day and half the night. Twice we were attacked by parties of Zodangan cavalry, but with little loss, however, and after darkness shut down they withdrew.

As soon as the last thoat was unloaded Tars Tarkas gave the command to advance, and in three parties we crept upon the Zodangan camp from the north, the south and the east.

About a mile from the main camp we encountered their outposts and, as had been prearranged, accepted this as the signal to charge. With wild, ferocious cries and amidst the nasty squealing of battle-enraged thoats we bore down upon the Zodangans.

We did not catch them napping, but found a well-entrenched battle line confronting us. Time after time we were repulsed until, toward noon, I began to fear for the result of the battle.

The Zodangans numbered nearly a million fighting men, gathered from pole to pole, wherever stretched their ribbon-like waterways, while pitted against them were less than a hundred thousand green warriors. The forces from Helium had not arrived, nor could we receive any word from them.[95]

Just at noon we heard heavy firing all along the line between the Zodangans and the cities, and we knew then that our much-needed reinforcements had come.

---

[95] Zodangans outnumber the Tharks ten to one, a ratio typical of the U.S. Army conflicts with Native Americans in the late nineteenth century. Burroughs himself had been a private in the Seventh Cavalry in 1896 (the same regiment that suffered ignominious defeat twenty tears earlier under the dubious leadership of George Custer at Little Big Horn, Montana), and was aware of the fact that a small number of disciplined, well-trained cavalry were capable of routing a more numerous force (Custer's failure at Little Big Horn notwithstanding). From his classical studies, Burroughs also had many examples of a small but determined force defeating an enemy with superior numbers.

Again Tars Tarkas ordered the charge, and once more the mighty thoats bore their terrible riders against the ramparts of the enemy. At the same moment the battle line of Helium surged over the opposite breastworks of the Zodangans and in another moment they were being crushed as between two millstones. Nobly they fought, but in vain.

The plain before the city became a veritable shambles ere the last Zodangan surrendered, but finally the carnage ceased, the prisoners were marched back to Helium, and we entered the greater city's gates, a huge triumphal procession of conquering heroes.

The broad avenues were lined with women and children, among which were the few men whose duties necessitated that they remain within the city during the battle. We were greeted with an endless round of applause and showered with ornaments of gold, platinum, silver, and precious jewels. The city had gone mad with joy.

My fierce Tharks caused the wildest excitement and enthusiasm. Never before had an armed body of green warriors entered the gates of Helium, and that they came now as friends and allies filled the red men with rejoicing.

That my poor services to Dejah Thoris had become known to the Heliumites was evidenced by the loud crying of my name, and by the loads of ornaments that were fastened upon me and my huge thoat as we passed up the avenues to the palace, for even in the face of the ferocious appearance of Woola the populace pressed close about me.

As we approached this magnificent pile we were met by a party of officers who greeted us warmly and requested that Tars Tarkas and his jeds with the jeddaks and jeds of his wild allies, together with myself, dismount and accompany them to receive from Tardos Mors an expression of his gratitude for our services.

At the top of the great steps leading up to the main portals of the palace stood the royal party, and as we reached the lower steps one of their number descended to meet us.

He was an almost perfect specimen of manhood; tall, straight as an arrow, superbly muscled and with the carriage and bearing of a ruler of men. I did not need to be told that he was Tardos Mors, Jeddak of Helium.

The first member of our party he met was Tars Tarkas and his first words sealed forever the new friendship between the races.

"That Tardos Mors," he said, earnestly, "may meet the greatest living warrior of Barsoom is a priceless honor, but that he may lay his hand on the shoulder of a friend and ally is a far greater boon."

"Jeddak of Helium," returned Tars Tarkas, "it has remained for a man of another world to teach the green warriors of Barsoom the meaning of friendship; to him we owe the fact that the hordes of Thark can understand you; that they can appreciate and reciprocate the sentiments so graciously expressed."

Tardos Mors then greeted each of the green jeddaks and jeds, and to each spoke words of friendship and appreciation.

As he approached me he laid both hands upon my shoulders.

"Welcome, my son," he said; "that you are granted, gladly, and without one word of opposition, the most precious jewel in all Helium, yes, on all Barsoom, is sufficient earnest of my esteem."

We were then presented to Mors Kajak, Jed of lesser Helium, and father of Dejah Thoris. He had followed close behind Tardos Mors and seemed even more affected by the meeting than had his father.

He tried a dozen times to express his gratitude to me, but his voice choked with emotion and he could not speak, and yet he had, as I was to later learn, a reputation for ferocity and fearlessness as a fighter that was remarkable even upon warlike Barsoom. In common with all Helium he worshiped his daughter, nor could he think of what she had escaped without deep emotion.

CHAPTER XXVII
FROM JOY TO DEATH[96]

For ten days the hordes of Thark and their wild allies were feasted and entertained, and, then, loaded with costly presents and escorted by ten thousand soldiers of Helium commanded by Mors Kajak, they started on the return journey to their own lands. The jed of lesser Helium with a small party of nobles accompanied them all the way to Thark to cement more closely the new bonds of peace and friendship.

Sola also accompanied Tars Tarkas, her father, who before all his chieftains had acknowledged her as his daughter.

Three weeks later, Mors Kajak and his officers, accompanied by Tars Tarkas and Sola, returned upon a battleship that had been dispatched to Thark to fetch them in time for the ceremony which made Dejah Thoris and John Carter one.

For nine years I served in the councils and fought in the armies of Helium as a prince of the house of Tardos Mors. The people seemed never to tire of heaping honors upon me, and no day passed that did not bring some new proof of their love for my princess, the incomparable Dejah Thoris.

In a golden incubator upon the roof of our palace lay a snow-white egg. For nearly five years ten soldiers of the jeddak's Guard had constantly stood over it, and not a day passed when I was in the city that Dejah Thoris and I did not stand hand in hand before our little shrine planning for the future, when the delicate shell should break.

Vivid in my memory is the picture of the last night as we sat there talking in low tones of the strange romance which had woven our lives together and of this wonder which was coming to augment our happiness and fulfill our hopes.

In the distance we saw the bright-white light of an approaching airship, but we attached no special significance to so common a sight. Like a bolt of lightning it raced toward Helium until its very speed bespoke the unusual.

---

[96] The last chapter set on Mars depicts Carter triumphant, having joined the two races of Martians together, having proved his mettle on the field of battle, and having won the heart and hand of Dejah Thoris. What is more, after nine years together in Helium, the two lovers await the hatching of an auspicious egg. Nevertheless, a crisis emerges involving the atmosphere plant and the specter of only three days left to live!

Flashing the signals which proclaimed it a dispatch bearer for the jeddak, it circled impatiently awaiting the tardy patrol boat which must convoy it to the palace docks.

Ten minutes after it touched at the palace a message called me to the council chamber, which I found filling with the members of that body.

On the raised platform of the throne was Tardos Mors, pacing back and forth with tense-drawn face. When all were in their seats he turned toward us.

"This morning," he said, "word reached the several governments of Barsoom that the keeper of the atmosphere plant had made no wireless report for two days, nor had almost ceaseless calls upon him from a score of capitals elicited a sign of response.

"The ambassadors of the other nations asked us to take the matter in hand and hasten the assistant keeper to the plant. All day a thousand cruisers have been searching for him until just now one of them returns bearing his dead body, which was found in the pits beneath his house horribly mutilated by some assassin.

"I do not need to tell you what this means to Barsoom. It would take months to penetrate those mighty walls, in fact the work has already commenced, and there would be little to fear were the engine of the pumping plant to run as it should and as they all have for hundreds of years now; but the worst, we fear, has happened. The instruments show a rapidly decreasing air pressure on all parts of Barsoom—the engine has stopped."[97]

"My gentlemen," he concluded, "we have at best three days to live."

There was absolute silence for several minutes, and then a young noble arose, and with his drawn sword held high above his head addressed Tardos Mors.

"The men of Helium have prided themselves that they have ever shown Barsoom how a nation of red men should live, now is our opportunity to show them how they should die. Let us go about our duties as though a thousand useful years still lay before us."

The chamber rang with applause and as there was nothing better to do than to allay the fears of the people by our example we went our ways with smiles upon our faces and sorrow gnawing at our hearts.

When I returned to my palace I found that the rumor already had reached Dejah Thoris, so I told her all that I had heard.

---

[97] A similarly dissipating Martian atmosphere is depicted vividly in the film *Total Recall.*

"We have been very happy, John Carter," she said, "and I thank whatever fate overtakes us that it permits us to die together."

The next two days brought no noticeable change in the supply of air, but on the morning of the third day breathing became difficult at the higher altitudes of the rooftops. The avenues and plazas of Helium were filled with people. All business had ceased. For the most part the people looked bravely into the face of their unalterable doom. Here and there, however, men and women gave way to quiet grief.

Toward the middle of the day many of the weaker commenced to succumb and within an hour the people of Barsoom were sinking by thousands into the unconsciousness which precedes death by asphyxiation.

Dejah Thoris and I with the other members of the royal family had collected in a sunken garden within an inner courtyard of the palace. We conversed in low tones, when we conversed at all, as the awe of the grim shadow of death crept over us. Even Woola seemed to feel the weight of the impending calamity, for he pressed close to Dejah Thoris and to me, whining pitifully.

The little incubator had been brought from the roof of our palace at request of Dejah Thoris and now she sat gazing longingly upon the unknown little life that now she would never know.

As it was becoming perceptibly difficult to breathe Tardos Mors arose, saying,

"Let us bid each other farewell. The days of the greatness of Barsoom are over. Tomorrow's sun will look down upon a dead world which through all eternity must go swinging through the heavens peopled not even by memories. It is the end."

He stooped and kissed the women of his family, and laid his strong hand upon the shoulders of the men.

As I turned sadly from him my eyes fell upon Dejah Thoris. Her head was drooping upon her breast, to all appearances she was lifeless. With a cry I sprang to her and raised her in my arms.

Her eyes opened and looked into mine.

"Kiss me, John Carter," she murmured. "I love you! I love you! It is cruel that we must be torn apart who were just starting upon a life of love and happiness."

As I pressed her dear lips to mine the old feeling of unconquerable power and authority rose in me. The fighting blood of Virginia sprang to life in my veins.

"It shall not be, my princess," I cried. "There is, there must be some way, and John Carter, who has fought his way through a strange world for love of you, will find it."

And with my words there crept above the threshold of my conscious mind a series of nine long forgotten sounds. Like a flash of lightning in the darkness their full purport dawned upon me—the key to the three great doors of the atmosphere plant!

Turning suddenly toward Tardos Mors as I still clasped my dying love to my breast I cried.

"A flier, Jeddak! Quick! Order your swiftest flier to the palace top. I can save Barsoom yet."

He did not wait to question, but in an instant a guard was racing to the nearest dock and though the air was thin and almost gone at the rooftop they managed to launch the fastest one-man, air-scout machine that the skill of Barsoom had ever produced.

Kissing Dejah Thoris a dozen times and commanding Woola, who would have followed me, to remain and guard her, I bounded with my old agility and strength to the high ramparts of the palace, and in another moment I was headed toward the goal of the hopes of all Barsoom.

I had to fly low to get sufficient air to breathe, but I took a straight course across an old sea bottom and so had to rise only a few feet above the ground.

I traveled with awful velocity for my errand was a race against time with death. The face of Dejah Thoris hung always before me. As I turned for a last look as I left the palace garden I had seen her stagger and sink upon the ground beside the little incubator. That she had dropped into the last coma which would end in death, if the air supply remained unreplenished, I well knew, and so, throwing caution to the winds, I flung overboard everything but the engine and compass, even to my ornaments, and lying on my belly along the deck with one hand on the steering wheel and the other pushing the speed lever to its last notch I split the thin air of dying Mars with the speed of a meteor.

An hour before dark the great walls of the atmosphere plant loomed suddenly before me, and with a sickening thud I plunged to the ground before the small door which was withholding the spark of life from the inhabitants of an entire planet.

Beside the door a great crew of men had been laboring to pierce the wall, but they had scarcely scratched the flint-like surface, and now most of them lay in the last sleep from which not even air would awaken them.

Conditions seemed much worse here than at Helium, and it was with difficulty that I breathed at all. There were a few men still conscious, and to one of these I spoke.

"If I can open these doors is there a man who can start the engines?" I asked.

"I can," he replied, "if you open quickly. I can last but a few moments more. But it is useless, they are both dead and no one else upon Barsoom knew the secret of these awful locks. For three days men crazed with fear have surged about this portal in vain attempts to solve its mystery."

I had no time to talk, I was becoming very weak and it was with difficulty that I controlled my mind at all.

But, with a final effort, as I sank weakly to my knees I hurled the nine thought waves at that awful thing before me. The Martian had crawled to my side and with staring eyes fixed on the single panel before us we waited in the silence of death.

Slowly the mighty door receded before us. I attempted to rise and follow it but I was too weak.

"After it," I cried to my companion, "and if you reach the pump room turn loose all the pumps. It is the only chance Barsoom has to exist tomorrow!"

From where I lay I opened the second door, and then the third, and as I saw the hope of Barsoom crawling weakly on hands and knees through the last doorway I sank unconscious upon the ground.

Chapter XXVIII
At the Arizona Cave

It was dark when I opened my eyes again. Strange, stiff garments were upon my body; garments that cracked and powdered away from me as I rose to a sitting posture.

I felt myself over from head to foot and from head to foot I was clothed, though when I fell unconscious at the little doorway I had been naked. Before me was a small patch of moonlit sky which showed through a ragged aperture.

As my hands passed over my body they came in contact with pockets and in one of these a small parcel of matches wrapped in oiled paper. One of these matches I struck, and its dim flame lighted up what appeared to be a huge cave, toward the back of which I discovered a strange, still figure huddled over a tiny bench. As I approached it I saw that it was the dead and mummified remains of a little old woman with long black hair, and the thing it leaned over was a small charcoal burner upon which rested a round copper vessel containing a small quantity of greenish powder.[98]

Behind her, depending from the roof upon rawhide thongs, and stretching entirely across the cave, was a row of human skeletons. From the thong which held them stretched another to the dead hand of the little old woman; as I touched the cord the skeletons swung to the motion with a noise as of the rustling of dry leaves.

It was a most grotesque and horrid tableau and I hastened out into the fresh air; glad to escape from so gruesome a place.

The sight that met my eyes as I stepped out upon a small ledge which ran before the entrance of the cave filled me with consternation.

A new heaven and a new landscape met my gaze. The silvered mountains in the distance, the almost stationary moon hanging in the sky, the cacti-studded valley below me were not of Mars. I could scarcely believe my eyes, but the truth slowly forced itself upon me—I was looking upon Arizona from the same ledge from which ten years before I had gazed with longing upon Mars.

Burying my head in my arms I turned, broken, and sorrowful, down the trail from the cave.

Above me shone the red eye of Mars holding her awful secret, forty-eight million miles away.

---

[98] Carter has been gone ten years.

Did the Martian reach the pump room? Did the vitalizing air reach the people of that distant planet in time to save them? Was my Dejah Thoris alive, or did her beautiful body lie cold in death beside the tiny golden incubator in the sunken garden of the inner courtyard of the palace of Tardos Mors, the jeddak of Helium?

For ten years I have waited and prayed for an answer to my questions. For ten years I have waited and prayed to be taken back to the world of my lost love. I would rather lie dead beside her there than live on Earth all those millions of terrible miles from her.

The old mine, which I found untouched, has made me fabulously wealthy; but what care I for wealth![99]

As I sit here tonight in my little study overlooking the Hudson, just twenty years have elapsed since I first opened my eyes upon Mars.

I can see her shining in the sky through the little window by my desk, and tonight she seems calling to me again as she has not called before since that long dead night, and I think I can see, across that awful abyss of space, a beautiful black-haired woman standing in the garden of a palace, and at her side is a little boy who puts his arm around her as she points into the sky toward the planet Earth, while at their feet is a huge and hideous creature with a heart of gold.

I believe that they are waiting there for me, and something tells me that I shall soon know.[100]

---

[99] In the late 1890s, Burroughs lived in Pocatello, Idaho, close to where his brothers operated a mine. Evidently, success at mining eluded them.

[100] Burroughs practically invented the cliffhanger ending that demanded an endless spate of sequels.

New Tales

of the

Red Planet

A Friend in Thark

by Matthew Stover

It was on that seemingly endless pilgrimage, across the dead sea-bottoms toward the throne of Tal Hajus in the ancient city from which the Thark take their name, that I first had cause to hope I might find fellowship among my warlike captors.

Martian night having fallen with its usual abruptness, Sola undertook her customary chore of arranging a warrior camp for my comfort—for though I was still formally a captive, I wore the metal of two redoubtable warriors. As Sola prepared the ground and spread ape-pelts, I released Woola to hunt among the avenues and crumbling structures of the nameless ruins where we'd stopped. The great beast bounded away with a savage growl that would have done credit to an earthly lion, though from Woola this fearsome rumble was only a purr of anticipation, such as might be heard from a contented house cat which has found cream on the floor.

As the lesser moon hurtled through the depthless sky, its reflected light illumined for a moment the figure of my captor himself, the warrior jed of the Thark, Tars Tarkas. He stood with arms folded across his chest, and his intermediary limbs akimbo, fists bunched against his mighty thighs. Staring at the empty darkness into which Woola had vanished, the Thark said musingly, "A curious master you are, Dojar Sotat. The Warhoon are not far behind, and the dead cities of these sea-bottoms are home to the great white ape . . . and yet your calot runs free in the night, far from your camp, where it cannot defend you at need."

"He will come if I need him," I said. "I am no master to Woola, Tars Tarkas, nor is he my slave. I had experience of masters and slaves in my native Virginia, and I have no great use for either. I prefer that he be my companion and my loyal friend."

"Friend," snorted the great Thark with derision. "Only red men use this word in the sense you mean. Among the Thark, friend is another word for fool."

"Then a fool I am proud to be," I replied. "Woola would die for me—and I for him, as you may recall." For he knew well how I had nearly met my end in Woola's defense, after the great beast saved me from white apes in the ruins of Korad. "Better a single friend than a hundred slaves."

Tars Tarkas paused there a moment. His shadowed face could not be read, but my growing proficiency with Martian telepathy gave me understanding that the great Thark was in some considerable distress; were he an Earthman, I would say he struggled with his conscience, but the green men of Barsoom had dispensed with such inconveniences as *conscience* millennia ago. At length he turned to me in great solemnity. "May I join your camp, Dojar Sotat?"

I forebore to mention the irony of such a request, coming as it did from my captor, whose huge green hands held the power of life or death over me; the grave courtesy of his tone inspired similar courtesy in my response. "I am honored, Tars Tarkas, and you are welcome."

Sola spread additional pelts, but it seemed Tars Tarkas had little desire for ease. Instead he crouched on one knee, and watched in silence while Sola built a small fire against the deepening chill. When at length she withdrew to make her own bed of skins and pelts, the great Thark finally spoke from his troubled heart. "I once had a friend," he said slowly. "A friend in the sense you mean. Many, many years ago."

This I found astonishing both in itself, knowing as I did the green Martians' view of tender sentiments, and also in that he would confess it to me, and I said so.

He nodded gravely. "He perished here, more than two hundred years past."

"Here? In this city?"

"Just beyond its walls. Less than two haads from where we now converse. He has been much on my mind this day."

"Of course—to return to the place where you lost your only friend—"

"I did not lose him, Dojar Sotat." His eyes seemed pools of night in which danced the campfire flames. "I killed him."

Whereupon he related the following tale, which I here present as he spoke it to me, saving only that it is translated from the original Martian.

"In my hatching day gauntlet, I was chosen by Sarkoja, whom you know too well already. She it was who instructed me in the arts of war and all necessities of manhood. Sarkoja is a hard woman, ruthless and bitterly vengeful, and males in her charge are reared to be like her, for these are virtues among the Thark.

"In my third year, a Warhoon slave raid captured some dozens of Thark females, and slew most of the juveniles these females had attended. The survivors, as is our way, were distributed among the other females, and to Sarkoja was given a boy of my own age, Malus.

"Him I had known already; we had often contested in the athletic trials we Thark use to strengthen body and mind. He was a capable opponent, swift and strong, though not my equal; yet he contrived to win as many contests as he lost to me, due to his wits—he was possessed of cunning remarkable even among the Thark, and was considered a fair prospect to become a jed, or even jeddak. We went overnight from being each other's fiercest rival to being the closest thing to a brother a Thark might hope to have.

"Malus and I made common cause against Sarkoja, repaying her harsh treatment of us with childish pranks, and devoting the balance our energies to evading her supervision and subverting her every command. This pursuit also practiced us in the power to deny telepathic access to our minds, for only thus could any of our plans succeed; Sarkoja was ever watchful for the slightest hints of our intentions.

"Sarkoja, for her part, responded to our campaign with ceaseless attempts to sow discord between us, setting us one against the other to maintain her authority. Only one of these attempts succeeded. It is the story of her one successful plot that I share this night.

"Our band had encamped beyond those crumbling walls that night, for sign of the great white apes had been discovered everywhere in this place, and the men of our band planned a great hunt for the morrow, in which they hoped to exterminate the entirety of the beasts. Mal and I, at only nine, were greatly grieved to be forbidden to hunt with the men; for though we had trained with sword and lance, we were permitted to bear only the knives of boyhood, little blades no longer than a hand's breadth.

"Sarkoja here hit upon a stratagem to once and finally divide us—a test our friendship could not survive. She set us a challenge: the first of us to steal into this city that night, to enter an ape lair by boldness or stealth, and to return to her with a trophy to prove we had done so, would win a prize. In this, dangerous as it was, her challenge was little different from the everyday training for young men of the Thark; the key to the stratagem lay in the prize itself.

"The prize was a green-Martian longsword—a fine, well-worked weapon with basket and grip bound in platinum wire and set with gemstones—that had been in Sarkoja's possession for some years. Malus and I both knew the blade well, and we coveted it without reservation. And yet the blade itself was not the true prize, but instead only the symbol of it.

"For a youth of the Thark to be awarded a longsword by his governess is the mark of passage from child to man; thus, the victor in her contest would get also not only the weapon, but would be released from her supervision forever—and would be free to join the great hunt on the morrow!—while the loser would remain in her charge, and suffer her undivided attentions for at least another year, a span of time barely comprehensible to our young minds. It might as well have been a sentence of death.

"Thus Malus and I set out into the night together for the last time. I cannot say what he might have been thinking, for we both were shielding our minds, to deny Sarkoja the pleasure of seeing what distress her cunning had wrought. For my part, I was in despair. I longed for the sword and all it would represent with a passion that burned beyond the power of language to describe, and yet should I win it, I would have to abandon Malus—my one true friend, my brother—to Sarkoja's infinite cruelties.

"By the time we had crossed the crumbling walls into this city proper, I had concluded that my honor and my affections both required that I contrive to lose this contest. Instead of abandoning Malus, I would see to it that he won the prize. I resolved that even should it cost my life, I would set my brother free.

"Malus, though, was my superior in cunning, as I have said. When he was sure we had entirely escaped the chance of being observed, he turned to me in great excitement. 'I have the answer, Tars!' he exclaimed. 'Whatever is done, we will do *together*! Just as when a war band goes forth, we will win or lose as one! We will return to camp arm in arm, as brothers—then we'll take our ape-trophy and cast it into Sarkoja's ugly face!'

"This outcome would have been more than agreeable to me, as we would be rewarded or punished as one. I enthusiastically assented, and we set off together.

"Locating an ape lair presented no difficulty; the city was so infested that we could scarcely avoid them. Our problem was rather the opposite: armed only with our boyhood knives, we dared not risk battle against even a single beast, and many of the lairs were home to whole families, or even clans, if white apes have such.

"Soon, though, fortune smiled upon us. We heard a terrible bellowing, that seemed to rise and ebb, to trail away to silence only to rise again. By following the awful noise, we came upon an ape who, we surmised, must have been vanquished in some bestial battle against another of its kind. It lay as though dying, its sobs of pain becoming roars of agony, and the air was thick with the reek of its blood.

"Our safest course of action would have been to simply wait for the beast to die, and then take its ears or a finger or somesuch as our trophy—but the great white ape is known to cannibalize its own kind, when an opportunity arises. The beast's cries would soon draw others of its kind, and our chance would be lost.

"Again it was Malus who hit upon a solution. In a narrow alleyway nearby—only a few dozen ads from this very fire, in fact—we found a half-tumbled building, with an upper wall of unstably stacked stone blocks. Malus proposed that one of us should creep close to the dying ape to cut away an ear or a finger by sudden attack. Then, should the ape prove capable of pursuit, we would lead it down this alleyway, where the other of us would lay in wait upon the upper floor. Once the first had passed, the other would push the stones of the wall into the alley, to delay the ape and perhaps crush it outright.

"This struck my childish imagination as a sound plan, and I said I would attack the ape while Malus stayed back, for we both knew that I was the swifter runner. But Malus said, 'Speed of foot will count for less than strength of limb, Tars. What if I cannot topple the stones in time? I could never live with myself if my weakness caused your death. Nay: you are the stronger as well as the swifter. Wait here, and do not fail me!'

"I swore I would not, my voice choked with emotion, for Malus there showed greater nobility of spirit than ordinary green Martians can even conceive, much less possess.

"I took my place, and it seemed that I stood there forever, waiting for his return, as though whole lifetimes had passed since our parting mere moments before. The bellows of the ape faded to silence, and did not return. As the silence stretched ever longer, I began for the first time to misdoubt Malus's intentions—I was nearly consumed by a growing apprehension that he had tricked me, and had stolen away already with his trophy. Suspicion grew into agony. Should I wait like a fool, or attempt to overtake him before he could get to Sarkoja and claim the sword? Yet I could not move, for fear that leaving my post might condemn my brother to an awful demise—and yet, I imagined that Malus had known I would be caught by this fear, and was now laughing at the thought of my lonely vigil.

"So it was that I nearly broke my word—my decision made, I was already turning to race back to Sarkoja when I heard a sudden roar of white ape rage, rather than pain, and I heard my brother sprinting along the alleyway and shouting for me. 'Now, Tars!' he cried. 'Now! The beast is upon me!'

"I threw myself against the wall with all my strength, thanking the immortal Issus that I had been spared betraying my brother unto death.

For an instant the wall held, but only that; the great stones fell directly upon the ape below. I paused on the floor above only long enough to ascertain that I had not crushed Malus as well, then jubilantly I made to leap away—but the stones, heavy as they were, had not been enough to slay the beast, only to knock it down and injure it. In its convulsions of pain and rage, the white ape kicked out and its furious strength brought down the rest of the wall upon it, and brought down the floor above, and me as well.

"Stunned half-senseless by my unexpected plunge, I scrambled to my feet, but my clumsy attempt at escape alerted the beast to my presence. One mighty hand closed around my ankle and hauled me back, and for the first time in my brief existence, I was forced to fight for my life.

"In that terrible fight, I called out to my brother but once, and that only to warn him, lest the ape overcome me and turn to savage him. Boy that I was, I should have been no match for the least of the great apes, but this one had been weakened by loss of blood, and injured further by the fallen stones. Two of its arms were broken, and its face was half-smashed, leaving it without one eye, and its shattered jaw left it unable to rend me with its jagged teeth.

"Still it tore at me with its huge claws, ripping bloody furrows in my flesh; it was then I heard a curious sound—my brother's voice, in fact—though I did not at the time attend to it, as I was fighting desperately for my life. I have no doubt I would have died there, but that one of my flailing attempts to slash it with my knife struck, entirely by fortune, at its remaining eye. It recoiled, and in its shock and horror released me to clutch at its new wound with both of its good hands. Now blinded, it was unable to find me again before I lifted the largest block of stone my strength could support, and brought it down upon the creature's head again and again, until finally I had crushed its skull, and the beast moved no more.

"I retrieved my knife, and called to Malus to join me in taking a trophy worthy of our adventure: the arm of a great white ape, slain by our own guile and courage. Malus, though, did not reply, nor could I discover where he might be . . . until I recalled the curious sound that had come to my ears during the fight, the one that I had been unable to attend to at the time. Now its memory struck at my heart like a dagger of fire.

"It had been the sound of my brother's laughter.

"I took nonetheless my trophy. Though I knew I had lost the contest, I was determined to acquit myself with as much honor as I might retain. I had, after all, accomplished my design: my brother would be free, and my virtue was unstained. Injured as I was, it was no small matter to cut the arm from the beast's shoulder with my little knife, nor was it an insignificant effort to drag the arm, nearly as large as I was, back through these ruined streets to our camp beyond the walls.

"On that torturous journey, my thoughts were much upon Malus, and his laughter. Not the fact of it—among the Thark, gore and slaughter are the highest of comedies—but in its tone: one of triumphant malice. It was that same malice I found on his face when at last I reached the camp.

"He strutted about, flourishing the sword his treachery had won, boasting extravagantly of his guile and daring—and of course saying nothing of me, until he noticed my return. Then his boasts turned to mockery; he made light of my wounds, and proclaimed that I had nearly been killed trying to bring back a mere piece of a corpse, whereas he, in contrast, had brought an entire ape.

"The great white ape, alone of the higher species of Barsoom, is viviparous; what we had taken for death agonies were instead the labor pains of a lone female struggling with a difficult birth. When finally the infant emerged, the mother lay exhausted, only semi-conscious. Malus had simply crept close and yanked the infant from her breast. The first squeal of alarm from the infant had roused its mother to instant fury. It was the mother, mad with rage and grief over the loss of her child, that I had killed in the alleyway.

"This, somehow, cut more deeply than had even his treachery, yet still I was determined to act with honor; he and I both knew the truth, and that was enough. Yet I could not let his mockery pass without reply, and so I summoned a contemptuous laugh and a jesting tone. 'You have your trophy, and I mine,' I said. 'You have won the sword, but my trophy is superior in every way.'

"This elicited general laughter, and he turned upon me a humorously pitying gaze. 'And how is that?'

"I proclaimed that it had been won in battle, not in burglary, and that I could feed a dozen warriors upon its meat, where the infant could be no more than a boy's midday snack. And that if he still would contend his was the better, let him take his trophy in his hands and measure it against mine in single combat—for the severed arm would make a formidable bludgeon, where the infant was more akin to a seat cushion.

"My sally met with general approval, and the matter should have rested there, but the men began to make sport of Malus. The sudden turn from admiration to ridicule overtook his temper, and he yanked his sword out from its hanger and lunged for me, shouting 'If you think it such a fine weapon, try it against a real one!'"

The great Thark fell silent, and only stared into the pale flame of the campfire for some considerable time. At length I said, "And the result?"

"The arm proved indeed a formidable bludgeon," Tars Tarkas said softly.

I noted that as he said this, his hand rested upon the hilt of his sword—a fine weapon, nearly as long as I am tall—and that this hilt was wound with platinum wire, and set with precious gems. "Is that the prize sword? The blade you carry even now?"

His great eyes were like pools of ink. "I bear it to remind myself of the penalty for friendship."

"A betrayal two centuries past?"

"Not his betrayal, Dojar Sotat." He rose, towering fifteen feet high. "But that I slew my brother. He was my friend, and I killed him."

With that, he strode off into the night without a backward glance.

I watched him go, marveling at his dark tale. "Sola?" I asked. "Did you hear this?"

She slipped out from the shadows nearby. "The tale of Tars Tarkas's duel with Malus is well known. This is the first I have ever heard of what passed between them in the city. It may be he has never spoken of it before."

"I am honored that he would confide it to me, though I am still unsure why he would do so," I said. "Is it all true, do you think?"

"No false word has ever passed Tars Tarkas's lips."

"And yet—for a man so sour on the very concept of friendship—I must say that it seems his own conduct was entirely above reproach. The finest gentleman of Old Virginia could not have behaved better. Perhaps it is not that friendship is foolish, but that he was unfortunate in his choice of friend. Perhaps he should instead choose a man whose honor is steadfast as his own."

Sola nodded thoughtfully. "And perhaps, John Carter," she said gravely, "that is why he told the tale to *you.*"

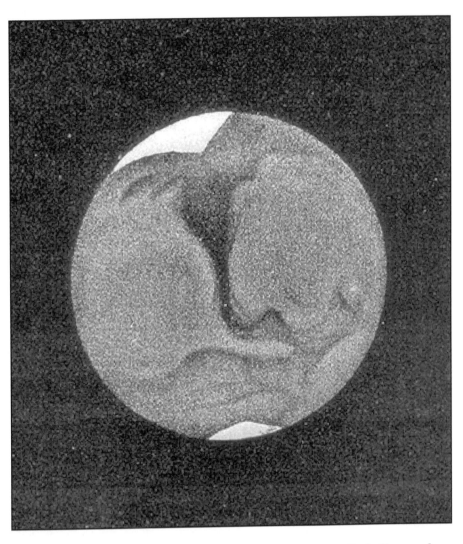

Drawing of the planet Mars by English astronomer Warren De la Rue, made from telescopic observations on April 20, 1856

GENTLEMAN OF VIRGINIA
BY MICHAEL KOGGE

Mars hung over Manassas. It shone as but a pinprick of red in the firmament, yet I saw little else as I rode into the night. The star drew me like a compass, guiding me through the fields and foothills of northern Virginia. When a passing cloud or an overhanging branch obstructed my view, I felt its presence all the same, its glow in my heart. What had for so long been the object of my fascination loomed now as the harbinger of my glory. The war to save the South was about to begin, and Mars gave its blessing.

Bellona relished the hard pace we took. She had hooves of steel and lungs that in the myths would have belched fire. When spurred to a gallop, she would not stop. My steed was the fastest thoroughbred in the land, winner of a Tennessee cup by ten lengths and a Carolina crown by more than fifteen. Such small victories did not satisfy her: Bellona had been born for more than derbies and fox hunts. She longed to prove herself in a greater struggle, a contest that called for courage as much as speed, honor as much as drive.

Battle was in her blood, as it was in mine.

We had been together not much longer than a day. I had been most recently a student in England, but once my beloved Virginia announced her secession, I procured passage on an Atlantic steamer as quickly as I could. Upon my arrival, word had spread that the Federals were massing to attack General Beauregard's camp at Manassas Junction, perhaps two days' ride from my family's plantation. Though there had been small skirmishes here and there, including the taking of Fort Sumter, a fight at Manassas would be the first major battle of the war—and neither Bellona nor I were going to miss it.

For the sake of speed, we avoided the roads. Other volunteers busied them, trudging north from the bluegrass and bayou, singing and carousing. I did not want to be waylaid by their idle conversation. I did not want their dreams to spoil my own. War was not an endeavor to be boasted about before its engagement. War was a deed to be done, to be felt, like love.

Bellona would have taken me all the way to the Potomac had I not whispered for her to slow. We were but a few hours from Manassas and she needed to save her vigor for the battle. I dismounted and watered her at a brook that ran along a tobacco field. It was the ideal place to rest. The smell of the brightleaf not only soothed my nerves, but drove away the mosquitoes. I could sleep unmolested under the stars.

Sleep never came. With my arms crossed behind my head, I lay on the soft turf of the bank and gazed up at the night, at Mars. I imagined the coming battle, the charge of the cavalry and the boom of artillery, a mêlée of horses, men, rifles, and swords. Death was there, but so was valor. Nameless men fought their way into history. Sacrifices were made for brothers just met at breakfast. Sabers sung melodies in the air, muskets blasted out dirges. Wave after wave, the enemy fell. It was like something out of the old tales.

Bellona whinnied. I turned from the stars just in time to see a dark shape approach her. She bucked, but the man managed to rip a bag from her saddle. I jumped to my feet and raced after him. I could see from the whites of his eyes he was a slave.

We ran through the tobacco fields. The slave had an uncommon speed, and knew the dips and ruts of the terrain that otherwise slowed me. I drew my revolver, though honor precluded me from shooting a man in the back, no matter what he was.

The distance between us grew, and soon pursuit became a lost cause. I gave up the chase. The saddlebag contained but meager rations that Beauregard's camp could provide. If this man was that hungry, he could have them.

I began to traverse the field back to Bellona. Although it was late July when tobacco ought be on the verge of maturity, this crop grew scattered, in clumps. In the moonlight I noticed a blue mold infected many of the leaves. The farm that tended these fields was on hard times.

A thunderous shot rang out.

I turned to see an old man run out of the nearby farmhouse. He carried a rifle and was dressed only in a night shirt and field boots. His shot had missed, yet it had been enough to stop the slave in his tracks.

"James, you goddamn fool, don't you be thinkin' of runnin'," the old mane shouted. Two mutts bolted past him, both lean and ill-fed.

The slave dropped the bag behind his back, probably in hope that the old man would not see his action in the dark. The mutts noticed. They dashed around the slave and pounced on the saddlebag, tearing it open to fight over my provisions.

The old man, whom I assumed to be the farmer, kept his rifle aimed at the slave. "Stealin' from me, too, are ya? Boy, you're in for a whippin' tonight. Get on your knees."

As the old man approached, the slave stood there, trembling. He wore no shirt, and his cotton breeches were ragged and dirty, tied around his waist with twine. Bits of briar clung to his hair. Still he was a proud specimen of masculinity, standing a foot over the farmer, and from this distance he looked to be of my age, in his third decade.

"Get down I said!" The farmer pressed his rifle into the slave's chest. Having devoured my provisions, the dogs joined their master in threatening the slave with snarls and barks.

The slave glanced in my direction, desperation in his eyes. Then the farmer smacked him across the back of his head and pushed him down onto his knees. The dogs pawed forward, snapping their jaws.

"Now listen. Only peep I want from your lips is beggin' mercy from the good ol' Lord Jesus, got me?" The farmer held the rifle with one hand and unclasped a bullwhip from his belt.

What I observed next repulsed me.

Perhaps in my youth I had been blind and ignorant to such violence, but not once did I witness my father, stern as he was, raise even a hand to any of our slaves, let alone a whip. He lived by the tenets of the ancient sage Seneca, who taught that the best master is the kind master, for kindness shall be rewarded with productivity. Seneca's counsel proved wise for my family. We had one of the most prosperous plantations in southern Virginia and not one of our slaves had ever turned fugitive. Everyone knew their place and was content. It was the Roman way.

Those were not the principles under which this master treated his property. The old farmer flogged his slave so savagely I felt that my own honor was being disparaged. Such cruelty went against our customs. This was conduct expected of a man of Arkansas or Alabama, not of Virginia. It only fortified the resentment of the slave while affirming the worst prejudices of the Yankees, who thought that Southern gentility was a ruse and beneath its guise we were but wicked and depraved tyrants. The forces arrayed against the Confederacy were immense; we did not need to topple it from within.

I came toward them. "Sir!"

The old farmer did not seem to hear. He cracked the whip again. The slave cried out in pain, on his elbows. Blood glistened in stripes along his back.

"Sir!" I called out again, nearing them. "That is not necessary. It was only my saddlebag."

The dogs turned first, growling at me. Then the farmer spun around with the bullwhip, letting the slave collapse into the dirt.

"Who the hell are you?"

I drew closer, revolver still in hand. "I am a gentleman volunteer for the Confederate Army of the Potomac."

The old farmer squinted an eye at me. "They're not musterin' here. You're well off the roads."

"I'm not taking the roads." I walked slowly by the dogs to pick up my shredded saddlebag. Their teeth had made it unusable. "This was mine."

"Knew it was stolen." The farmer spit on the slave, then lifted the whip for another blow.

"Sir, as I said, that is not necessary."

"I'll be the judge of that."

Before he could crack the whip, I grabbed its leather fall and clenched it in my fist. The old man sneered. "What the hell do you think you're doin'?"

"You have punished him enough."

The old man tried to wrench the whip free. Its leather fall cut into my palm, but I held onto it. Unable to match my strength, he let go of the whip to bring his rifle to bear on me.

"You're one of those uppity abolitionists, aren't ya?"

The mutts began to snarl and bark at me. I thumbed the hammer of my revolver, but did not raise it. "Sir, I request you put that rifle down or I will haul you to Richmond for treason."

"Only thing you'll be haulin' is your goddamn soul to hell." The old man stepped back and cocked his rifle. I did not move.

"Father!"

The moon favored a figure running barefoot through the field, a young woman in a shawl and a summer dress. At the sound of her voice the dogs turned tail to rush her, whimpering like puppies wanting to play.

The old man scowled. "Dora, get back in there this instant!"

He could have said the same to the wind for all the good it did. This Dora was a stubborn girl, not bothered by the roots and pebbles of the field that soiled and cut into her feet. She came right up to him, shooing the dogs away.

"Dora, I told you—"

"You were flogging James again."

She reproached her father with such a glare that he lowered both his weapon and his head. He let out an angry breath. "Boy was runnin' away," he muttered.

"I doubt that. James has been loyal to our family all these years." She looked past me as if I was a field varmint. "James, were you trying to run away?"

Between groans, the slave on the ground behind me murmured what sounded to be a negative.

"He lies!" said the old man.

"And how can I believe you, father, when you said you had put down the whip for good?"

The old man grumbled some more. He nodded my way without looking. "Just ask this soldier here. He'll tell you."

"The man you were about to shoot?"

"Yea—I mean, no. Thought he was trespassin'."

Now Dora's eyes fell on me. I holstered my revolver and gave her a nod. "Ma'am. My apologies for bothering you. I was just passing through to water my horse."

Dora looked me up and down, suspicious. She was not a beauty, though she carried herself with such pride that her spirit was her allure. Strands of her brown hair drifted across eyes that glinted even in the dark.

"You are a soldier for Virginia," Dora said to me.

"I aim to be," I said. "My family name is Carter, though you may call me Jack."

"Where is your horse?"

"A few acres that way." I canted my head in the direction where I had left Bellona. "A pack fell off my saddle. I came to retrieve it." I hoisted up the saddlebag.

"Another bald-faced lie," said the old man. "Our boy stole it from him. This man even told me so himself!"

Dora's eyes did not move from me. "Is my father right? Did James steal from you?"

I could feel the slave moving in the dirt behind me. His moans had grown softer. As had the distrust in Dora's eyes. She was suspicious only because that was the nature of the world in which we lived. That was the nature of the South.

"Tell her!" the old man said to me.

Honor dictates many points in life. Live by its code and one will never vacillate. As I could not shoot a man in the back, I could not tell a lie to a woman.

"It was removed from my saddle," I said.

Her father grinned, showing a mouth half full of blackened teeth. The slave defended himself only with his groans. Dora sighed.

"Since our slave caused you this loss, the least we can do is invite you inside for the night."

"What? Dora, this man is a stranger!" said the old man.

I declined at once. I did not wish to impose myself on these poor people, and on this night I honestly preferred the stars as my blanket. Dora would hear none of it.

"You insult me if you remain out here. A man who is willing to lay down his life for our home deserves a proper night's sleep in a bed."

She silenced her father's protests with a glare, then leveled her gaze on me. She conveyed such intensity, that I, like her father, had to look away. As it would be uncouth to further refuse her generosity, I reluctantly accepted.

"I must first get my steed," I said.

My father claimed I had not been more than two when I first pointed out the red star. He had taken me out one summer evening, and I had sat there on the hillside, listening to the songs of the slaves in their huts, staring up at the sky. I could not peel my eyes away from the brightest star that night, for it was imbued with the most color, surrounded by a nimbus of red. My father told me its name.

Mars.

"Ba . . . Mars," I repeated, and as the legend goes, according to my father, it was the first word I uttered beyond the *bar-bar* gibberish of babyhood, my first word in the language of men. It was the word that drove me north to fight for the South.

It was the word that my father regretted ever speaking to me.

My father devoted his days to running our family's plantation, making sure that the fields were irrigated, the soil was turned, enough hay was purchased for the horses, and that the slaves were doing their job. He could be a hard taskmaster, his orders exacting, but he never demanded anything he himself would not do. Often he would roll up his sleeves, loosen his collar, and throw himself into the fields, hoeing and picking like any other laborer. But when the sun went down and the work was done, he laid aside all thoughts of tobacco, cotton, and beans, and turned his mind to the gods.

My father fancied himself an amateur classicist, though I will profess with a son's admiration that he was more than that: my father was a scholar of the first-rate. During the wee hours of the morning, when all were asleep in our house, he took coffee in his study and then consumed himself in the writing of tracts and monographs about Ovid and Virgil, Varro and Livy, Tacitus and Suetonius—always Romans, never Greeks. He felt the Romans had triumphed where the Greeks had failed. In his mind, the Greeks laid the foundation for society, then abandoned it to engage in petty rivalries and meaningless philosophical discord. The Romans, on the other hand, had the sense to gather the broken remnants of this Grecian vase, fit its sundry fragments together by inserting bits of their own design, then glaze and polish it into what became the greatest civilization mankind had ever known. They organized the chaotic muddle of Greek democracy into the fairest and most efficient form of representative government, the republic, and occupied their minds not in the philosophizing of the laws of Nature but rather the application of those laws, engineering aqueducts, forts, roads, and new devices that improved man's life and connected him to the world. As they bent Nature to their wills, they were unafraid to confront the heavens, shaking the frost off Mount Olympus until the gods themselves fell in line with Roman virtues and values.

At dinner, my father would regale us with these theories under the blush of wine, debating and discussing opposing arguments, never without a jab at his nemesis in the study of antiquity, a man he identified as "that cretin from Charleston." Since I was too young to partake in libations, as he called his generous sips, I understood very little of what he said. My sister and mother seemed equally incognizant, nodding and smiling whenever father wanted shakes and scowls. Still, I listened, and in the Roman method of picking up fragments here and there, formed my own juvenile conception of what made a civilization strong and great.

"Take the red star, for example," he said to me one night, after the others had gone to bed. "The one named after the Roman god of war."

"Mars," I said.

"Very good," he said. He poured another glass from his crystal carafe. "What perturbs me—what irks me—is that even today, in our advanced and elevated study of antiquity, some scholars continue to correlate the Greek pantheon with the Roman, as if gods could be swapped for different names, as if they were the same. As if they were!"

I hesitated, then shook my head. My father must have approved, because he also shook his.

"What offends me the most—oh it riles my soul!—is the erroneous association of Mars with his lesser Greek cousin, Ares. How could anyone confuse the two, a Roman for a Greek? How? It defies comprehension."

He stabbed a finger at the journal that had arrived this afternoon in the post. "But that cretin from Charleston, that fool, he does just that. His latest article is an affront on Southern scholarship. He makes us look like rubes!"

He picked up the journal and pointed it at me. His voice lowered down to the stern tone he used to instruct the slaves in a new task. "So you never make the same mistake, let me remind you of the difference.

"War to the Greeks was the engine of destruction. They feared the god, Ares, because of the fury he could unleash, the vast devastation he could lay waste upon life and land. To the Romans, however, war was the engine of civilization. They knew its price, yet they understood its reward. They worshiped their lord of war, Mars, not out of fear, but with all the solemn dignity he deserved. To them Mars represented the greatest virtues of mankind, those of duty to your countrymen and your home, the resolve to shed blood, including your own, for all that you believed was right and good. If it cost you your life, then so be it. The Romans knew you could not have stability without its threat. You could not have the rule of law without the rule of the sword. If you want peace, you must make war."

He shook the journal so hard its binding cracked. "That is why you should never mistake the Romans for the Greeks. That, my boy, is why this newest article by the cretin from Charleston is so grave a sin."

I was only five or six, and I did not know what a cretin was or how one measured the gravity of sins. But I was frowning and nodding at all the right moments and that seemed to please my father to no end. He ruffled my hair and drank. Libations made his face red.

"Good gracious. I should not let myself become so agitated. Passions can spell the end of us." He put down the journal and took another sip.

"Mars," I said.

Bellona was not by the brook where I had left her.

I drew my revolver and immediately regretted all my decisions that night. Gunshots would not have spooked Bellona—she was too well trained—though if there was one fugitive on the loose there could be a second.

I bent down to the mud of the brook. There was a mess of prints from the slave's approach, but I was able to isolate Bellona's hooves going into the stream. Fortunately, there did not seem to be a second set of prints. I walked through the water and discovered her tracks again on the other side. I was careful to keep head low when I peeked over the bank.

In a thicket Bellona picked apples off a tree.

I laughed at myself for doubting her, holstered my sidearm, and climbed up the bank. Bellona nickered when she saw me coming. I smiled, plucked an apple she could not reach, and fed it to her. She licked my palm clean.

In all of the derbies and hunts in which I had participated, I had never seen a more beautiful horse than Bellona. It was an assessment that few shared, including my father. Bellona's skin was mottled from a condition that had affected her since she was a foal. One of her ears had a nick from a bite she suffered from her brother, and her tail was stunted, as it had been when she was born.

Her birth was one of those singular events in a man's life he remembers more clearly than anything. After Bellona's mother had foaled her brother, the stablehand and my father went to wash up, leaving me to make sure the new colt got its legs. The colt did not need my help. The mare licked the last of the birth from the colt, and slowly he rose, teetering and tottering. But my eye moved from this miracle to another. A second foal was pushing herself out of the mare. She was so small, her mother did not seem to notice, not even issuing a grunt.

The foal fell out into the hay, bloody and wriggling in her birth sac. She could not get out of her own accord, and as her mother was ignorant of her arrival, I tore her free. I feared I was too late already. She was not breathing and I felt no heartbeat.

But when her eyes opened her eyes, they were wide and bright. And she saw me.

Twins were a rare occurrence in horse breeding. If it happened, the runt seldom survived past its first few hours. Even then, it usually was disregarded by its mother, for maternal energy needed to be spent in raising the stronger foal for life. So I took the tiny foal into my own care, cleaning her up, rubbing ointment onto her bare spots and picking out hay from her thin hair. And since her mother showed no interest, I helped her get her legs.

It was a process that took hundreds of trials and many days. My father said I was squandering my time. Our stablehand counseled we should sell the foal to the local butcher, who was French and was always looking for tender meat. Only my mother, bless her soul, came to my defense. She bottled warm milk from which I suckled the foal to health. And the day the foal gained her legs, I gave her a name.

Now as I looked into Bellona's eyes and held her, I could feel her heartbeat pumping through her veins. Her mane brushed and tickled my cheek. Her breath was hot. If a man could ever die for love of his horse, I was that man.

I stabled Bellona then went to the farmhouse. The door was open. I watched in silence as Dora stitched James's wounds in the kitchen. He sat in a chair and gripped the table. The shackles that now bound his arms and legs shook as the needle went in and out of his flesh.

She dropped the bloody needle into a basket. "Can you make a dressing out of this? We don't have any gauze." Without even a glance at me, she pulled the cotton shawl off from her neck and held it out. I had to step into the kitchen to take it.

"Tear them long enough so I can wrap then around his chest." She found a whiskey bottle in a cabinet and sprinkled what little was left onto James's back. He tensed, biting his lip so hard it split.

I tore the shawl into horizontal strips and gave them to Dora. She laid them over the stitched wounds, tying the ends around James's chest. When she was finished, he looked up at her with both relief and gratitude. Dora did not look at him.

"To your quarters," she said.

James began to speak, but she dismissed him with a wave of her hand. Shackles rattling, he teetered up from the table without further comment, bearing the look of a man who did not know whether he was alive or dead. He lumbered past me into the hall, the chains around his ankles dragging on the floor.

"Sit. I will make tea." She went over to the stove and would not heed any of my declinations. "And take off your boots. We only have James. I do the cleaning up around here."

Knowing there no use arguing with her, I sat down in the chair the slave had occupied and removed my boots. I placed them on a mat next to the farmer's pair.

"Has your father already gone to bed?"

"After he shackled James like a dog, he did," she said.

We did not talk while the tea brewed. Bereft of the shawl, her neck was visible, long and slender, one that swans would envy. She remained by the window, looking out, and when she moved she did so with a sad elegance. Barks echoed outside.

I glanced at my timepiece, absently winding it. I would have to be up in a couple hours to make Manassas before dawn. If there was a battle to be fought, it would surely be at first light.

"Milk?"

"No, thank you."

She poured the tea into two cups, added milk to one, and gave me the one without. I nodded my gratitude. She sat across from me. We both drank. A howl joined the chorus of barks.

"You have more than those two mutts?"

"Five," Dora said. "You met Nutmeg and Finley, but we also have a beagle, a pit bull terrier, and a Great Dane."

"I love dogs. Tell me about them."

It was as if I had given her a rose. Her face blossomed and all her melancholy vanished. I drank my tea and listened to her speak of these animals as if they were her own brothers. Nutmeg you could throw a steak, but he would abandon it in a second for a pickle. Finley had a tendency to sprint from garden post to garden post, and would probably run until death itself if someone did not call him into the house. Alexander the Great Dane had a gimp leg but the meanest growl in the South. Pincher, the pit bull, had a heart of gold, and once returned a baby robin to the sycamore tree from which it fell. The beagle, Malcolm, had picked up some marching tunes played by trumpeters and could howl the first bars of "Dixie."

"I would like to hear that," I said.

"Do you have any dogs?" she asked.

"At the moment it's just me and Bellona, my horse. We had a pair of border collies on the plantation, but they both fell ill while I was away at Oxford."

"You were in Mississippi?"

"England. I was at university."

"That seems a far way to travel for your studies."

"I was not going north to Harvard, that was for sure. And it was always my father's wish that I head to Oxford, for the best scholars reside there."

"You don't strike me as a scholar."

I chuckled. "Much to my father's regret, I am not. At Oxford I spent more time outside the classroom than in it. I prefer to learn things on my own."

"Like war?"

The bluntness of her question cut short my laugh, and had caused all the bloom of her cheeks to vanish. She averted her eyes and rose.

Without thinking, I reached out. My hand, sticky with apple, lingered on hers before I realized what I had done. I pulled it away.

"I apologize. That was not called for. I should go—"

"No."

She placed her hand back atop of mine.

"My hand," I said. "It is not clean."

"Neither is mine," she said. Hers was soft and cold and made me sad.

"Mister Carter—"

"Jack," I said.

"Jack," she said. "I see you are a brave man. But," she paused. I waited. "Do you fear what tomorrow may bring?"

"Not at all," I said. Her voice had such sincerity I did not dare laugh. "In fact, it is why I returned to Virginia with such haste. Tomorrow is the day of which I have dreamt my entire life."

"You could die."

"I could, yes. But I would die with honor, defending the Virginia that I love."

"Virginia." She scoffed. "What honor is there in death?"

"You sound like my father."

"Perhaps he is right." Her hand slipped from mine.

I should not have expected to her to understand. She was a woman and naturally possessed a different view on the merits of the sword. Her gender had come into this world to suckle, not to slay. But it did not stop me from wanting her approval.

"Dora."

On my tongue her name felt as soft as her hand. "Dora," I said again. "The Yankees would destroy everything we cherish. They distrust our traditions, particularly our hospitality, believing it disingenuous. They doubt a fine lady would be so accommodating to a stranger on a journey. While we Southerners practice the tried-and-true methods of our grandfathers and are blessed by bountiful harvests year after year, the Northerners bow to the altar of industry, trusting the gears of machines more than the labor of their hands. It would bring them great joy to plow through our fields, smash our mills, and erect towering smokestacks to exhaust the fumes of their factories. They would cloud the night."

"What of our slaves?" she said.

"The slaves?" I was struck by her question. "The Yankees would claim to free them, but then would put them to work in the most miserable of conditions and pay them the most meager of wages."

"Men like James would not be shackled by chains."

"No, they would be shackled by poverty and the machine," I said. "Their lives are better in the South. Under fair and kind masters, they flourish."

"Yes, under fair and kind masters," she said.

"I did not mean to imply—"

"I know what you meant. And on that count—on that count only—you are right."

I looked at her, into her proud eyes, and I began to understand. "Did you," I said, hesitating, "did you let your slave run free?"

She put the tea cups in the washing bin. "I must show you my brother's bedroom."

I rose from the table. "It is already late. Perhaps I should depart."

"I have seen enough suffering in my life. I will not allow a difference of opinion to cause more. Since you have accepted my hospitality, please do not reject it."

Her stubbornness endeared her more to me.

She beckoned me into the hall where the slave had gone. The Great Dane sat before a door that was slightly ajar, through which I could hear the old man's snores. The dog began to growl, but Dora shushed it. I walked past the beast slowly and followed Dora up a flight of stairs.

She led me into a small room. The furnishings were spartan. A daguerreotype of a young man sat on a dresser in a picture frame. His hair was wavy. A black tie fixed his collar. He looked out with all the hope of the world.

Dora saw me looking at the picture, but she did not furnish any information, nor did I ask. She untucked the blanket and plumped the pillow. "I hope this will be comfortable."

"This is the most that any soldier could ever wish for," I said. "And I apologize for any misunderstandings. When I go into battle tomorrow, I will be thinking of the kindness you have shown me. If there is anything I can do for you, it will be done."

She nodded, then walked to the door. But she did not leave. She stood at the threshold for a few moments, then turned back to me.

"There is something," she said.

What she asked went against the very traditions for which I was prepared to fight, but she had shown me such kindness I could not refuse. Or perhaps a part of me knew what she asked was right and true.

I did her the favor as quickly as I could.

When it was done, I returned to the bedroom. The red star burned bright through the window. I stared at it, putting my finger to the glass, as if to touch it.

My father could not have been more proud of my acceptance to Oxford, nor could I have been more forlorn. I had mastered Latin from his books, penned an article about the Roman-Parthian wars for a quarterly, could recite Cicero, Caesar, and Cato upon request, and even fashioned my own *gladius* as another blade to wield in my fencing lessons. To my father—and to the dons of Oxford—I represented the model American scholar, classically trained, genteel, versed in the pen as well as the sword, and he offered libations in that regard.

"What if I refuse the offer?"

He nearly spit out his wine. "Has the grape soured your mind already?"

I had not yet partaken. "War is on the horizon, father. I want to be here, to defend Virginia, if need be. I want to be ready."

"By the gods, war is always on the horizon. It's been on the horizon since the founding of this damned republic."

"But if it comes and I am not here?"

"I have not saved my precious dollars to throw my only son into the foams of Scylla and Charybdis! You will go abroad to Oxford, where you will study, row the Thames, and author a stellar thesis on Roman history that will shake the foundation of classical scholarship. Events in Virginia shall never cross your mind. Gentlemen of leisure do not worry about such matters."

I looked at my reflection in the wine. It glistened red and black in the chandelier's light.

"What of Mars, father?"

"Of Mars?" It was as if he had forgotten my childhood. His own words. His own gods. "Drink," he said, "then pack your belongings. We will talk of this no more."

I partook of the libations, said goodbye to Bellona, and went to Oxford.

I woke with a start to the faint boom of artillery. The bedroom was dark, the window shutters latched, but upon opening them I squinted in the brilliant sunshine. Dawn was a distant memory; from the position of the sun, it was well past noon. Smoke tendrils touched the clouds in the distance. The battle of Manassas had already begun.

I ran down the stairs. Dora prepared food in the kitchen. She wore the dress as before, with evidence of her run in the fields staining the hem. Her hair hung free and unbraided. She looked as if she had not slept.

"You did not wake me," I said.

"You are our guest," she said.

I sat down in a chair to strap on my boots. She laid down a plate of eggs and bacon on the table before me. I shook my head.

"It's not wise to go into war on a full stomach."

"So you would rather suffer on what may be your last day?"

"I do not intend to die, ma'am."

"And I don't intend my guests to starve. Eat."

The smell of her food convinced me to stay for a few moments longer. I proceeded to shovel spoonfuls into my mouth, having not realized how famished I was. The last full meal I had consumed was on the boat, and this was much better than that or any camp rations. Peppered just right, it was one of the most splendid breakfasts I had ever had.

"When did they start fighting?" I asked, scraping the last bits of egg off my plate.

"I was not listening."

"I do not know how I could have slept ever through it," I said.

"Perhaps you do not want to go."

I finished the coffee, which was strong enough to gird twenty men, and rose, rejuvenated. "You kept this soldier well. Thank you. I should say the same to your father."

"He is already out searching for James."

A long pause lingered between us. "I see. Well, I must be off."

She leaned against the sink and said nothing else.

In the stable, Bellona circled ceaselessly, scraping her hooves against the stall. The sound of gunfire was driving her mad with anticipation. She wanted to be let loose, to join the battle. I called her to me, then stroked her mane to sooth her. I told her the words I had used to woo her in days past, of the glory we would have. They sounded false when I said them now, yet Bellona eased. Soon I had her saddled, light one bag.

I rode out of the stable, tall on my horse. The house looked empty when we passed it.

Minutes later when I glanced back, Dora stood on the porch, the dogs jumping about her. The breeze rippled her gown and her chestnut hair caressed her neck. A tremor came over me. All my goals, my dreams faded at this vision of her. I wanted nothing but to sit at her table, play with her mutts, eat her breakfast and enjoy her company.

Bellona broke into a gallop.

Dora. Her name meant "gift" in Greek. My father never would have approved.

"You are not going to Manassas," my father said. "You are going to get back on that boat and return to Oxford at once."

He had aged noticeably during the time I was abroad. The blush of red around his nose had become permanent and he appeared shorter, diminished in stature, now requiring the use of a cane. A cranky petulance replaced his otherwise stern and unmitigable demeanor; at moments he seemed to regress into the fits of a child who could not get his way.

This was one of those moments. He stomped his foot and pointed his cane at the door of his study. "Get back on that boat, I said."

"That is impossible, father."

He pushed the tip of his cane into my chest. "You would flaunt your disobedience? In my own house?"

"The Yankees have blockaded our ports. There is no boat to take."

"Then how did you get here?"

"I was on a fast British steamer. We managed to run the blockade."

"Surely there are other vessels that can do the same."

"I have signed my volunteer papers, father. I would look like a coward."

He snorted, lowering his cane and jabbing it into the floor, more than once. "Who put you up to this? A colleague? A ladyfriend?"

I hesitated to give him an answer he already knew.

"Who?"

"You did, sir."

The cane trembled in his grip and ended with another stab at the floor, as if to punctuate his anger. "The cretin from Charleston has won! You have handed him victory!"

I looked at my father in confusion. He walked back to his desk. "While I wither away in obscurity, my articles rejected, my scholarship mocked as the ramblings of a rube, that cretin's idiocy will creep into the Old World and bear bitter fruit, spoiling the study of antiquity for generations to come. You were to stop that, but alas, it seems I have born no fruit at all."

I thought he had partaken of his libations early. Yet there neither was a glass on his desk, nor could I spot the crystal carafe from which he always poured.

"You too think I ramble."

"No, father. It is only that I do not understand. How did I hand your nemesis victory?"

"The cretin has a son at Cambridge. Another at the Sorbonne. And a third a year away from choosing any university he desires. From the rumors I hear, they all will be researching the purported equivalence of the Greco-Roman pantheons."

"I was not aware."

"Now you are." He fell into his armchair. "Get out of my sight."

"Father—"

"Go to Manassas, if that is what you want! But do not return here, for your mother's sake. She must think you are at Oxford."

I sighed, nodded, and walked to the door. There I turned to face him. "You have not born bitter fruit, father," I said. "When this is over and the South is at peace, I shall return to Oxford, and finish my studies."

As my hand turned the knob, he spoke one last time. "Your thesis. Had you chosen a subject?"

"Mars," I said.

Bellona's nostrils steamed. Her hooves barely touched the ground. I clung to her neck with both hands as she thundered at a pace faster than I had ever seen. Today her lungs belched fire.

It was all for naught.

When we arrived at Manassas, the battle was fought and done. What lay before us was its detritus. Shattered musket shells. Bayonets staked in the mud. Overturned tents. The whiff of clay powder in the air. Blood painting the grass crimson and congealing on the dead.

They were everywhere, the corpses. In various uniforms and various poses. Curled like babies, sprawled out with open arms. Face up, face down, without a face. Slumped, sitting against logs. Burnt from the coals of a fire pit. Dinted by grapeshot, wedged inside a cannon. Pieces. A leg, an arm, an eye. Hands in prayer, lips on letters. Standing but still dead, dead but still twitching. Hundreds. Man, horse, and dog.

Bellona slowed to pick her way over the bodies. Occasionally her legs buckled as this was not sure ground. I tried to keep my gaze forward, on the lookout for any sizable contingent of Beauregard's forces with whom I could rendezvous. Most of the soldiers I saw were in singles and pairs, tending to their injured brothers-in-arms or dressing wounds themselves. All avoided my glance.

I called out to one man who wandered in front of us aimlessly. A bandage was wrapped around his head and grime so caked his uniform that I could not distinguish whether he was Federal or Confederate.

"Who won?" I asked.

The soldier looked at me, his hand gripping his jaw, and shambled away.

I rode the length of the field to a broken wooden fence, which was built to stop bulls from plunging into the tributary called Bull Run. It had not stopped men.

The dead littered the banks and bobbed in the waters, filth swirling in brackish silt. The current tugged a few bodies free of the streambed and sent them adrift along with a woman's feather hat, a picnic basket, ribbons and tin medals. One body caught my eye. I dismounted and climbed down into the stream.

I pulled the man out of the water. He wore no uniform except breeches and his flesh. Strips of cloth wound around his torso and stuck to the lash marks on his back. Blood oozed out from under the stitches. There was a wound that was not dressed or stitched. A penny-sized hole where flies swarmed. I swatted them away.

The slave, the one Dora called James, had been shot in the back. His eyes were open and now they stared at me in horror.

I grew sick. Here was the first of my victims. A man killed not by my pistol, nor by my blade. But by my honor. Because I had done what Dora had asked.

Last night, after she had quieted the Great Dane and the other dogs, I had slipped into her father's room and stole the key to the shackles. Then I went to the slave's quarters to free him. He did not want to run. He feared what the old man would do if he was caught. He feared the dogs. I told him Dora was with the dogs and this was his only chance. I had to force him to go at gunpoint.

When James ran off, I felt a serene sense of relief, as if my spirit had lifted, as if I had done a great and noble deed. I had both saved his life and kept the honor of the South. We were not the cruel tyrants the Yankees supposed us to be. We were just and could amend our own wrongs. We were in the right.

Now this man was dead. Because of my actions. Because of my honor. Either the world I knew did not exist, or I was a traitor.

Trumpets sounded in the near distance. A quarter of a mile to the west on a stone bridge, a regiment of troops reassembled under a flag. Whether it was the Stars and Bars or the Stars and Stripes, I could not tell. I did not care. For a long time I held James's body in the waters.

The sky darkened. Twilight came. Soldiers splashed by and spoke of victory, their families, glory. I did not move. To them I was just another one of the dead. Above their chatter a dog howled "Dixie."

I looked up and was too late. The gunshot did not pierce my own flesh, but it sank into my heart all the same. A neigh followed, high-pitched and urgent, and then my dear steed Bellona tumbled through the fence to crash into the water.

I sprang up and ran to her side. She screamed and thrashed, kicking up waves. I had to duck one of her hooves to kneel next to her. Blood gushed from a gaping wound near her throat.

With all my strength, I pressed both hands down onto the wound to staunch the flow. It was like trying to hold down a geyser. Her life spurted out between my fingers. When her legs ceased to move, I knew the shot had penetrated deep into her spine. Still I pressed. I had helped her get her legs as a foal and I would do so again if it took all the patience of mankind.

"A horse for a slave. Not a fair trade, if I may say. I'm thinkin' you owe me more," said a weathered voice. Silhouetted against the night, Dora's father stood atop the bank, holding his rifle, with the beagle pawing the dirt next to him.

"I will kill you," I said. On instinct, I almost went for my sidearm. But if I drew, I would have to let go of Bellona.

The old man knew it too. He laughed. "Then come up here and do it. You're a man, ain't ya?"

Bellona screamed and at once I forgot the old man to look down at her. Her ears drooped and her eyes rolled in their sockets. I leant close and whispered her name. Over and over I said it, Bellona, faintly, sweetly. The gush of blood eased.

I released my hands to hold her head. Her eyes found mine and relaxed. In her pupils I saw my reflection, cast against the stars.

When I rose from the stream and climbed the bank, the farmer was gone. Thousands of Beauregard's troops were regrouping on the battlefield, yet no one had seen the old man or a beagle. They were too full of jubilation to search for a horse-killer. The Confederacy had won its first big victory and had sent those damned Yankees skedaddling back to Washington. The heavens had blessed the Southern cause.

"You see that, young soldier? Good omens, indeed," said a sergeant who wore epaulets snatched from a Northern officer. He held his cup of wine up to the sky. There the red star hung, bright, the color of blood. "Mars is on the march, my boy."

That night, I did not dream of war.

ZERO MARS

BY AARON PARRETT

eometry is to the universe what *keffrar* is to space," explained the pale-skinned wise one, as her bright-eyed pupil manipulated the polyhedrons stitched together with frozen bands of the eighth and ninth rays. "When you fully grasp the relationship between these unities, you will understand that your location in time is like a dream that you can control at will."

Her student was not yet two years old, but she was far beyond the others of her cohort, and already she had learned to nest the five perfect solids with a few deft flicks of her wrist, and to fold the interior regions without crossing their vertices.

Her name was Maizy Theta, and it had been clear from the moment of her hatching that she was a most unusual child. The caretakers of the incubators noticed that thirty-seven days before the breach of her shell a very faint lattice of perfect hexagonal stripes began to appear, as if the very framework of her origin bore testimony to her destiny. As the day of breaching drew closer, the lines glowed ever more brightly, and at the final moment, the shell burst like a frozen bubble of dioxide at one of Barsoom's poles, its perfectly shaped remnants falling like flower petals. Maizy had stepped out from the shell onto the soil and instinctively walked with faultless coordination toward the wise one, the one known only as "Bejanda," or "Teacher." Maizy began her lessons within moments of taking her first breaths of the thin Barsoomian air.

That had been many centuries ago, though Maizy remembered her first few moments on Barsoom as if they had occurred just yesterday. Her natural predilection for learning and her facility with numbers set her apart from the moment of her inception, and she steadily and effortlessly mastered the wisdom of the Therns and the ancient secrets of the first Barsoomian races.

But of what avail was almost two thousand years of her mastery of Barsoom's deepest mathematics and philosophy now? The Therns had not reacted with the sort of appreciative amazement she had anticipated when she exploited her newly discovered abilities to twist knots into the numerical fabric of distance between Barsoom and its nearest neighbor, Jasoom, in such a way that she could at will walk atop the strange green grass of the world its natives called "Earth," or wander the cobbled streets of its villages and cities—cities like Alexandria, which was like an entire nursery school of green jeddaks valiantly trying to puzzle out simple equations for waging wars.

Maizy recalled the occasion of her first arrival through the geometrical portal of the *keffrar* on Jasoom. All the images she had seen through Barsoom's viewers could not have prepared her for the real thing: the alien odor of its many trees and lush foliage, the frantic energy of its human beings, the strange specter of the sun and its moon shifting back and forth so readily.

She awoke from her transport and mentally sorted the dwindling rays emanating from the small ring she wore on her thumb. She knew the humans of this planet knew nothing of the eighth and ninth rays, if indeed they knew of anything beyond the first four. With a crisp snap of yellow light, her body emerged from its point of origin nearly one hundred and forty million haads away on her native planet.

When at last she stood on Jasoom, the ring on her thumb no longer glowed with its vibrating swirl of light; now it gleamed no more than a dull and ordinary local metal.

She had set her arrival at coordinates she calculated from the viewers, choosing a city at the nexus of commerce and learning so that she would not immediately be marked as an enemy. As she wandered its streets of limestone cobbles, lined with buildings of pink granite, she somehow felt at home—even though the cities of Barsoom were many thousands of years older and mostly abandoned now. This Jasoomian city was young and vibrant, yet it deported itself with an air of doom and decay that she read in the furrowed brows of its inhabitants.

Her light tunic and scarf were not much different from the dress she observed on those around her. Anyone looking closely would have seen her skin did not quite match any tone of flesh known on Earth. As for the language of the Earthmen, she had spent much time listening to their rhythmic chatter through the *keffrar* portal and had decoded their vocabulary and syntax so she could speak with relative ease.

But the men, at least, were put off by her lack of deference.

"What can a woman know of numbers?" scoffed the sages of the primitive cities on Earth when she sought to engage them in discussion.

They saw before them merely a woman, young and lithe, with skin of a rich ruddy tone that would have drawn cautious stares in a smaller town. Her eyes were grey as sword metal, but they glittered with an unfamiliar light. It was obvious that she was exotic, but that was true of many of the strange characters wandering the streets of Mediterranean cities.

Nevertheless, she struck the men as a foreigner on the verge of violating custom.

"But I know all of the operations you practice, and more," she insisted.

Her petulance was too much for the men of this world. "Bah! It is too much to expect a woman to count her own children and tally up the cups of grain she wastes in a week. Go—run your household, wherever it may be," said the men, laughing among themselves, annoyed by her daring and distrustful of her unfamiliar accent.

Baffled, she withdrew from one circle and another, before she even had a chance to scratch a triangle of her own in the dust.

Then, one afternoon, a soft voice followed her as she scurried down a narrow lane of crumbling stone and anxious chickens.

"I, too, have tried to join them," said the voice. "But a man cannot hear what a woman says unless she whispers in his ear."

Maizy Theta smiled. The voice belonged to a sturdy woman, barefoot and plain, but who stood with her shoulders back and her chin thrust forward.

"And do you know the mathematics over which they converse?" she asked.

The woman nodded. "I know what they know, and so much more. My father was a brilliant man who did not deny his children the light of his mind simply because they were girls. He taught me to read and write as soon as I could speak. He taught me all that he knew about numbers and shapes and the mysteries of the circle and the square."

"My name is Maizy Theta. I would trade words with you regarding all these things."

The woman looked puzzled, but took the hand Maizy offered to her. "Your name is quite odd. Alexandria is a town of many tongues, but I do not recognize your accent or know what land your name might fit. And I must confess I have seen all manners and shades of human being, but never one with skin like . . . yours."

"Perhaps one day I will tell you how it is that I arrived in your wonderful city, but for now I must remain something of a stranger given the attitude of your men."

"I understand."

"But you have not told me your name—or perhaps you have something to hide as well."

"Forgive me! My name is Hypatia. Please—follow me. I will take you to my dwelling place and give you food and drink."

Hypatia regaled her with stories of Earth, of its people and their strange emotions. She demonstrated geometrical proofs regarding most of the features of the five solids and a simple quadratic formula for solving polynomials of the second degree, showing a distinct pride in what for Maizy Theta was as simple as breathing.

"And you do these things without the nullity?" marveled Maizy Theta.

Hypatia looked puzzled. "I do not know that word."

Maizy cleared the dust and tapped a handful of holes in the fresh surface with her fingertips. Into each light depression she dropped a pebble, which seemed to be the local custom for calculating. A radium machine would have greatly speeded things, but Maizy Theta was patient and respectful.

"This is a quantity." Maizy swept the dust and made the motions to indicate other orders of magnitude—tens, and then hundreds. And then she removed a few of the pebbles and circled the depressions that were left with her index finger. "Now tell me if you know what these are."

Hypatia frowned. "They are the difference in sums . . . " she began, then shook her head.

Maizy Theta tapped the dust and swept a light round circle around the depressions. "This is the nothing that is something. The other men around this place sometimes speak quietly of it—as if they are afraid. I heard them call it the 'nullity,' or 'nullus.' Something like that."

"An absence of quantity."

Maizy Theta's eyes gleamed in appreciation. "In some cases. But not in others. Here, I will show you."

The two of them knelt in the dust of the hearth of Hypatia's home, deftly twitching out formulae and figures, too caught up in their work to recall that they had come for food and rest.

Over the course of many Earth days, the two women shared words and wine and spoke of numbers and the distances between planets. Maizy Theta perceived that Hypatia was a singular intellect among the humans of earth, though Barsoomian mathematics was far beyond even her. If Maizy could conceive a way of conveying Hypatia to Barsoom, perhaps the woman could understand.

In the end, Maizy was able to explain the *keffrar* only in its most feeble form.

"So, this quantity that is empty of quantity is called *keffrar*?"

"Yes, but it is more complex than that as well. It can be more than just the nullity."

"*Psephos*, that is what it should be called in my language."

"It is the number of numbers, and the emptiness that contains all the ranges of all things that can be counted. You will have to catch your breath when you can see what it will do."

Hypatia mastered all of the simplest aspects of the *keffrar*, but she remained baffled by simultaneity of *is/not is*, which Maizy Theta understood as simply as she knew the planets circled the Sun.

"In my country, we call this quality *qubit*," Maizy explained. "An emanation—like light, for example, or a number—"

"How can light be like number?"

Maizy smiled. She tapped the dust and made a small impression, into which she placed one of the small pebbles the Jasoomians used for counting. "Do you see, beneath the one pebble, the nullity rests? They are there at the same time." She lifted the pebble. "You see? Nothing." She dropped the pebble back into its little crater. "Now something."

"Is it not one or the other?"

"The power of the 'nullity' is that it can hold something within, like this pebble in the emptiness beneath it. Standing above the emptiness is a quantity, a something."

"As if it is waiting to be swallowed up . . . "

"Precisely! Only if you can think of it this way: it is all the time, always *being swallowed up.*"

Hypatia looked puzzled, but recalled a quip of wisdom from her own youth. "One of the ancient philosophers of my country said that '*Being is like a worm coiled at the heart of Nothingness.*'"

"What a way of putting it!" Maizy nearly clapped her hands together. "And someday you will see that light and number are like the stone and the dust."

Her hours with Hypatia were rich with profit for them both—Hypatia absorbed the mysteries of the *keffrar* with aplomb, while Maizy Theta luxuriated in the thick warm air of this strange planet, delighting in the oily richness of its food and the bubbling sweetness of its mead.

Eventually, however, the tireless conflicts among the men and women of earth—all of whom looked so much alike that it was a mystery to Maizy Theta why they fought at all—wore on her and she longed for the relative tranquility of Barsoom. It was true that some of the races of Barsoom lived only for combat, and the green men in particular were a nuisance, but here it seemed that no one got along for long.

Each time she transported herself and returned, she realized that was paying for her visits with a loss of her being—almost as if some part of her mass disappeared and with it, the continuity of her identity. She came to understand why it was strictly forbidden to leave the bounds of Barsoom, and that it was largely for her own good.

Nevertheless, Maizy Theta moved back and forth from Barsoom to its neighbor Jasoom with careless frequency. She spent many afternoons with Hypatia, drinking strangely flavored and strong Egyptian wine while patiently leading her through the logical manipulations of the *keffrar*. Hypatia was an avid learner, though she seemed perpetually frightened.

"They took my husband, you see," explained Hypatia when Maizy asked about her furtive glances at the door while they worked equations on the crude wax boards the Earthmen used for calculating devices. "There are many around us here who feel such knowledge is forbidden."

"What was his discipline?"

"He was a logician. He was adept at dismantling the proofs of others. One of our wisest philosophers devised a proof of God's existence, which my husband exploded with efficient delight. The very men who laughed at the facility of his demonstration and ridiculed its author came later and escorted him away."

"I am sorry for your loss. And now you think they will come for you?"

Hypatia nodded. "The neighbors have warned me that I am being watched. They are aware of your visits, and no one knows you, or where you come from. I do not mean to frighten you, but I tell you—these methods you have shown me—they would execute you."

Maizy smiled. "Men who would kill over their gods are superstitious, not holy. It is sometimes the same where I am from."

Noise from the street jolted Hypatia. She ran to the window. "I told you! Look, they swarm like angry flies!"

A mob was gathering in the street. The men were shouting for Hypatia to show herself. Instead she drew the curtains together defiantly and turned toward Maizy.

"I will show you the way to the alley. If you leave now, you will escape them."

Maizy looked at her thoughtfully. "There is another way . . . "

The shouting and tumult were growing in intensity. They could hear voices out in the hall at the bottom of the stairs.

Maizy Theta took Hypatia by the hand and led her to the low couch against the wall. The two of them sat facing one another while Maizy swept the dials of the ring clasping her thumb. The room became flooded in the confluence of rays. The dazzling light took Hypatia's breath away. Suddenly the room was filled with men shouting, their beards flecked with angry spittle, but by now Hypatia could hear nothing.

Maizy held her hand and probed her mind. *It is . . . nothing,* she felt Hypatia thinking, and she responded telepathically: *Yes. It is nothing.*

Then the room disappeared as the two lost consciousness.

For her offenses, which included the unauthorized transport of a Jasoomian to Barsoom, Maizy was issued a summons to appear before Bledzok the Wise, first among the Therns. She sought out her teacher for counsel.

"Bejanda, why do Bledzok the Wise and his lieutenants insist on curbing my desire to teach and learn? They are well aware that we are not alone in the skies."

"You are precocious, but naïve, my precious Theta. You deny your body in deference to your mind. You cannot use the transport of rays without suffering grave danger."

"Is not the mind simply a system of the body? Like our digestive system, or our nerves?"

The teacher smiled. "Quite so. But the mind and the body interact along lines that unfold according to the logic of what we represent with qubits."

"And whatever result the qubit yields in one scenario, it must necessarily deny in the other—yes, I know."

"Ah, so we have been through this before. Recall the rhyme about the calot in the box:

> *In a box, a calot hides,*
> *I cannot see him with my eyes,*
> *A black calot walks through the door*
> *Where white the calot was before.*"

Maizy narrowed her eyes. "That rhyme is for children, Bejanda."

"Yes, but it is a warning to us all. I cannot put it more simply than to say that you let your flights of mental fancy take you too far away from the business of life itself. We are flesh and blood, and therefore the soil of Barsoom and nothing much more."

"But the wisdom of the numbers and the folding of the rays lead so clearly to other worlds, to an infinite—"

"In a way," her teacher interrupted. "But when you use them as you do, you must suffer a concomitant loss of actual existence here. All quantities in the end balance out."

"Oh, the repercussions are far worse than *you* make them out," thundered the growling voice of Graddok, one of the Wise One's closest lieutenants. They had not heard him enter, but now his rough whiteness clouded the room and his harsh voice grated their ears.

"You cannot imagine what havoc you will wreak on Jasoom by giving men gifts they cannot possibly hope to understand for centuries to come. Our world is nearly as old as the sun—theirs is like an unhatched egg that has not yet begun to glow. And here you go, showing them tricks that will doom them surely."

Maizy Theta resisted the urge to argue.

"What is worse—they will probably hasten our end as well, and take us with them to their doom," said Graddock.

She could remain silent no longer. "But perhaps we will one day need them to help us—to save our civilization!"

Graddok laughed. "We have watched them for millennia. We should sooner expect succor from the Black Pirates."

"Well. You cannot stop me, and I will teach any student who is willing."

"We shall see about that. As speaker for the Wise Ones, I hereby enforce your summons and call you to a trial in the Hall of Rays before the Circle of the Wise."

At her trial, Maizy Theta pled innocence of the charges—interfering with interplanetary peace and evolutionary processes by misuse of the sacred rays, insubordination, and corrupting the pure strands of time enfolding Barsoom—but she knew that the hearing was a formality. Simply calling her to account was an indication that a verdict had long ago been reached.

"We wise counselors of the race of Ancient White Therns do hereby condemn you to abstraction for a period sufficient for us to assess the damage and to conjure up some method of repair, if it should be required and if we are able. We do not believe in punishment per se, but we wish your abstraction to be an exhausting experience that will perhaps impress upon you the grave nature of your offense. We have spoken."

Maizy Theta understood that her fellow Barsoomians were distinct from the people of Jasoom in many respects. By and large, they were incapable of emotional attachment or what those on earth understand as *conscience*, and the punishments they impose upon their criminal classes were purely punitive and never administered with any fantasy of rehabilitation in mind.

Thus it was that the administrators of the Therns, led by the Lieutenant Graddock deemed that Maizy Theta must be restrained from further experimentation involving the sacred rays.

It was her prodigious skill in mental artifice and her finesse with formal logic that determined the precise nature of her imprisonment: she was to be inserted into the framework of one of the most complex and baffling mysteries of number theory. Given the singular nature and focus of the Barsoomian intellect, an apparatus of ratiocination that cannot evade its own drive to the solution of problems—whether it is a search for water on the ruddy plains of its dead seas, or a strategic maneuver in battle—this was for Maizy Theta a veritable prison of impenetrable stone and steel. She had to admire the cunning of her oppressors: the Barsoomian mind finds itself unable to resist the challenge of a problem subject to the critical faculties. Ordinarily the problems she encountered would not have posed any particular challenge and so would never have been as incapacitating. But the mind of a Barsoomian abhors paradox and is compelled to resolve it like an Earthman instinctively seeks water when he finds himself in the midst of desert sands.

Many paradoxes belong to that species of mental conundrums which tickle but do not perplex. *This statement is false* arouses a smirk, then a wrinkled brow, and then a dismissive sniff. Certain words and phrases simply can't be self-referential, we observe, and let them pass. Meditation on such trifles we leave to children bored at recess, or to philosophers who have already earned tenure. Other paradoxes create more respectable and enduring problems. How can an electron have either velocity or location but not both? How can a time traveler move back into the past without impinging on her future? From what possible vantage point can it be meaningful to remark that *all motion is relative*? From what lofty epistemological ledge can one say with certainty that *truth and meaning are matters of perspective*?

The interior of the abstraction to which they had condemned Maizy Theta echoed with the haunting groans of collapsing geometrical proofs. The very structure of her thoughts became tangled in knots around her as she sought to grasp the threads that would connect the mental dots and lead her outward, back into the light that flocked around irreducible axioms, self-evident truths, and inviolate precepts. She surveyed a cerebral terrain whose horizon glowed dimly, as if a fading sun had set just beyond her reach. Her mind raced to grasp the last rays of light ahead of an inevitable gloom that would envelop her mind and leave her locked in forever. Copulae and operators hummed and oscillated through her like geometric bursts of electricity. The *keffrar* of her youth—the essence of her life's purpose—had become inverted, turned inside out, and she was falling across the edge of its infinite and indefinite border.

Outside her mind, the material red sands of Barsoom swirled and shifted without ceasing in throes that marked the dying of a planet. The vanishing of its once vast seas had marked the beginning of ten thousand years of slow decline—an interval plenty long enough for its inhabitants to become accustomed to the idea of disappearance.

On Jasoom, it was another story.

"We fear that their thirst for territory and their inhuman lack of empathy will lead them to exterminate us without prejudice, O Wise One," reported Zabrisk, number two among the Therns to Bledzok, who was number one.

"Do they not understand that their survival on their vibrant young planet depends in part on us?" Bledzok could not grow used to the foolish notions of the primitive Jasoomians. They would not merely bite, but chew off and devour the very hand that fed them. "How soon will they come here of their own accord?"

"Yes, I'm afraid they do not understand anything beyond their irrepressible compulsion to wage constant battle among themselves, on the most feeble of pretexts. According to our algorithms, they should begin migrating here in a few thousand years."

"And we lack the power to repel them?"

"Well . . ." Number Two hesitated. "We are not completely without the means to subdue them. But I fear the cure is worse than the disease."

"Pray tell, what in Diis does that mean?"

Number Two smiled wryly. "I mean only that we could release Maizy Theta from her abstraction. She could use her facility with travel beyond the *keffrar* to find a solution that might avoid undue bloodshed."

"Can we not effect such a solution on our own?"

Number Two frowned. "Probably. But it would take time to discover methods she has known since her infancy. After all, we condemned her to abstraction for a reason."

"I'm failing to remember what it was we found so threatening in her methods."

"Sir, you will recall that she has retrieved an Earthwoman from Jasoom and deposited her here."

"What of that?"

"The woman needs to be sent back, Wise One."

"Why? Surely no single female could disrupt the fabric of Barsoomian time enough to cause damage."

"She is of no consequence. It is her egg. I have peeked through the *keffrar* to witness the line of her brood," said Number Two.

"And what did you see?"

"I saw one of her progeny who could become the greatest jeddak among the green hordes. Great enough to challenge us."

The leader of the Therns recoiled in disgust. "Impossible."

"What is more is that this jeddak occupies a slot of timespace on Barsoom in which he counts as his closest ally a woman who is descended from Theta herself."

"We must not let this happen. We must kill this Earthwoman."

"We cannot, Wise One. Our thinkschools counsel her death will cause irreparable damage to the timestream. There will be no hope of mastering the *keffrar*. She must be sent back, so that her egg never hatches on this planet. But I would not risk sacrificing the essence of any of us in doing so. Maizy Theta caused this, she should fix it."

Number One rubbed his ears, coughed, and sighed. "Break Maizy Theta from her abstraction."

"You needn't have retrieved me," Maizy insisted emphatically. "I was on the verge of unraveling your abstraction."

Number One smiled. "I admire your self-confidence, but you must know that that particular abstraction is especially frustrating because the solution seems just out of reach."

"A few more attempts—"

Number One did not wish to quash her exuberance. "If anyone could . . . *circumvent* that abstraction, it would be you, certainly. The fact is, we need you. That is why we hastened your retrieval."

Maizy Theta was pleased to hear the leader hint that she was capable of retrieving herself from the abstraction. "How may I serve the Therns?"

Number One sighed. "I must warn you, this duty comes at a considerable cost to yourself."

Maizy noted the slight emphasis on the word 'duty,' but it was unnecessary. As with all highly evolved Barsoomians, the instinct for species preservation ran deep.

"From what I was told before immersion into the abstraction, my years on Barsoom have been shortened by centuries."

"Yes. It is impossible to pursue qubit manipulations involving spacetime transport and not lose actual mass. It is like gaining immortality at the cost of experience. Your instantiations will continue to reverberate down the avenues of those ninth ray emanations you effected, but at the very real cost of any localized mass."

"So I will—"

"You will continue in a fashion, but there will be no 'I' there."

"The only way the calot can be black and white is for there to be no calot inside the box at all."

Number One laughed. "I thought you would be more distressed."

"State my duty and I will do it."

"Yes, of course. It seems the Jasoomian woman you retrieved must be immediately returned. She fulfills a function in the path from which you snatched her that is critical to developments on Jasoom that almost certainly affect us."

"But I was told that manipulations of this sort are forbidden."

Number One admired the flash of measured insolence in her eyes. He had had a similar streak in his own youth.

"Oh, they are. But please recall that this involves factors beyond the scope of either this planet alone or that."

"Do you refer to what on Jasoom they call 'God'?"

Number One frowned. "That mistake in reasoning is perhaps the most frightening flaw in their primitive minds. How little do they understand how that habit in their thinking is actually like a hidden charge of radium that may do them in before they have a chance to develop themselves into something useful to the solar system." He sighed, again. "No, that is hardly a concept large enough to contain all the statistical truth of the universe."

"That is what you mean? The statistical truth?"

He nodded.

Maizy understood and was quiet. Number One was telling her the truth, but not all of it. Still, this was her duty and she must attend to it.

She also saw other possibilities, visions the *keffrar* had provided. Perhaps what was good for her kinsmen on Barsoom would be even better for her friends on Earth.

Hypatia returned to consciousness before Maizy. The tumult of angry men had vanished, and the room was still. Hypatia leaned back into the cushions and tried to retrieve snatches of the strangest dreams she had ever had. She must remember to stick with less potent wine!

Maizy's eyes fluttered briefly and then she spoke.

"How do you feel?"

"Exhausted. But . . . was it not a dream?"

"In a sense, yes. I wish I could explain more fully, but we haven't much time." In fact, she was not sure how much time she actually had, but instinct told her it was imperative to hurry. "Have you any idea where your husband is held?"

"Why, yes. They have locked him in a building not a half mile from here."

"We must go there immediately. I must ask you—do you trust him absolutely?"

"I do. What is all this about?"

"A day soon will dawn in which you must make a great sacrifice. It is clear to me that you do not have much fear of men, and that will help you, but in the end it will fall to someone else to pass on what I have shown you."

"So the mob of men was not a dream?"

"No, they are real. You will escape them for a time, but eventually . . . "

Hypatia nodded. "And you? What will become of you?"

Maizy smiled. "I must . . . disappear. Now, take me to the dungeon where your man is held."

As they scurried through the alleys, avoiding the faces that they passed, Maizy Theta tried to explain the riddle of the calot. It was impossible to convey without a more thorough grasp of the *keffrar*, but Hypatia accepted the urgency of the situation and did her best to follow.

Outside the walls of a plain stone chapel, Hypatia pointed to a narrow window with iron bars. "We cannot see him, but if I whisper his name, he can reach out his hand."

"Good. I will only need to be close. As soon as he is outside the walls, you must vanish. Leave this land and travel west. If you disguise yourselves as monks, you will make it far."

"Where shall we go?"

"I'm not sure. But you will know when you get there. And remember, you must write everything you know down as soon as possible. Have copies made. Your husband will do this for you?"

Hypatia nodded.

"Then follow me. Call his name when we are close enough."

When the weary man inside his tomb heard his wife's sweet voice, he slowly stirred and reached his hand through the bars. No sooner had he noticed that it was not his wife's, but a stranger's hand in his grasp, than he found himself barefoot in the dust outside the prison.

"What miracle is this?" he cried, embracing his wife.

"Thank you," Hypatia said to Maizy, kissing her cheek. "I wish you well."

Already Maizy Theta was beginning to fade, the color in her cheeks pulsing as the eighth and ninth rays enveloped the last of her mass. The furious guards from inside the chapel were screaming and brandishing knives of oyster shell and bronze.

"One last thing," Maizy said to the couple. "Have children."

Hypatia was puzzled at this sudden remark, but her husband pulled her away to flee into the evening twilight.

The would-be captors were astonished when they reached the point of their prisoner's escape to find nothing left in the air but the lingering wisp of a smile and a dull ring of lead in the dust.

THE WHITE APES OF ISS
BY MARK D'ANNA

I am going to die because of love. We all are. I have been here for eight hundred years, most of that time alone, walled off from the world. There is just machinery here. Machinery and walls. The machinery is very loud. Nothing else here is. We revere it, this machinery. All Barsoomians do. They hold me in a certain esteem, too. I am the soul of this planet. I give life to this machinery. I give life to the whole of this world. I am practically a god.

I have no present, no future. Yet I go on indefinitely, condemned to walk these same halls, stare at these same walls for all eternity. I have only past, only prologue. My life ceased along the River Iss on that day so long ago when the white ape attacked. No matter what I do, I cannot forget it. What I have been experiencing since that day cannot rightfully be called life, nor can it be called death. It is somewhere at the intersection of the two, in that watery gray all Barsoomians fear so completely. I see it every day. I know its size and its shape. For me this place is not so much a factory as it is a tomb.

I can still see it so vividly, the hulking white animal, the long, powerful arms, the eyes deep-set and black, filled with one desire—to kill—and nothing more. Its silhouette overtook the waning light of the fire and cast a shadow across the entirety of the campsite, plunging it into darkness. The place was thick with vines and outcropping rocks from the surrounding valley, and we were cornered there. The ape had hunted us across the long expanse of dusty, red landscape, followed us along the shorelines, along the valley rim and to the floor below. It moved quietly at first, as if in some vain attempt to prevent the waking of an even greater evil better left sleeping. It waited until we were cornered, vulnerable and tired, before it attacked. I remember the awful sounds, reverberating along the stony walls, ascending into the void of the surrounding night and sustained forever in memory.

Jerrak is dead now. So is Thena. Their fates played out centuries ago. Yet I persist, hobbled by age, driven nearly mad by loneliness. The choice I made that day was to do nothing, and because of that I am sentenced, doomed to a long existence without joy or love or companionship. Condemned to do nothing but operate the machinery in this factory, so that the rest of Barsoom might go on living. I know nothing but this persistent, purgatorial tedium. I exist nowhere but in memories and regrets.

It is midday. I have checked the pumps. They will not need checking again for another hour or so. I wander down the long corridor. It is dark, cold, my robes weigh heavily on me today. The shuffling of my feet creates a strange echo far down the corridor. I close my eyes as I walk and imagine it is someone else down there, another one like me, slowly working his way to the pumps. And there we will meet and talk and exchange a friendly word. But he only moves when I move. And he moves away from me. Always going away from me.

The ceilings in my tomb are made of a thick, clear composite. The walls are like that of a fortress, deep, impenetrable. No one is permitted in and no one may leave. I am allowed a short leave each year, at which time an assistant relieves me. But the bulk of the time here is mine alone. The machinery is too valuable to allow others access to it. All life on Barsoom depends upon the safety and function of this factory. But Barsoom is a perilous, dangerous place. Once peaceful cities now lie in ruin, overrun by wild beasts, destroyed by war and famine. People here know only greed and murder and violence. They live in fear of random and meaningless attack, at all times. So they have made the task of isolating me from their murderous habits a top priority, second only to their interminable desire to kill one another. The machinery housed here within my tomb provides the atmosphere that makes this planet livable. And with the life I give them, all Barsoomians want to do is kill.

I ascend the stairwell to my turret. Climbing these stairs has grown increasingly difficult over the years. I have fashioned a long rope, which I use to pull myself up. A sad, weak spectacle it must be, but it is all I can do to reach the top. I fear one day I will no longer be able to make it. This turret offers me a small window, which is my only means of viewing the outside world. Were I to be robbed of this window, of this view, I would have nothing around me all day but dark, dirty walls, shadows, and gray. Coming here, sitting down, and looking into the distance is the only respite I am afforded. It is the only time I still feel free.

I take my seat at the window and survey the surrounding lands. Occasionally I will see a small horde of the red men passing in the distance, hunting, fleeing, it is hard to tell one from the other. They all look the same, riding high astride their thoats, weapons at hand, layered in the dust of these wastelands. Watching the warriors pass in the distance is a troubling thing for me. The wars have always been fought here. They always will be fought. I cannot help but question it. Sometimes I think how easy it would be to let it all fall by the wayside, to allow the machinery stop pumping, and watch the atmosphere wither and die. I think of the warlords, the princes and princesses, how they live their lives, consumed by their own importance, their own self-appointed value. How easily I could take it all away from them. And maybe they deserve it. A just punishment for the violence they inflict upon one another. I am alone, centuries old, a weak, feeble man. Yet I hold the power to destroy the greatest warlords of the land, to eradicate violence and greed and lust for power once and for all from this place. It is a strange thing.

I sit here in my perch for a very long time, surveying the landscape. I am tired, fading in and out of wakefulness. I think I see a movement in the distance. I look again, thinking it some trick of the mind. It was a good distance away, on the horizon. There it is again, some creature moving slowly across the landscape. Whatever it is, it appears small and weak, possibly injured. It crawls across the dusty landscape, slow and deliberate, as though its fate were cast by some other agency than that which rules this place. It pauses on an outcropping of rock. Perhaps it will die there, so sad and sickly is its gait. I can see it better. It is dusty, dripping from the trials that have brought it here. It is a man-shaped thing, male from the look of it. He has a calot at his side. The man looks at my tomb and I look down at him and for that brief moment I think maybe he sees me. But such a thing would be impossible over such a great distance. He moves again. He is coming in my direction.

He is not a red man nor is he green. I don't know what he is. He is of a different hue, a manner of being I have not seen before. He is small, a pale color. His calot is injured. They are both in bad shape, weakened by their travels, by war. Why he should seek me out I do not know, but there are many possibilities. I do not move from my perch.

He is almost to the doors of my tomb. I don't know what to do. I laugh. This man is a pathetic sight. He will probably be dead within a day and that is likely a good thing. Any Barsoomian would have too much sense to seek my aid here. The law strictly forbids me from taking visitors of any kind. But this man, he seems different.

He arrives at the front entrance of my tomb and bangs on the door. I should leave him there, let him die sad and alone. But something draws me to him. I know it is a mistake, but I do it still. I stand up and descend the stairs. I shuffle down the long corridor until I arrive at the gated entrance. I put my hands and head against the door. I push softly against it, and it pushes back. He is still there, on the other side, demanding to be let in. I laugh some more.

Thena and I were meant to be together. That is what I believed. I still believe it. We were together in Greater Helium as children. I had been identified early on and brought into the program. I was said to be unique, to possess certain, rare characteristics. I do not know what they saw in me. But few children were chosen. Jerrak was with us too. He was also chosen. We were educated together, trained together, matured together. Oftentimes we would sit across from one another talking of nothing for hours. I saw Thena regularly. We were the closest of friends. I knew Jerrak had eyes for her as well. I would see him looking at her and I knew what he was thinking. We never spoke about it. Such feelings were forbidden in the program.

As we progressed, it became clear that Jerrak was the likely candidate to assume the position at the factory. He was stronger, smarter, possessed of a considerably greater mind and spirit than any of the others. I did not excel at combat training, at the sciences or any of the mental labors. Jerrak was the one everyone admired. He was considered a great and selfless person, a gift to all of Barsoom. He would be the savior of our people someday. This was something worth respecting.

It was a quiet afternoon, a few days before the trials to determine the successor at the atmosphere factory were set to begin. Thena and I had sneaked away, wandering into the farmlands north of the city. We were alone for the first time in a long time. We had a view of the river valley. Thena wore a beautiful golden bracelet on her wrist. She fingered it absentmindedly as we spoke.

"Where did you get that?" I asked. "It's quite beautiful."

"Are you afraid?" she asked me.

"Afraid?" I asked.

"Of the trials."

"No," I said.

"They will be difficult," she said. "You will be alone, tested. Most do not return."

I smiled. Thena was concerned for me. "I have been well trained," I said.

She looked at the horizon. Helium lay sprawling before us, bustling with life. I felt no connection with the place any longer. It was the city in which I had grown up. It was supposedly my home, but I had been severed from it years before, not allowed to have a normal childhood, normal relationships. Thena was my only friend. I cared deeply for her. I took her hand in mind. She was soft, innocent. Mine. I thought I would kiss her but didn't. I couldn't. I was too afraid. We sat in silence for a long time, staring at the city, listening to the sounds floating up from it. I asked her if she would meet me here again, in two nights, my last night before the trials. She said she would.

He has been at my door for some time now. He has grown tired of his banging. Instead, he yells ceaselessly, boorishly. In my training I was taught to fear everyone. There would be no end to the attacks I would be subjected to in this position. I was to consider everyone a threat to my personal safety. People only came here for one reason, and that was to kill me, to destroy everything I once swore to protect, to eradicate all life on this planet. My safety is the safety of everyone. This incredible value is my curse. It means isolation. But I am intrigued by this man. His origins are unknown, and he appears to be dying. And I am so alone. If he is not of the countless warring factions that pollute this ridiculous planet, what cause do I have to fear him? I can think of none.

I can see the man through a small inlet in the door. He struggles to his feet, almost as if he can sense some movement or thought nearby. He examines the door, perhaps searching for a breach, a way in. There is a speaking tube there. He examines it closely. He leans towards it, about to speak. I interrupt him. I will have the first word. It is better that way.

"Who are you?" I ask.

The man says nothing. He is frozen, too scared to respond.

"Where are you from and what is the nature of your errand?"

I watch him, looking him over more closely than I had before. He does not respond. His is a sad visage, a cold, white pallor on his face, his body torn and tattered. Even his calot looks defeated and dying. I try to read his thoughts but I am unable. It is strange. I can read the thoughts of any man or beast on Barsoom, yet this man's mind is entombed, protected from a harsh world that seeks to violate it. Does he think about war and violence and murder like all the other creatures of this place? Is he here to plunge a weapon into my chest? I doubt it. Such people do not usually bang on your door and demand entrance. I cannot read his mind but his face tells me more than I need to know. This man is docile. He is peace-loving. He has fought before, I am certain of that. But he is done now. He is lost and lonely and in need of help. And so am I.

Finally, he speaks. "I have escaped from the Warhoons," he says. "I am dying of starvation and exhaustion."

"You wear the metal of a green warrior and are followed by a calot," I say, "yet you are of the figure of a red man. In color you are neither green nor red. In the name of the ninth day, what manner of creature are you?"

"I am a friend of the red men of Barsoom and I am starving," he replies. "In the name of humanity open to us."

A friend of the red men of Barsoom. Humanity. These things mean nothing to me. An escapee of the Warhoon warriors of the north. This equally means nothing to me. I hold no allegiance to anyone. I am neither of the north nor the south. I am neither green nor red nor white. I am of no city, no planet, no home. They are all murderous, lecherous beasts to me. I stand still for a moment, watching him. Of course my duty to my post dictates one thing and one thing only. If a visitor arrives at the gate, unannounced, of unknown origin or purpose, I am to turn him away. I am to send him back into the harsh deserts from which he came. The will of the many outweighs the needs of the one. For the good of all Barsoom.

I cannot do it. I won't do it. I feel something I have not felt in a long time. It is a spark inside me. A long forgotten connection to someone living beyond these walls. I am suddenly happy to be standing here talking to another and having him talk back to me. When was the last time I communicated with anyone? I cannot say. I do not communicate. I stay here, in my tomb, and I watch, and I wait. On the rare occasion when I am allowed to leave and my assistant arrives, I am kept in equal isolation. No one must know my whereabouts, ever. It is too risky. My life means too much to too many people. But now there is suddenly something I can do about my loneliness. I can exert some power, some manner of free will, and I can make it so I am not lonely anymore. I take a step back from the door. It can only be opened by uttering a silent incantation, a prayer known only to me. I stare down the massive doors that separate me from the rest of the world. I close my eyes, recite the incantation, and listen as the doors slide open.

It was the morning of the trials. I had remained alone on the hill the night before waiting for Thena to arrive as she had promised. She never did. I wandered back to my room in the early morning hours, alone through the darkened streets of the city. I saw a group of old women who had been upriver gathering food all night long. To me they were ghosts, fates wandering the land of the living, warning us. The night was bright, full of two strange moons. Another woman knelt at the door of her home. She had built a small fire there. She poked at it with a stick, blew back a flame from the ashes. This will be the last time I see this city, I thought, and I have no one to share it with.

All our young lives had lead up to the trials. This was our fate, our destiny, written out for us by birthright and nothing more. Each of us was to be sent down the River Iss. We would go alone, on a single raft. The River Iss was the passageway to the Valley Dor, the halfway world between the living and dead. A place devoid of life and of death and a place no living thing was meant to return from unless there was something more to him. If we survived and returned, then we were newly born, ordained agents chosen by the gods and destined to assume the care of the atmosphere factory. The others never return, and are lost to the afterlife.

I looked out at the river, cold and dark, indeterminate. It was stormy with wind and rain that day. The gods were angry. I could think only of Thena. I had hoped to spend my last night with the woman I loved but instead I spent it alone. I would not return from the Valley. Men like me do not return. We go down the cold, dark waters, we slip quietly to the other side and whatever strange eternity awaits us there. Last night I had planned to tell Thena that I loved her, that had circumstances been different, I would have spent my entire life with her. Now it was too late.

The elders went through their final incantations, eyes closed, hands raised, offering prayers to the river and sky in equal portion. We were silent, covered in the garb of our trade, the armor, the ceremonial daggers and headgear. Jerrak was at the front of the group. The sun bowed down ahead of him in the distance, and his shadow fell long and cold across the group. The air grew colder in it. To the west, further down the river, we could hear the howls of the strange animals that lived there. Apes and banths, all of them creating horrible, malingering noises, noises that cut through you. I stared at Jerrak and he was unfazed. He held his dagger in his hand. We all did. The sun lingered longer in the distance then appeared to quiver, to move slightly, and something on Jerrak's wrist caught the light just so. I closed my eyes, turned my head away from the bright reflection. The prayers of the elders continued unabated. I tried to pray with them but I couldn't. My eye was drawn back to the glinting adornment on Jerrak's arm. I could see it clearer now. It was Thena's bracelet, which had caught that reflection, which had blinded me to all things. Jerrak wore it now.

What a fool I had been. Thena had been with him last night. She had left me waiting alone on that hill, and had been with Jerrak instead. He stood so proudly in his armor, solitary amongst the group, strangely unassuming for all of his prowess, gazing out over the heads of his adversaries. I hated him. Together they must have laughed at me the whole night through. Laughed at my foolishness in thinking she would choose me over him. I felt a clammy movement throughout my body. I gripped my dagger tightly. I could run it through him before anyone got to me and that would be the end of it. I listened to the lull of the river water, the incantations that surrounded me. I was scared, too scared to move. There arose a low rumbling in the distant sky like a rainfall was gathering, and suddenly the sun was gone behind a cloud again, the reflections it had brought suddenly gone, and all the world lay in cold shadow.

The door to my tomb moves very slowly and deliberately. I move myself back, away from the door, positioning myself in a secret inner chamber. From here I can see the man, watch him, even interact with him, yet stay safely hidden. This traveler wears the battle garb of the green warriors, yet his stature is more similar to that of the red man. He appears to be neither red nor green. He is a strange sight, seemingly wrought from the very wildness of this place. He is clearly a warrior, but he has long since flung his implements of war and destruction in favor of survival, of retreat. If he is a warrior then he is a failed one. He comes to me a victim, a supplicant.

He crawls slowly into the entry chamber. His movements are labored and difficult. His calot follows close behind him. They are nearly inside my tomb. But the man pauses, looks around, perhaps sensing my presence nearby, some uneasy feeling overtaking him. I keep myself hidden. I am miserable and weak, and to an outsider I would cast an odd and alarming visage. That of a man who should have long ago passed from this world and into the next, yet lingers here stubbornly in the in-between of life and death. It is dark inside my tomb and I watch the man and his calot standing there at the entry, as if dangling cautiously over some great and bottomless precipice, until they finally relent and move forward, passing into the main entry chamber, into the shadows and shapes and darkness which so well becomes them.

I dare not show myself yet. The food I had prepared for my own supper the man now considers. With my voice I urge him to satisfy his hunger and feed his calot. The man eats carefully, suspiciously, sharing with his calot. The spectacle is so sad. I wonder what struggles have brought them here. Without me they would have died. I am certain of it. I let the man eat but I watch him closely. He does not feel safe. It is obvious and I cannot blame him for feeling that way. No one is safe on

Barsoom, anywhere. This is a place beset with warfare and hatred, with lunatics in high places, with murderers and soldiers who would sooner gut you than look at you. This man and his calot are the sickly byproducts of this evil, having run the course of that awful system to be cast out and left at my doorstep to die.

The man finishes eating. He stands up, looks around. His stature seems to have grown with nourishment. I can get a better look at him now. He has long black hair and angry eyes cast deep within his skull, eyes that scan the interior of my tomb with malice, cutting through the blackness, the darkness, studying the gray, the walls, looking for some breach. He is ready to defend himself. He wears boots, a few tattered articles of battle, and he is cut and bloodied, having survived thus far the awful affairs of Barsoom. I close my eyes. I look through him and into him. I take inventory of what I see there. His head is oddly shaped, small, egg-like and soft. His muscles are short and lean, powerful. His heart is equally strange, small and confounding. It is bulbous and very weak, stimulated by something within his body, the origins of which I cannot pinpoint. His lungs and kidneys are scattered and backwards, creating a perilous architecture that is wrong and unsustainable. He is built like nothing I have seen before. He is a creature assembled from the leftover parts of the various beasts that roam these lands. I cannot account for what manner of god created him, what laws of science allow him to live.

I speak to him. My voice echoes effortlessly throughout the chamber. My body remains concealed in the inner chamber. "Your statements are most remarkable," I say, "but you are evidently speaking the truth, and it is equally evident that you are not of Barsoom. I can tell that by the conformation of your brain and the strange location of your internal organs and the shape and size of your heart."

He looks around the room, searching in desperation for the origin of my voice. I am unable to read his thoughts, which is troubling, as my telepathy has been finely tuned over the years. But I do not need to peer inside his mind to know what he is thinking.

"Can you see through me?" he asks.

"Yes, I can see all but your thoughts, and were you a Barsoomian I could read those."

The traveler does not respond. His posture is grateful, appreciative. I am not afraid of him. He is not here to kill me. A wall still separates us, but I open it now. I have no reason not to. The wall slides open with a booming, thunderous movement. A brilliant reddish light suffuses the hills behind him, just beyond the walls of my tomb. The sun reflects off the highest peaks in the distant north, and darkness still lingers in the foothills. I shield my eyes from the glare. Air rushes into my tomb. Dust is kicked up and moves throughout the tomb's small interior. The air is cool and alive with smells, with a kind of feeling I have not known in a long time. I see just a silhouette of the traveler before me. I hear the wispy, labored breathing of his calot. We remain in that strange silence for a time, then I instruct him to follow me, and we go deeper into my tomb. I close the main entrance behind us, sealing us in. We reach a small antechamber and I instruct him to sit, so we can talk.

"Tell me your name," I say.

"My name is Captain Carter," he says. "Of Virginia."

"An unusual name."

"I have traveled a great distance," he says, "but my travels are not yet finished."

"Your travels?" I ask.

Captain Carter does not answer at first. He looks down, sadly. Then he proceeds to tell me of his trials on Barsoom. He has met with many hardships, he says. He has killed many times and fought in dozens of wars. He is not from this place yet he has fought and killed in the name of Barsoom. He tells me he is going to Helium to be reunited with the princess there. Her name is Dejah. He tells me they are in love.

"Love," I say.

He nods. I laugh.

"This amuses you?" he asks.

"You do not yet know."

"She was captured by the Tharks," he says. "They sought to hold her, to torture her and kill her. They would kill me for my association with her."

"It's a falsehood, my friend. It is a lie."

"I don't expect one like you to understand it."

"I understand that love cannot exist amidst killing and murder and hate, that any love found here is poisoned and will soon die."

"I love Dejah," he says. "There is no limit to the things I will do to be united with her again. I have laid waste to many soldiers already and should any more stand in my way then I will lay waste to them as well."

"Love and murder, Captain Carter, they cannot associate. It has always been the way. I warn you to be cautious of such things."

He does not respond.

"You must be a great warrior then?" I ask.

"I was a great warrior on my planet. Here I have been able to survive."

"But you wear the medals of the Thark warriors."

"They took me in. They cared for me. During my time with them I bested many of their warriors on the battlefield. I did what I needed to do in order to live."

"So you are a warrior."

"If you must define me, then yes, I am a warrior."

"There are too many warriors in this place. I am locked away here, because of warriors. I am forced to live in absolute solitude and isolation, behind these thick walls, in this tomb, because of warriors. Everyone here is trying to kill someone and you are no different. I owe the awful circumstances of my existence to the greed and short sightedness of warriors."

He looks at me. There is something in his eyes. Anger. Pain. I do not know what. My telepathic powers are useless against him. Yet he is trying to read me, to understand me. For a long moment our eyes meet and I grow concerned. This is a man overcome with pain and secrets and violence, capable of anything.

"I abhor many things," I say.

"Is that so?"

"Barsoom is a violent, disgusting place."

"There is beauty here too."

"Beauty," I say and laugh.

"I have seen it," he says.

"What beauty there was here once before is now gone. Beauty and love cannot live in so violent a place."

Carter gestures at the surrounding walls, at my tomb. "What is this place?" he asks me.

I take a step towards him. "You talk about love," I say. "Yours is a love born of war, of hate. Can't you see that?"

"It does not matter to me," he says. "I love Dejah Thoris and I will fight for her."

"Of course you will. You will fight for her and kill for her and you will eventually be together. That is the strength of your love, I suppose."

Carter says nothing.

"Do you know what I long for more than anything?" I ask.

Again, he says nothing.

"Peace," I say.

"Many feel the same way. I can assure you."

"I do not believe you."

"People here do not fight for love of fighting," he says. "They fight to secure the safety of those they love. They hope their fighting will one day bring peace."

"I knew love once myself," I say. "But it was stifled by violence, by hate. All things eventually are."

He looks at me again, assessing me in a most peculiar way. "May I ask you again?" he says.

"Ask me again?"

"This place where you live."

"Yes."

"What is it?"

"This place?" I say. "This is my tomb."

The prayers and incantations continued, the evening growing cold, solemn and meaningful. I knelt behind Jerrak. Most everyone was deep in prayer but my eyes remained open. I was not a great warrior but I was good enough. He would be unprepared for attack. It would be swift, effective. I raised my dagger slightly, slow and deliberate, as we had been taught. Jerrak was so deep in concentration, so lost in prayer. I concentrated too, on myself, on my body, on my hatred. I willed myself to move, to rise and to take action. But I was unable or unwilling, or too afraid. And I let the moment pass.

Jerrak rose from his prayer. His expression was clouded but unperturbed, having no idea what danger had nearly befallen him. Others rose around me. It was nearly time for our departure. People spoke in low voices. I returned my dagger to its sheath. I hated everything about Jerrak, but mostly I hated the fact that Thena adored him. The ceremony continued uninterrupted. We were blessed by the clerics, we were anointed and told of the journey that awaited us. It was to be the single most important journey of our lives, lives that we had long since given up to the health of Barsoom. There were twenty of us that were to be conveyed down the river, but only one of us would return. The gods would choose. They would sift through us. They would determine who was worthy of giving his life to the caretaking of the atmosphere factory. The chosen one, whoever it may be, would accomplish something no other living creature could, save the previous caretakers. They would travel down the river, into the afterlife, and then they would return.

We were each given a small vessel, big enough only for ourselves and our weapon and a few days of supplies. Nothing more. Most of us would not need to worry about the return trip. And the weapons were merely ceremonial, never intended to be used. We had no hand in deciding who would survive the trials. If we were meant to survive, then we would. It was all determined by our worthiness, by the content of our souls.

I boarded my raft when the time came. It was small, made from the wood of the local forests. It would hold for a few days. The river was choppy that day, the waters thick and muddy. A thin haze of fog lingered above the shoreline but dissipated downriver. The way into the Valley Dor led through the red gorges, along the base of the mountains and then south. The terrain was rocky and thick with moss and vines, surviving there would be difficult for even the best trained among us.

I shoved off from the landing with my brothers. Everyone was quiet. We were blessed again by the elders. They placed flower petals into the water. They floated around us, formed half-shaped circles until their shape could no longer hold and they drifted away. There was music too, played by someone unseen back on shore. I could hear the lapping of the water against the rafts. I did not paddle, did not steer, opting to let the tide take me wherever it would. Jerrak was some distance ahead of me. I preferred it that way. He was crouched in the center of his raft, in a posture of absolute concentration and prayer.

While we drifted we were not permitted to speak or interact with any of the others. Eventually the tides separated us and I found myself on a vast expanse of water, drifting silently and alone. This was the transition world, the halfway point between the known and the unknown. I was not dead, nor was I alive. I was nowhere, nothing. There was not much of a shoreline to speak of, just a cloud of fog broken only by the rocks on the shore and the ponderous cliffs that loomed overhead. I heard the strangest sounds from the shores. The high-pitched yelps and howls, the anguished plaints of the creatures that lived there. I would imagine movement on the shoreline, as though some wild thing were stalking me, marking my movements, my passage between worlds. But there was never anything there.

By the second day on the river my surroundings had grown much darker. I had drifted towards the back of the group. Most of the others were now far ahead of me, and some had likely already entered the Sea of Korus and their final fate, whatever that might be. Around me the shoreline grew taller, and more impressive, looming higher and further than I had ever thought possible. Sheer cliffs rose overhead, rocky shorelines surrounded me. Ahead the river disappeared into a dark, narrow nothingness. I was entering the Valley Dor. The Sea of Korus would not be much further. There was nothing to do now but wait.

The river here was sizeable and it curved along enormous boulders and some waterfalls fell from the high-perched rocks. The waters became more treacherous and violent the further I went, lapping at my vessel harder and harder with each passing hour. It would not be long now. I was getting closer. The water around me seemed to be teeming with activity, with flashes of life, just out of sight below the surface.

Along the rocky shorelines, there was no doubt the apes were now there. I could see them, barely silhouetted against the swirling fog, but they were there. They looked their heads up as I passed, twitched their ears and lowered their heads again, browsing for fish on the shoreline. I had never seen one before. They were massive in stature, an incredible awareness painted across their faces, deep set in their eyes. They knew who I was, why I was there.

I had lost track of Jerrak, but he was ahead of me. I was certain of that. Perhaps he had entered the Sea of Korus already. If so, I had little doubt the gods would return the elders favorite son safely back to Barsoom. The idea of him walking back to the shoreline, held aloft by the clerics and citizens, praised as the returning hero, conqueror of death, chosen by the very gods themselves to bring long-lasting life to all of Barsoom, sickened me. I was consumed with rage and jealousy, driven nearly mad by the solitude of that river, by the silence, the sense of my own impending doom.

I always thought I would dutifully handle whatever fate awaited me at the end of this river, when my time came. I had prepared all my life for it. But some new feeling grew inside me now, a feeling born of anger and of hate and of pride. I knelt down and placed my hands into the water of the River Iss. It was cold. I cupped some of it and felt it run through my fingers. I dipped my hand again and brought it quickly to my mouth and this time I drank from it. I prayed silently there and then I took more water and doused my head with it, anointing myself. Only man can enslave man and I was prepared now to be the keeper of my soul. No longer would I defer to the clerics and arcane Barsoomian law. My life was my own and whatever evils existed down this river did so without my awareness and without my consent.

I pulled my raft towards the shoreline. The water was rough here, seemingly pawing at me, trying to pull me back in. To take my raft ashore in such a manner was a gross violation of law, but I didn't care. I hid my raft among some brush and found myself sitting on a small, rocky outcropping, with all the vastness of the River Iss before me. I looked down the river, where the black waters disappeared into a smoky mist, and the rocks jutted out too far to see around. Beyond that point was the river's mouth, where many of my brothers had already met their own noble and heroic deaths. This was the intersection of the living and the dead, and I had a choice to make.

Without reservation I chose the living.

I dug up silt from the riverbed and used it to sink my vessel, putting it safely out of sight. I was going to make my way back on foot. There were many legends about the dangers that lived on the shoreline's here. I knew them all too well. They kept me awake many nights in my childhood. They were the reason the men who undertook the trials did not do what I had just done. Better to take your chances in the Sea of Korus and to die nobly, than to be torn apart by the wild apes. I set out on foot, walking slowly, sticking to the shoreline. Movement and sounds seemed to come to life all around me, the darkness alive with them. I had my dagger and my protective armor, but did not expect they would do me any good. I didn't know how long the journey back would be. But I intended to move quickly.

Captain Carter walks ahead of me. He moves slowly, having grown somber now, calm, neither with pain nor anger on his face. He seems a solitary man, a man of no race, no city, no people; entirely lost and alone, like me. He tells me he wants to stay the night within my tomb, and in the morning he will leave me.

"Where will you go?" I ask.

"To Helium, as I have said."

"And there you will kill, and take back your princess. Is my assumption correct, Captain?"

"I do not go anywhere with the intent to kill. I want only to be reunited with the one I love."

"All murder is in the name of something."

"I am no murderer."

"I give life to everyone on this planet," I say. "What men chose do with it is beyond my control, I suppose."

Captain Carter looks at me, strangely and intently, probing with his dark and clouded eyes for some answer. I wonder what the question is.

"You fear an attack here," he finally says.

"Should we not? Barsoom is a violent place," I say.

"How did you manage to unlock and move the massive doors for me earlier, while you were in the interior chamber?" he asks.

"That is a secret I cannot divulge."

Captain Carter laughs. "Of course," he says.

He thanks me for my kindness and generosity. I can see reflected in his eyes the fires that maintain the machinery, the very same fires that breathe life into Barsoom and thus sustain all the killing and greed and violence here. The fire burns in Captain Carter too. I can see it so clearly now and I know what he intends to do when he leaves here. His kind traffics in pain and hatred and in blood. He will lay waste to men and women and children if they dare stand in his way. On his body are the scars and trinkets of war and murder and chase, all of them so glaring as to singularly justify my every fear, and to find all that fear embodied here in this one strange man.

I know what I must do. I cannot let him leave here. I cannot let anyone else die in the name of love.

"Before you leave in the morning," I say, showing Carter and the calot to their room, "I will give you a letter to a nearby agricultural officer who will help you on your way to Zodanga, the nearest city."

"Thank you for your kindness," says Captain Carter.

"But be sure that you do not let them know you are bound for Helium as they are at war with that country," I say.

"I will," he says.

"And so good-night, my friend," I say, "may you have a long and restful sleep."

I was not a day into my journey back upriver when I saw a good distance up the shore a small fire burning. Its light stood out amongst all the darkness of those rocky shorelines, burning in a kind of divine defiance to all the coldness and death that pervaded this place. There was no need to wait for nightfall since darkness was almost a permanent state this far downriver. I moved towards the flame, sticking close to the water, moving carefully across the slick and naked rocks. All around me was thick brush, everything alive with otherworldly noises.

I drew closer to the camp and saw a solitary figured hunched beside the fire. Against the flames, he was nothing more than a silhouette. I ascended an outcropping of rocks and found myself perched on the topmost rim of the surrounding hills looking down at the fire. It was Jerrak, hunched beside the fire with a small notebook open in his lap.

I sat there and watched him for a time, not knowing what else to do. I did not know how he would have come to this place so far ahead of me. It was clear he had not gone downriver, faced whatever elements were to be faced there, only to be safely delivered by the divine hands of the gods.

Jerrak was just like me.

Afraid.

Unwilling to risk his life to an ancient belief. His fire flickered and I thought it might die. He placed his notebook down and watched the fire and I did too. Soon the fire died and it was all darkness and the shadows that danced around Jerrak and his small camp were gone.

I passed the night on those rocks and followed Jerrak upriver the next day. We both moved on foot, slowly and deliberately. He kept his notebook handy, always making entries there. I did not know what he wrote. I remained a good distance behind him, tracking him carefully, always keeping him in my sight. There was no easy route along the bald and slippery rocks, the ponderous slopes. Jerrak opted to stay close to the water, as had I. I could hear the apes, deep inside the surrounding forests. Their cold, plaintive howls rising up like prayers, echoing across the canopy of rock and plant life that surrounded us, and conveyed directly to heaven. I had no mission, no plan. I just meant to follow him. It would be at least a four days journey back, and the gods would not allow both of us to return, if we were to believe the old stories. The reality was I had not gone all the way to the Sea of Korus and neither had Jerrak. We were both liars, both of us living in defiance of Barsoomian law and every belief that our people held fast too.

On the third night I set up camp down the shoreline from Jerrak. I had kept a safe distance from him, careful to conceal my movements and my fire. I heard only the sound of the water lapping gently against the rocks. The apes were quiet, the darkness around me stilted and thoughtful, resting. I wondered about Thena. What was she doing? Who was she with? Did she pine for my return? I didn't think so. I missed her terribly, but I could no longer see a version of the future in which we were together. From birth, my life had been a long journey towards one kind of death or another; either a quick end in the Sea of Korus, or the prolonged, living death that is life within the atmosphere factory. Each was noble, honorable, but I was too selfish to want either. Nobility and honor meant nothing to me. I was in love with Thena.

That night I slipped off to sleep, only to be awoken later by horrible sounds. There was a high-pitched screeching, a yell, a wild struggle. My fire had gone out. Just darkness. I heard a long and impossible howl.

The apes had come alive.

They were moving. Then there was another yell. It was Jerrak. I grabbed my dagger and my shield and moved quickly towards his camp. I stumbled across the slippery rocks, falling, moving blindly. I drew closer to his camp and he yelled out again, this time in pain, invoking the names of the gods, begging for help, for some kind of deliverance. I had only the sounds to guide me, so I ran down the inner rim of a small interior valley to where I could pinpoint the origins of those sounds. There I found Jerrak. He was scared and corned, his sheath on the ground, dagger drawn. He was injured, bleeding. Before him stood a towering and shadowy white form. It had its back to me. I could see the heat coming off it, steam rising as if its anger had become manifest. Its ears twitched. It raised its four arms and howled that awful sound.

Captain Carter is asleep. I head into the great hall and remove a long, thin dagger from the cupboard. It will be easy, quick and painless. It will be for the betterment of all. Carter is no better than any of these other Barsoomians. He is greedy and deceitful. He lies without forethought. He is a man willing to kill, to inflict unspeakable pain and suffering on others, just to get what he wants. That men like Carter freely kill under the umbrella of life I provide for this planet disgusts me. I have done so much for these people, suffering endlessly and needlessly, and yet I am repaid only in blood. I will not allow it any longer. There is a great stone here in the hall, which I use to sharpen my old ceremonial dagger. I am a little nervous, the weight of the task at hand dragging heavily on my body and my mind. But I have no reservations. No doubts.

I hear something shuffle behind me, something deep in the shadows. I pause, frozen, counting the moments quietly and under my breath. I have the sense something is here in this room with me. I turn to look, but my eyes are too old and tired. They do not cut through the darkness like they once did. My telepathic powers are much more attuned, but there is nothing here that I can see. It is some mere trick of the mind. I go back to sharpening my dagger.

It is very late now and my mind grows tired. It is about the time of night when the moon is highest. I cannot see it for all the walls of this place, but I can imagine it. It is time. I head towards Captain Carter's room. My tomb is cold and dark, my long shadow stretched out before me. I try to be quite, but my old body will not cooperate. I raise and lower each leg so slowly, deliberately, in a vein attempt at stealth. I cannot shake the feeling that I am being watched, that there is still someone here with me, marking my movements, my passage from corridor to corridor. I think about the noise I heard earlier. I think there is movement behind me, all around me, something hiding in every darkened corner, but when I look there is nothing. I remember the white apes on the River Iss, from so long ago. The way they hunted under cover of night, how they stalked their prey for days at a time.

When I arrive at the Captain's door it is shut, just as I left it. I remove the dagger from my cloak. Carter is clearly a great warrior, and I have no doubt that should my dagger fail to find its target on the first attempt, he will likely kill me here. But I cannot stray from my task. There is too much at stake. Slowly, carefully, I push open the door. I move as quietly as is possible. I am mindful of his calot. That despicable beast sleeps somewhere here, dutifully at his side. I will have to rid myself of him next. I stand beside the bed. There is no sound of breathing. Of life. I strain my eyes, trying to see through the darkness, but am unable. I must act quickly, before it is too late. I raise the dagger and drop it with as much strength as I can muster. Then I pull it back and do it again. But the dagger finds no purchase. Captain Carter's bed is empty. Both he and his calot are gone.

My first thought is the pumps. But I think better of it. Carter would not tamper with the pumps. He is not interested in dooming all of Barsoom to a slow, painful suffocation. He is interested only in his petty revenge. I make my way towards the entrance of my tomb. I am ever mindful of my surroundings. Captain Carter may still be here, waiting for me. But I make it to the doors safely. I don't know how he has managed it, but the doors have been opened. I move to the entrance and stand there with all of that dusty red Barsoomian night laid out before me. I scan the vastness of the deserts before me and find nothing there. In the distance the mountains are hazy and lifeless, the moons casting a sinister glow across the tallest peaks, whiting them out against the dark and looming nightfall. Dust swirls within the confines of my tomb. There are footprints, leading away, out into the night. A man and his calot. Captain Carter has escaped.

I called to Jerrak and told him not to move. He was hurt but I could not tell how badly. The darkness around us was the all-encompassing kind, broken only by the occasional flicker of the dying campfire. Scattered around the campsite were conspicuous flecks of blood that had pooled up in some places. Sometimes they would catch the glow of the campfire just right and flicker with an unexpected beauty.

Jerrak rose to fight. He was armed only with his dagger, but he had managed a respectable defense from the mostly useless weapon. He turned to look at me and if he were relieved by my sudden presence he would not dare to show it. I think at that moment he came to understand what I had known for a long time, that we were both sinners on a savage and mad pursuit of something simple but unknowable, and if it was absolution we sought we would not find it on this night.

The ape was huge and there was a constant and baneful growl that seemed to emanate from the very core of it. It raised its head and then dropped it violently in what was some quivering and primal display of aggression. It hissed and it heaved and pounded its massive chest with its four massive arms, letting forth with an awful and ear-piercing bellow that circled the rim of the valley and rose into the night sky, marking all this land and the heavens above it with his murderous intentions. Jerrak stood rigid, with his dagger pointed at the animal. "We need to work together," he said to me.

I said nothing, too afraid to move or to speak.

"I can keep him distracted. You will need to strike from behind."

Again, I said nothing. I had no reservations about what I had to do. For all my hatred of Jerrak I had a moral obligation to help him. The ape looked at me then back to Jerrak. It was growing disoriented, struggling to ascertain who among us was the larger threat. It looked at me and I met its stare and saw in its eyes naked blackness and not even the light of the fire reflected there. I looked once more across the dying flames at Jerrak and took a step backwards into the darkness. Jerrak stood uneasily but with bravery. His armor was on the ground in front of him and he bled from his chest and his arms. He jumped up and down, making a clamoring noise, waving his arms and yelling. The ape moved towards him. Its back was turned to me. For the first time it was vulnerable.

Jerrak's eyes danced nervously between the ape's and my own. He was waiting. I could see it on his wrist still, after all of this. Thena's bracelet. I raised my dagger. I took a step forward, into the light of the campfire and within striking distance. The ape was twice my size. Its shoulders strong and broad. It hissed and it bellowed, the echoes rattling all around me and scattering into the night, each of them reiterating a simple idea, that we were invaders in his land and he meant to defend it or die in the attempt.

"Now," Jerrak yelled. "What are you waiting for?"

"Jerrak," I said.

"Do it," he said.

I didn't move. I couldn't. Something held me back and I cannot say what it was, a divine hand or my own cowardice or something else entirely. I remained frozen in that shadow. I couldn't move or maybe I didn't want to, and instead I let play out before me whatever awful things were meant to. The ape was upon Jerrak in almost no time at all. It raised its hand and with a single stroke swiped his head from his body. A thin stream of blood rose from his neck and fell to the ground, feeding the other pools that had already gathered, and with that the fight was over and Jerrak was dead. I wanted to retrieve Thena's bracelet from Jerrak's wrist, but instead I left that place quickly, whether from fear or shame or both, and I made my way further upriver.

That was eight hundred years ago. Today I stand here at the opened door to my tomb, staring at the vastness that surrounds me. I cannot leave. I will never leave. Some blind allegiance still holds me fast, and the only things I will ever know in the world are entirely of my own making now. I cannot forget the faces of the elders when they saw me returning up the river. It was still in the dark of the early morning. They were standing on a rise of ground in a small group, and they were looking west. There was shock and surprise and some sadness in their expressions, and I could not blame them for feeling the way they did.

They had been waiting for five days for the gods to deliver them the next caretaker of the atmosphere factory. Everyone knew it was supposed to be Jerrak. He was the most capable, the most deserving. But the scripture is very clear. He who is returned from the River Iss shall ascend to the hallowed position. And I was the only one to return. I was the one who knew the secret—to save one's life, to save Barsoom, one must defy the gods.

One of the elders fell to the ground and placed his hands upon his chest and closed his eyes, and he remained in that manner for a long time. He muttered some half silent prayers and I didn't know if they were prayers of thanks or lamentations of another kind. Eventually they surrounded me, offering me rudimentary civilities because it was written in scripture that they should do so. I scanned the crowd for Thena but did not see her. I was already alone.

The elders brought me up from the river and into the surrounding mountains. I said nothing of Jerrak or of my cowardice. We trod a narrow trail through the mountains and up to the greatest peak. A thin column of light from the moons fell upon the ground there, and figures passing close were careful to avoid it, as if that light brought with it a certain understanding they were not yet ready to experience. I was prayed upon and anointed as the next caretaker of the atmosphere factory. The ceremony was quick and full of meaningful songs and gestures. It was cold and the breath of the elders plumed out of their mouths as they prayed and sang and thanked the gods for their wisdom.

I had no choice in the matter. Neither did they. I had been delivered by the gods and their word was law and all were subject to it. It was a responsibility most would accept with a certain degree of pride and self-sacrifice, but for me it was something else. I thought only of Thena. Even if I could not be with her, maybe I could provide for her a healthy and beautiful world in which to live. She would no doubt hear about the sacrifice I had made for Barsoom, and she would fall deeper in love with me. Jerrak was gone and for all that had happened maybe I was starting to see that as a good thing. I would pay a price, but in this way Thena and I could be together.

The first few months at the factory moved quickly. Every day I went to my perch and surveyed the surrounding lands. I was looking for Thena. I had little doubt she would come see me. She would be conveyed here by complicated feelings of respect and love and apology. She wouldn't want to see me. She would need to. Overcome with guilt for the way she had treated me before I left, she would arrive at my door and beg my forgiveness, speaking softly of a newly formed void within her, something once filled with love but now just a deep and bottomless fissure threatening to take over the whole of her being should I not grant her absolution from that suffering. I would tell Thena I loved her and that I forgave her. I would look into her eyes when I said that, and we would live here together.

But weeks became months and months became years and eventually it was clear Thena would not come. I do not know why she would again leave me alone and waiting. All on this world are put here for a purpose, and I suppose sinners are here to sin. But I had always thought Thena was not subject to such moral failings. How many hours did I pass alone in my perch, scanning the surrounding landscapes for her? How well did I learn the luminous red hills and rocks of the land here? It was a land washed almost transparent by the sun and the winds that swept through here daily. A place so lacking in life that even the lowest creatures wouldn't pass within eyeshot of my tomb. A poison exists in loneliness like this. It lives in the air and the dust and the dark. It covers your body and infects your bloodstream and all you want is to find someone or something that might abate that feeling but there is nothing. And now Captain Carter has left. I do not know how he slipped out last night, but he is gone and on his way to Zodanga where he will lay waste to those who have done him wrong, and the violence and vice that is Barsoom will continue.

I step out of my tomb for the first time in I don't know how long. I feel the dirt and the rocks under my feet. The windswept deserts stir with my movement and wisps of dust are scattered. I think about the hills surrounding my old home, where I used to sit with Thena in the high grass, all the living world laid out before us. We were closer to the gods then than ever before and such an exalted place I have not yet returned to. I kneel down in the dirt and pick some of it up and hold it aloft in my hands. I let it run through my fingers and watch it fall to the ground and disappear into nothing again. I say a short prayer for Barsoom, and then go back into my tomb.

How many have breathed their last breath in my atmosphere? And how many more must die before the cycle is broken? I could not prevent Captain Carter from leaving, but I can still prevent him and anyone else from killing again. I owe this to Barsoom. I head into the tomb and inspect the pumps. There is enough radium for another few days of operation, and then the machinery will stop and the atmosphere will cease pumping. I take my dagger and leave my tomb for the last time. The great door is sealed tight behind me. The only other who knows the secret to open it is my assistant, but I will find him and I will kill him. These pumps will never run again, and Barsoom will die.

I stand in the shadow of the tomb and let the desert winds affect me. So high are the walls of this place, so distant their reach, they seem to offer direct passage to the heavens themselves. But I know the truth. All life on Barsoom comes from this place and now comes a judgment long overdue. I have given life to this planet and that life has been abused and molested, so now I will take it away. When the pumps stop all the warlords and soldiers and murderers will have but a few hours to contemplate their lifetime of sin and vice, to beg from the gods for a forgiveness that is not in the offing. Then they will fall to their knees and lament their lot, and with their dying breaths will come a great crying and gnashing and they will ask the heavens why.

Uncle Jack

by Daniel Keys Moran

My name is Jack Anderson. I'm told Anderson is a northman's name, on Earth; on Barsoom, and especially in Helium, it's merely an alien one. Jack isn't unheard of, though John is commoner—common to the point of tedium; I must have known two dozen Barsoom-born Johns in my life, most of them named after our long-dead Warlord.

I was the second child born on Barsoom of Earthman parents, Angelique Gutierrez having preceded me by two days, back before the turn of the century. I'm told the media on Earth had speculated about our future together even before either of us had been born—no one in Helium cared at all, of course, and they were correct not to: I never liked Angelique, and never married her, or anyone else; and never had children.

And now it's late in the twenty-first century, and I'm dying, alone and forgotten in the Ptarthian Home for the Elderly in Lesser Helium.

The young man who's begun visiting me is named Jack too, Jack Voerman.

"I had an Uncle Jack when I was a boy," I told him. "Named for him." I peered at him. "You look a bit like him, if I recall."

"Do you recall?"

I looked away—couldn't say why the question irritated me, but it did. At eighty-three I was younger and stronger than humans of previous generations—modern medical technology couldn't cure the cancer I was fighting, but it had kept me fit enough otherwise.

"I'm eighty-three, young man. Memory is treacherous."

Jack nodded as if he understood, and sat by my bedside in apparent comfort. I had the bed tilted up until he and I were at eye level—I had two chairs and a small table in the room, but I wasn't feeling well that day—the drugs more than the disease. I was thinking about stopping taking them. It would hasten things, but I was almost ready for that.

Jack was a tall fellow, handsome in a rugged way, with black hair and colorless eyes. He wore old-fashioned Earthstyle clothes, unusual these days when most humans aped the fashions of the red Martians of Greater Helium, and appeared unarmed—he'd a belt from which he might have hung a sword or gun, but hadn't.

I'd been reluctant to let him visit. Those of us in the home who lack family still have the option of visitors—they were almost always Earthborn or the first generation descendants of Earthborn. Earthborn and their children still have some sense of the sacrifices we made, those of us whom the United States Space Force sent to Mars in the late twentieth century. While I appreciate what those volunteers are attempting to do, there's nothing wrong with my mind—it's my body that's betrayed me. With the cube at my bedside containing a thousand times more books and movies in its atomic matrix than I could possibly consume in my remaining months of life, I didn't feel much of a need for company.

But young Jack was persistent, I don't know why. He'd come by twice and the nurse, a manic-depressive green Martian whose name was either Zaavog or Jill depending on where she was in her cycle—Jill, lately—turned him away without mentioning it to me. Tim Burke, my next-door neighbor, an engineer from San Diego who'd come to Barsoom as a grown man back around 2050, told me about it over a game of chess. "Did she let you know?" he asked.

"No," I said, "but she was right. I don't need to be cheered up and I don't want to entertain some stranger with my dying."

Tim nodded sympathetically. He was dying of colon cancer himself and the last ship from Earth hadn't brought the new treatments we'd both heard of, and in which we'd placed our last, faint hopes. They'd probably arrive with the next wave of ships, the next time the two planets were in conjunction—two years from now, roughly, and since neither Tim nor I were going to see another New Year's Day, it didn't matter to us.

Tim beat me on the fifty-third move with a discovered check I hadn't seen coming, and then gloated about it until I declined a rematch and went back to my room.

The next day I told Jill to send the stranger on up if he came back again. She peered at me doubtfully. "You're sure?"

"Unless he cheats at chess," I told her. "I've had enough of that from Tim."

"I don't cheat at chess," Jack informed me. "I'm not sure I can see how you could."

"Distract a man with idle chatter," I said. "Move when he's not prepared, sort of thing."

Jack grinned at me. "Some men are without honor." He said it in a joking tone, but still as if he meant it.

I shrugged. "I wouldn't know. I've been a water engineer my whole life. With waterworks you're competent or you're not. Courage doesn't keep the canals flowing."

He shook his head. "I spoke of honor, not courage. Honor and courage are merely cousins. A man can be brave and dishonorable, though it's hard to be an honorable coward. At some point honor holds you to commitments, to sacrifice, and that requires bravery."

"You're opinionated, Jack. I'm not even saying you're wrong, but life isn't about those things most of the time. Mostly it's work. It doesn't require bravery to get through, just consistency. Getting up even when you're tired, working even when you're bored. Consistency."

"Well, yes," Jack said slowly, "I suppose that's true in some cases. But didn't you make choices that put you into the circumstances where that would be true?"

I thought about it. "I'm not sure I ever made any choices worth making. My father was an irrigation engineer—originally just for the immigrants, but later all over Barsoom. I learned enough of it from him that it seemed the sensible career, when I came of age." I looked at him. Oddly, I felt like I was justifying myself. "It's had its moments, as a career. I've seen almost every part of Barsoom worth seeing, traveling to repair and extend the canals."

"But no adventures to speak of."

I shrugged. "The age of adventures is over. It was over by the time Space Force first landed on this world. The Warlord pacified this planet, before he and Dejah Thoris died."

"Dejah Thoris," he said softly, and left it at that. "The Warlord didn't pacify the entire Solar System, though. Jupiter is out there, and Saturn. Why do you think the Prince of Helium died?"

"Couldn't begin to guess. Old age, a bullet, a blade—"

"Why do you think he died at all?"

"Their tomb"—his and the Princess's, both—"is less than five klicks from here," I said mildly. "I've seen it."

"His body is not there."

That was true; only the Princess's was. "No one lives that long, Jack. Not humans, not red Martians—not even with today's medical technology. Look at me dying, lad."

Young Jack was a bit of a crank. "Doctors," he said dismissively. "Scientists, doctors, all too proud of what they know. Often wrong," he added.

They weren't wrong about the cancer eating me.

"Look," I said, "John Carter was thirty or so in the late eighteen sixties, no? The painting that hangs in the tomb shows him that age, and it was painted not long afterward." I peered at him. "You look like my Uncle Jack, if I remember, but you also look like John Carter, at least like the painting."

I'd seen the painting a lot more recently than I'd seen Uncle Jack—I was ten, the last time I'd seen Uncle Jack, the day of my mother's funeral.

He shrugged. "So I've been told. I don't see it myself."

"Anyway, the Warlord is long dead, whatever happened to his body." I laughed. "It's approaching 2100, man!"

It was the day of my mother's funeral.

There was only one Christian church in Helium, in those days, and one Jewish temple, and one Muslim mosque, and they were all the same building. Today it was a Jewish temple, that being my mother's religion.

Uncle Jack showed up at our house as my father was leaving. He was a tall man, dark haired and grey eyed, and he wore a gun—unusual even then, when things were a bit unsettled following the beginning of immigration from Earth.

Even under the circumstances seeing Uncle Jack made me feel better. He'd been a constant in our lives, and I didn't remember a time when he hadn't been there.

"How long do we have to wait?"

Uncle Jack shrugged. "An hour, boy. No more. Your father has business to conduct before the funeral, he didn't want you there for it."

I didn't care. I just wanted everything over with—I wasn't angry, wasn't even really sad, yet, though later I would be both. I was in a sort of shock, I suppose. Uncle Jack tried playing Jetan with me, but I couldn't keep my mind focused, so we switched to chess, and I did no better, so we just sat quietly, in the living room my mother had decorated. I wished I were still young enough to sit in Uncle Jack's lap, but it had been two or three years since I'd done that, and I wasn't going to embarrass myself by asking now.

We took his skyship to the temple, and parked it on a structure across the way from the temple.

And then we had to cross the street.

It was eight lanes wide, one of the broadest avenues in Lower Helium, and busy enough that I was scared to cross it. Uncle Jack stepped out into the street and I froze on the walkway. Uncle Jack looked at me curiously, and to my humiliation I started to cry.

He came back to me and held out his hand. "Come on, son," he said softly. "We'll cross the street together."

"I dreamed about Uncle Jack last night," I told Jack the next day. "You *do* look like him."

He smiled. "Thanks, I suppose. You liked your uncle?"

I thought about it. "It was a long time ago. I was just a boy, but he was kind to me. He and my mother are the only people I can recall who were, when I was a child."

That seemed to surprise him a bit. "Your father wasn't?"

"Dad . . . " I shook my head. "He had something against me. I don't know what."

Jack seemed to think about that. "Perhaps he thought you might not be his?"

In eighty-three years the thought had never occurred to me. "No," I said slowly, "he had to know I was. Back around my sixteenth birthday everyone in the colony had their DNA sequenced with gear just arrived from Earth."

"You were a man by then," he said.

I smiled. "Sixteen."

"A man," he repeated. "Old enough to carry a sword and gun, and use them. But you say he wasn't kind to you as a child—"

"He wasn't unkind. Just . . . distant. As if I were an obligation." I shrugged. "Maybe he wasn't sure, before the DNA sequencing. I don't know. I don't know if he loved me. Before he died said he was sorry he hadn't been a better father, but I never held that against him. He worked hard. He did his best for me, however he felt." I shook my head a bit irritably, abruptly aware that I was doing the old man thing, chattering away about times long past as if they mattered.

"What do you do, Jack? Where are you from?"

"I'm a fighting man," he said, "when I can find a fight. That's not as often as it used to be. You're right, about things getting civilized hereabouts. I suppose that's a good thing—"

He didn't sound convinced. "Where was your last fight?"

"Moons of Saturn, a few years ago. The Methane Men of Titan."

I looked him over. It was possible. The Titanians had been whipped more than once, but they didn't learn and they kept coming back for more. "How was that?"

He shrugged. "Boring, to tell the truth. Not like in the old days. Practically a 'police action.'" He spat the phrase with real contempt.

"The old days look good to you, do they?"

He was slow answering. "I suppose they weren't good for everyone. But for a fighting man . . . cunning foes, desperate odds," his voice got faster and stronger, "great chases, running battles, good *God*, Jack," his voice rang out, "who wouldn't prefer *that* to *this?*"

When he came back the next day I had Jill tell him I was too ill for visitors. It was true. I'd just had my drug therapy, and I lay flat on my bed, dizzy and having difficulty breathing.

The following day I was out on the balcony, sitting in one of my two chairs, when he came to see me again. It was noon—not Earth's noon, the Barsoomian day is twenty-four and two-thirds hours long, more or less, and we hadn't tried keeping Earth time since the very earliest days on Mars. Barsoom noon, and warm as the nights were icy cold. I'd shucked my shirt and wore only a pair of shorts.

Jack called out my name, our name, when he entered the room, and then I heard him moving things about. Not much in the room to move—just the bed, table, and two chairs, one of which I'd already brought out onto the balcony.

After a few minutes he came out onto the balcony to stand. He stood silently a while in the sunlight, watching the skyships move across Helium. Finally he said, "You don't look like a dying man. Dress you like a red Martian, give you a man's weapons, they'd think twice about crossing you even in the worst cities on Barsoom."

"May not look it, but I am." I knew what he meant, though—I'd practiced various martial arts even into my middle years, and as I'd aged had shifted to yoga, tai chi and weight work to stay fit. I was still muscular and hadn't lost a lot of weight—and wouldn't, before I died. "Mostly my wind's gone. I can't run, can't walk long distances. I'll likely be in good shape when I die, except for my wind."

"Have you ever held a sword?"

"Me?" I laughed at him. "No. I spent my whole life working with water, Jack."

He looked at me. "Not even as a boy?"

"No, my father—" I hesitated. A ghostly memory had risen up. Uncle Jack . . . Uncle Jack had taught me to hold a sword. Taught me some basics of stance, some strokes—

"Come back inside with me."

He'd pushed the bed into the corner of the room, and turned the table over and put it on the bed, and put the second chair onto the table. It left a large empty space, maybe four meters in length.

A pair of swords, still in their sheaths, lay in the middle of the room. Jack picked one up and tossed it to me. I caught it out of the air and he grinned. "Not dead yet," he observed.

"Where on Barsoom did you get *these?*"

The sheaths were new—hardened leather—but the blades, once removed, radiated age. The blades had seen use, the bronze guards and pommels were nicked and scratched. The hand grips were dark green leather, darkened further by years of sweat.

"The Barsoom longsword. The blades are carbon steel," Jack said. "The guards, silicon bronze. The grips are banth skin, dyed green."

Banths were extinct on Barsoom—near a hundred years.

I gripped the sword he'd thrown me, hand within the guard. It felt light, like an extension of me. I waved it, just a bit, let the point drop toward Jack.

He tapped it aside with the barest flick of his wrist. "Do you remember the stances?"

I had to think. "The ox," I said slowly, "the plow, the fool, the roof, and the tail."

"Show me."

I moved through each position, holding it as best I could remember—it must have been close enough, because he grinned. "Your Uncle Jack would be pleased you'd remembered this much of his teaching, after all these years."

I let the point of the sword drop. "And how would you know he was the one who taught me?"

He stared blankly at me for a moment. "Lucky guess," he said finally. "Let's practice until you're tired."

I slept that night as well as I'd slept in months.

The next morning I went to breakfast in the home's common room. I sat next to Tim and we ate eggs and drank our coffee together.

He looked bad. He hadn't dressed; he was in his robe, wearing slippers. Gray-skinned, and he shuffled when he walked and looked as though he were about to fall over at any moment. I wondered if he'd make another month, and it was clear he was wondering the same.

After breakfast I went back to my room and dug out the cube. Most of the files on it were fiction, but a few were documentaries. I pulled up the one I wanted. It was an Earth documentary—they called the planet "Mars" rather than "Barsoom," but they had what I was looking for.

"That John Carter was from Earth," the narrator said, "seems evident. He was not a red Martian—who are merely humans themselves, also from Earth, though they were brought to Mars in the distant past. The puzzle of John Carter, how he came to be upon Mars, is not one to be easily solved. Records on Earth indicate that he returned to Earth at least once, after his initial visit to Mars. How he managed this, during an era when no civilization on either planet was capable of space flight, is a mystery that endures. Talk of astral projection is patently foolish, but the options, that he was transported by leftover technology from the more advanced past of Mars, or that he was transported by the beings of some other civilization entirely, are equally hard to credit . . . "

I paused the video as the image of John Carter appeared on the screen. It was a photo, from the days of the American Civil War on Earth, a now-famous photo found around 2020, long after the fact. It showed a troupe of men in uniform, with one man, standing a bit off to the side, who was alleged to be John Carter. I frame-advanced the video—from the photo they went to the painting which hung in John Carter's tomb, and then back to the photo.

The photo and painting were clearly of the same man, and that man, John Carter, the Warlord of Mars and Prince of Helium, was the very image of the young man, Jack Voerman, who had been visiting me the last two weeks.

Voerman, the dictionary told me, was Dutch for "carter."

"I don't age," he said. "I don't know why."

I half believed him, but only half, even then. "Tell me about my mother."

"We were friends, Sonja and I. I thought your father was my friend too, but later I found that there was jealousy there—unnecessary jealousy, I tell you; your mother was faithful to him, and I was respectful of their marriage." He looked up at me. "There was fire in that woman. She married beneath herself. And your father knew it. It ate at him, and then she died, and left you to be raised by him. He thought you were mine, I suspect, until the day came that he knew better—but it was too late, by then."

He stood, moving restlessly around the small room. "You asked where I was from at one point. I feel as though I remember knowing, once—but I don't remember now. I don't remember being other than I am. I don't remember a childhood, or parents."

"What do you remember?"

"Virginia," he said softly. "I remember Virginia."

"Where did you go, when I was a child?"

The question brought him back to the present, for a given value of "present," I suppose. "Titan. I was kidnapped by the Methane Men. They'd caught wind of who I was, that I was John Carter of Barsoom, and not really one of the new crowd from Earth. That was the first of my battles on Titan—" He grinned. "Much better than the pale skirmishes we've had there lately. They're not what they were."

"Nothing is, I take it."

"No." He paused. "I've got to leave again. Tomorrow is my last day on Barsoom, I think for a while."

"Oh." I wasn't sure I believed him, even then, but I knew I wanted to. "Jack . . . Uncle Jack . . . I'll be dead when you get back."

"Doctors and scientists," he said softly. "What do they know about anything?"

"I'm pretty sure they're right about this one, Jack."

Those gray eyes drilled into mine. "I'll see you tomorrow, before I go."

It might have been the longest day of my life. Certainly it was the slowest. I half expected him not to show up at all—if it was Uncle Jack, if it was John Carter, he'd certainly never taken his leave last time, when I was a child. He'd left me with my father, at the temple, and shook my hand a bit solemnly, and I'd never seen him again.

Tim Burke didn't even make it to breakfast.

He was in the room next to mine, and I checked on him after I'd eaten. He was gone, already cold in his bed by the time I looked in on him.

I didn't watch them take his body out. I went back to my room, back to waiting.

I didn't eat lunch.

By dinner time I still wasn't hungry. I was due for another round of treatment the next day, and I'd already decided to decline it.

What if it was all a sham? I found myself sitting on the balcony as afternoon shaded into evening. A young man, sick, sadistic, looked a bit like John Carter who looked a bit like my Uncle Jack. I was well known enough, second child to be born on Mars to emigrant parents, and it wouldn't have been too hard to find out enough about my past to spin a story a dying old man might fall for—

It got cold, and the sun sunk to the horizon, and I didn't move from my chair.

There came a knock on the door, and I heard Jill's voice. "You've got a visitor, Jack, your young man. Visiting hours are almost up—do you want to see him?"

I took a deep breath. No point in getting too worked up. Sham or remarkable reality, it was all over after today. I levered myself out of the chair, and came in off the balcony.

"Send him up."

The lights were off in the room when Jill ushered him in. She hesitated, then turned them on. "Twenty minutes," the green Martian told Jack.

He nodded. "I won't be long."

She closed the door and left us.

He was dressed for travel—a long coat, warm pants, sturdy boots. He'd a gun strapped to his belt, and his sword strapped across his back, the hilt showing over one shoulder. Incongruously, across the other shoulder he had a backpack quite like those young people used when exploring along the canals.

In his right hand he held the second of the two swords we'd practiced with.

"You're going, then."

He tossed me the sword. "You'll need this."

I caught it by reflex.

Jack unslung the backpack. "You look about my size, so I brought you my clothes." He pulled a coat and pair of heavy pants from the bag and tossed them toward me. "Put them on." A gun came out of the bag next, with a holster and belt. "And this." Finally, a pair of boots, and the bag was empty.

"I take it you're going somewhere cold?"

He hesitated. "I think so. I'm not completely sure. But we can always shed clothes if it's hot."

"We, again. You want me to come with you."

"Yes."

"Jack, I'm dying."

He shrugged. "So is everyone."

"Except you."

"Are you coming or not?"

We stood on the balcony together. "Look," Jack said. "There."

He pointed.

"It's a star."

He nodded. "It's a bright star. Capella, they tell me. Not a sun like ours. Four suns. Two giant stars in a binary pair, two red dwarfs in a binary pair orbiting the giant stars. The scientists don't know if there are planets, but I think there must be, or I wouldn't feel what I do."

"Feel what?"

"I'm being pulled there, Jack. I'm being called. We're heading there, tonight." He turned slightly to face me, his features lit only by the lights of the city of Helium. "Now."

At the very end, I did believe, and I had tears in my eyes. "You really are him. You're my Uncle Jack."

He smiled at me. "Yes, Jack, and I'm sorry for everything that went wrong, for the life you should have had. Let's make it right." He reached out his hand to me. "Hold my hand, son, and we'll cross the street together."

When Jill came back, just a little later, to tell the visitor it was time to leave, the light was still on in the room, but Jack Anderson's room was empty, the door to the balcony open, and the wind blew in through the open door.

An Island in the Moon

by Chuck Rosenthal

If I am insane, it is not simply so. The lines between the lived and the dreamt are seldom delineated by consciousness and sleep. A silver crow, for they are silver here in this silver land, silver when the light splays at silver angles from the nearest silver sun, the silver crow alights upon a grave, and who, not I, can say it is not the same blue crow who alit but hours ago in the blue light of dawn, or the black crow in the black night, invisible, who is only her cawing, the flutter of her wings, the wind of them on my ears as soft as feathers, for if not feathers, what else could they be?

I am John Carter. John Carter still. Living on and on in my prime, in my childhood, in old age, in my grave, never born so never dead, buried again, awakened again every time your eyes alight upon my grave, a page of stone: *Here Lies John Carter. Regrets.* Buried on a starship heading for Richmond, Virginia; Richmond, England; Highgate London (East or West?); Tarzana, California; Barsoom, Mars; at least these are the things I'm told when I step outside my vault. Who tells me? My companions here, dead starmen all, and women too, and children and their pets, and monsters, fairies, creatures green and red, the quiet dead, the rattling dead, the Romantic dead.

> I am John Carter, once the King of Mars
> Buried on a starship, buried in the stars.

The next time you step into a graveyard, remember that you're traveling at the speed of light (a little faster? a little slower? We discuss that here, we phantoms, worried that we were launched in some primitive time and we'll arrive at our next destination having crawled near light speed to a universe already dead or a dimension already abandoned).

Sometimes I am old, sometimes young. Sometimes I see things very clearly. Sometimes the ghosts are so thick I am walking in a fog of them, then I can't tell one from the other; that's how I know that I'm alive and they are dead, because they can't tell themselves apart, each one appears like the play of light upon a mist, my queen, Dejah Thoris, déjà vu, when I turn around, is that my life I see ahead?

This is how I went back to Mars one more time; a planet I had saved again and again and now was dead. There was a time, near the end of my last stay, when red cities were falling in upon themselves and the great incubators that breathed Mars' air gasped and droned, when Dejah touched my cheek (was it for the last time? How many times can the last time happen?). I can feel her long fingers now, feel my long breath circling them with my dreadful hope. She didn't say to me, Don't go. Don't leave me again. She said, "I don't know why I want to live at all." I didn't have the answer, I didn't know if on Earth I slept and on Mars I awoke or if on Earth I dreamt and on Mars I fell asleep; I knew her less than I know her now, but then I thought that when I spread my arms before a precipice of blue sky, Mars took me. Yes, Dejah, why live at all if I must live on Earth, my feet grounded, my mind asleep, if on Mars I could leap a hundred yards; if on Mars I was a warlord.

Who's to say if I am mad, just because I can fall asleep and travel from one planet to the next? This time I awoke on Mars inside a translucent tent, a red plain stretching around. I could see that portals with flaps led to other tents, and around me sat white and black boxes, some bigger than a man, made of what I later learned to be polymer, a kind of durable plastic. This tent, a dome on top that fell to vertical walls, had a diameter of about ten feet, the walls moving in and out like a slow pulse. I sat up. A man appeared before me, in his fifties? His seventies? I couldn't tell. He was six feet tall, at least, his hair white, but full, combed back, his gestures confident, assertive. He wore a one-piece suit, some kind of rubbery boots of a material I couldn't identify. Not surprisingly, he regarded me with great suspicion.

I assumed I'd come again to Mars because I always came to Mars, but this was a Mars very different from the one I'd left, one in decay, but yet with plants and water, if irrigated, unless I was now in a region of desert near the south pole; I didn't know how much or in what way Mars had changed. I'd never seen anyone dressed like this on Mars, never been in a tent like this one.

"Are you a Red?" I asked him. I spoke in Barsoomian, the prevalent Martian language. In it, Mars was Barsoom. The Reds were like us, like Earth humans.

"That isn't a language I've heard before," he mumbled. He opened his palm and an image, mine, appeared in front of him. He pointed at it, twitched his index finger and it disappeared.

"English," I said to him, but as I spoke another image appeared in front of him; I later learned that these were holograms. It was of a woman, eyes piercingly dark, almost black, and gray hair that fell softly on her shoulders like a young woman's hair.

"He speaks English, and something else, at least," said my host.

"Armed?" said the woman-image, though I couldn't tell where her voice came from.

"No, not apparently," the man said. "How did you get here?" the man said to me.

"Are you a Red?" I asked him again, this time in English, for in any case Barsoom could not have changed so much that the intelligent species, the human-like one, were not Reds. But were there Greens and other species? Other ambiguous monstrosities?

"Red what?" said the woman. "I'm coming over there."

"Nobody's used that term for a century at least," the man said to me. He peered at me now, squinting, rubbing his chin.

The woman now came through a flap in the tent. Though there was nothing remarkable about her size, she didn't move like a Barsoomian, but as I did on Mars, steady, both sliding and bounding, to adjust for the gravity only one-third of Earth's. She came to the man and they touched fingertips below their waists, very softly, his left hand to her right. He gently put his lips on her forehead. A kiss!

I tried to get up. The man put out his palm. "Please stay seated," he said. "We don't know who you are."

"We stand up for ladies where I'm from," I said to him.

The woman turned to me. "I am Elise Alaya," she said. "And this is Randall Word." After a moment she turned to Randall. "He doesn't recognize our names." She was right, though I didn't understand how she knew, or then again, why I might know their names. Had she read my face? My mind?

"Those don't sound like Barsoomian names," I said.

They stared at me silently.

"Martian names," I said to them.

"And you are?" said Elise.

"John Carter."

"That doesn't sound very Martian either," said Elise and she laughed, just a little.

"Are you Martian?" I said. "You've never heard of me?"

"Where's your survival gear?" said Randall. "How did you get here?"

"Is there yet water here now?" I asked. "Are there still canals?"

"This is a joke," said Randall Word. "They've sent a new pod, but this is too early for anyone to have arrived."

"We'd have seen it," Elise said slowly.

"A pod," I whispered. I studied the pair in front of me. My head was beginning to clear and it might have been time for quick action. Though they didn't appear to possess weapons, they'd demonstrated the ability to conjure images and sounds simply by opening their palms. Maybe they could hurt me like that, make me disappear, though it didn't seem likely. And they'd displayed no aggression, just cautious incredulity.

And though I knew I was on Mars the way I'd know I was sitting in my own backyard, even with my eyes closed, I didn't know *when* I was on Mars or where.

"He's not old enough to have been a colonist," Elise said to Randall.

Pods. Colonists. Spaceships then. Ships to Mars had happened. "You came in spaceships," I said.

"And you didn't?" said Randall.

In however many ageless years I'd lived, I'd learned that the truth could be as deceptive a weapon as any lie. I told them that I couldn't explain precisely how I'd arrived, but that I'd traveled from Earth to Mars and back, and back again. I spoke of the Mars I'd known and ruled, Barsoom, the green monsters, the red men, the flying battleships, the black ancients and white apes, Tars Tarkas, the Tharks, my beloved, my princess, Dejah Thoris. That I had overcome evil here and given the dying planet back its breath.

The two of them listened quietly. They sat down in front of me.

"There's no archeological signature for any of that," Randall said.

"The canals," I said.

Randall looked at me directly. "There have never been canals."

We sat together in the breathing tent, saying nothing more for quite some time.

"I guess things have changed," I said softly.

Randall averted his eyes, looked at Elise. "Burroughs?" he said.

"William Burroughs?" said Elise.

"Edgar Rice Burroughs," said Randall.

"I invented him!" I exclaimed. "I pretended he was the author of the books I wrote about what happened to me here."

"In what universe," whispered Elise.

"To say he's mad explains nothing," said Randall.

"You're talking about me?" I said. "Why am I not to believe that if I walked outside this tent, in a mile I'd find a canal, and boat, and soon I'd arrive in one of my Martian cities, greeted by the throngs who worship me as a hero?"

"You're welcome to try that. I don't encourage it," Randall Word said.

"That you aren't two maniacs, banished to this asylum," I said.

Elise whispered again, this time looking in my eyes. "Eternity is in love with the productions of time."

"What are you talking about?" I said.

"She's quoting William Blake," said Word.

"Or like 'Night Meeting,'" she said. "In Bradbury's *The Martian Chronicles*. Did you write that, too?" She spoke with such baffling, senseless precision, leaping around me instead of saying things straight, as if she moved through and around my thoughts.

"I don't know about any of that," I said.

Then Randall stood up. "Enough of this," he said. "Let's eat something."

I'd apparently established that however mysterious my intrusion, I was not a dangerous one.

We went under a flap and down a short tunnel into another tent, this one like a greenhouse, where some of the larger bushes and small trees were rooted in a kind of soil, but most of the vegetables and fruits grew out of tanks of circulated water, hydroponically, they said. Another tent housed rabbits and chickens, roaming freely. There were two calico cats who moved about as they pleased. "Where there is food, civilization, there are rodents," said Randall; he didn't know how they got there—he said that while meeting my eyes with a bit too much intention—but they got there. Elise had artificially inseminated the younger calico, she would have one kitten before the older cat passed. Elise had been a doctor on Earth and learned veterinary skills for the expedition. Even into middle age, she said, she'd always wanted to be a surgeon.

Even into middle age? How old was she now? But you didn't ask that of a woman, on Earth or Mars.

We passed into their main living space, its wall hung with thick, colored cloth, the floor a maze of strange abstract sculpture.

"Our sunny dome, our caves of ice!" said Elise, spreading her arms.

"Coleridge," said Randall Word.

"You did this?" I said to Elise.

She went on:

> How do you know but every bird that cuts the airy way
> Is an immense world of delight, clos'd by your senses five?

"Indeed," said I.

"Blake again," said Randall. "We use hydrogen-powered generators from water piped from the north pole and other underground sources."

"Not radium?" I said.

"We're on the cheap," said Randall. "We couldn't even afford a nuclear reactor to power the ship."

"Nuclear,," I said. "We simply used gravity. The eighth ray of propulsion."

He gave me that piercing, questioning look again, as if he were trying to penetrate my mind from under the brow of his right eye.

"Now my indeed," said Elise. She was, at times, quite impossible to follow.

"I don't understand," I said.

"Oh, you understand," she said.

"We're here," said Randall, "because there were indications of an element beneath the surface that could instigate fusion."

"Have you ever read Capek's *The Factory of the Absolute*?" Elise said to me. "A scientist invents a fission device in nineteen forties Prague, but it turns out that pantheism is true and God gets out everywhere."

"Disastrous?" I said.

"All deities reside in the human heart, Mr. Carter," she said to me.

"He'll catch on to you," said Randall to Elise. "Then what?"

"What fun that will be," she said.. "But he'll have to read some poetry to catch up."

Though Word was right, poetry aside, I was catching on. And becoming oddly enchanted by Elise Alaya. In a moment time cascaded around me and I imagined, more, I saw, the woman in front of me as young, spilling with manic ideas, words, magic, adventure, and beauty as well; she seemed, suddenly, a gorgeous young woman, and as she turned from me with a quick, light step, it appeared that she was growing not older, but younger; this banter, her verbal dancing, seemed the flirtation of a girl.

I stared after her. "You're a lucky man," I said to Randall Word.

"Don't condescend to her, or me," Randall said, "even if it's true."

He was slightly taller than me, if more slender, and I learned over our dinner of lasagna and wine (the lasagna heated in seconds in a small, buzzing oven and served in single, ready-made plastic containers, the wine from a small, metallic barrel) that he'd once been a decathlete and later a political essayist of sorts, too idiosyncratic, he said, to be very successful.

He made a living, for a while, teaching, and though American, met Elise in London on assignment.

Elise, though a British citizen, was Somali. I didn't know what that was.

"Somalia?" said Elise. "East Africa?" African. Her skin was slightly dark, her deep eyes almost black.

Randall Word gave me another piercing stare, wondering how I could be so ignorant.

They raised a daughter, a son. Their daughter died at eighteen, in an auto accident in Nevada. Their son died in battle in a foreign war that both Randall and Elise had opposed. He'd enlisted.

Around that time the European economy collapsed and soon after, the world economy. Among the things all that put an end to was space exploration, for decades. Randall said that before all that, he thought he remembered something about a movie that had been titled with my name. He hadn't seen it, but he thought it was about John Carter, of Mars. He gave me his look again.

"A documentary?" I asked.

Elise leapt up. She almost sang. "Is the Red King dreaming about us? Or are we dreaming of him?"

"Do you mean me? I said.

"It's *Alice in Wonderland*," said Randall.

Elise put both her hands over the fingers of my right hand that rested on the table. "You know very well that none of us are real," she whispered.

Beguiled, but a little off balance now, I looked at Randall Word.

"You're supposed to say, 'I *am* real!" he said.

I looked at the two of them. I stuttered, "But I am! All of this is real."

"Are you a real character?" said Elise.

"At a tea party?" I said.

"Regardless, you're a little young to be John Carter," said Randall.

"Maybe he's from the movie," Elise said.

It was baffling enough, even to me. If for over a hundred years I'd retired from Mars to my vault in Richmond, Virginia, only to awake, ageless on a Mars unchanged, I'd now awakened to a Mars apparently destroyed for a billion years or more. "What would you call it now?" I said to them. "Time warp? A worm hole?"

Randall Word became even more stoic, but a flash of empathy and recognition crossed Elise's face, her black, sky deep eyes holding me as if

I were traversing the dark space between the two planets. There was something that we shared.

"We volunteered for this," she began. She said it would be senseless to try to explain how they'd decided, but they answered a cyber-ad from a corporation called UCorp that offered to send humans to Mars to explore under the surface for an element that might enhance fusion. It had been suggested by some meteorite samples, some exotic equations, and earlier robot exploration. Simply, UCorp could increase the odds on their investment if they could send a lot of people to explore a lot of area, none of whom they'd have to bring back if they were already old, elderly people willing to retire and die exploring Mars. Elise and Randall were part of the first colony of ten. UCorp sent four more colonies, spread around the north pole, where there was water, where the element was thought to be. The colonists were selected based on technical skills, fitness, and personality compatibility. Elise, who had among other things, been a poet ("a poet," I said, and she bowed her head slightly), was once a doctor. After a teaching stint, Randall had become a holo-tech expert, proficient with throwing around those images he called holograms with his hand. And if elderly people were less mobile, they were usually more patient, needed less activity in space travel, and on Mars were one-third their Earth weight.

It would take a book to get from there to where they were now, Elise said, but she and Randall grew disillusioned, struggled with the other colonists, and one day, on one of their explorations which required setting up camps like the one we occupied now, they took enough supplies and equipment to get by on their own and never looked back.

"There are a lot of gaps in that story," I said, "speaking of stories and gaps."

"For another time, tomorrow, at least," said Randall.

But in the meantime he left the chamber and returned with a small device, no larger than his hand. It looked like a saucer with wings. Indeed, when he let it go it hovered in space.

"A robot?" he said. "Yes?"

I nodded. "I've heard of them," I said.

He sent it from the chamber and the next I saw it, it was outside the wall of the tent. In the air in front of us appeared a picture of the terrain outside our walls, calibrations beside it. The temperature was -100 centigrade.

"I've been here on a summer day," I said. "Eighty degrees."

"Fahrenheit," said Word. "At the equator. And that's on a rare summer day. The average right here is about minus two hundred-and-seven Fahrenheit."

The air pressure was only eight milabars. Almost nothing. He sent the robot out farther. It moved quickly over the red ground. I watched long enough. Nothing but desert. No water. Not even clouds.

"All right," I said.

"So how did you get here?" said Randall.

"I spread my arms," I said.

"Can you do it now?" said Elise.

I spread out my arms and stood in front of them.

'It doesn't always work," I said.

"But sometimes it does? she said.

"Come on," I said to her. "I thought you were a poet!"

A man who falls asleep and awakens years and worlds apart from his last abode is a bit cautious about lying down to rest. I have been, all my life, a man of action, not of thought. Aside from passion and freedom, I've found nothing else worth dying for. The ideas of men fade before they sleep or die in the light of the first dawn. It never mattered what I thought of power or justice, but for how it fell from the muzzle of my gun or the edge of my sword. I turned to my bed, and like a character in a cheap novel I fell asleep, but awoke not someplace else but in the depth of the Martian night.

I crawled through the tunnel of my tent chamber, back into the dome where the three of us had dined. Along the brocaded walls, like the inside of an Apache tipi, bags hung, a nomad's chest of drawers, and I began to rummage through them randomly. Never before had I felt so unsettled, so alone. I found inexplicable tools, small screens that lit up to my touch; sometimes the images on them leapt into space, expanding and contracting as I opened and closed my palm. I wondered at them. Obviously they could be sent, could speak, could even listen. Could they be sent invisibly then, to spy, as well? Was someone watching everywhere all the time? Who?

I found another image. Opened it. It was like a photo in three dimensions, of Randall and Elise, arms around each other, smiling, the red planet stretching endlessly behind them through a translucent wall; oddly, I felt a twinge of jealousy about Elise, before noticing that faintly, around each of them, ran the outline of a shady obelisk, like the graves of two lovers laid to rest. On the one behind Randall, words shimmered: *If the doors of perception were cleansed, everything would appear to us as it is, infinite.*

Behind Elise: *Till love and fame to nothingness do sink.*

In the chamber next to where I now stood, on the other side of the tent wall, I heard the passionate sighs of Elise Alaya and Randall Word making love.

I enlarged the photo image. Upon closer inspection what I found was that the two of them, in that picture, were very, very old.

"You were in our files last night," Elise said to me the first thing she saw me in the morning.

"That's the bad news," said Randall. "The good news is that you didn't send them anywhere."

"I wouldn't know how," I said to them.

"That's good news, too, I suppose," he said.

"What would you do," I said, "kill me?"

Randall laughed. "Please," he said.

"It hardly matters now," Elise said. She walked to the counter and brought me a cup of hot coffee. She handed me the cup. "You say you came from a graveyard."

I sipped the coffee. Good and very strong. The container was made from the same polymer as everything else, it held the heat of the coffee without getting hot.

"We'll show you something," she said.

We put on space suits like thick jump suits, boots, gloves, air packs, helmets with wide visors. We left the installation through an intermediary chamber that could pressurize and depressurize air. Outside, this Mars had almost no air or air pressure, no running water, and was too cold for life. Elise drove us in an open vehicle like a jeep. "It's not far," she said. "When we found it we built our installation nearby."

"The element?" I said.

"No," said Randall. "No one ever found that."

"You were born quite some time ago," Elise said to me.

"Inexplicably long ago," said Randall. "You say you travel here from Earth, but you can only account for your time here."

I remained silent as the vehicle rumbled listlessly over the cold, red dust. Elise guided the vehicle, meandering through a plain of small boulders, following a narrow path. I could see it was not a created road, but a found one.

"Correct," she said, anticipating my observation before I spoke.. "We found all this on foot the first time, then figured out a path big enough for the TV."

"Terrain Vehicle," said Randall.

"Do you read my thoughts?" I said to Elise, for when I first arrived on Mars I found I could anticipate the intentions of the red Martians.

"You send them, don't you?" she said. "I can send too."

It seemed the closer we moved toward explanation, the more everything became more inexplicable, though Randall Word was always ready to explain, even if it made things less understandable.

"In your book you said you could read Martian minds," he said.

"In my reports," I said.

"Stories," said Randall.

Elise said, "Mind-reading is simply a synthesis of close observation, induction, and intuition. No one can see another's secrets, unless he's revealing them. 'But first the notion that humanity has a body distinct from its soul is to be expunged.'"

"Too display . . . to display . . ." I found myself mumbling, stuttering.

"Go ahead," said Elise. I felt as if she were silently throwing words at me.

"The infinite," I finally said.

"You see?" she said. "Poetry is everywhere and eternal. It's even in you."

"In any case," said Randall Word, "it seems she can do it and you can do it, but I can't."

We'd stopped in front of a mound of boulders some twenty feet high.

"We figured out that you must have come from here," Randall said. "Somehow."

As you can see, though it is late for me to point it out, conversation with the two of them was not the easiest. It leapt and meandered both, while at the same time, between them, it danced in simpatico, like a tango, lyrical, like a poem almost, and as I tried to speak with them I felt I was being written, danced, into it, though the author was apparently not Randall Word, but Elise Alaya.

"Come with us now," said Elise to me, "and maybe we'll find out how you got here."

Still in our suits and helmets, Randall led us from the TV, but in that moment, following Elise Alaya into the rocks, I recognized a defiant strength in her stride; my memory fell through a shaft of my unconscious to Dejah Thoris, my Barsoomian queen, a billion years of loss burst through my heart and I almost collapsed under an infinite roaring love, yes, infinite, but not for Dejah—rather for the woman in front of me, Elise Alaya. I wanted to take her, consume her, murder Randall Word and rule the barren planet and our little outpost alone, eternally.

She stopped and turned to me. "We're there now," she said. She spread the palm of her right hand across my chest. "Don't try to reconcile the love and destruction, the hate or creation, young Werther."

"Carter," I said. "John Carter."

She turned again. We'd come to an old door, like to a vault. Randall opened it and we stepped in. Before us swept a huge graveyard with black, winding paths between caverns of black monuments. Grass, weeds, and wild bushes pushed at the graves beneath the drooping branches of sycamores and willows, maples, hickory, and oak.

"You can take your helmet off," said Randall, and he did so with his.

Elise removed her helmet and gloves. I removed mine.

"This is quite impossible," I said.

"Yes," said Elise, "this, too, is quite impossible."

We walked. Not all the graves were black or large, some were gray, their surfaces effaced or worn. Tree roots pushed from underneath the vaults, cracking them open. Until we came upon a silver slab, erect and clean, the weeds shorn away, fresh flowers planted round. It said, *John Keats, 1795–1821.*

"Who could have done this?" I said.

Elise bent on a knee, plucked away a few weeds from the grave. "Me," she said.

I didn't find out how I got to Mars, not during that visit, but now, there, this is how we spent our days, not in science or research, or searching for lost elements or new worlds, but manicuring the graves of famous dead, each a different one on each a different day. And if you wonder how a man who conquered a world could now spend his days walking lazily through a graveyard, it was that I'd fallen in love, with graves, with death, with the flowers of death, and with Elise Alaya, the poet who tended the graves of the Romantic dead: William Blake, Percy Bysshe Shelly, Christina Rossetti, Samuel Coleridge, Byron, Wordsworth, Elizabeth Browning,

Emily Bronte, Goethe, even Yeats. And as you see, not just any poets, but Romantics. As we walked and stooped to manicure the graves, the faces of my new friends glowed with vibrancy and life and, as well, I felt my own pulse revive as if I were but twenty and just ran a hundred yards with the least of effort. Each of us was growing younger everyday. Our skin grew smooth, our hair darkened. There was simple joy in it, being young, being immortal, as the young must ever be, amidst the graves, the dead. I was filled with exuberance as if it were a drug. We walked among the graves and for days I lost time and thought of nothing; in the evenings, drinking wine, we read to each other the poetry of love and death. *Les ballades d'amour et de mort*, Elise said. Yet so often, even in this ecstasy, I gazed at Elise and envied Randall Word so deeply, that he had her constant love, and then my heart ached in despair that she would never look at me the way she looked at him.

Until one day Randall Word took me aside before we were about to leave for the cemetery.

He fidgeted with the flying robot. Numbers flashed out from it and into the air, counting down. "UCorps ETA," he said. "But you see what happens. You forget. You forget about everything." He told me they didn't discover the graveyard, that it came from the sky. They saw it land.

"A Flying Dutchman," I exclaimed.

"A very peculiar one," he said. He talked about a sect of Buddhists in Tibet who believed the cosmos was all in their imagination. The short of it was that when they died, on the way toward their next reincarnation, they went through a place or state of mind called the Bardo where they encountered deities and devils and other supernatural beings. It happened to everybody who died, or so they believed. But the beings that non-Tibetans saw were the beings of their own particular beliefs, say, for Christians, angels, for Islamists, genies. He thought the graveyard worked something like that.

"So it's all in our minds," I said. "Made up."

"Or as real as anything. Or as made up as all this," he said, spreading his arms.

"Can all of us be making it up?" I said.

"It's Elise's graveyard," he said.

"Where are your children's graves?"

"It's not a matter of will power."

We were quiet.

"Your son was a soldier," I said. "A soldier's death is a noble death."

"No death is noble," said Randall Word.

"I lost a son," I said. "Here. Somewhere. It must be long ago now."

"I'm sorry," he said. "My daughter, she was just a wild little thing. A bird. It ended our lives."

He wasn't the sort of man I was used to dealing with. He was not a fighting man, a leader or even a follower. I imagined I'd have had more in common with his son. It was Word's mind that made him unique, his concentration. He was in command of his mind.

And so he and Elise came to Mars, a planet they presumed so dry and lifeless it could not remind them of life or death. It was his idea. I saw that now. No woman, not Elise, would choose it. But in the passion of her soul something, someone, the graveyard, had given her the path to immortal love, the only way that death was conquered.

"It's a fountain of youth," I said.

"I don't know. But if we don't go, we age. Odd, isn't it, that a graveyard would do that?" He explained that when they were a part of the colony they had to be careful, visiting less frequently so as not to show the bloom of youth, but eventually it became impossible, so they left.

"Why didn't you tell them?"

"You mean share it? Really?" he said. "To what end?"

"And the colonists now?"

"All dead," said Randall Word. "For quite some time."

"How old should you be?" I said.

"Quite old," he said. "Like you. Impossibly old. But it doesn't matter now. As we've told you, they've sent a ship. We dropped out of communication, tried to hide our signature, but UCorp has found us." He held up the little machine. A red light flashed. "They're coming." He put down the saucer and looked at me. "So best if you go without me today. There are things you need to find out very soon."

When I went to the pressure chamber Elise was waiting.

"Randall isn't coming today," she said.

"No," I said.

"They're coming, you know. UCorp."

"He reminded me. What could they want?"

"They want us, of course. They want our secrets," she said. "We're still alive."

"Do you have a plan?" I said.

"Yes," she said, "to go find out what you're hiding."

We drove to the graveyard and went inside. We disrobed from our suits. She let me take her hand. We walked for quite a while like that, hand in hand. I felt like a teenager in love. Finally we turned up a crooked path that suddenly broke into a circle. There, a beautiful, twisting stone seemed to dance in an eerie light.

"My favorite," said Elise. "Mary Shelley."

"She wasn't a poet," I said.

"Without her, neither you nor I would exist," said Elise.

"In your graveyard," I said.

"Are you my Frankenstein monster, John Carter? Let's go over there," Elise pointed. "Maybe you'll find some novelists now."

I was dumbfounded. I am yet dumbfounded. Gliding like a phantom into a wide hall I followed her. At first it seemed like we were amidst a sea of crumbling monuments, but slowly a grave would emerge with a name: Hawthorne, Jewett, Melville, Verne, H.G. Wells.

"I can't imagine," I whispered.

"But you are imagining," said Elise.

"Where are we?" I said.

"An island in the moon," she said. She faced me. "That's a metaphor."

"I get that," I said.

Elise pointed across the way. There, in a secluded corner, sat my vault in Richmond, Virginia.

"Is that where you come from?" she said.

Yet when I reached the vault it didn't have my name on it. It said, *Edgar Rice Burroughs.*

"I guess you two are going to have to work that out," said Elise Alaya.

"I can stay here," I said to her.

"It seems you have. More than once."

"And so can you," I said.

"On a graveyard starship," she said. "In this eternal twilight."

She could read my thoughts and I hers. We were alike. It could be an eternal dawn, as well. We both felt it. "We are the same," I said. "Meant for this. Fated for this." I lifted her hand and kissed it, then her forehead, then her lips. I hadn't felt the joy of such love since my first kiss. She touched my cheek. Then she turned from me and walked away, and I followed.

At the installation Randall had wine waiting. His machine put a hologram between us, the numbers counting down. "You found yourself in the graveyard I assume," he said to me.

"This UCorp," I said to him. "Can't we fight them?"

"They will have unimaginable weapons," he said.

"We can figure out a way to fight them!"

"Shall we sneak up and hit them on their space helmets with spoons?" said Elise.

Word took me by the arm and led me away from Elise and into the neighboring chamber. "When they arrive the grave ship will just leave. Then we will age quickly and die," Randall said.

"Then we can leave on it!"

"I cannot," said Randall Word. "I can't be buried there. You didn't see the graves of any political essayists or holo-techs, did you?"

"Imagine them!"

"It doesn't work that way. Only Romantic artists," he said. "Or apparently their warrior creations."

"Elise?"

"She could have a grave, like you."

"Just get on," I said to him. " Like you do now. One escape at a time! That's how it's done. I'm an expert at escape!"

"On Mars maybe," he said. He faced me.. "John Carter," he said, "any man would fall in love with her. I forgive you."

"Then let her come with me."

Elise came into the chamber now. She went to Randall Word. He took her hand. "I should leave the two of you alone again for a bit," he said.

When he left it was I who now took Elise's hand. "He's right. Come with me," I said to her. I looked into her eyes. She felt my passion. How could she not? "Randall is doomed," I said to her. "We'll stay with him until the end."

"What end?" she said. She withdrew her hand from mine. A dozen emotions crossed her face. Her brow tightened, then relaxed. Her dark eyes filled with tears, but they didn't fall.

"You could love me," I said.

"Of course," she replied. "Of course I could." Then she got up, turned away, and left.

At that moment I felt as if my heart had turned to lead. For the first time in my life I was gripped by utter despair. And in the same moment I remembered Mars, Barsoom, its canals punctuated by bright cities filled with women and men; there were yet streams, and clouds beneath its moons; I saw a leaf fall from a tree, contemplated a single, tiny white flower, its petals spreading, infinity within, and I was filled with such joy that I wept. I couldn't stay there and die with them. And I couldn't make Elise go with me. I thought, then, of ending my life. What was the difference between a moment of joy and eternity? What will it matter how long we have lived in that moment when we face the end?

In the coming weeks Randall and Elise didn't return to the graveyard and I watched them quickly age, their skin wrinkled, their hair again turned gray. If much slower, I began to age, too. As for them, how they fell together into the pit of feebleness, you don't need the details. A few nights we sat together in the main chamber of the tent, drank wine and read poems. Other nights they were too weak. Until finally, Randall shook my hand, and Elise kissed my lips. Her eyes. Her eyes were yet young. Then they disappeared into their bedchamber for the last time. I waited a week, went in, and found them on their bed, two skeletons, their hands upon each other's cheeks, entwined in the embrace of death.

For a day I wandered between the tents before taking stock of what I must do. I set the green house and animal tents into their automatic controls, hoping the invaders would have souls. I erased everything from the image pads in the storage pouches, then destroyed them as well as I could. I went to the small bookshelves and found this poem that we had once read together, copied it in my own hand, and placed it near Elise's head.

> When you are old and gray and full of sleep
> And nodding by the fire, take down this book
> And slowly read, and dream of that soft look
> Your eyes had once, and of them shadows deep;
>
> How many loved your moments of glad grace,
> And loved your beauty with love false or true
> But one man loved the pilgrim soul in you,
> And loved the sorrows of your changing face.
>
> And bending down beside the glowing bars,
> Murmur, a little sadly, how love fled
> And poured upon the mountains overhead
> And hid his face amid a crowd of stars.

A ship arrived and circled the planet. From it a pod ejected and slowly fell to the surface. UCorp was here. I drove the jeep to the graveyard, entered, and shut the door, returning to my vault. *My* vault. It read *John Carter* on the door. I entered, then felt the rumble beneath me as the Flying Dutchman launched.

And now I travel in the starship of graves, of ghosts, yet to land, heading for some planet light years ahead, guided by I know not what or whom. Am I doomed? No. I think I shall escape again, on another planet around another star. After all, I am John Carter.

ABOUT THE CONTRIBUTORS

BOB ZEUSCHNER wrote *Edgar Rice Burroughs: The Exhaustive Scholar's and Collector's Descriptive Bibliography* and has contributed numerous articles to the *Burroughs Bulletin*. He holds a doctorate from the University of Hawaii at Manoa and serves as a professor of philosophy at Pasadena City College, specializing in Asian philosophy.

MATTHEW STOVER is the author of numerous *New York Times* bestsellers, including *Star Wars: Revenge of the Sith* and his own science-fiction series from Del Rey Books, the *Acts of Caine* (*Heroes Die, Blade of Tyshalle, Caine Black Knife*, and *Caine's Law*).

MICHAEL KOGGE is a screenwriter from Los Angeles. He has written most notably for Blizzard Entertainment and Lucasfilm, having garnered accolades for his screenplays and *Star Wars: The Despotica*. His original comic book series, *Empire of the Wolf*, is due out in 2012.

MARK D'ANNA's short story collection, *Big Brown Bag: Stories*, was called "an exciting debut" by the Midwestern Book Review. He served as the literary editor for the journal, *Silent Voices*, from 2007–2009 and currently works in International Creative Advertising at 20th Century Fox. His first novel, *Distortion*, will be published later in 2012.

AARON PARRETT is a Professor of English at the University of Great Falls in Montana. In addition to short stories, he has published *The Translunar Narrative in the Western Tradition* (Ashgate), an academic study of science fiction, and wrote the introductions to the Barnes & Noble editions of Edgar Rice Burroughs's *A Princess of Mars* series.

DANIEL KEYS MORAN is a writer and programmer who is best known for his series *The Tales of the Continuing Time*. The most recent volume in that series, *The AI War, Book One: The Big Boost*, was published in March 2011 and is available on *amazon.com* and *barnesandnoble.com*. He coined the word "webcast" in 1987 and has performed on-air commentary for National Public Radio.

CHUCK ROSENTHAL has won many awards for his novels and short stories, including nominations for the Pushcart Prize, the National Book Award, and Critics Circle Award for his sci-fi novel, *The Heart of Mars*. He has published eight novels, a memoir, and a book of Magic Journalism. His next book, *West of Eden: A Life in 21st Century Los Angeles* will be published in the fall of 2012 by What Books.

DAN PARSONS is an award-winning comic book artist and illustrator.

BIBLIOGRAPHY OF RESOURCES
BY AARON PARRETT

Edgar Rice Burroughs's Life and Works

Brady, Clark A. *The Burroughs Cyclopaedia: Characters, Places, Fauna, Flora, Technologies, Languages, Idea and Terminologies Found in the Works of Edgar Rice Burroughs.* Jefferson, NC: McFarland & Company, 1996.

Cohen, Matt. *Brother Men: The Correspondence of Edgar Rice Burroughs and Herbert T. Weston.* Durham, NC: Duke University Press, 2005.

Heins, Henry Hardy. *A Golden Anniversary Bibliography of Edgar Rice Burroughs.* West Kingston, RI: Grant, 1964.

Lupoff, Richard A. *Barsoom: Edgar Rice Burroughs and the Martian Vision.* Baltimore: Mirage Press, 1976.

Fenton, Robert W. *The Big Swingers: A Biography.* New York: Prentice-Hall, 1967.

Holtsmark, Erling. *Edgar Rice Burroughs.* Boston: Twayne, 1986.

Porges, Irwin. *Edgar Rice Burroughs, The Man Who Created Tarzan.* Provo, UT: Brigham Young UP, 1975.

Roy, John Flint. *A Guide to Barsoom: Eleven Sections of References in One Volume Dealing with the Martian Stories Written by Edgar Rice Burroughs.* New York: Del Rey, 1976.

Valdron, Den. "H.G. Wells' Barsoom!" *ERBZine* Vol. 1404. Web. <http://www.erbzine.com/mag14/1404.html>.

Zeuschner, Robert B. *Edgar Rice Burroughs: The Exhaustive Scholar's and Collector's Descriptive Bibliography.* Jefferson, NC: McFarland, 1996.

Other Classic Mars-oriented Science Fiction

Asimov, Isaac. *The Martian Way and Other Stories.* New York: Fawcett, 1981.

Bradbury, Ray. *The Martian Chronicles.* New York: Garden City, New York: Doubleday, 1950.

Brown, Frederic. *Martians, Go Home*. New York: Dutton, 1955.

Dick, Phillip K. "We Can Remember it for You Wholesale" in *The Collected Stories of Philip K. Dick*, Vol. II. New York: Citadel, 2002.

Dick, Philip K. *The Martian Time Slip*. New York: Vintage, 1995.

Wells, H.G. *The War of the Worlds*. London: Heinemann, 1898.

Weinbaum, Stanley. *A Martian Odyssey and Other Great Science Fiction Stories*. New York: Lancer, 1972.

Technical and Scientific Works about Mars

Lowell, Percival. *Mars*. Boston: Houghton-Mifflin, 1895.

Lowell, Percival. *Mars and its Canals*. New York: Macmillan, 1906.

Lowell, Percival. *Mars: The Abode of Life*. New York: Macmillan, 1908.

Nelson, M. and W. Dempster. 1996. "Living in Space: Results from Biosphere 2's Initial Closure, an Early Testbed for Closed Ecological Systems on Mars." *American Astronautical Society: Science & Technology Series* Vol. 86: 363–390.

Zubrin, R. *The Case for Mars*. New York: Free Press, 1996.

Zubrin, R. *How to Live on Mars: A Trusty Guidebook to Surviving and Thriving on the Red Planet*. New York: Three Rivers Press, 2008.

Zubrin, Robert. *Mars on Earth*. New York: Tarcher, 2003.

Books on Pulp Fiction

Chambliss, Julian and William Svitavsky, "From Pulp Hero to Superhero: Culture, Race, and Identity in American Popular Culture, 1900–1940," *Studies in American Culture* 30.1 (October 2008).

Goodstone, Tony. *The Pulps: 50 Years of American Pop Culture*. Bonanza Books, 1970.

Goulart, Ron. *Cheap Thrills: An Informal History of the Pulp Magazines*. New York: Hermes, 2007.

Reynolds, Quentin. *The Fiction Factory: Or from Pulp Row to Quality Street: The Story of 100 Years of Publishing at Street & Smith.* New York: Random House, 1955.

Photography

Jay, Bill. "Images in the Eyes of the Dead." First published in *The British Journal of Photography*, 30 Jan 1981, and later edited and revised for *American Photographer*, July 1985. <http://www.billjayonphotography.com>.

Films

Mars Movie Guide. The Mars Society, San Diego Chapter. Website. <http://marsmovieguide.com>. (Devoted to movies about Mars, beginning with Thomas Edison's 4 minute film from 1910, *A Trip to Mars*. After Earth, more movies have been filmed about Mars than any other planet.)

Mars Attacks! Dir. Tim Burton. Warner Brothers,1996. Film.

Mission to Mars. Dir. Brian DePalma Touchstone, 2000.

Red Planet. Dir. Antony Hoffman. Village Roadshow, 2000.

Total Recall. Dir. Paul Verhoeven. TriStar, 1990.

War of the Worlds. Dir. Byron Haskin. Paramount, 1953.

War of the Worlds. Dir. Steven Spielberg. Dreamworks, 2005.

John Carter. Dir. Andrew Stanton. Walt Disney, 2012.